Y0-EIY-616

The Voyeur

Books by Henry Sutton

THE EXHIBITIONIST
THE VOYEUR

The Voyeur

by
Henry Sutton

published by
**Bernard Geis
Associates**

© 1969 by David R. Slavitt and Lynn M. Slavitt, as Trustee
All rights reserved under International and Pan American Conventions
Manufactured in the United States of America
First Printing, December, 1968
Second Printing, January, 1969
Library of Congress Catalog Card Number: 68-26006
Designed by Elliot Epstein

To Sheldon S. Cohen
and all the guys down at the office

The Voyeur

1

A city is an act of faith.

In order for men and women to be able to live together, millions of them, crowded together in a small space, piled on top of each other in offices and apartments, they must rely upon one another and share in some minimal belief in the benevolence of mankind. They depend upon each other, even for the most basic necessities.

To be in a city is to be a part of civilization, for a city is a monument to commerce, to culture, to industry, and to all of man's highest aspirations. And the city dweller depends upon his neighbors for his food, for his clothing, and for his very safety. Most of the time he is right to do so. He wakes in the morning to find eggs from the poultry farmers, milk from the dairy farmers, oranges from the groves of Florida and California, coffee from the remote plantations of Brazil, all ready and at hand. At night the city dweller locks his door, but doors can be broken and windows are frangible. Policemen patrol in cars, but they cannot see everything, so the city dweller must trust his neighbors for his very life. To trust millions of neighbors is to trust mankind.

The masses of lights that, from the air, seem to be clustered beacons of trust, have an attractive glitter that is especially fascinating to the young who come to the cities from their villages and small towns, drawn to those lights like so many moths.

Marcia Church had been living for two years in the apartment in what had once been a grand town house on Beacon Hill, but even after all that time, she still felt sometimes that same excitement she remembered from the day she had moved in, and the same apprehension, too—lest she should wake up and find that it was all another one of her elaborate daydreams, and that she was still in Mr. Olson's English class back at Montgomery College. But, no, she looked around the apartment, which was simply but strikingly decorated with Swedish modern furniture on an orange nylon-pile carpet, and walked to the window to look out at the golden dome of the capitol of the Commonwealth of Massachusetts. By craning a little, she could see it, burnished by the light of the late afternoon sun. She was here in Boston, with a great apartment, an exciting job—as a photo researcher for *Tomcat*—and a subscription to the Thursday evening series of the Boston Symphony Orchestra. It was a good life.

She distributed the pile of wrought aluminum ashtrays she was holding in convenient places around the living room, glanced about, nodded to herself approvingly, and went off to the bathroom to shower. As she took off her wristwatch and put it on the edge of the marble washstand, she checked the time. She had two hours, still, before he would come. There was plenty of time for her to dress and set out the hors d'oeuvres—which had not yet arrived. She wondered where the hell her order was.

Oh, well, she thought to herself. If it hadn't arrived by the time she was out of the shower, she could call them again and complain. She turned the water on full blast and adjusted the temperature so that it was nicely tepid. It had been a hot, muggy day and she felt sticky. She got into the shower and stood there for a long time, feeling the lukewarm water, enjoying it as it pounded down, massaging the back of her neck and relaxing her. She closed her eyes and just enjoyed it.

She did not hear the doorbell the first time it rang, but the second ring—a long, insistent peal—brought her back suddenly. She turned off the water, reached for a towel, and ran into the kitchen to buzz the delivery boy in. Then she went to the bedroom, leaving wet footprints along the orange rug, to grab a cotton shift that she could slip into quickly. With one long motion she zipped it up the front.

The upstairs bell rang, and she went to open the door. "Frankie?" she called.

"Yes, Miss Church, it's me."

She opened the door and held it while Frank Scully carried the Campbell's Soup carton containing her order into the small kitchen and put it on the counter.

"It sure is hot," he said.

"Yes, I know. I was just taking my second shower today."

"Can I help you put the things away?" he offered.

She opened the refrigerator and he started handing her the cheeses, the soda bottles, the cold cuts, and the bottles of beer.

"Sorry to be so late with this," he said, "but it's so hot. Nobody is going out for groceries today. They're all having them delivered. I don't think I've been in the store for five minutes all afternoon."

He pulled a rumpled handkerchief from his pocket and mopped

his brow. "Hey, could I have a glass of water?" he asked, handing her the last of the beer bottles.

"Would you rather have a beer?" she asked.

His face lit up. "Gee, Miss Church," he said, "that'd be swell."

"I think I'll join you."

She took one of the bottles from the refrigerator, pried off the cap, and they sat down at the tiny table together to drink the beer. Marcia Church had known Frank Scully for a year and a half, but she had not spent twenty minutes in his company during that time. Two or three times a week he appeared to unload the groceries he had brought, said something cheerful and banal, and left. He was, she guessed, about eighteen. His hair was long and rather greasy, and he had a cluster of blackheads on either side of his nose. He was none too bright, but he was pleasant enough, always cheerful, and always very respectful. She was happy, after all this time, to extend to him this small gesture of kindness, allowing him a moment's rest and a glass of cold beer.

She had no idea, however, how much this moment meant to him. To Frank Scully, Marcia Church was a special person, a frequent figure in his most intimate dreams. In a way it was confusing for him for the two Marcias to come so close to each other. The one who lived in the swell apartment and who was so friendly and so casual with him looked exactly like the other Marcia Church, the complaisant dream slave who obeyed his every whim and who was so secret that he had never even mentioned her existence to his priest. But here she was, sitting at a table with him and sharing a beer, and if he looked at her, as he was doing, he could see the outline of her damp breasts, to which the thin cotton of her shift was clinging.

"This your day off?" he asked, making conversation, the way they did in the movies.

"Yes," she said, and took a sip of her beer.

He could smell the perfume of the soap she had been using. It filled the small, warm kitchen.

"Having a party?" he asked, nodding toward the refrigerator where he had just put all the groceries.

"Just a few people in for cocktails," she said.

He nodded, feeling hurt. He had never been to a cocktail party.

She took out a cigarette. He reached for a packet of matches in the pocket of his tight jeans, and deliberately dropped them. As he bent down to retrieve the matches, he looked up from under the table to see the swell of her thighs where her legs crossed. He struck a match and lit her cigarette. The wavering flame betrayed a slight tremor of his hand to Marcia. She looked at his face, but he was not looking at her. She smiled, amused.

"You have a girl friend, Frankie?"

"Sort of," he said, unwilling to admit that he did not.

"Is she pretty?" Marcia asked, with a slight edge to her voice.

"Not as pretty as you," he said, meeting her gaze for the first time.

She looked back at him with cool insouciance.

"No, but I mean it, Miss Church."

Finally, she said, "You're very sweet."

She finished the last of her beer, beginning to feel just the slightest bit uncomfortable under the intensity of his gaze. She got up, took her glass to the sink, and rinsed it out, suddenly conscious that the shift was glued to her buttocks. She had not had time to dry herself from the shower before putting it on. She began to wish that he would go.

He finished the last of his beer and walked over to the sink. She held out her hand for the glass, but he turned the water on and rinsed it out for himself. As he turned the glass over on the drainboard, he brushed against her and froze.

She laughed nervously. There was a definite odor of stale sweat about him that was unpleasant and almost suffocating in the tiny kitchen.

"What're ya laughing at?" he asked, turning red. The Marcia of his dreams never laughed. Certainly never at him. It made him angry.

"I just thought of something funny," she said lamely. "I wasn't laughing at you."

She touched him lightly on the forearm to reassure him of her good will. Then she left the kitchen, expecting him to follow her into the living room and go on out through the door, out of the apartment. But he hung back in the kitchen, staring at her. He could see the outline of her hips and buttocks clearly through the cotton shift, and the sight of her, silhouetted against the window, excited him, even more than her nearness in the kitchen had done. He took advantage of the moment when her face was averted from him to adjust his jeans, which were suddenly painfully tight.

She still had the dish towel in her hand, and as she crossed the rug she noticed the wet footprints she had left earlier. Forgetting for the moment that he was there, she bent to blot them up.

Perhaps if she had not noticed those wet footprints, or if she had waited until Frank Scully had left the apartment before she tried to dry them, or if she had been wearing something other than the clinging cotton sheath, nothing might have happened. But suddenly there she was, bending down to mop up the wet spots and aware of his intense stare. She looked behind her and saw him leaning against the doorjamb, now openly looking at that part of her thigh which had been exposed by the rising of her shift.

"Enjoying the view?" she asked. Her intention was to be cool and somewhat hostile, but such subtleties were lost upon Frank Scully, to whom no girl had ever spoken in just this way before, except perhaps the other Marcia Church, the one in his dreams.

This was, clearly, the moment. Deliberately, slowly, the way he had pictured it to himself so many times, he walked over to her and bent down beside her. He put his hand on her thigh. All he was intending, all he was able to imagine, was one kiss, which he could later embroider upon and enlarge, and perhaps that was all that would have happened if she had not said, "Take your hands off me, you silly little kid!"

She said it without even turning around, dismissing him completely. A wave of rage came over him, and a kind of contempt. Who was she to talk to him this way? He could feel the softness of her thigh, the yieldingness of it. He knew the strength of his own body. She could not bully him. Not vulnerable, there, the way she was.

He pulled her to her feet and clutched her clumsily, mashing his lips against her cheek, for she had turned her head away. She struggled, but he enjoyed that because he was so much stronger than she was, and the feeling of her struggling against him was exhilarating. The softness of her breasts as he crushed her against his sweat-stained T-shirt intoxicated him with a feeling of power. He could do anything he wanted. It was a wonderful feeling.

"God damn it, Frank, let go of me!"

She tried to bring her knee up to his groin, but he blocked her with a turn of his body. With one hand he held both of her arms, and with the other he rubbed at her buttocks, pulling her up close against the bulge of his dungarees. She was frightened now, and in terror and rage she sank her teeth into his upper arm, biting as hard as she could. He gasped in pain.

"Son of a bitch!" he shouted, and pushed her away from him.

Perhaps if she had fallen in some other direction, nothing more would have happened. But as she fell, her head grazed the corner of the coffee table, and she was stunned for a moment. He stood over her inert form, looking down at her. The dress had ridden up high on her thighs. He bent down and touched her arm, but she did not move. He touched her breast, but still she did not move. He noticed the zipper that ran down from the top of the shift to the bottom, and slowly he pulled it down. The dress fell open, exposing the slender white body. What especially fascinated him were the moist ringlets of her pubic hair.

He could control himself no longer. Tremblingly, he unzipped his fly and fell upon her, pushing her legs apart and entering her roughly. She moaned slightly. He took it to be a moan of pleasure. He was, anyway, past caring.

He moved quickly and almost immediately shuddered convulsively as he reached the moment of his climax.

He looked down into her face. Her eyes were wide with horror. Slowly he struggled to his knees, stunned, now, almost as much as she. He turned away from her to zip his fly. She took advantage of his movement away to get up and stagger to the kitchen. He followed her, not knowing exactly why. There was something still to explain, something to say. There had to be something.

She opened the drawer of the cabinet and pulled out a bread knife. "Get out," she said, holding it toward him.

Only to protect himself, now, he picked up the empty beer bottle that was still on the table. Holding it by the neck, almost automatically, he broke it and held it so that the jagged end was pointed at her. He took a step toward her and said, almost pleadingly, "Put down the knife."

She did not move.

"*Please*, Miss Church."

It was not what he said but the step that he had taken toward her that made her lunge at him. She cut his arm just above the wrist.

"Bastard!" she said. Over and over again, "Bastard! Bastard! Bastard!"

He was not listening. He saw the rivulet of his blood dripping onto the floor from the gash she had made in his arm.

"Whore!" He screamed as he plunged the beer bottle into her neck, severing the carotid artery. Her blood spurted in gushes that hit the ceiling. Silently her body slumped to the floor, the blood continuing to spout out of her neck. The only sound was the clatter of the knife she had held as it fell onto the linoleum.

The blood, dripping from his arm, stained the orange carpet as he fled. He dropped the beer bottle in an ash can a block from the apartment. It was not until then that he noticed he was still carrying it.

When the lights began to come on in the city of Boston, the windows in the apartment of Marcia Church remained dark.

When Charles Stanley rang the bell downstairs in the alcove for the third time and got no answer, he checked his watch. It was puzzling. It was two minutes to seven. He was not that early. She had to be there. He rang once more, trying to listen for the ring of the bell inside. He was considering going off to find a phone booth from which he could telephone upstairs on the chance that the bell was out of order, when an elderly gentleman leading an elderly English bulldog walked up the front steps and into the alcove. He produced a key, opened the inner door, and went on inside, and Charles Stanley caught the door just before it closed. He waited for a moment and then went on in himself.

He climbed the stairs to the third floor and was rather reassured to see that the door was slightly ajar. Obviously she was expecting company. Perhaps she had gone to the apartment across the hall to borrow some ice or something at the last moment. He tapped lightly on the door, and called out, "Marcia?" There was no answer. He waited for a moment, and then, tentatively, he pushed the door slightly further ajar and went in.

The apartment was almost dark, illuminated only by the half light that came from the northern exposure. It was very still. He could hear the sounds of traffic below. Puzzled, he called out once more, "Marcia?"

He turned on the light and saw the blood on the carpet.

"Marcia!" he called. He assumed that she had cut herself somehow and had gone to get help, but his supposition lasted only a fraction of a second. He followed the blood to the kitchen and saw her lying on the floor.

"Marcia!" he shouted for the last time. And then he saw all the blood on the floor, and he saw her throat. He vomited. Shakily, he made his way back to the living room and picked up the telephone. He dialed "O" and asked the operator for the police.

It was a curious and difficult thing to do. The operator wanted to know what number he was calling from, and he had to look down and read numbers off the telephone. Then he had to tell the desk sergeant who answered the phone that he had discovered a body. The desk sergeant asked for the address, which seemed reasonable, but then he transferred the call to a lieutenant in homicide to whom he had to tell it all over again. Then he had to give his name. It seemed so very complicated and difficult, rather as if he were dreaming that he was running through some sticky, clinging substance. And the taste of the vomit in his mouth made it all the more nightmarish.

At last the lieutenant said that they would be right over, and warned him not to touch anything.

The two of them sat there on the blue couch, smoking cigarettes and looking at each other. All around them was the activity of specialists from the homicide division and from the crime lab, but Lieutenant of Detectives Dan Prince ignored them, keeping his eyes on Stanley. It had to be either Stanley or one of those millions out there. Prince could not help hoping it was Stanley. It would be lots less work that way.

"All right," he suggested, "let's go over this one more time." He was still polite. He could afford to be. The opportunity to question a suspect at the scene of the murder did not come up very often. It was, he supposed, a little corny, and rather like the last chapter of any mystery novel, but there was a psychological advantage in it that all those mystery writers had recognized and that his professors back at Michigan State—where he had studied criminology—had mentioned several times.

"You got here at what time?"

"Seven o'clock. Two minutes of."

"You're sure of that?"

"Yes, I checked my watch downstairs. I rang the bell and there was no answer and I happened to look at my watch, just to make sure I wasn't too early."

"And you used your key to get in the door?"

"No, no. I told you, I didn't have a key. I don't have a key," Stanley protested. "There was a man downstairs who came in. With a dog. I followed him."

"What kind of a dog?"

"A bulldog."

"And how did you get in here?"

"I told you. The door was open."

"Open wide?"

"No, just a little bit. I rang the bell. No, no, I didn't. I called. And I knocked. But there was no answer. I called again. I think I did. Anyway, I pushed the door open and came in. I saw the blood. I found her in there. And then I called the police."

"Right," said Prince. "Now, tell me, Mr. Stanley, were you working this afternoon?"

"No, it's a Saturday."

"I know what day it is. Where did you say you work?"

"John Hancock. I'm a computer programmer."

"What were you doing this afternoon?"

"I was at home watching the ball game on television."

"Friends with you?"

"No, I was at home alone."

"What game? And what was the score at the end?"

"The Yankees," he said. He meant the Red Sox–Yankees game, but that was understood, in Boston.

"It was a good game, wasn't it?"

"Yes, it was."

"You do remember the score, don't you?"

He tried to remember, but he couldn't. "No," he admitted. "I don't. I can't."

Lieutenant Prince got up, walked to the window, and flipped his cigarette end out of it.

"Had you and Miss Church been friends for long?" he asked, after a moment.

"About three months."

"See a lot of her?"

"Some."

"Well, twice a week? Three times a week? What?"

"About twice a week, I guess."

"Sleeping with her?"

Stanley did not answer. Prince turned from the window, looked at him for a moment, and asked again, "Well, were you?" He came back to the couch, stood over Stanley, and remarked, in almost an offhand way, "She was raped, you know, before she was killed."

The young man looked up at him. He seemed to take it pretty well.

"Were you in love with her?"

"Yes. No. I don't know. I mean, yes, I was sleeping with her. I don't know whether we were in love. I didn't do it."

"You were sleeping with her, but you didn't love her."

"I liked her. I liked her a lot. But I wasn't ready to settle down. She wasn't either. She had lots of friends."

"She was sleeping with them, too?"

"Some of them."

"How do you know that?"

"She told me."

"It bother you?"

"I don't know. Maybe a little," he said. And then, "No, not really. I have other friends, too. Look, it was just civilized. We enjoyed each other's company. We enjoyed each other."

Prince nodded. The nod was partly one of comprehension and partly one of anticipatory fatigue. If that's the way she was, he thought, then it might be a long, drawn-out, messy investigation.

"Do you know any of her other friends?" he asked.

"A few. There were a lot of them that I'd never met. And I forget the names of some of the ones I did meet. Look, I've told you what happened. Can I go?"

"Not just yet," Prince said, but he smiled while he said it. "Anybody call you while you were watching the game?"

"The game?"

"This afternoon. You said you were watching the ball game."

"Oh, yes. Uh, no. I don't think . . . Hey, wait! Yes."

"Yes?"

"My mother called."

"Do you remember about when that was?" Mothers, he knew,

were useless. They would say anything. But, still, he supposed he could hurt nothing by asking.

"You mean the time?"

"Yes, the time."

"I don't know the time. But Mantle had just hit a triple."

"Okay, we can find out the time from that," Prince said. "Where does your mother live?"

"Chatham. It's down on the Cape."

The detective nodded. Chatham would be a toll call. There would be a record of it.

A sergeant called to him from the door. The lieutenant got up, said, "Excuse me," and went to the door to hear the sergeant's report. He had found a man on the second floor who owned an English bulldog and who remembered coming in at about seven. Between the toll call from Chatham and the man with the bulldog, it looked as though this Stanley was off the hook. The coroner had said that from the way the blood was congealed, he supposed the girl to have been dead for at least two hours.

He sighed, went back to the couch, and told Mr. Stanley he could go home. He went back to the window and looked out of it.

Somewhere out there was a rapist and a killer.

Somewhere out there too, he hoped, was the top half of a beer bottle.

2

From the pay station near the wharf Nina Kirby called the house on the island.

"Tomcat House," the pleasant voice of the switchboard girl announced.

"Boathouse, please," Nina asked. "This is Nina Kirby."

"Certainly, Miss Kirby," the switchboard girl said, and connected her.

"Boathouse. Captain Preston."

"Jack? Nina Kirby. Will you come and pick me up, please?"

"Yes, ma'am. I'll be there in a few minutes."

It took only four or five minutes for the hydrofoil, starting from the island headquarters of Irvin Kane's publishing empire, to maneuver through the busy waters of Boston harbor to the wharf on the mainland. Nina tied a thin blue chiffon scarf around her hair and enjoyed the cool breeze from off the water. It would have been perfectly possible for her to have taken the launch along with the rest of the guests, but her position—she was the feature editor of *Tomcat* magazine—entitled her to such special perquisites as the use of Irv's hydrofoil.

Most of the time Nina went out to the parties at Tomcat House with Bud, but this evening she was alone because Bud had gone to Logan to meet Fred Postman's plane. Postman was the guest of honor this evening, the author of the novella that was featured in the September issue. The novella, *The Monkey House*, was startlingly and even shockingly frank, but its literary merit was undeniable. Even more important, Postman's position as the *enfant terrible* of American letters, his literary reputation, and his stature provided Irvin with a certain degree of insurance against prosecution. It had also worked to Postman's advantage, enabling him to command an extraordinarily high figure—even compared with the usually high rates that *Tomcat* paid.

The hydrofoil approached the wharf at a great curve, sending up a spray of water behind it. The roar modulated as Captain Preston reduced the speed of the engines. The boat settled down in the water, slowed, and pulled up alongside. Preston jumped ashore, tied the boat to a piling with a mooring line, and helped Nina down onto the deck.

She had offered to go out to Logan with Bud to keep him company while he waited for Postman's plane, but he had insisted that she go on out to Tomcat House. It was hot and unpleasant in town, and it would be cooler and more comfortable out on the island.

The boat made its way through the choppy water of the harbor and approached the island. Nina could see the great cylinder of poured concrete that was Tomcat House. It looked like a massive pillbox, and its military aspect was emphasized by the lack of any landscaping on the island. There was nothing but the boathouse, the road leading to the house, and the house itself, the top twenty feet of which were perfectly smooth, uninterrupted by any windows.

Irvin Kane was an insomniac, could not sleep, and was afraid of not being able to sleep. He had decreed—God knows how many years ago—that it would always be daytime when he was awake. Night could come on only after he had fallen asleep. He never went to bed. He took catnaps in one of the innumerable Barcaloungers that were scattered all through the house. It was ironical, Nina supposed, that there were no beds in his private quarters. What pleasure he took with women he took on those Barcaloungers or on the thick pile rugs on the floor. It was also ironical that his attempt to decree perpetual day had brought upon the house something very like perpetual night, for it was always brilliantly lit inside, but with artificial light. There were no windows through which the light of the sun could shine, or fail to shine.

There were no clocks, either, in any of the rooms in which Kane ever set foot. And he never wore a watch. The only places that Nina had ever been that had been anything like this were the gambling casinos in the Las Vegas hotels. Of course, you could always ask one of the guards there what time it was. But you had to ask.

Nina got out of the boat and walked fifteen feet to the little red Triumph that was waiting to take her up to the house. Captain Preston followed her, and then, running a few steps ahead, opened the door for her. The automobile had nowhere to go except the four hundred yards that ran from the dock to the front door and back. It had never been out of second gear. But Kane kept it there to save his guests the trouble of walking, and himself, too, if he ever had occasion to go out, which was rare indeed.

Usually Nina liked to walk after the boat ride, but tonight she let Captain Preston drive her. Even here, out on the island, it was warm and muggy.

The little car pulled up to the stainless steel doors, which opened silently as she approached. The doorman inside had been watching her on the closed-circuit television.

"Good evening, Miss Kirby," the doorman said.

Nina smiled and asked, "How are you, Berney?"

"Fine, thanks," he answered. "Big crowd tonight."

"Good, good," Nina said, smiling again. She went on, up the stairs. Her smile had faded by the third step. She did not enter the huge living room but continued up another flight to the elevator that went up to Kane's private quarters. She pushed the button, the door closed behind her, and the elevator rose noiselessly. It stopped, but the door did not open. Kane, inside, had to push a button at his console of monitors and electronic gadgets to complete the circuit of the elevator door mechanism. The door opened and she stepped out.

"Nina, good to see you!" Irv said. "Come in and cool off."

"Thanks," she said. "Miserable night."

"Drink?"

"Yes, thanks. Gin and tonic."

He went over to the little bar that was ordinarily hidden away behind a panel in the wall and mixed her the drink.

From a chair at the far end of the L-shaped room, Mimsy Perkins, Irv's current girl, waved languidly at Nina but hardly took her eyes from the television screen on which she was watching the Sport of the Week in living color.

Irv Kane was wearing his regular costume for his Saturday night parties, a beige silk V-neck pullover with matching beige slacks that had dark brown stitching down the side seams. He was barefoot. His face was attractive but bland, and his straight, black hair was brushed back without a part. The point of the widow's peak, exaggerated by the recession of the hairline above the temples, gave an angularity to his otherwise roundish face. He was neither short nor stocky, but compact. In splendid physical shape for a man of thirty-seven, or indeed for a man of twenty-seven, he worked out in his gymnasium frequently and swam in his pool two or three times a day. But the energy was more than physical. It was almost a spiritual condition. It had, however, the peculiar effect of making his stature seem to be a momentary thing—as if he were a coiled spring that at any moment might expand, grow taller, leaner, huge.

It took a while before one began to sense this odd quality of his. At first glance, he seemed unimpressive, ordinary. But the gestures, the intensity of his concentration on whatever was at hand, the energy in him, made him seem larger than he was. Indeed, she would not have been surprised to find that he could make his hair stand up, the way animals do when frightened or angry.

Nina had been struck by this quality the first time she had met Irv Kane. She had come up on assignment from a ladies' magazine in New York to interview him. She had come to report and had stayed to work. And it had been as much the magnetism of the man as the challenge of the job or the lure of the phenomenal salary that had kept her at *Tomcat*.

And yet it was not simply a physical attraction that he had for her, nor even that fantastic energy. It was the way in which that energy was improbably combined with a kind of vulnerability that had aroused in her what she could not deny was love. But it was a hopeless kind of love—with which she had learned to live as a fact of life.

Irv preferred young girls of eighteen or nineteen, never older than twenty. They were beautiful mindless creatures—she thought of them as "the hardbodies"—in endless succession. She had been able to discover little pattern to these relationships. Some of them lasted as much as a few months, others lasted only a matter of days, or, for all she knew, hours. She could not take them seriously; they were relationships of a kind she could not even comprehend. Irv had no idea how she felt about him, but in the course of their work together she had earned his respect and his friendship and that was enough to feed the fantasies she occasionally allowed herself.

Her fantasies, she supposed, were no more peculiar or any more absurd than his were. But neither were they any less adolescent. The only difference was that she knew this. But, then, perhaps he did, too.

Cato, the Filipino houseboy, entered through the service door bearing a fresh pizza and set it down on the table near Irv. He took one of the wedges of the pizza and bit into it. "Have some," he said, chewing. "This one's anchovy."

Downstairs, in the kitchen, they went through a cycle of thirty different kinds every day. Anchovy wasn't so bad, Nina thought as she picked up a slice. It was the lox pizzas she couldn't stand.

"Great," Irv said. "Isn't it?"

"Very good," Nina said.

"Mimsy," Irv called, offering the girl a slice.

"You know they're terrible for my figure," she answered archly.

"You can afford it," he said.

Nina suppressed a smile. It was a nice decision the girl had to make. She was damned if she did, and damned if she didn't. Nina gave her another couple of weeks at the outside.

"Hey, we've got a terrific flick tonight," Kane said. "Remember the girl who was in the gatefold last year? November?"

"Priscilla something," Nina offered.

"Yeah, that's the one. She's got a bit part in this. It's real small, but . . ." Just then the buzzer sounded. Irv threw a switch on the console and, suddenly substituting for the Sport of the Week, a view of the interior of the elevator flashed onto the screen. Bud had arrived with Fred Postman in tow.

Irv pushed the button, the elevator door opened, and the two men stepped out. Even before Bud had a chance to introduce him, Fred Postman stepped—virtually lunged—forward, seized Irv's hand in his, pumped it vigorously, and said, "A pleasure. Great boat you've got there. Crazy house." He finally released Irv's hand, stepped back, slung his jacket, which he had been carrying onto a chair, looked first at Nina and then at Mimsy, and silently surveyed the entire room. Irv introduced him to the two women.

"I've looked forward to meeting you," Nina said quietly.

He looked at her for a moment, smiled, and then surprised her by the authority of his simple "Thanks."

He was a big man, tall, broad-boned, beefy, and even gone slightly to paunch. His hair was worn long, and it curled on the back of his neck. But the effect of Postman's appearance was rather the opposite of what Nina supposed was his intention. Instead of looking like an elder statesman of letters, he looked all the more boyish. And the way he had of jutting out his lower lip only emphasized that boyishness. He was, after all, a very young man for the kind of eminence he had achieved. He had started out as a boy wonder with a big war novel, and then had gone on to pioneer with the disaffected, disaffiliated, disengaged novels that had caught the restlessness of the fifties and had made him such an idol on campuses and among intellectuals. For their part, the intellectuals seemed to adore him all the more for his contemptuous dismissal of academic writers, academic critics, academic anything. Postman had taken up spearfishing, boxing, sky-diving, and continued Hemingway's bully-boy cult. And all the intellectuals loved him for it.

"Would you play host?" Irv asked Bud.

"Sure," Bud said, and he asked Fred Postman what he wanted to drink.

"Jesus, but I wish you'd told me what you really do," Fred kidded. "I wouldn't have been so hard on you on the way out here. I mean, for Christ's sake. Bartending is honest work!"

"I do other things, too," the managing editor said.

"I'll bet you do, sweetheart. I'll bet you do. But you can get me a gin on the rocks, and it will be recorded in the book up there that you have done a good work. I'll even let the angel put me on the scale holding the damned gin. That'll balance out a lot of magazines, now, won't it?"

"You disapprove of *Tomcat*?" Irv asked.

"No, not at all. I never knock any man's racket. And I like tits as well as the next fellow. No, I think it's fine. But it's not what I had in mind for old Biddle here."

"Biddle?" Mimsy asked.

"Yeah, Biddle. Bud, here. Biddle Mellon Sloat. Ain't that a gas?"

"I don't understand," Mimsy said.

"Oh, knock it off, will you?" Bud said, as good-naturedly as he could manage. He handed Fred the glass with the gin in it.

"Anything you say, old Bud-bud," Fred returned, smiling. He raised his glass. "Well, here's to tits. Long may they wave!"

"There are other things in the magazine," Irv protested. "Your novella, for instance."

"Sure. But I was acknowledging that fountain—or should I say those fountains?—from which all the other blessings flow. Okay?" And he winked at Irv, as one conspirator to another.

Irv thought for a moment, then relaxed and smiled.

"When it comes down to the wire, you cop out and get pleasant," Bud suggested. "Is that it?"

"That's me. The old arch-cop-out! You got an eye for it, haven't you?"

"All right."

"Do you mind if I ask you a question?" Nina broke in.

"Not at all."

"Why are you needling him?"

"Because he's a friend. And because I don't like to see him taking himself so damned seriously."

"What makes you think he takes himself too seriously?" she asked.

"On the way over here, we heard about a rape-murder. On the 'Twenty-twenty' news, or some such thing. It has to do with the time, rather than with the clarity of vision with which they report. Anyway, some kid got herself done and done. And Buddy-boy here took that text as the occasion for a sermon on the hang-ups of the *homo Americanus,* and then delivered himself of a peroration on the spiritual value he thought society just might derive from the contemplation of *Tomcat* magazine."

"You don't agree?" Irv asked.

"Nope."

"Why not?" he asked. He almost snapped the question.

"Because I don't believe that books—or magazines or newspapers—*do* anything. Nobody gets hurt by books, or helped by them. If they did, we'd have seen some improvement since Plato, say, or *Candide,* or—for God's sake—the Bible."

"But you write."

"For the fun of it. And for the money. But not for the betterment of mankind."

"You don't think that betterment of mankind is worth thinking about?" Nina asked, hoping to make the subject more general.

"It's worth thinking about. But it may not be possible. And if it were possible, I'm not sure that editing a tit-book would be the first place I'd think of starting."

"We all do what we can," Irv said.

"Yes, we do that. But we shouldn't fool ourselves any more than we have to. There may be a lot of foolishness in me. Or in you. You and I may need that to keep going. But Bud here shouldn't need it. Or Miss Kirby, here."

Nina could feel his gaze upon her as if it were something of weight, like the touch of a hand. She was trying to figure him out, to decide not so much whether she liked him or disliked him but what it was that had gone into that weird concoction of a personality now confronting her.

The aggressiveness, even the unpleasantness, she had seen before in other authors who felt uncomfortable about the fact that their work was appearing in *Tomcat*, who disliked themselves for needing the money or, anyway, for taking it, and who turned their dislike against Irv, or against them all. But Fred Postman wasn't coming on quite that way. Nina was rather inclined to believe that his concern really was with Bud—whom he had known well enough to know his real name. Biddle Mellon Sloat! Irv knew it, of course. It would have been on the personnel records. And she knew it. But then she had been sleeping with Bud off and on for a year now. And Fred knew it.

Bud had told Nina that he knew Fred, but had not said much more than that. Which was typical of him. Fred's was a name he would not drop, not only because of his own modesty but because the affirmation of such an association, of such a friendship, would have been the affirmation of his past and its promise. Bud had been a novelist, too. He had published three novels, all of them quite elegant and impressive, and . . . But, as he'd said, himself, you can't eat reviews. He had latched onto Irv Kane, and had intended to stay only a little while, in order to earn his grubstake for the fourth book. That had been seven years ago. Long enough to labor in any man's vineyards.

"You don't think of yourself as improving the lot of humankind, do you?" Fred asked Nina, jutting the lip again.

"I don't know," she said. "I think there may be some good effects that the magazine may have. Repression and fear are not good things. *Tomcat* may be doing a little to get rid of some of that."

"Tell that to the Church girl," Fred said.

"The Church girl?" Irv asked.

"The girl who got herself killed," Fred said. "Martha or Marcia. Or maybe Margaret. But Church."

"Marcia, I think," said Bud.

"Not *our* Marcia Church!" Irv turned to Nina. "We have a Marcia Church. In photo. You know her."

"Yes, I think so."

"She didn't get killed, did she?"

"It was on Beacon Hill," Fred volunteered.

Irv crossed the room, picked up the phone, pushed a button, and was connected immediately to the Kane Building in Boston. He asked for Marcia Church's address. Then he hung up.

"Beacon Hill!"

"It's not an uncommon name. There could be two or three Marcia Churches living on Beacon Hill."

"That'd set your crusade back a few miles now, wouldn't it, Buddy!" Fred said.

"That's not very funny, Mr. Postman," Irv snapped. Then he asked, "What the hell time is it? There ought to be a news program on somewhere."

Without waiting for an answer, he went back to the console and turned knobs and dials. Radio stations blared and died as he searched for a voice, for news, for something other than the beat of pop songs and the blandishments of commercials. It took a few minutes before he got a news summary. They all stood there, listening, as the few facts that had been released to the press were recited again. The girl's name and address, and the expectation that the murderer would soon be apprehended. And then the weather.

Irv turned the machine off.

"Jesus!"

Irv rubbed his forehead with his thumb and forefinger, and then turned and pointed at Fred Postman. "This is just what I mean when I tell people that *Tomcat* is liberating. This kind of thing happens because guys are afraid of real sex. Rape is a cop-out."

"That depends," Postman said.

"What are you talking about? You don't know what you're talking about!"

"Do you? Have you ever raped anyone?"

"I've read about it. I read a lot here."

"So do I read a lot. But the guys who go around raping people don't read so much! Not even *Tomcat*. Not even street signs."

"Look," Bud said. "We've got to think about this, but we've got to do it calmly. And later. There are people downstairs waiting for us . . ."

"You all go on down," Irv said. "You, too, Mimsy. I'll be down later on. I . . . I've got to send flowers. And to think."

"Look," Fred said, "I'm sorry about the girl. I mean, I wouldn't have come on this way if I'd know that she worked for you. That you knew her."

"No, no. I understand. That's okay," Irv said, and, abruptly, he shot out his hand to Fred Postman, who shook it in what appeared to Nina to be a gesture of spontaneous warmth and even gentleness.

Then they went into the elevator, Fred, Bud, Nina, and Mimsy, to go downstairs, to the living room and the thirty or so guests. And the movie.

Twenty minutes later, after Bud had introduced Fred to the other guests, they sat down to watch the screening of the film. It was a comedy, but not funny enough to engage Nina's attention. She sat there, between Bud and Fred, and let her mind wander. She thought of Marcia Church, whom she could not imagine as being dead, much less violated and murdered. And she thought of herself, there in the dark room with men on either side of her and, through the ceiling, above her.

Which was odd. It struck her, abruptly, that she was including Postman in that constellation. She glanced to her left and looked at his profile. And saw him glance at her. She turned back to face the screen.

So, it had not been pure fancy. He was, in however trivial a way, interested. There were the vibrations. She had enjoyed, before, the way in which the novelist had hardly noticed Mimsy, and had resisted the temptation to turn that into something. She would have liked to think that a real man would be interested in a woman more than in one of those polyurethane hardbodies. And all the sensitive little indicators suggested that with Fred Postman that was exactly the case. But she had been reluctant to make a thing out of it because it was all so treacherous. For all she knew, Fred's attention to her might have been a way of putting Irv Kane down. To ignore or despise Mimsy was, in a way, to despise Irv. And to send out unspoken messages to her was, in a way, to affront Bud. But then Fred couldn't possibly know that Bud was her lover. Could he? No. Even allowing for the intuition of novelists, it was nonsense.

Why, then, best of all, it was to her, directly and without any strategic reason at all, that he had responded, sounding his civilized version of the bull-moose call of choice. A glance, an intonation, a pause of just a beat or so in the lighting of her cigarette, and it was all as clear as though it had been bellowed out through the thick silences of evergreen forests, echoing against rock outcroppings, and fading off into the cold bowl of the sky.

She tried to push all this out of her mind and to watch the film, but she couldn't. It was just no good telling herself that she was imagining it, because she knew better. Her antennae were a lot finer tuned than they had been that first time, when she had seized upon Jon. That affair, and marriage, and divorce had taught her something, surely. At the very least, it had taught her to rely on the kinds of intuitions and hunches that presented themselves to her sometimes. She had known, deep down, that Jon was different. It had been his delicacy and his refinement that had attracted her, and the challenge. What had been the warning—or should have been—was that sense of challenge. For she had known, down under all the reason and intelligence and education, in the bedrock of her nerves and glands, she had known that he was a homosexual, and had taken it as a challenge, had taken it upon herself to convert him, with all the high purpose and fervor of a missionary among the heathen. And like many missionaries she had been lucky to escape alive, without having been thrown into the huge stewpot by cannibals.

She ventured another glance to her left, this one lasting only an instant. And she was reassured. Yes, she was right, absolutely right. The beginning of the paunch, the carelessness about his clothing, the curls at the back of his head, all pointed to the same thing—that he was a man, confident enough of his phallus to be able to relax about the rest of his body and even let it go a little to fat and sloppiness.

And Bud? That was a difficult question. She had avoided it because she knew that he had avoided it, but now, for no reason at all—or, perhaps, for the only reason, the only real reason—Postman was raising it: what responsibility did she and Bud have toward each other? If any.

Oh, what they said to each other was all so intelligent, so sophisticated and civilized . . . But did she believe it? Did he? He was, after all, a convenience for her. As she was for him. And they had admitted as much to each other, and delighted in their maturity and their honesty. But after a year of sharing each other's bodies, was it still true? Didn't they owe each other anything?

It had begun in such a ridiculous way, with each of them telling the other how very sensible it was, and all the while knowing that it was never sensible, that its only sense could be stupid necessity and a need that transcended sense. But he was comforting her for Irv's unavailability, and she was comforting him for—everything. For that fourth novel that he had never written, and would probably never write. And for his two divorces. And for his softness in allowing Irv to keep him on the hook with toys like the Maserati and the apartment, and the American Express card and the money.

And yet, after all, it was so banal. What was it but an ordinary little office affair? Or, no, she was being unfair. They had had good times together, liked each other, were good in bed together. Wasn't that enough? Wasn't that all she wanted, all she was willing to take—from anyone? As if to apologize for her peculiarly disloyal thoughts, she reached over with her right hand and took Bud's, holding it. A moment later, Fred took her other hand.

It was as if he knew what she had been thinking. She flushed with emotion and embarrassment, but she did not try to withdraw her hand. It was exciting to experience such intensity of feeling—even if of embarrassment and shame. It was, at least, an indication that she was alive, fully and entirely alive. And that kind of intensity was rare for her—or, she suspected, for anyone. The only thing was that, now, with both of her hands immobilized, she wanted to scratch the side of her nose, which tickled. She remembered that an itchy palm was supposed to be a sign of physical attraction. But a ticklish nose?

She wished that the movie were funnier, because she felt like laughing. And the more she thought about it, the funnier it seemed. The question of etiquette, for instance, was deliciously fine. If she did decide to scratch the side of her nose where the tickle was, which hand should she abandon? In those pornographic books that Bud had in his apartment, in which one woman satisfied two or three or seven Cossacks or Tartars or Mongols at once, such small, but important, questions never arose. Which was the trouble with those books.

She endured the itching. And, most curiously of all, she tried to think about something else. About Irv, upstairs. She wished, in a way, that he could see her now. It would serve him right, after that first interview. She remembered—she was afraid she would always remember—that interview. There had probably been nothing quite like it in the annals of journalism.

She had come up all crisp and efficient, with her two matched leather suitcases from Mark Cross and her Hermes portable, had taken the launch out to the island, and had met Irvin Kane, the mammary mogul, the fearless publisher, the nervous, occasionally brusque, but nevertheless fascinating man. The angle her editor in New York had suggested was clever enough—what could this man who was so successful in marketing female sexuality suggest to females who were, in one way or another, trying to market their own? It had been light and catchy, and easy enough.

But he had been surprisingly serious, and had furrowed his brow, rubbed it with thumb and forefinger, and had considered, as if for the first time, the relation of his magazine to the women of America. "They benefit from it," he had said, "in two ways. Or perhaps three. The first is that when men are less inhibited and less afraid of their own sexuality, women will naturally be the beneficiaries. But that is fairly abstract and indirect. More important, I think, is the opportunity that the magazine provides for fantasy and voyeurism. Men are always looking for variety in their sexual lives, and as between actual extramarital affairs and imaginary ones with the pictures in *Tomcat,* I think the majority of women would prefer the latter. Voyeurism—which is deriving sexual satisfaction, or at least sexual stimulation, from *looking*—is comparatively harmless, and yet it satisfies some of that sexual curiosity that all men have without threatening any of the real relationships upon which they've built their lives."

"And the third reason?" she had asked.

"Women like to look at other women. On the street, when you see a couple together, you look at the woman first, don't you? You check the man. And then you look at the woman again. It's as if you were a comparison shopper, working for Macy's and looking at the displays in Gimbel's. Whether it's a Lesbian thing or not, I don't know. But it's there."

He had been interesting, and interested, engaging and engaged. But Nina had interviewed many people who had been good subjects. What intrigued her, what hooked her, had been the peculiar finale to their conversation. They had been sitting in a kind of breakfast nook upstairs, in the private quarters, and Bambi—the hardbody of that moment—had come in, joined them, sat down, and started to eat. Froot Loops! Of all foolish things! And Nina had asked Irv one of her trick questions.

"Who are you?"

"What does that mean?" he had asked.

"Who are you?"

"Irv Kane, of course."

"Yes, but aside from that, who are you?"

"I am the founder and publisher of *Tomcat* magazine."

"And aside from *that,* who are you?"

He had looked at her, looked up at the ceiling, and then, with a smile, had thrown it back at Nina. "That's a good question. Really sharp!"

"Thank you," she had said. "And what would the answer be?"

"I'd have to think about that, now, wouldn't I? Let's see . . . Cato, this coffee is cold. And . . . and I need a cigar. No, no I don't. A piece of coffee cake. Or, no, that's not it. What I need . . . what I need is a piece of ass. That's what I need. Would you excuse me for just a moment?"

Nina had looked on in disbelief as Irv Kane had got up from the table and walked off with Bambi obediently following, still chewing on a mouthful of Froot Loops.

And Bud, who had been there, had noticed the visceral reaction she'd had, and had tried to comfort her. Even then, even that first time.

"He builds up a lot of pressure," Bud had offered.

"You don't say."

"He makes his own rules."

"You don't say."

"Still, you've got to admit that it wasn't a bad answer to your question, now, was it? I mean, if you sit there posing Zen questions, you're likely to get some Zen-ny answers, aren't you?"

And it had been, she had supposed, a Zen-ny answer. The sound of one hand clapping and all that mysterious stuff. Or maybe it had been another Zen-ny question, for when he had come back and found that she was still there, unruffled, because she had refused to seem ruffled, or let on that her instincts for sexual competition had been at all aroused, he had offered her the job of feature editor. Or maybe it was because he needed the kind of acceptance, the kind of permissiveness that she seemed to be giving him by the blandness and the poise of her smile and her matter-of-fact resumption of the interview.

Yes, that had to be it, and it also had to be that his performance, his going off with Bambi that way, had been in some part for her, to impress her, to try to shock her, the way a teen-ager will tell a dirty joke or pull a girl's braids, not to hurt her, but because he finds himself attracted to her. It had never happened since that time, but then, there had been no reason for it to happen again. A bond of that kind, however strange and inexplicable —or perhaps because of its strangeness and inexplicability—did not need to be re-established or repaired once it had been established. Neither of them ever made allusion to it. But it was there, somehow, all the time. Nina felt it, and felt that it enabled her to continue to work with him. For instance, when they discussed the facial expression or the legs or the breasts of various centerfold candidates, it was almost as though they were a husband and wife discussing these things. There was an intimacy, a closeness that enabled them to communicate the slightest nuances of preference.

It was the appearance of Miss November on the screen that had made Nina think of that. But the banality of the movie kept flipping her thoughts back, the way the levers at the bottom of a pinball machine send the ball back up for further adventures among the ringing bells and flashing lights and bumpers and springs. And still, on either side of her, the two men, each of them holding her hand, and in every way except the merely physical and literal, tugging at her. And the thought of that, the awareness of it in the forefront of her mind made that tickle return to the side of her nose—which was, she speculated, the only undiscovered, unexploited erogenous zone. "Nonsense."

"I beg your pardon?" Bud asked.

"Nonsense," she said, again, startled that she had said it aloud the first time. It was not the ideal situation for talking to oneself aloud. "The movie, I meant."

"Well, of course," Fred said. "What did you expect?"

She was about to answer when she felt Bud withdraw his hand. Quite naturally, when Fred had spoken, Bud had turned to look in his direction, and had noticed, had seen—must have seen—that he was holding her other hand. And had released the one that he had been holding. Which meant?

She glanced to her right, but his face was riveted to the screen as if in utter absorption. It was not—could not possibly be—that he was giving his approval, was telling her to go and have fun, to enjoy herself. It was something else, jealousy or defeat, or both. He had backed down, not even locking horns with Fred, but merely hearing that bull-moose bellow and turning to run.

Or, no, that wasn't right. These metaphors were tempting, but finally misleading. For they were none of them savages. And she was drawn all the more toward Bud because of this new defeat piled on all the old ones, and the way they had acquiesced, yielding without a struggle.

It was ridiculous, but she felt a prickle at her eyelids—more natural and reasonable than a tickle at the flange of the nostril, but all the more absurd for that—as though she were about to cry. With the now-free hand, she reached up and brushed at her eyelids, lightly, carefully, so as not to smudge her mascara. And she took a deep breath.

And then, thank God, the film came to an end, and the lights came on, and Irv appeared, and the food was announced. And she could have another drink!

"I ordered a hundred dollars' worth of flowers from the staff of *Tomcat*," Irv told her, *sotto voce*. "Do you think that was too little? Or too much?"

"No, that's fine. Just right," she answered.

And Postman came up, drink in hand, to say, "It really is a hell of a fine place you've got here!"

"It's fun," Irv said, enjoying the praise.

Postman looked around at the huge semicircular room, admiring the reds and blacks and whites of the abstract tapestries, the marble tables, the leather chairs, and the cleanliness of line that quietly murmured of money. It was a big room, but neither barny nor cold, which was admirable.

"You have anything to do with this?" Fred asked, waving his hand around the room.

"No, I just edit," she said.

"Strange job," he said.

"How so?"

"Well, isn't it? A woman editing a magazine like this?"

"Not at all. Who would know better how to interest men than a woman?"

"And do you?"

"Do I what?"

"Do you know how to interest men?"

"That's what I get paid for."

"You only do it for pay?" he asked. "What do you do for relaxation, then? For fun?"

She looked at him. She looked away from him, and noticed Irv, who had stepped away a few moments before to greet a latecomer. She saw that he was watching her, watching the two of them, deliberately waiting to bring the newcomer up for an introduction when the moment was right. But it wasn't that at all. He was watching to see what she would do. And it pleased her a little, more than a little, to know that he was watching, to know that he was learning that, even at the advanced age of thirty-two, she could be attractive to men—even to important men, manly men like Fred Postman, men who had been bored by Mimsy . . .

"Are you propositioning me?" she asked, half playfully. And half not.

"I might be. I don't know. Yeah, I guess I am."

"You don't seem quite certain."

"I'm out of practice."

"I don't believe you," she said, playing him, coquettish and pleased with herself.

"It's true. I *am* out of practice. You get to a certain point, you know, and everything changes. It isn't the way *Tomcat* says it is at all. Suddenly, you get to be twenty-five or twenty-eighty or thirty-three, and you aren't running after girls any more, or propositioning them even. They're running after you. And it's even worse—or better—if you're a celebrity. And whether I'm a writer or not, I am, Lord knows, a celebrity!"

"I'm sorry not to have been more forward," Nina said.

"Not at all. That's what I like about you. It was fun, after all. Sometimes it was fun. It's fun now."

She looked at him, decided that she liked him, and smiled.

And he smiled back, nodded slowly, and said, "Yeah, I'm propositioning you."

She looked at him, feeling good, feeling very happy, but not knowing what to do. Or what to say.

"Let's cut out, shall we?" he asked.

"I can't. Not now. Later, perhaps."

"Perhaps?" he asked. "Only perhaps? Well, okay."

And Irv brought up the new guest, a cartoonist.

After the introduction, Irv turned to her and said, quietly, "You two seem to be hitting it off splendidly."

"He's very amusing," she answered, trying not to gloat.

"Yes, I guess he can be."

A little while later, when the drift and eddy of the party deposited Bud beside her—or had he sought her out?—she tried to get some sort of reaction out of him. But he refused to give her one, withdrawing into himself.

"Interesting man, Postman," she said.

"Oh, yes."

"Do you like him?"

"I did. I guess I do. He's . . . he's awfully tough on his friends . . ."

"I'd noticed that," she said.

"But he's tough on himself, too. I suppose the toughness is what it takes. Not just the talent, or maybe not even the talent so much as that toughness . . ."

He trailed off, reluctant to bring himself into it, unwilling to make the comparison in any further detail between his career and Postman's. "Yes, I like him," he said, and he took a long pull at his drink.

So he would not say anything, would not fight. But then, to be honest, she had to admit that he had already made his comment, earlier, during the movie, when he had withdrawn his hand. And she remembered the way the tears had come to her eyes.

She hated herself for it. She could see it as a pattern, one that suddenly presented itself to her with ghastly clarity. Jon, Irv, Bud —they were all of them lame ducks, hurt in one way or another, and it was the hurt as much as the men themselves that had drawn her toward them. Fred Postman was robust and healthy and successful and confident. And she knew that she would not leave with him. And felt sorry, because she liked him. And found him attractive. Oh, God, yes. But she could not leave with him, not this time, not with Irvin watching her, and Bud . . .

And she would not sneak.

Later on that evening, Fred came up to her, stood in front of her, smiled, jutted out his lip, and asked, "Well?"

"No," she said. "Thanks, but no."

"It would have been good," he said.

"Yes," she said. "I know."

He looked at her for a moment, a long, searching look, which she returned with a steady, sure gaze.

"Okay," he said, and shook his head.

She was not surprised to see him talking with the young, rather pretty, but quite boring wife of the travel editor not fifteen minutes later. It hurt her, but then she thought how that hurt had been exactly what Bud must have felt. She went over to him and said, quietly, "Let's leave soon, huh?"

"All right," he said.

She felt a little disappointed. But then what had she expected? That he would be grateful? For an instant she regretted the choice she had made.

But it was too late, now, to go back.

3

Jerry Farber heard the phone ring, sighed, and put down the piece of the Sunday *Globe* that he had been reading. He got up from the glider, padded barefoot across the rattan rug, and went into the house. It was a nuisance, he thought. He was sure the call was for his daughter, Naomi, who was still asleep upstairs. Letty was down in the cellar doing the laundry, and he did not want her to have to race upstairs. She worked hard enough all week in the store with him.

It was already beginning to get hot in the house. The porch had been comfortable, and it was comfortable, he was sure, down in the cellar, but in the little entrance hall where the telephone stood on a small cherry spool-leg table, it was very warm. He picked up the phone and said "Hello?"

"Jerome Farber, please," a crisp voice requested.

"Speaking."

"This is Sergeant Rice of Homicide. We're checking a few facts on the Church murder."

"Church?" Farber asked, confused. He was an occasional worshiper at a synagogue, but a church? He had not read anything but the sports section of the *Globe* so far that morning.

"Yes, sir," the sergeant explained, patiently. "A young woman on Beacon Street, Marcia Church, was murdered yesterday."

"Oy Gott!"

"We're checking all the groceries and delicatessens in the area. Did your store send out an order to a Marcia Church any time yesterday?"

"Yes, yes we did."

"Did you deliver it yourself, sir?"

"No, I have a boy."

"And his name?"

"Frankie. Frank Scully."

"Do you remember what time that was, sir?"

"It was a busy day. Nobody wanted to go out yesterday. It was sometime in the afternoon."

"Did he return after the delivery, sir?"

"No, as a matter of fact, he didn't. It was late in the afternoon. It was on his last trip. I guess he went home after that. Funny, I'd paid him on Friday, but I owed him some overtime. I'd told him I'd give it to him after work on Saturday, but he never came back for it. I figured it was just the heat."

"Can you tell me, Mr. Farber, do you remember if there was any beer in the order?"

"Yes. I'm almost positive."

"Do you have an address for this Frank Scully?"

"Hold on just a minute," he said.

He put the phone down and went to the cellar door.

"Letty?" he called. "Letty!"

"Quiet," she said. "Naomi is still sleeping, no?"

She came to the foot of the cellar steps and looked up. "What is it?" she asked.

"That Frank. That Frank who delivers for us. Where does he live?"

"Why?"

"Never mind with why. Where does he live?"

"Somewhere in Dorchester."

"Where in Dorchester?"

"It's in the books. In the desk. It'd be on the withholding."

"Oh, yes. Yes."

"Do you want me to come up?"

"No, I'll find it."

On the way to the desk he stopped at the phone, picked it up, and asked the sergeant to hold on yet another minute. He would look it up. Then he went on out to the enclosed sun room, where he pulled out the top drawer of the secretary, located the books, and, after a few moments, found the address. He went back to the telephone and told the sergeant the address.

"Thank you very much, sir," the sergeant said. "We'll be in touch with you."

"You're welcome," he said, and hung up the phone.

Quickly, he went back to the porch and found the first section of the paper. There she was, on the front page, that nice Miss Church, staring out and smiling.

He read the first couple of paragraphs of the story, shaking his head. A terrible thing, he said to himself. He thought of his own daughter, Naomi, sleeping upstairs, shook his head, and said, once more, but this time, aloud, "A terrible thing."

It was difficult not to leap to a conclusion. Dan Prince tried, sincerely tried, to keep his mind—and the investigation—open. He was not trying to ignore the signs. Not at all. But he did want to try to keep alert to other signs that might yet appear, and that might point in other directions. Still, it was difficult to dismiss the increasing weight of the evidence. The cardboard carton in the Church kitchen had led him to the perfectly reasonable inference that a grocery delivery had been made. The five bottles of beer in the refrigerator, the glasses in the sink, and the shards of the beer bottle on the floor of the kitchen, all made it seem more than likely that the murder had taken place after the delivery. The beer bottle, they were now sure, had been the weapon. The medical investigation, which had turned up two minute glass slivers in the neck of the dead girl, had proved that. And they had found the murder weapon itself—the neck and body of the beer bottle—in a garbage can a block away from the dead girl's apartment, complete with blood stains of the correct type and two smudged fingerprints.

And now there was this delivery boy, with beer in the order, too.

Sergeant Rice parked the squad car half a block from the rooming house in Dorchester where Mr. Farber had said that Frank Scully lived. They had taken an unmarked car, and now they sauntered down the street until they stood opposite the rooming house. It was a shabby, three-story structure of gray shingle with a wide porch in front that was much in need of paint.

They crossed the street and went up the steps quickly, into the tiny foyer. There was one bell, and, beside it on the wall, a sheet of code rings for each of the tenants. Frank Scully's was three longs and a short.

"Shall we ring the super?" Rice suggested.

"Why bother?" Prince asked. "The door's open anyway."

It had been left ajar, propped open by a cast-iron Boston terrier in the hope that some air might penetrate into the closeness of the hall and stairwell.

"Silly!" Rice said, and shook his head.

"Yeah," Prince agreed, but with a smile.

They were, both of them, on edge.

They went inside and climbed the stairs quietly. Frank Scully's room was 3-B, the sheet in the hall had said. They climbed to the third floor.

"Which one is B?" Rice asked.

"That's F over there," Prince said.

"Then where are A,B,C,D, and E?"

"The F is probably for front. B must mean back."

"Well, that's the back," Rice said, nodding with his head.

"Yeah, I think so. Cover me, will you?"

Rice took his gun out of the holster, switched off the safety, and stood by the door. Prince knocked. There was no answer. He knocked again.

"Frank?" he called.

"Yeah?" a voice inside asked.

"Open the door."

"Who is it?"

"The police," Prince called out. "We want to talk to you."

"No."

"Come on, now. Open up!"

There was no answer.

Prince drew his gun, too, nodded at the door, and together the two of them ran at it, shouldered it, and nearly broke it open. They stepped back, charged it again, and it gave way.

It was a tense moment. The thing was to get in there fast, find the man, and estimate his intentions and dangerousness, all in a split second. That split second passed, and Prince could feel the adrenalin that still surged through his blood, even as he smiled and indicated to Rice the figure in the bed. Scully was lying in bed, with the covers drawn up to his neck.

"Take your hands out of those covers," he ordered.

"Why should I?"

"Because I told you to," Prince said. He was pointing the gun at Scully.

"You got a warrant?"

"You got life insurance?" Rice asked. "Come on! Let's see those hands!"

Scully took his hands out from under the covers. "You can't come breaking into a guy's room this way!" he said. "I know my rights."

They didn't answer him. Prince looked around the room. It was a pig pen. There was underwear strewn around on the floor, and dust along the walls. The walls themselves were covered with gatefold pictures showing nude and seminude girls in all sorts of poses. There were even girlie pictures taped to the ceiling. And written on the pictures, in broad, crude letters made, he supposed, with one of those felt-tipped pens, there were comments in balloons, as in comic strips: "Put it in me, Frankie!" "I want to suck your big cock!" and "Give me your fuck juice, Frankie!"

Prince stood there, holding his gun, while Rice went around the room, opening the closet, opening drawers, rummaging around to see what he could find.

"Hey, what do you guys want with me?" Scully asked. "I mean, what is this, anyway?"

"You don't know?"

"No," he said, belligerently, "I don't know. You tell me."

It was the same belligerence he had learned in school, or earlier than that, at home. But it was practiced. He had polished the technique—the half roar, half whine, with the lower lip protruding—by using it on principals and guidance teachers, on social workers and the juvenile court people, and on the police, too. There hadn't been anything serious, but the truancy and malicious mischief had been enough to teach him the manners. He hadn't learned it in the movies. The movie hoods were never quite so mean and nasty as the real ones. They didn't have that shade of sniveling that discolored the tough talk.

"This is one filthy guy," Rice commented to Prince, as if Scully were not there. "Jesus, what filth!"

"I see," Prince said.

"Look at that."

Rice was pointing to a Coke bottle, about a quarter full of Coca Cola, which Scully had been using as an ashtray. Wet cigarette butts were dissolving in it. It looked like a miniature toilet bowl.

"Even without that, it'd be bad enough," Rice went on. "The stink in here!"

"Hey, what the hell do you guys want?" Scully asked.

"You think about that," Prince suggested.

"I didn't think they made these things any more," Rice said.

"Made what things?" Prince asked.

"These dirty comic books. Popeye. Flash Gordon. Another Flash Gordon."

Rice had been looking through the top dresser drawer.

"Nudie playing cards, too," he said. "You wouldn't think he'd need them with the walls he's got in here, would you?"

"He needs any help he can get."

"What do you mean?" Scully asked.

"I mean you need any help you can get. You're not very good at it, are you?"

"Very good at what?"

"Sex," Prince said.

"I don't know what you're talking about."

"You play with yourself a lot, don't you?" Prince asked him. "That's what you were doing when we came in, wasn't it?"

"No."

"Sure you were."

"No, I wasn't."

"Throw that blanket off. Slow, now."

Scully threw the blanket down. He had been lying in bed in his dungarees and his T-shirt.

"See?" he asked.

"Look at that sheet!" Prince said.

"No, thanks," Rice answered.

Prince put the gun away.

"You know what I think?" he asked.

"What?" Rice asked.

"I think he raped her after he killed her."

"You think so?"

"Sure. He likes them dead. Don't you, Frank? Don't you like them dead? They don't fight with you when they're dead. They don't argue with you. They don't scare you when they're dead, isn't that right?"

"No. I don't know what you guys are talking about."

"Sure you do. All these damned pictures. It's pathetic. 'Give me your fuck juice,' huh? Your laundryman gets it all."

"If he's got a laundryman," Rice said.

"And so you found yourself a nice girl and you killed her. And then you slipped it to her, right?"

"I don't know anything about it. You got the wrong guy."

"I don't think so. You made the delivery to Marcia Church, yesterday, didn't you?"

"Sure. But I didn't kill her."

"Why didn't you go back to the store, then?"

"Why should I have gone back? That was my last delivery."

"What about the overtime Jerry Farber owed you? He was going to pay you Saturday night, but you didn't go back for it."

"I forgot about it."

"You forgot about money he owed you? You got so much money you don't bother to keep track?"

"I—I forgot because I had a bellyache. I didn't feel so good. All I wanted to do was come back and get into bed."

"And eat fried chicken?" Prince asked. He touched the Chicken Delight box with his toe.

"That was from the night before."

"He's not the neatest guy in the world, is he?" Rice asked.

"It's a crime to leave a box around in your room?"

"No, but murder is a crime."

"But I didn't kill her. I swear to Christ I didn't!"

"Then you got nothing to worry about, right?" Rice asked.

"That's right."

"Then why didn't you open the door?"

"I was sleeping."

"In your jeans?"

"That's a crime too?"

"Hey, tell me something, would you?" Prince asked.

"What?"

"What's it feel like to screw a dead girl?"

"I wouldn't know."

"Kind of crawly, wouldn't you say?" Prince asked.

"He's a crawly kind of guy, though," Rice said.

"I didn't. I wouldn't do anything like that. You don't know what you're talking about!" Scully said. He was angry now, and disgusted. As bad as it had been, what he had done had not been as bad as what Lieutenant Prince had suggested.

That, of course, was what Prince was counting on. The class prejudices of these people were reliable—even among rapists and murderers.

"You going to tell us about it?" Prince asked.

"There's nothing to tell. I didn't kill her. I didn't touch her."

"How'd you get that cut on your arm."

"I fell."

"On a beer bottle?"

"What do you mean? Where'd you get that?"

He did it pretty well, Prince thought. It had taken some self-control and some willpower to hide the fright. And he had done it pretty well, but not quite well enough. The timing had been off. The pause had been just a beat too long. He had just missed it.

"The beer bottle. You remember the beer bottle."

"I don't remember any beer bottle."

"Tell us about it."

"About what?"

"About the groceries you delivered to Marcia Church."

"What's to tell? I delivered the groceries. She let me in. I put the groceries down and then I left."

"Try it again. Tell us more. You can do better than that."

"No. That was what happened. That was the way it was."

"You helped her put the stuff in the refrigerator, didn't you?"

"I might have."

"And you had a beer with her, didn't you?"

"No."

"If you're going to lie, you've got to know when to lie and when to tell the truth. The glass on the sink had your prints on it."

"I had a beer with her. Yes. But then I left."

"That's better. Now you're coming along. But you still aren't making it. Tell us how you cut yourself."

"I told you. I fell."

"On a beer bottle."

"No, it wasn't a beer bottle."

"We found the bottle, Frank. It's got your prints on it, Frank. We found it in the garbage can where you left it."

"It wasn't a beer bottle."

"Your prints are on it, Frank."

There were prints on it, and by now Prince was sure they were Frank's prints. So it was true, even if the prints were smudged.

"I didn't . . ." he started to say. And then he turned his face to the wall. "I didn't . . . I didn't . . . I didn't mean to . . ."

"But you did, didn't you," Prince said.

"Did you rape her afterward, or before?" Rice asked.

"It was before, wasn't it, Frank?" Prince said. "He wouldn't screw a corpse, would you? You raped her first."

"Yes," he said, almost relieved that they believed him, because it was less horrible than the other way, less horrible than the way they had first said it was.

"And then you killed her."

"I—I didn't mean to kill her. She came at me with a knife."

"After you'd raped her?"

"Yeah. That was how I got cut."

He turned his face back to the wall. Prince and Rice stood there for a moment, waiting for him to recover himself. They looked around the room. It was an evil-smelling, drab, horrible room. The girls on the walls only made it worse.

"All right, get your shoes on," Prince ordered.

Slowly, as if he were recovering from a long, wasting illness, Scully got up. He went to the closet and pulled out a pair of scuffed loafers. He put them on. Prince had been watching Scully as he went to the closet, watching very carefully. Rice had been watching, too. Neither of them had known what kind of improvised weapon might be in there—a baseball bat, a shoe tree, even. But he'd got the loafers and returned to the bed.

"You see that in there?" Rice asked.

"What?"

"Those magazines?"

Prince looked into the closet. There was a pile, nearly four feet high, of back issues of *Tomcat*.

"Funny thing, isn't it," Rice asked, "her working there?"

"Yeah," Prince said, shaking his head.

"All right, let's go," Rice said.

The young man got up. The two detectives took him downtown.

It was going to be a difficult time. She could see that. Bud's silence on the way back across the harbor and in the car back to his apartment hung in the air like a blanket. The heat and the mugginess were easier to take than the oppressiveness of his mood. Over and over again, Nina fought down the feeling of regret at the decision she had made. After all, wasn't this moodiness an indication of the depth of Bud's feeling, of the extent of his need for her? And not just for her body but for the assurance, the starveling ration of self-confidence that she could smuggle to him in that tower of arrogant and—yes, admit it—self-pitying loneliness?

He said nothing, and she took advantage of the silence to contemplate, to think about him, to study him. It was, after all, an unusual opportunity. She could look at him, even stare at him, and he just sat there, gripping the steering wheel, an object like a museum porcelain.

She looked for outward and visible signs of the inner condition of the man, but there was nothing she could focus on and declare with any certainty that, yes, this was it. There were no deep furrows in the brow, no heavily worn frown lines, no tracks of doom around the eyes. He looked to be the cheerful, gangly Southerner that he had once been, and that he still seemed to be most of the time. But somewhere along the line, for no reason that he had been able to determine, or perhaps for no reason at all, the luck had run out.

He had explained it to her. Nearly a year ago, when they had first started to sleep together, he had opened up in the intimacy of the darkened bedroom, in the first flush of the intimacy they had established with their bodies, to tell her about the golden youth he had been, the charmed life of the bright boy from Tupelo. There had been a wedding in Tupelo, the wedding of a cousin, and a relative of the groom came down to the wedding—and saw Bud playing baseball for the Tupelo High team. From that chance moment—chancy because it had been a good day for Bud out on the field, and chancier still because the relative just happened to be a big wheel in the alumni organization of Phillips Exeter Academy—everything had followed. The scholarship to Exeter, and the scholarship to Harvard, and the Clare Fellowship to Cambridge, and the first marriage.

"If I had had to work harder, to scramble more, and if I'd had it tougher, maybe everything would have been different. But then maybe I'd never have done anything at all. But it was all dished up to me on the old silver salver, and I just stuffed my face and filled my pockets and had me a good time. Even the novels came easy. Well, you know, I'm facile and fast. But what I got out of it, what I figured out was that it's all a gift. That nobody earns or deserves or works for anything. Oh, you can work, all right, but whether you actually get what you're working for is another matter entirely. That's luck. That's just a gift. Well, I had those gifts, and they stopped. They just stopped, that's all."

"And you've given up?" she had asked.

"No, I've still got my hand out, and I'm ready to take if there is anything else that wants to get itself given to me. But until that happens, I lie low and hide out, I wait."

And, of course, that was what he was doing now, with her. His career, his writing, even his women, had taught him this singular strategy. Yes, even his women. His first wife, the good one, had collapsed into melancholia and was in a mental hospital where she would probably stay for the rest of her life. And the second wife, the rich one, had come along, had picked up Bud—and the bills for the first wife at the mental hospital—and then had got bored with both and gone off with a Fort Lauderdale yachtsman, leaving Bud ripe and ready for Irv Kane's offer.

"Silence, exile, and cunning is what Joyce prescribed," Bud had told her, "but you don't have to go into exile, and you can yammer all you want. And as a matter of fact, you don't even have to have much cunning. Patience will do. Or impatience but endurance. Or maybe not even that. Maybe it's what I've thought all along—nothing. You don't need a damn thing. You just wait and maybe something will turn up. And again maybe not."

"I've turned up," she had said.

"Yass'm! And I am most sincerely pleased that you have," he had said. And almost certainly they had made love again.

But now, beside her in the automobile, he was not so sincerely pleased, not with her, not with himself, not with anything. And he was too good and too valuable a man to just let go into disappointment and sourness.

She put her arm up along the edge of the seat, and touched the back of his neck. He did not react. Not a smile, nor a look, nor anything. She took her hand away.

"What is it?" she asked. "What's the matter?"

"Nothing."

"Nothing?"
"That's what I just said, didn't I?"
"You said it. I'm not sure that you meant it."
"I meant it."

Well, then, she would have to gamble, have to try something bolder and more direct.

"Postman propositioned me this evening."
"He does that."
"I turned him down."
"Oh? Are you sorry?" Bud asked, turning to look at her for an instant.
"No," she said. "I'm not sorry." And then, after a pause that was partly calculated, she asked, "Are you?"
"That's a crazy question, now, isn't it?"
"I don't think so. Is it?"
"No, maybe not," he admitted. And then, after a while, he said, "I'm glad you turned him down. I don't know why you did, but I'm glad you did it."
"I wanted to be with you."

He glanced at her again, but didn't say anything.

"I thought about it," she said, "but I wanted to be with you."
"I'm glad," he said. And he smiled. It was, she suspected, a forced smile, a willed, deliberate gesture, but she was satisfied. At least he was trying a little, as one tries in prayers by beginning with the words, and hoping that after a while the meaning and the belief will follow, and that the prayers will become real. She put her hand back and stroked his neck again, and although there was still no smile, no murmur, no outward sign of his acceptance, she could feel it, as if this time the chemistry of the surface of his skin were different.

She kept her hand there all the way home.

She held the large glass ashtray under her chin. The cigarette flared in the semidarkness as she took a deep drag and passed it back to Bud. She kept her mouth closed in order to hold the smoke in as long as possible. By the time Bud had taken his drag on the cigarette and returned it to her, she had exhaled very slowly and was ready to puff again and to fill her lungs as deeply as possible with the dry, pungent smoke.

The glass ashtray felt cool against the flesh of her throat. She was peculiarly sensitive to the cool, smooth, brittle feel of it and she wondered whether her awareness of its weight and of its surface was an indication that the smoke had begun to take effect. But, no, it was too soon for that. They had only shared one cigarette, and were on their second. The only effect so far was a slight tingling sensation in her legs and in her fingertips. And their mutual silence.

The quality of the silence, though, was entirely different from what there had been, before, in the car. Now, sharing the marijuana, they were close again. That it was a pharmacological closeness did not matter. The end justified the means. Besides, it was more than a feeling of closeness. It was a way by which she could join him in that inner retreat he had constructed for himself, a bridge, a connection . . .

In a sense the sharing of the marijuana defined their relationship, for with it they could lie together in bed, as they were doing now, naked and sharing the pot. And it was a beautifully sensual and yet strangely disembodied experience that they could not only share together but, more important, could share without pretense.

She took back the cigarette from Bud's fingers and, holding it upright so that the long coal would not fall and burn the sheet, took another drag.

"You high yet?" he asked, stroking the outside of her thigh with the tip of a speculative finger.

"Still climbing," she answered. She loved the dizzying sensation at the beginning of each high. Part of her mind was cold and analytical, watching the other part do strange things, as if it were performing an elaborate, courtly dance with the reasonable part, with her body as the ensemble providing the music for the dance. She became increasingly aware of the rhythms of her own heartbeat and respiration, which became more and more interesting. And the weight and density of her flesh and bones transformed themselves into acoustical resonators, enhancing the music of the dance.

Bud had introduced her to the marijuana a year before, late one night after a sticky ride back across the harbor. Tired from an extremely long day, relieved that the deadline had been met and all the copy and proof was off to the printers, and perhaps depressed, too, by the brusqueness that Irv could show when the pressure was on, he had invited her up for a nightcap. She had agreed, and had followed his car to his apartment house, and had come up for the first time to the rooms that she now knew so well.

He had shown her the view of the Charles from the huge picture window and then had turned the switch that closed the draperies automatically. And had turned the lights up slowly with the rheostat.

These were the toys that Irv Kane had provided for his amusement, and her visit was, apparently, one of those rare occasions when the gadgets actually were amusing. Mostly, they were millstones around Bud's neck, for he had accepted them as gifts not only of Irv but of that goddess in which he believed—Fortune, or Luck, or Chance, or whatever her name was. The ironic thing was that they didn't belong to Bud. Irv had the lease and paid the rent on the apartment. So it really was a gift. And thus there were strings attached.

He had mixed a pitcher of martinis, and she had occupied herself by inspecting the books. It was impossible not to notice them, or not to glance at their titles. They stretched along for twenty feet, covering a whole wall. She had had the feeling of prying, as if she had been looking at the contents of a medicine chest rather than a bookcase, but then it would have been so studied, so artificial *not* to look.

The books were impressive. It was to these that he repaired, and by them, she was certain, that he repaired himself. They were not simply there as possessions or for show, but appeared to be well handled and much used. This bookcase, these books, gave him that hard shell into which he could invest himself, like a spore waiting for a better moment. She noticed with a certain satisfaction the orderliness of their arrangement, and followed along a nearby shelf with her eye, running over the names—alphabetical by author within a field—of the poets nearest the Barcelona chair: Roethke, Seferis, Skelton, Slavitt, Snodgrass . . . On the opposite wall there was a low table with a hi-fi turntable, and, in a corner, on a large black pedestal, a shiny bronze Tovish head.

Bud had returned from the kitchen with the crystal pitcher of martinis, had poured them, and had seated himself next to her on the Regency loveseat. They had sat, sipping their drinks, not saying much, and yet not quite comfortable with each other's silence, and he had asked her whether she liked the sitar.

She had confessed her total ignorance of the instrument, and he had put a record of Ustar Hali Jaffar Khan on the turntable. Suddenly the room had been filled by the intricate development of rhythms of the raga, and, even more, by the tranquility that came out of the slow, carefully molded music. It was then that he had done what she had been afraid he might do—and, for that matter, what she had been afraid he might not do—put his glass down, reached around her, pulled her to him, and kissed her, lightly at first and then with increasing fervor.

At first she had returned the kiss, but then she had broken away from his embrace.

"What?" he had asked. "What's the matter?"

She had taken a sip of her drink before answering. It was all so difficult, so complicated. "It's not you," she had said, "but me."

"Oh?"

"I'm . . . I'm just too tense."

"You don't have to be."

"It isn't that I *want* to be . . ."

"Then relax."

"I would, if I could."

"Do you want some help?"

"What do you mean?"

"Have you ever tried pot?" he had asked.

"No," she had answered, truthfully.

"Try some. Here," he had said, and had reached for the silver cigarette box and offered her a marijuana cigarette.

She had held it in her fingers, had sniffed it, and then had tried to decide. The boldness, the simplicity, the suddenness of the suggestion were all too puzzling for her, too difficult for her to sort out. He had explained to her with clarity and frankness, what marijuana was like, how it often had a mild aphrodisiac effect, but how essentially it was relaxing and—interesting. They could do it, he had suggested, in a quietly experimental way, smoking a little together in the privacy and safety of his apartment. And she might find that it was helpful.

Nina had always thought that people who used drugs had turned to them to escape from the reality of their ugly or dreary or unsatisfying lives. And she had been surprised at Bud's offering it to her, and surprised by the fact that he obviously used it from time to time. After all, here was a man with a body of work, four novels, a fine job, culture, resources, success. He grumbled about his work, but he did the work with great competence and, his protestations to the contrary, even occasionally with relish and delight. He was hardly an unwashed dropout from society.

She had known people in college who had used marijuana or pep pills. Things like that. But she had had an instinctive aversion to anything that would cause her to lose control of herself. An aversion, and even fear. And for that reason, she had never been more than mildly high on alcohol.

But what did she have to show for all this care and restraint? A spectacularly successful life, a great marriage, a fine sense of fulfillment? None of these things. And the safety and reasonableness of the apartment and of Bud, himself, had been reassuring. And the frustration she had been living with for a year or so, having that absurd crush—which was what she had come to call it—on Irv Kane, had produced a kind of pressure that was enough to overcome her natural caution, her inertia, and make her want to experiment.

She could, she had told herself, try it just this once. Even if it was for people who had something wrong with them, didn't she qualify? And if it made her do dreadfully irresponsible things, weren't they the same things that she had been toying with the idea of doing anyway? She had come up for the drink with the idea that she might, after all, get seduced. With the marijuana, she would have an excuse for herself if it worked out badly.

So, she had accepted the proffered lighter, and had smoked the cigarette. She had been rather disappointed after the first cigarette, for nothing had happened. But Bud had reassured her that it took a little bit more than that, the first time. So she had smoked a second one with him, and the now familiar light-headed feeling had started to hit her. And then they had smoked a third, and he had begun to stroke her arm, and she had been puzzled by the preternatural clarity of the sensation. It was exactly what he had said it would be—interesting.

His fingertip on her arm was more absorbing, more intense a sensation than even the kiss had been, and yet she felt none of that tightening of nerves, no apprehension. Indeed, she could hardly connect it with anything else. Time seemed to stop under the influence of the marijuana smoke, and everything became so discrete, so detached, so beautifully isolated from everything else.

She watched his fingers as they traveled up and down her arm, and observed with a curiously remote eye as his hand wandered down from her arm to her breast. She had felt slightly dizzy and she could still hear a kind of singing in her head. It was a kind of choral singing, as if her heartbeat were somehow orchestrated.

"Lie down," he had instructed, and they had moved to the velvety gray rug. And it was on the rug that they had made love, but with a kind of lovemaking that she had never experienced before—not so much sexual as more generally sensual. She had been aware of him not simply in a genital way, but in a completely unfocused, dreamy manner. Her elbows had been as sensitive as her nipples, and her neck as responsive as the inside of her thighs. And it had been with a beautiful undersea languor that they had floated into the ultimate, intimate embrace.

And even then, there had been no urgent drive toward a climax, and therefore no possibility of fear lest she not arrive at one. In almost wavelike undulations, they had cruised around it, and practically without her noticing it they had arrived at a peak so intense that she had not been sure where her body stopped and his began. Neither had there been any sudden drop-off or withdrawal into postcoital tristesse. They were ineffably close, and her happiness was exhilarating. She remembered how strange it had been, not feeling close to him as an individual but as a glorious extension of herself. It had been a relationship of bodies, but neither gross nor crude. It had been a relationship, really, of idealized bodies, of improved bodies, as of two statues or paintings brought to life. She remembered how she had fallen asleep with him still in her and how they had awakened an hour or so later, not hung over, not at all depressed, but quite gay and ravenous.

And garrulous. She had been suddenly easy and talkative, and had told him about her marriage to Jon, and her discovery of his homosexuality and the shock that that had been to her, both as someone who loved him and also to herself as a woman, as a female. And she had told him about the brief, unsatisfactory liaisons she had attempted after the divorce. And she had even told him about her "fixation"—as she had called it—upon Irvin Kane.

He had not laughed, but had thought about it quite seriously for a little while before suggesting to her that it might be a "safe" sort of emotional outlet, because nothing could come of it. Or, digging deeper, that her work on *Tomcat* might be a reaction from the disappointment of her first marriage, a way she had found to try to prevent other young men from turning queer by showing them the most attractive faces and breasts and thighs, and getting before them the most effective kind of fiction and articles for the propagandizing of heterosexuality.

It had not mattered whether she agreed or disagreed with his analysis, whether she accepted it or not. But the intelligence of it, and, even more important, the seriousness with which he responded, could not help but impress her, and please her. It had been so long since any man had listened to her seriously, attended to what she was thinking and feeling, showed any real interest in her. . . .

Well, she had been grateful, she supposed. And that evening

had stretched out into weeks and months. And it was a year, now, that they had been coming up here, and smoking pot, or not smoking pot but making love, or not doing either, but just talking. Or even, sometimes, just being with each other, reading, or working, but sharing the comfort of having another body, another mind, another personality there in the room. And yet it was not love, had never pretended to be that. There had been a kind of unspoken bargain between them, an agreement that up to this line and no further would either venture—or allow the other to venture.

She had been just as pleased, or at least at the beginning she had been pleased. It was more than enough to find, at last, a reasonable and pleasurable relationship with a man through which she could channel her normal, healthy, and even exuberant sexuality. And she had told him at the very beginning about her feelings for Irv, and he had accepted them. Only it wasn't just that, either. During the weeks and months that followed their first night together, she discovered his own peculiar passivity, which was not sexual—he was not at all passive in bed—but general and even philosophical. There was in him an unwillingness to commit himself to anything. Or to anyone.

But then why had Bud reacted this evening to Fred Postman's making a pass at her? Or to Postman's perfectly obvious feeling of some necessity to put Bud down, to be insulting? Surely Bud could see that Postman was angry at himself and simply redirecting his anger at Bud! Or was it something else entirely?

Whatever it was, she had felt the heaviness of his mood, and she had been the one who had made the suggestion that they turn on. For his sake, more than her own, she had suggested it, hoping that the effect of the hemp might be somehow to dissolve that knot she had been building in Bud all during the evening.

She touched the fine hairs on Bud's chest.

"Another?" she asked.

"Sure," he said, and he reached over to the night table beside the bed for another cigarette, which they shared.

The smoke, and the tangy smell of it, hung in the air, and Nina could see it eddy over the night table lamp. She felt as if she could, with only a little effort and a little skill, contrive somehow to float on the swirls, rising up from the bed and floating around in mid-air, supported by the smoke itself. But, then, it would be sad to do that and leave poor Bud behind, down on the bed, all heavy and depressed.

"What bothered you tonight?" she asked.

"Postman."

"I thought so."

"Something he said. I . . . You do these things . . . I'm not making very much sense, I'm afraid."

"No hurry," she answered.

"I don't care about the hard struggle and the purity of the artist's life. I really don't. But you make up excuses for yourself. We all do. We all have to. Even Postman."

"Yes, even Postman."

"But what he said this evening about the magazine not doing any good, not helping . . . I guess I had let myself believe Irv more than I'd realized. I wanted to argue with him. I really did. It made me angry."

"Why didn't you argue?"

"He'd have cut me up. He'd have called me a sellout, and a company fink, and all that. And he'd have been right, I guess, but that wouldn't have had anything to do with what I wanted to talk about, or what I wanted to argue about."

"Whether the magazine helps get rid of hang-ups and inhibitions?"

"You see? That's Irv's phrase. You've swallowed it, too!"

"Nibbled maybe," she admitted.

"A nibble here, a nibble there. You can eat a peck of dirt that way."

"Mental dirt?"

"That's the worst kind!"

"You want to vomit it up?"

"I don't know. But I felt a little queasy there."

"I know," she said.

In a way, she was disappointed. She had hoped—no, she had been convinced—that it had been Postman's advances toward her that had bothered Bud. And she had liked the idea of Bud's being at least a little bit jealous. Would she be jealous of him? Was she falling in love with him? Did she want him to leave *Tomcat?* To take her away with him? To take her away from Irv Kane and . . .

No, she didn't. Or she didn't think so. It was too difficult to think anything. Her brain was all muddled. From the pot. She realized that she had been thinking very hard, with her forehead all furrowed and her eyes shut tight, and she opened them. She noticed the way the light from the night table seemed to silver the hairs on Bud's chest. And she became quite fascinated by the way it sprang from his skin, coiling up out of the follicles. And then she was struck by the odd, giggly thought that it would be funny to have hair on her own chest.

A silly idea, but, having thought of it, she wanted to feel his hair against her own breasts. She rolled on top of him and pressed herself against him, rubbing her breasts against his chest. And she felt a surge of desire.

She wanted him, and she slid her hand down and found him ready for her. She sat up, moved down his body with both hands, and lowered herself onto him. He clasped her buttocks and muttered, "That's nice. That's very nice. It's so silky tonight."

"Velvet," she said.

"No, silk!"

"You're velvet. I'm silk," she said, and they both laughed.

She shifted her position and lay down on top of him, and he stroked her back, reaching up occasionally to touch the short hairs at the back of her neck. They kissed, a long, lingering exploration of each other's mouths. She shifted slightly so that she could make ever-increasing circles upon him—and then the phone rang, startling them both. It took a moment before they even figured out what the sound was. It was so gradual, as though it had come from a long way off, as though the ring had begun at the other end, and had wandered casually along the wires of the New England Telephone Company to arrive, rather lackadaisically, in the bedroom.

"It's the phone," Bud said, as though discovering a great and mysterious truth. "Who could it be at this time of night?"

"Irv?" she asked. "It has to be Irv."

"No, it wouldn't be Irv," he said, thoughtfully.

"You'd better answer it," she suggested. "At least it will stop ringing."

Without changing position, he groped with a hand and found the telephone that was on the shelf under the night table. He and Nina were still joined together. He took the receiver off the hook, brought it to his ear and mouth, and said, "Hello?"

"Bud? Mike Barnacle! I didn't wake you, did I?"

"No, you didn't wake me," Bud said, and then, after a beat, he asked, "What's up?"

"I'm in the city room, and I've just heard the news. That Church kid that got killed, you heard about her?"

"Yeah, I heard."

"Well, they found the guy. And his whole goddam room was covered with those centerspread pictures from *Tomcat*. I thought you'd want to know."

"Thanks, Mike. I appreciate it."

"I don't know what the hell there is you can do about it, but this way at least it won't hit you cold in the morning."

"Yes, thanks."

"Well, I got to get back to work. And you've probably got to make some calls, or think, or—I don't know—pour yourself a stiff drink."

"Yeah, but . . . Thanks for calling. I'm grateful to you."

"Any time, old buddy!"

Bud put the phone back on the hook, and then, looking up at Nina, asked, "Did I do all right?"

"You did fine! You sounded as though you'd been asleep. I was afraid I was going to laugh."

"That would have been funny."

"It would have been terrible," she said.

"No, it would have been funny. Which was why you wanted to laugh, don't you see?" And struck by the intricacy of that thought —which, under the pot, seemed to be endlessly complicated and rich, he started to laugh himself. The laughter racked his body and, as the heaving waves of glee grew more and more intense, they caused Nina to respond, and, quite unexpectedly and ridiculously, brought her to her climax.

Then, amazed by what had happened to her, she began to laugh herself, and her laughter brought him to his.

It was only later, after they had separated and were lying beside each other, resting and smiling, enjoying the nonsensical marvelousness of what had happened, that Nina thought to ask, "Who was it?"

"Who was who?"

"Who called? On the telephone."

"Oh. Oh, my God!"

"What?"

He told her, then, about Mike Barnacle, his friend at the *Globe*, and the news about the murderer's room being covered by *Tomcat's* Kalendar Kitty pictures.

"I wonder whether we should call Irv."

"What for? He'll find out in the morning."

"Wouldn't it be better to find out sooner, and from one of us?"

"What difference would it make?"

"I don't know," she said. "But *your* friend called you, didn't he?"

"Yes," Bud admitted. "But there's nothing we can do. And nothing Irv can do."

"He can think of what to say when the reporters get to him."

"He'd be better off not to say a damned thing."

"Well, he could have some time to think and decide that for himself."

"He doesn't think. He reacts. You know that."

"Look, Bud," she said, sitting up, "what has that to do with anything? We ought to call him!"

"Then call him," Bud said.

He got out of bed.

"Where are you going?" Nina asked.

"To the bathroom, if that's all right with you?"

She picked up the phone and dialed the number for Tomcat House. But the switchboard girl would not put her through. Mr. Kane had left orders that no calls were to be put through to him. From anyone.

Well, she had tried.

And it bothered her that she felt worse for having tried. Bud had been right, after all. She resented the fact that Irv, up there in that room with Mimsy or—for all she knew—some new hardbody, could cut himself off that way. Why was his sexual pleasure so much more important than Bud's or hers?

No, that wasn't fair, either. They could have taken the phone off the hook. But even so, she felt that there was a difference. They didn't have a switchboard. They hadn't left orders that no calls were to be put through. Not even her insistence to the switchboard girl that this was an emergency, not even her position as feature editor and friend had been enough to get the girl to ring the bedroom.

Bud came back from the bathroom.

"Any luck?"

"No."

"Well, he takes his pleasure very seriously, you know. Built a whole magazine on it, I guess."

"Why?"

"Why, what?"

"Why do you suppose he takes it so seriously?"

"Because, my dear, he is a convert. He converted to sex, the same way that people convert to the Catholic Church or Communism, or vegetarianism. And converts are always very serious."

"What do you mean, he converted?"

"I don't know, exactly. But he didn't just grow into it the way most people do. It was a conversion. He's never talked about it, but it happened. In Japan, I think."

He sat down on the bed beside her.

"Hey," he said, "I'm sorry about not wanting to call him. It's funny, but . . . I guess I was jealous."

"That's sweet," she said, and kissed him on the cheek.

"And now I'm hungry."

"That's fixable," she said, kissed him again, and got up to go and scramble some eggs.

4

In the canvas sling-seats of the MATS plane, it was hard to get comfortable, but none of them was complaining. The revving of the engines, the gathering of momentum, and then the giddy feeling of lift as the plane took off were small details that none of them had dared imagine, even a week before. If there had been any hope of getting out of Korea, it had been a vague, undefined hope. Back in the trenches, Irv Kane would have been willing to settle for simple warmth. To be dry and to be warm and to wear clean clothes had been the entirety of his dream. He had even forgotten that night could fall and not bring with it the rattle of small-arms fire and the heavy thud of shells. He had been living from moment to moment; at first in the hot, dusty summer there had been fear, but as the days had gone on the fear had given way to a kind of indifference and fatalism. He had stopped worrying about which bullet it was that had his name on it and had begun to long only for some relief from the heat and from the stink of night soil on the rice paddies that the hot wind occasionally blew into their trenches on the line, or into their tents behind it. The heat had given way to the rain and the slimy ankle-deep mud of fall. He had yearned for firm ground underfoot—which the freezing of winter brought. And that had been worst of all. The bitter, unbelievable cold, and the dampness, which made the cold penetrating and worse than anything he remembered back in Indiana, had been so bad that the attacks of Joe Chink aroused in him a kind of fury at having to take his mittens off in order to squeeze the trigger of his M-1.

Korea seemed to have only one pleasant season—the spring, which had just begun. But Kane was not sorry to be missing it.

Beneath him he could see patches of green and brown laid out in neat squares under the random clusters of marshmallow-fluff cloud. It was like going to heaven and looking back. Even with the noise of the engine and the cold in the cabin as the plane gained altitude, he could not help wondering if he was not imagining the whole thing, or fearing that it might turn out to be some kind of hallucination, a mere mirage. He remembered Dunford and how, after he'd been hit, as he lay there dying, he'd laughed. It had seemed to be a laugh. It had been closer to a giggle, really, something between a giggle and a whimper. But, no, that had been because of the shallowness of the breath. It had been a kind of laughter. Maybe Dunford had seen back, from some undreamed-of and mysterious height, from even higher than the plane's cruising altitude, the rows of trenches, the no-man's land, and the other rows, and the tiny figures shooting at one another. Maybe it had seemed funny from up there. Or maybe it had seemed so lousy, so stupid and lousy, that there was nothing to do but laugh.

In a way, it had been one big joke all along. It hadn't even been a war, but a "police action." And it hadn't been that, either, but some kind of fucking Boy Scout outing, the point of which was to accumulate points. Thirty-six points for rotation. The big merit badge, and you got to be a Life Scout—they let you live.

It had all seemed pretty safe back at Camp Hood. Irvin Kane had just finished basic when Malik proposed a truce at the UN. And a couple of weeks or so later, the talks had begun at Kaesong. It'd be a piece of cake, they'd told each other, and had believed it, too. Some joke. He'd arrived just in time to join in the battle at Bloody Ridge. The phrase the newspapermen used for it was "baptism of fire," and appropriately there had been a ceremony, with a kind of sermon for the occasion. General Boatner had addressed the new replacement troops, and had instructed them in the commandments of war. There weren't ten, but only three. "When you're on the hill," the general had said, "if you stand up, you'll get your ass shot off. If you get off the paths or roam, you'll get your ass blown off by mines. And when you take a hill, you'll be tired as hell, you'll want to poop out, slap your buddies on the back, and take it easy. But remember, as soon as you take a hill, just as water comes out of a spigot, the mortars come in on you, and blooey! It's too goddam late then to dig in."

They'd had six days of special conditioning and training, and then had been sent in. And it had been crazy. It had been so crazy that nobody could believe his own eyes and ears. You had to figure out comparisons first, work out indirect ways of understanding what the hell was going on. You had to notice, in a curiously calm way, that the flashes of artillery fire were so frequent as to be nearly continuous, and what made you notice this was not the artillery fire itself, but your realization that, if only it were a little quieter out there, you could read. At two o'clock in the morning. By the light of the explosions of the shells, and the flares and tracers. You could goddam well read! Maybe it had been something like that that Dunford had been thinking of when he'd gone out with a giggle.

It was supposed to be modern warfare, but it looked for all Kane could tell exactly like the battles in World War I. Trenches opposing trenches, and shells tossed back and forth, and then some kind of abrupt charge. Nobody got anywhere. Finally, the 23rd Infantry went around the hill, flanked it, and the NKPA withdrew. And that had been the biggest joke of all, their belief that the North Korean People's Army was on the run. Behind Bloody Ridge, there was Heartbreak Ridge, and behind that a thousand more, stretching away in the distance all the way up to the Yalu. So they dug in, and sweated and froze. And put on salve for the creeping crud, and watched the fungus eating their feet up, and turning their toenails into yellow, fibrous growths. And they got picked off, and tried to pick off the Chinks in their armored bunkers and pillboxes and trenches. Most of the time, except when there was a skirmish, you couldn't even see them. You just knew that they were out there, keeping the odds up against your chances of getting those thirty-six points.

Nothing was happening. The peace talks had been resumed, at Panmunjom instead of Kaesong, and there was a cease-fire line. Nobody could move. It was just a matter of keeping up the pressure, and not even for military reasons so much as for the sake of the negotiations. It wasn't just one soldier's crazy idea that the whole war was a game. The generals were running it like a game too. A big game of flinch. For the generals, it was easier to play. They didn't get shot at, and they didn't have the stink of the creeping crud in their crotches and in their armpits and behind their knees. It was a worse smell than shit; it was the smell of the whole goddam war.

He looked out of the window again, and was just in time to

see the coastline. He looked down and watched the east coast of Korea slide back, and the blue water slide in to take its place. Further east was Japan, and then, across the Pacific, the States. It was difficult to believe. He felt about the way he supposed his father would have felt it, after he died, he went to heaven and found out that there was a heaven, after all, except that Jews didn't set much store on heaven. Of course, his father had not been very religious about his religion; if he had been he probably wouldn't have married out of his faith. It had been Irvin's mother who had given him his religious background, although precious little of it remained with him. But after the nine months he'd gone through on the line, Kane didn't think that imagining hell was much of a problem. It wasn't even interesting.

"Have a slug?"

"Of what?" Kane asked.

"Brandy."

Beside him, Big Bill Buchanan held out a small silver flask he'd picked up that day they'd had in Seoul.

"Go on," Buchanan said. "It'll keep out the cold."

Kane accepted the flask and took a slug of the brandy. He felt the warmth spreading down through his throat and chest. "Thanks," he said.

Buchanan took the flask back, raised it in a toast, and said, "Well, here's to I & I." He took a slug.

"I & I?" Kane asked.

"Sure. It's like R & R. But the real thing."

"What do you mean?"

"Intoxication and intercourse," Buchanan explained, and laughed. "I'm going to get me some of that good old Jap tail. Tokyo nookie-oh. I've been imagining it, studying on it now, for months. We'll check into some good hotel with clean sheets and lots of towels and hot water, and we'll get cleaned up, and then we'll go out to the Ginza and get a good edge in one of the bars there, and then we'll find ourselves a pair of broads. Right?"

"No edge for me," Kane said. "I want to get smashed."

"You can't do that," Buchanan protested, almost as if he were explaining a lesson. "You have to have just an edge for the broads. Smashed is too much."

"I'm not so sure about the broads. I've waited this long, I can wait a few weeks longer. I'll be seeing Cal then."

"No, you've got it all wrong," Buchanan said. "You come at your wife after a year out in Korea, you'll wound her. Come on now. Don't you want to find out whether it's true what they say about those Japanese girls?" He winked and took another swig of brandy.

Kane thought for a moment and then answered, "I would, Bill, but I'd be taking a hell of a chance. I mean, you've seen those pictures about VD . . ."

"Oh, is that all that's worrying you?" Buchanan asked. "Well, Jesus! Look, a few pennies more, go first class. You can get yourself a virgin for fifty bucks. What would you say to one of those Japanese cherry blossoms? That's a great idea! I haven't had me a virgin since I was sixteen." He laughed, remembering it, and added, "And I was too young to appreciate it then."

Kane lit a cigarette and wondered what the appeal was about virgins. He'd had a virgin once, too—his wife, Carol. On their wedding night. And he'd been a virgin, too.

The drone of the plane engines reminded him of the hum of the air-conditioner in the motel they had stayed in just outside of Indianapolis. He had done everything right, exactly the way the books had said. He'd got into his pajamas and had let her have the bathroom while he'd sat in a Danish-modern chair smoking one cigarette after another, and drinking the too-sweet champagne that the management had provided for the newlyweds. After what had seemed to be a year, she'd emerged from the bathroom, clad in a white nightgown and matching white peignoir, She'd been very pale.

She had stopped when she had got to the center of the room, and he had gone to meet her.

Their courtship and even their engagement had been extremely chaste. He had kissed her, had touched her breasts, and, once, timidly, she had touched him on the outside of his clothing. That was all they knew of each other's bodies.

They stood there, in the middle of the motel room, kissing. At last, he broke away from her and said, with some embarrassment, "We might be more comfortable on the bed."

She laughed nervously and followed him to the big double bed that dominated the room. They lay down together on top of the covers, and he kissed her again. After a minute she asked, "Why don't we pull the covers down?"

They got up and, methodically, carefully, almost as if she hated the moment to end, she pulled the covers down and folded them with painstaking precision. He flopped down on the sheet and she lay down beside him. She stretched out and lay there, almost as if she were ready for some sort of human sacrifice.

He untied the ribbons holding the peignoir and slid it down from her shoulders. She wriggled out of it. Then he kissed her and ran his hands up and down her sides.

"I love you, Mrs. Kane," he said, softly, into her ear.

"And I love you," she said, opening her eyes very wide.

He looked at her for a moment, and smiled, "Relax, Cal," he said. "Remember, it's me. Irv."

It had said in the books to be gentle and patient, and he was as gentle and patient as he could be. But at the same time, he worried about it because he had never made love to a woman, and he wondered who was going to be gentle and patient with him. Almost conscientiously, he "stimulated her erogenous zones."

It had been a long engagement, and a frustrating one for Irv, and he wanted her very much. She neither spoke nor moved. He had, by this time, taken off his pajamas, and had worked her nightgown up above her breasts. Finally, he rolled on top of her, and she opened her legs like an obedient child. It struck him, suddenly, that she must have been reading the same books, and he almost laughed. But he didn't.

"Do you want me?" he asked.

"Yes, Irv, I love you," she answered.

He was not quite sure whether she was ready or not. She was shy, he knew, and frightened. It was all new to them both. "And I love you, Cal," he answered.

He tried to insinuate himself into her body, but with no success. She was not resisting, but he was not succeeding. He reached down with his hand to guide himself, and, as he did so, he touched her there. She was moist enough, he thought, ready for him, as the books said. He took his penis in his hand and tried to guide it home. The head slipped between the lips and he felt encouraged. He pushed slightly with his hips but could go no further. He pushed again, harder. She gasped slightly.

"Am I hurting you?" he asked.

"A little," she admitted, "but go on."

Again he moved, harder this time. She lifted her hips slightly to meet him, but it was no use. Each time he thrust, he was stopped by a tough, unyielding membrane. Finally she said, "Please, Irv. I'm sorry, but it hurts."

He rolled off her and, lying by her side, stroked her hair and said, "It's all right, baby. Why don't you take a warm bath. Maybe it would be better."

Several of the books had suggested warm baths for this kind of difficulty. She went into the bathroom, and he followed her.

"Let me run it for you," he said.

"Irv," she said, in a quavering voice. "I don't know what's the matter."

"There isn't anything the matter," he said, firmly. "There isn't anything to worry about."

He adjusted the temperature of the bath and slid the nightgown over her head, then held out his arm for her to steady herself on as she got into the tub. He sat down on the edge of the tub and looked at her. He had never seen her naked before.

"You're very beautiful," he told her.

"Thank you," she said, smiling shyly.

She lay in the tub, swishing the water with her hand. He lit a cigarette and gave her puffs of it. When the cigarette was finished, he helped her out, and dried her with one of the big bath towels the motel supplied. He kissed her again, and led her back to the bed.

Twice more they tried, and twice more they failed. It was impossible. She sat up, and cried softly.

"I'm a failure," she said. "I'm a terrible wife."

The tears ran down her face. She used the pillowcase as a handkerchief.

"No, honey," he said. "Don't worry about it. It's all right."

They lay down together, cuddled next to each other, and, after a long time, fell asleep. The next day they went to a gynecologist in Indianapolis. He looked at her and said, sternly, "You should have come to me before you got married. You'd have saved yourself some grief."

Deftly, in a few seconds, with a small surgical scissors, he cut the tough, leathery hymen.

For Irv, the next night—the last night they had had together—

was all he had ever known of warmth and passion. She had been loving and sweet, and they had both been so very proud of themselves and of their success.

During the furlough he'd had after basic, Cal had been having her period. And so it was the memory of that one night that he'd carried with him to Korea, a memory to be taken out very sparingly, only in his moments of greatest depression. It had never failed to warm him, to make him feel, even if only for a moment, happy and safe.

To follow that night with a night on the town with Buchanan and his Tokyo nookie or his Japanese cherry blossoms seemed a desecration.

In the Army his attitude was considered a little peculiar. He had, nevertheless, maintained it. He didn't mind the dirty talk so much. That didn't bother him. He suspected it was mostly a pose anyway. Since he was married, and since he carried the picture of his lovely wife with him, no one could accuse him of being a fairy. He was, they thought, a straight arrow, but that was all. And that was okay with him.

He liked Big Bill Buchanan a great deal, and was going to stay with him; but, as he explained, he would rather spend the money on a transoceanic telephone call to Cal than on some Japanese whore.

"Well, just don't get it caught in the coin-return slot," Buchanan warned him, laughed at his own joke, and killed off the brandy in the silver flask.

The plane began to descend. Below, Irv could see the harbor, the island, and the Tokyo airport.

They left their hotel, got into a cab, and gave the driver a slip of paper the doorman had given them that contained an address in

Japanese characters. The cab darted with incredible speed through the crowded roads to the Ginza. On the small side streets, on either side, were restaurants and bars, one after another, with bright lights and signs both in Japanese and in English. Occasionally, the blare of music reached right into the cab. Buchanan signaled to the driver to stop. They got out and walked along Namiki-dori, found a bar that looked inviting, and went in. Two hostesses in bright kimonos, with the broad obi sashes bound around them, bowed and led them to a table in the bar. Both girls were tiny, and beautiful in a doll-like way. Their English was flawed, but all the more amusing for that.

"You like sake? Whiskey? Gin?" one of them asked.

"Do you have bourbon?" Buchanan asked.

"Bourbon whiskey? Ah, yes."

One of the girls went off to get the bourbon. The other slid onto the banquette next to Kane.

"My name Mariko," she said. "You have fought in Korea?"

Buchanan told her they had just got in from Korea that afternoon.

"Oh, then you will want plenty bourbon whiskey," she said, giggling.

"That's right, baby," Buchanan answered, patting her on the arm.

The other girl appeared, carrying a bottle of bourbon, four glasses, a small bucket of ice, and a pitcher of water. With great delicacy and grace, she set the glasses down on the table, put the ice in them with bamboo tongs, and poured the drinks.

"You like water with bourbon whiskey?"

"No, thanks. Just on the rocks," Kane said.

"Water ruins the flavor, Buchanan said.

"Rocks? Oh, rocks. Yes," she said, pointing to the ice cubes. She giggled, too.

She sat down beside Buchanan.

"Here's how," he said, and they drank.

They sat in the bar for an hour, talking and joking with the girls. No matter what either of the soldiers said, the girls giggled, and it was sort of fun to sit there and drink, and make them laugh. They were nice to have around, pretty enough, and very efficient at refilling glasses. Mariko also shelled some kind of nuts, tapping them with the base of her glass on the table top, and offering the meats to the two men. It was a great pleasure to see women who were pretty, clean, and so far removed from the agonies of the war from which they had come.

At the end of the hour, Mariko suggested that they get a new bottle to replace the one they had just finished, but Buchanan was eager to go on with his program. His face was flushed, his eyes were bright, and he was ready. He had his edge.

They paid their bill, tipped the girls, and left. Outside, Buchanan hailed a cab. Just before he got in, he opened his wallet, took out a wad of bills, and handed them to Kane.

"Hold on to these for me, will you? They can't steal what I don't have."

"Sure," Kane said. "Be glad to. I'll see you back at the hotel."

"Right."

"Have a good time."

"No fear," Buchanan said, laughed, and got into the cab. Kane heard him, enunciating carefully, direct the driver to the Yoshiwara district. The cab pulled away at enormous speed, as if the driver himself had been affected by Buchanan's eagerness and lust.

Kane went back to the Ginza and walked along the street, looking into the windows of the stores. He stopped in front of Matsuzakaya to look at the kimonos and wondered about bringing one back to Cal. He tried to imagine her at home in their bedroom in a kimono. It was a funny idea. Down the street a short way, he looked in the windows of Mikimoto, where there were pearls of all sizes and colors. He looked around to get his bearings, thinking that perhaps he might come back the next day to go in and price a pair of earrings. Cal had always liked pearls.

There was a sudden, loud report as the engine of a motorcycle backfired. Kane crouched, and it was only with great effort that he refrained from flinging himself flat onto the pavement. It took him a moment to realize that it had been nothing but a motorcycle. He straightened up, feeling stupid and self-conscious. He looked around. Nobody was staring at him. Well, he thought, it was probably not that uncommon, anyway.

He felt very tired. Too many nights, sleepless and under fire, had had their effect. He decided to go back to the hotel and hit the sack. He flagged a cab, held out a card with the name of the hotel printed on it in Japanese, and sat back as the driver sped through the traffic. He could still feel the sweat on his palms and on his forehead from that bang of the motorcycle. He wondered how long it would take him to get used to the ordinary world again.

It was a quarter past four when Buchanan came into the room. He tried to be quiet, but the noise, slight though it was, of the door's closing was enough to cause Kane to sit bolt upright. He looked around, startled to discover that he was not in a trench, did not have to grab for his gun, was in Tokyo. He lay down again.

"Have a good time?" he asked, sleepily.

" 'Roll me over, in the clover, roll me over, lay me down and do it again,' " Buchanan answered, "but not tonight. Man, you missed a great evening. A truly great evening," he repeated, and flung himself on the bed, fully dressed.

He was asleep before Kane could answer him.

The following morning, Kane was finishing his second cup of coffee and enjoying the view of Hibiya Park in the morning sunshine. Buchanan was snoring lightly. Even if it was not the sleep of the just, it seemed to Kane that Buchanan was enjoying it nonetheless. The telephone rang, and Kane crossed the room quickly so the ringing would not disturb his sleeping roommate. It was the hotel operator.

"Your call to Ames, Iowa, is ready, sir," she said.

He had booked the call the night before. He reached for the cigarettes on the night table, lit one, and listened to the variety of beeps and crackles that went on for several seconds until he heard Cal's voice.

"Hello? Irv?" she said.

"Hello! Cal! Can you hear me?" he asked.

"Yes. Can you hear me?"

"Yes. How are you?"

"I'm fine. And how are you?"

"Just fine. What time it is where you are?"

"It's eight o'clock at night," she said.

"It's ten o'clock in the morning here."

"That's funny," she said, and laughed.

"I love you," he said.

"And I love you."

"What?"

"And I love you!" she repeated. Her voice was clear enough, but its volume wavered, as if she were retreating and advancing, or as if they were not talking on a telephone connection but through a medium at a séance with only uncertain contact with the spirit world.

"You're all right, aren't you?" she asked.

"Yes, I'm just fine," he said. "I'm in Tokyo, you know."

"Yes, the operator said it was Tokyo. What are you doing there?"

"What?"

"What are you doing in Tokyo?"

"I've got a five-day leave here, and then I'll be waiting for assignment to a troopship."

"You're coming home?" she asked. Her voice rose with excitement, or he thought it did.

"Yes," he said. "You'll meet me in San Francisco?"

"Yes!"

"And we'll finish our honeymoon! Oh, I miss you!" he burst out. The longing in his voice was clear enough, even over the thousands of miles that separated them. There was a moment of expensive silence, until she said, "Yes, Irv. Oh, yes."

"What are you doing now?" he asked, wanting to fix her at that moment in his mind.

"I'm talking to you on the telephone. And . . . I was studying in the dormitory. You remember how noisy it was."

"I remember," he said. "What are you wearing?"

"A blue flannel bathrobe. I've just washed my hair."

"And you're fine?" he asked.

"Yes, I'm fine, and my parents are fine. I spoke to them tonight."

"Give them my love," he said.

There was another pause, longer this time, as he tried to think of what to say, something that would not just be small talk for a telephone call but that would break through the distance to make the kind of real contact for which he had so much yearned. But there was nothing that occurred to him, and nothing that occurred to her, either. For fifteen seconds they listened to each other's breathing, or perhaps it was nothing more than the surface resistance of the cable that lay on the floor of the Pacific.

The operator broke in to warn them that their three minutes were up. Almost with relief, Irv repeated, "I love you. I miss you. I'll see you before too long."

"Yes, darling," she said. "And I love you. Write me and let me know when your ship will be coming in so I can meet it."

"I will," he said. "Good."

"Good-bye, darling," she said.

"Good-bye, honey."

He hung up. He was unwilling to admit to himself that he was disappointed or let down, or, if he was disappointed, then he was sure that it was because he had expected too much. What could people say to each other on a long distance telephone call, anyway? Much as he tried to avoid it, though, it was still true that he felt a kind of frustration and uneasiness. He walked back to the window and, without thinking, took a sip of the black coffee. It had not even had time to get cold.

He sat down in the chair by the window and looked at the sleeping mound that was Buchanan. It annoyed him that he knew more about Buchanan—his habits, his quirks, his state of mind, even his physical state—than he knew about Cal, his own wife. Of course, Buchanan had the advantage of being there, where Irv could see him, and the two of them had shared more, had plumbed together greater depths of experience than he and Cal had ever known existed. But he could blame that on the war. It had been the war that had separated him and Cal anyway. Just as it had precipitated their marriage in the first place.

Cal was the first girl he had dated seriously. They had gone together from the middle of their freshman year. When he failed the deferment test and found suddenly that he would have to go into the Army, Irv was less distressed about the prospect of the military service than he was by the fact that he would be leaving nothing behind. Nothing and no one. His father had died when he was fifteen and his mother when he was eighteen, and, while he had managed perfectly well, the idea that there were no connections to any real life from which the Army would be taking him upset him enormously. They sat in Cal's car, parked off a country road, drinking the 3.2 beer that was all the county allowed, and he told her that he was going into the Army. She cried, and he comforted her. He had touched her breasts, and she had touched him through his trousers.

And maybe that was all there was to the impulse that came over him and produced his sudden, "Look, let's get married!"

She had burst into tears—and agreed. And they had spent the next weeks together talking, finding out about each other, telling each other about themselves. Her favorite author was Wordsworth, and her favorite color was blue, and her favorite song was "Just One of Those Things." And for his part, he told her about his parents, and how his father had been Jewish and his mother Catholic, and how his name should have been Irving Cohen except that his father, as a young man coming to Indianapolis, had changed the Cohen to Kane, and his mother had dropped the final "g" from the Irving when she had filled out the birth certificate, and then told him about it after his father's death.

But in that span of weeks, neither could really discover what the other thought, how the other looked at the world. Neither could get to know the other. And sitting in the chair in the hotel room in Tokyo, he felt a shudder of nervousness at the brashness of what he had done, of what they had both done by getting married.

And that made him feel guilty. He promised himself that he would go back to Mikimoto to buy Cal the biggest and most beautiful pearl earrings he could afford.

With a groan, Buchanan sat up in his bed and asked, "What the hell time is it, anyway?"

"A quarter past ten," Kane told him.

"Jesus Christ!" Buchanan exclaimed. "You wouldn't think after a night like that a fellow could wake up with a hard on, now, would you?"

Buchanan noticed that he still had his clothes on, laughed, got up, and started to get undressed to take a shower.

"Order some coffee for me, would you, buddy, and a big breakfast. Ham and eggs, if they got it."

"Okay," Kane said.

"Hey, do you know what ham is?" Buchanan asked as he disappeared into the bathroom.

"No, what?" Kane called after him.

"A piece of pig's ass."

The water from the shower drowned out the noise of his laughing.

At five-thirty that afternoon, Kane and Buchanan emerged from another bar just off the Ginza to which they had gone partly to rest up from their day of shopping and sightseeing, and partly to restore Buchanan's edge for his foray to another whorehouse. They had gone to see the judo at the Kodokan Hall, and then had gone out to Asakusa to Ueno Park, where they had walked around, passing the lake and the beautiful Toshogu Shrine, until they had found, quite unexpectedly, the little Ueno Park zoo. They had stopped to eat pork cutlets at the Horaiya, and had then gone back to the Ginza and Mikimoto's, where Buchanan had bought a cameo brooch surrounded by small pearls for his mother and Kane had got a pair of pink pearl earrings for Cal.

"Look, pal," said Buchanan, "you don't have to worry about the clap. I mean, they're legal here. They're inspected. It's like the goddamned food and drug act. And they're beautiful. I mean, really good looking. Not so big in the tits, but legs? Up to their necks!"

"That's a hell of a place for legs," Irv said. "Besides, tonight is my night to indulge my stomach. I'm going to Benihana to have a really first-class Japanese meal. It's supposed to be even better than that place we ate in in San Francisco the night before we shipped out."

"Yeah, that was good," Buchanan agreed.

He had lost interest in the conversation. Kane saw that he was already scanning the streets for a cab. His mind was already at that whorehouse, and impatient for the body to catch up with it. He stepped off the curb to try to flag a cab, then stopped and, remembering about his money, came back to the sidewalk. He took out his wallet and extracted the bills, a couple of which he kept for himself. He thrust the rest into Irv's hand.

"Don't wait up for me," he said, and, chuckling, stepped back out into the street. He turned back. "Have a good feed, old pal," he said.

"Don't worry about me . . ." Kane started to say, but he broke off. "Look out!" he called.

But it was too late. "Bill!" he cried out, but even as he did so, he watched the kamikaze cabbie's attempt to swerve, heard the squeal of brakes, and saw Buchanan ride up the fender and bounce off the windshield and up into the air.

Three hours later, Kane opened the door of their hotel room. His hotel room, now. He stood in the doorway, reluctant to turn on the light. It was, he thought, the biggest, the most outrageous, the dirtiest joke of all for Buchanan to have lived through all those months on the line and then come back to get killed by a cab on the streets of Tokyo.

First there had been the police and the ambulance and the doctor, who had shaken his head and had covered Buchanan's face with a cloth, and then there had been the military police, who at least spoke English, and to whom he could explain what had happened. Finally, they let him go, and told him to pack up Buchanan's belongings and send them over to Graves Registration. They would notify the family. They would take care of everything.

So there was nothing Irv could do, except go back to the hotel room, and . . . And what? He flipped on the light, closed the door behind him, and then crossed to the telephone. He called down to room service for a bottle of brandy. Sitting down, heavily, on the edge of the bed, he slowly unlaced his shoes and eased them off his feet. With the brandy, the hall boy brought in the packages from Mikimoto. He bowed and smiled. Kane tipped him and he disappeared.

There was a glass on the tray, but Kane ignored it. He drank from the bottle. The point was to get drunk enough so that he could feel something, so that he could let his feelings come out, so that maybe he would even be able to cry. But after all of the deaths he had seen as ordinary parts of the day's routine in Korea, tears were not so easy to find. It was just lousy. It was the lousiest thing he could think of. Just shitty.

He drank about a third of the bottle and then stopped, because he knew that if he drank any more he would fall asleep, and that was not what he wanted. He had not been able to cry, but he was at least feeling suitably morose. He felt absolutely alone. If he had been given the news that Cal was dead, he knew he could not have felt any more bereft. Probably less, he had to admit. And in a peculiar way, he was annoyed with Cal because he knew that she could not possibly understand the kind of loss that he was feeling now. Even if she had been there, and he had been able to tell her about it, he knew she still would not be able to understand. He looked around the room, trying to find something on which to focus his attention. He wished they had booked a Japanese-style room instead of this one. The straight lines and the bland colors in which the room had been decorated offered no resistance, no diversion, nothing on which his mind could snag and break its train of thought. He kept looking at the bed in which Buchanan had slept. It had been turned down by the maid and was ready to receive him. It had no idea that he was dead. In a peculiar way, with his mind fuzzy the way it was, he felt terribly sorry for the bed, and sorry, too, for the prostitutes whom he fancied to be waiting for Buchanan to appear. He knew that it wasn't true, it was just the brandy, but, still, he felt it ought to be true. The world should have felt a space.

And then he thought about the prostitutes themselves and Buchanan's eagerness and lust for them, and he thought of his own reaction to Buchanan's evening plans. It seemed prissy, stupid. Why had he refused to join him? What the hell difference did it make?

If he had gone with Buchanan, Buchanan might still be alive. There would not have been that fumbling with the money. Or they might both be dead, which maybe would have been better. But the world was a stupid place. To try to live in it with some crazy kind of high school rules was impossible. With Buchanan dead, what the hell was the point of making a big fuss about the whores anyway?

The more he thought of it, the more it made him laugh. He felt almost silly now from the brandy. That's what he would do, he thought. He would go to one of those whorehouses. It wouldn't be a monument to Buchanan—that would be stupid—but a monument to the vitality of the guy, to what he had learned from Big Bill.

If only people could learn from the experience of others, he thought, they'd be a lot better off. What he had learned from Buchanan's life and death was not so much, maybe, but if he was going to get hit by a cab tomorrow he would, by God, go out like Buchanan—well laid.

It didn't make a damned bit of difference anyway. It didn't, he thought, smiling, make any fucking difference at all.

He reached for his shoes and put them on.

For a long time, Kane stood on the sidewalk where the cab driver had left him. There was a marquee that looked as though it belonged to a theater or a taxi-dance hall, and the photographs in the glass case bore out that latter resemblance. In those days, before the 1957 Prevention of Prostitution and Rehabilitation of Women Act, the *machiai* were legal and open. They had lost the great luxury and style they had been famous for, before the war, but there were still traces—such as those pictures of the girls, which were, in fact, surrogates for the real girls who, in other times, would have displayed themselves in person, magnificently coifed, resplendently clad, and surrounded by incense and the delicate music of the samisen.

The samisen music had survived, and it tinkled forth, even if only from the loudspeaker of a phonograph. Kane examined the photographs of the girls, and remembered Buchanan's delighted report about how their legs went up to their necks. It was impossible to tell from the pictures, which showed them all clothed in kimonos. Their faces were pretty enough, but with the elaborate maquillage, there was a kind of unreality about them. They looked like dolls more than like real girls. In a curious way their artificiality made it easier for Kane to avoid any crude, abrupt confrontation with himself and what he was doing.

Shortly before he had been killed, Buchanan had told Kane about the odd system that the Japanese *machiai* used: "They have this kind of box office thing in the front, and you pay before you go in. You'd think it would be kind of commercial and horrible that way, but it really isn't, because once you've paid and have gone in, it's kind of social. I mean, they make you feel at home, and don't rush you or anything. None of this crap about putting twenty dollars on the dresser, or handing it to the girl before she gets her clothes off.

"Jesus, I remember a house I visited once in Steubenville," Buchanan had told him, "when I was a kid, I mean. It was full of railroad men and coal miners and some college kids, and it was just goddam crude. I mean, really hairy. The girl took me into the room and asked me whether I wanted it straight, French, or half-and-half. I swear, I had no idea what the hell she was talking about. And she wouldn't let me take my shoes off, either. I mean, for Christ's sake, there was canvas across the bottom of the bed where the shoes went. But here, in this place I was at last night, you just go on in, and they serve you sake in those little cups, and there are lots of girls around, smiling and giggling. It's like a goddam sorority house or something."

Kane doubted whether he would find it anything like any of the sorority houses at Ames, but the comparison was comforting. He wondered whether poor Buchanan had ever been in a sorority house. He supposed so.

Walking up to the booth, he felt more as if he were in some kind of an amusement park, paying admission to get into the fun house, but it wasn't really him. It was one of the distortions that he would see in one of those funny mirrors they have that make you look tall and skinny or short and fat, or sort of wavy looking. He wondered if he was still feeling the aftereffects of the brandy. But, no, that had worn off by this time. The fresh spring air and the long ride out to the Yoshiwara district had pretty much sobered him up.

The charming, middle-aged woman smiled at him, revealing a row of bright gold teeth.

"How much?" he asked.

"Twenty dollar American."

"Twenty?" he asked.

"No short time. Only long-time house here," she said.

It took him a moment to figure out what she meant, but once he had done so, it seemed to make sense. He could stay as long as he wanted, but that didn't mean he had to stay any longer than he wanted. He gave the woman two crumpled ten-dollar bills. She smiled, pressed a button, and indicated to him that he should open the door. It worked the way automatic vestibule doors of apartments work. He stood for a moment with his hand on the doorknob, and then, with the noise of the buzzer insistent in his ear, he turned the knob, pushed the door open, and went inside.

It took a moment for his eyes to adjust to the dimness of the hall. A girl in a brightly flowered kimono came mincing up to him, wearing high-heeled cork sandals. She took his overseas cap and knelt on the tile floor to help him take his shoes off. She put the shoes on a small rack on one wall, and, from a closet on the opposite wall, produced a black robe upon the back of which was a caligraphic symbol in bright red strokes.

"You put on a happi coat?" she asked.

He did so, with her help. He let her tie the sash for him, and then, with a slight bow, she indicated that he should follow her. She went to the end of the hall, slid open one of the shoji panels, and escorted him into a large, low-ceilinged room.

It was just the way Buchanan had described it. It looked like a large living room in which there was a party going on. The only odd thing was that there was no furniture except for a few low tables, on top of which a few delicate sake jugs and cups were set on trays. In the middle of the room, sunken in a pit, there was a charcoal brazier that sent faint wisps of smoke into a chimney above it. The brazier was used both as a heat source and for cooking the rice-balls and shrimp hors d'oeuvres the girls passed around from time to time. There were about fifteen girls and eight or ten men in the room, all the men wearing "happi coats." Some of the men were Americans, and the rest were Japanese. The girls were all wearing the same flowered, loose kimonos. Two of the girls came up to him, smiled, and led him to a low table, where they indicated that he should sit down. As best he could, he got down on the tatami next to the black lacquered table.

"Sake or Suntori?" one of the girls asked. "The Suntori is like your Scotch," she explained. Her English was flawless.

"I've never had sake," he admitted. "What's it like?"

"Try it," she suggested, and smiled seductively.

She took a small white jug from a kerosene burner where it had been keeping warm, and poured what seemed to be a thimbleful into a tiny white porcelain cup. It was warm, and relaxing, rather sweeter than whiskey. Something between whiskey and wine. He asked for another thimbleful, and the girl poured him a second drink.

They introduced themselves and sat down beside him. The taller of the two was named Haruko. She was lithe and willowy, and taller than he had thought Japanese women got to be. She also seemer bustier than most of the women he had noticed in the bars on the Ginza. The other girl, Satsumi, was tiny and delicate. Her bones were small, and her large almond-shaped eyes burned out from the soft petal-like complexion of her face. She was the quieter of the two. Haruko talked to him with ease and animation, asking him whether he had been in Korea, and congratulated him when she heard that he was on his way home. Satsumi merely sat quietly and smiled, and, in a curious way, he felt rather sorry for her. She seemed to be uncomfortable, or shy. Less at ease than the other one. Or it might have been that he felt something in common with her, because he was not entirely comfortable and assured himself.

At one point, he looked around the room and noticed a couple rise from the tatami mats, open a panel in the shoji screen, and disappear, closing the screen after them. Their exit had seemed perfectly natural. No one had paid the slightest attention to it.

Haruko noticed his glance, and said, "If we do not please you, we can introduce you to some other girls."

She said it perfectly simply and in a straightforward way. He appreciated the gesture she had made, but still, he felt it would have been insulting and crude to accept her offer. He did glance around the room, rather furtively, and he saw that all of the girls, while attractive, looked very much the same. One girl was fleshier than another, or taller, or more delicate of face, but essentially the dark hair, the slightly slanted eyes, the bright kimonos, and the air of repose that all the girls shared made them seem as much alike as flowers in a garden.

Satsumi poured him another cup of sake. The conversation somehow had lapsed into silence. The three of them had been quiet for some moments. He had tentatively decided upon Satsumi, and he wondered whether it was not up to him to indicate that to her, or to let her know that he had chosen her and that they might go off now to wherever it was that couples went. Not knowing quite what to do or what to say, he reached his hand out toward Satsumi's. She took it. Her fingers were smooth and cool. She asked Haruko if she would please refill the sake jug. Haruko smiled, got up, fetched another jug from the kerosene burner, poured the sake into cups for the two of them, smiled again, bowed, and went off to another part of the room.

It was already done. He felt a great sense of relief, and only later, when he went over it all in his mind, did he come to appreciate how tactfully and adroitly they had handled the situation. He was still feeling that relief at having maneuvered successfully— or at having been maneuvered—through the last hurdle, that he was not even apprehensive about the next step, which Satsumi took rather abruptly and yet with a kind of subtlety, when she suggested, quietly, "Perhaps you might care for a bath?"

It seemed to him not at all unreasonable. Sensible, actually, from the point of view of the house. If these girls were going to go to bed with men off the streets, then the least they could do was to make sure that the men were clean. It was just like the "Y" back at Indianapolis, where the rules required that you shower before you went into the pool.

"Sure," he said.

He followed her out of the room, up a short flight of stairs, and down a long corridor lined with the same shoji screens as he had seen downstairs. Halfway down the corridor, she stopped, opened a panel, and led him in. The room was, like the one downstairs, relatively bare. There was a large low bed and a large round wooden tub on a small platform. There was also a shelf on which a gnarled bonsai tree was growing beside a small willow-colored vase containing two sprigs of quince with pink blossoms.

Satsumi helped him out of his happi coat and his uniform and carefully hung the clothes up in a small closet, concealed by the panelling of the screens. A dumpy elderly woman with white hair and thousands of tiny wrinkles all over her face came in bearing an impossibly heavy cauldron of hot water, which she poured into the wooden tub. She bowed, left them for a moment, and then returned carrying a large pitcher of cold water, a sponge, and a pile of fluffy white towels. Kane waited until the woman had left before he allowed Satsumi to take off the white cotton undershorts he had bought a few days before at the PX in Seoul.

Satsumi produced a small vial from a fold in her kimono and poured its contents, some kind of fragrant oil, into the tub. She took the sponge, dipped it into the steaming water of the tub, and then motioned to Kane to get onto the platform. She sponged him all over and then told him to get into the tub. It was very strange. There had been something impersonal, almost clinical, in her washing. It had been very pleasant, but not at all sexual. He was in no way aroused, but had found it all relaxing and soothing. For the first time that evening, it struck him that this would be a good thing to remember when he got home to Cal. The time they had spent together had been so painfully brief and so terribly strained and awkward.

Satsumi again told him to get into the tub. He climbed gingerly over the edge and tried the water with a foot. It was scalding hot. He withdrew the foot.

"It's too hot," he protested.

She smiled and nodded. "That's right. It's supposed to be hot."

"No, no. It's too hot." He pointed to his bright red foot.

"Yes," she said. "You get in. I will take care of it."

Very slowly, and with great apprehension, he eased himself into the incredibly hot water. He was just about to jump out when she poured the large pitcher of cold water over him. He gasped, and sat down abruptly in the tub. It was a shock to his nervous system, but, having passed through it, he had to admit that it was the most refreshing bath he had ever had. All his nerve endings seemed to tingle. She scrubbed his back with a long-handled brush, then picked up a large white towel and held it up.

He climbed out of the tub, and she wrapped the towel around him. She spread another on the bed and indicated to him that he lie down on it. He did so, and felt what little tension there was left draining from his muscles. So relaxed and serene did he feel that it crossed his mind in an idle, dreamy way that he might very well fall asleep. Which would be a great joke, he thought. But he didn't care. He had never felt so good in his life, at home with himself and with his body.

Then he felt her hands massaging the backs of his heels. Gently and yet firmly she kneaded the muscles in the back of his heels and calfs and then moved up and down from his heels to the back of his knees. It was wonderful. He had the beautiful feeling that he was melting into the bed. He turned his head to tell her how good it felt and saw that she was naked.

Her skin was the color of old ivory. Her breasts were small and pointy and the tiny nipples were a delicate shade of creamy brown. Her legs were not so long as Buchanan had promised, but they were slender and shapely, and his eyes climbed along the line of her legs and thighs up to the dark tangle of feathery hair. The steam from the bath had given her skin a moist sheen that he thought was deliciously sensual. Her hands moved up to the backs of his thighs, paused for a moment, and then continued up to his buttocks, which she massaged with firmness but with tantalizing slowness of rhythm.

He felt a certain disappointment as she moved her hands up from the buttocks to message his back and his shoulders, but after a few moments he felt the tips of her breasts grazing his buttocks as she leaned over him to massage the back of his neck. It was the slightest sensation, and he was just barely aware of it, so it was the idea of it as much as the physical contact that excited him. He felt desire move in his loins.

He rolled over and reached out for her, encircling her tiny waist with his hand. He pulled her down to him and kissed her on the mouth, a long lingering kiss. He pulled her tightly down on top of him so that her breasts were crushed against his chest. They rolled so that she was beneath him. Her thighs parted.

Until this moment he had felt eager and keenly excited, but somehow the blunt way she had spread her thighs and her total submissiveness chilled him. He felt his desire shrivel. She responded by pushing him over, gently, so that he lay on his back. Methodically, and yet tenderly, she began to move her lips over him, descending inexorably from the chest where she had begun toward his penis. It may have been that he was still nervous and distraught from his precipitate failure a moment before, or it could have been his vague realization of the methodical nature of her expert attentions, but, whatever the reason, he failed to respond to her delicately engulfing lips.

After some time had passed, she realized the extent and seriousness of his inability, and, fearing that she might embarrass him by continuing, she got up and went to the corner of the room, where she pulled a bell rope. The old woman with the wrinkled face appeared, and Satsumi said a few words in Japanese. The old woman disappeared and Satsumi explained to Kane that she had ordered some sake. The woman returned, bringing the jug and small glasses, and Satsumi poured him a cup of the warm, nearly clear liquid.

"It must be very bad in Korea," she said.

"Yes," Kane answered, not entirely sure whether she was offering this as a possible excuse for him, whether she meant that this was a fairly common occurrence, or whether she was merely making conversation. She perched on the edge of the bed and they drank their sake in silence.

Without saying a word, she got up, padded quietly across the room to turn out the light, and then came back to the bed. She leaned across Kane's prone body, and opened a panel in the screen that separated their room from the adjoining one. She opened it only a slight crack, but it was enough. She smiled, put her finger to her lips to command silence, and pointed to the opening. Not knowing quite what it was that she wanted him to look at, Kane sat up, shifted his weight and put his eye to the crack.

In the room next to theirs, a room identical to the one they were in, there was a couple on the bed. The man was a large, burly Japanese, and he lay on top of the girl, who had locked her legs around his back. From his position at the screen, Kane could see his buttocks contracting as he moved vigorously, plunging into the girl beneath him. Kane watched, fascinated, as the rhythmic movement increased in intensity. The copulating couple breathed heavily, and Kane could hear over the continuance of their breathing the occasional slap of flesh against flesh. Curiously, even frighteningly, he felt himself grow rigid. He had never been so excited before. Satsumi was on her hands and knees, with her eyes glued to the crack in the screen. As if he were making a comment on the activity in the next room, Kane climbed on top of her and entered her from the rear, still watching the other couple next door.

That couple continued, until the husky Japanese shuddered, groaned, and collapsed on the girl. Satsumi braced herself on one arm and, with the other, slid the panel of the screen shut. By this time, Kane's excitement knew no bounds. Almost immediately, he came, with such a sharp spasm of pleasure that it made him cry out.

Bathed in sweat, he rolled off and collapsed onto the bed. Satsumi got off the bed, went over to the platform, got the towel, and dried him off. She lit two cigarettes, handed him one, and stretched out beside him on the bed. Kane lay back, amazed by the pure joy of what he had just discovered. It had been so easy, so simple, so sublime. He did not allow himself to think consciously about the other couple in the adjoining room, but he was nevertheless aware in some groping way of a whole world of sex into which he felt he had now been initiated. He reveled in the freshness of the experience, and through pure ebullience he laughed aloud. He felt at one with himself and with all of nature. It had nothing to do with the lovemaking he had known with Cal. That had been pathetic, really, compared with this, but that had not been their fault. They had both been victims of some hideous misconceptions about the joy and truth of the body, and had been warped and inhibited by their families, by their society, even by their religion. But lovemaking wasn't like that at all; it was beautiful and simple, and beautiful in its simplicity.

Satsumi looked at him inquiringly, and, perhaps out of politeness, giggled. He was touched by this, and, in return, he touched her, playfully and with gaiety, tracing his fingers along the length of her smooth body. He would, he knew, make love to her again. He was in no hurry. He was enjoying each moment as it came.

On the way back to the hotel he felt no fatigue, even though the sky was beginning to lighten in the east. He was not tired, but he was light-headed. So much had happened in twenty-four hours that he had not been able to digest it yet. Still, he had never felt so much in command of himself, and he knew that when he was ready he would be able to sort it all out. Partly as a demonstration to himself of the power that he felt he now had, and partly out of his own wonder at the curious absence of any feelings of guilt, he allowed his mind to drift back to the most uncomfortable moment he could remember, a moment he had for so long studiously avoided thinking about.

He had been fourteen years old at the time. It had been a hot Saturday afternoon in July, and the still heat had shimmered outside his bedroom window. He had worked for a neighbor in the morning, mowing her lawn and trimming her privet, and then had returned home to an empty house. His lunch had been waiting for him in the refrigerator. He had eaten, and then gone up to his room to stretch out on his bed. The coolness of the sheets had promised some relief from the closeness of the room downstairs, closed against the heat. He had taken a shower and then gone to his room to lie down, still wet, and had turned on the electric fan, which oscillated slowly. He had closed his eyes and had been able to feel the fan's motion as coolness on his body, where as the current of air hit him, the moisture evaporated. The fan was on a chair next to his bed, and the sweep of the air over his body had caused him to have an erection. A few months earlier he had discovered the pleasures of masturbation, but before now it was something he had only done under the covers, in the dark, at night. And he had felt guilty about it and had resolved each time never to do it again. But now, in the empty house, in the half light that came in around the edges of the shades, and with the fan blowing on his body, it had seemed somehow entirely innocent. He had just begun to stroke himself when he had been seized by an odd idea, which, however, seemed no more odd or bizarre than what had already happened in a perfectly spontaneous way—a desire to watch himself. He had got up from the bed and had gone across the room to the full-length mirror on his closet door. He had begun pumping himself, watching his reflection with great interest, and eager for the moment when the real and the imaged figures would meet in a small opalescent splash on the surface of the glass.

Because of the noise of the fan, an old fan that hummed quite loudly and clattered at either end of its oscillation, he had not heard his parents return. Suddenly the bedroom door had opened, and his mother had entered. She had gasped in horror, and he had tried to cover himself, but, furious, she had seized him by the ear and dragged him after her, out of his room, down the stairs, and into the kitchen where his father had been putting down bags of groceries.

The moments after that were blurred still, but he remembered how the shame of it had stayed with him for years, though yet it seemed to him now to be nothing more than an intellectual construct. He could smile at it now, and the fact that he could smile at it reinforced his feeling of euphoric transcendence over all of the taboos and the furtive secrecy of his youth. He could even feel a detached kind of pity for his parents. He doubted that sex had brought them any great joys such as those that he had just discovered. He resolved to share those joys with Cal when he returned. And, having resolved that, he felt entirely liberated, entirely righteous, entirely wonderful.

Three days later, with only sixty dollars in his pocket, he was assigned to the *Stephen Ford*, a troopship bound for San Francisco. Each of the nights he had spent waiting in Tokyo he had passed with Satsumi, who had taught him more ways in which the human body could take delight than he had ever imagined. He felt out of place on the troopship. So many of the men were still shaken from their experiences in Korea, but all of that seemed so ineffably remote. The only carry-over he felt from the war was his friendship with Buchanan. He felt a sense of loss and of obligation, and knew that he would have to pay a call on Buchanan's parents. Buchanan had died in a stupid, unheroic way, but he had been a good soldier, and, more than that, Kane felt that he owed his buddy, in a peculiarly direct way, for the whole new attitude toward life and sex that he had almost accidentally acquired. He was grateful for that. He would not be able to explain that to Buchanan's folks, but he would go, anyway. He would pay his respects.

But most of all, he was looking forward to his reunion with Cal. Now their marriage could really begin.

The *Stephen Ford* was a small old ship, crowded with soldiers. Below decks it was stale and stifling, so the men spent as much time as they could on deck. At night sleep was impossible, and the only place to go to get away from the dark, fetid hold was the head, where, by the dim light, some of the guys played cards. They had all been in Korea long enough so that money had lost its value. They knew it could buy things when they got back to the States, but even there, on the ship, the States seemed to be some kind of dreamland in which they were still afraid to believe. They played poker every night, all night through. Kane joined the game. It was a reckless game, but because of his feeling of omnipotence, which had not yet left him, and the confidence he had now, not only about his own body but about the entire world, he did well. He played surely, confidently, taking chances when a more cautious player would have folded, and in unlikely and improbable ways finding the chances paying off. By the time they passed through the Golden Gate Bridge, while some soldiers were weeping with emotion at seeing that symbol of the States again, Kane was counting his money. He had $2,654, more than he had ever had at one time in his entire life.

There was a band playing as they trooped down the gangplank. Kane knew what the homecoming would be like from all the movies he had seen from World War II, but, corny as it was, he still felt the prickle of tears forming in his eyes. The crowd at the quayside was thinner than it had been in those shots in the movies when Gable had come off the ships, but most of the men on his ship were from the East, and they still had a while to go before they were reunited with their families. But the crowd was thick enough so that it took him a while before he spotted Cal, standing there and looking for him. She was wearing a navy blue suit and a yellow blouse with an absurd yellow hat to match. She was scanning the faces of the men as they walked by, looking carefully, almost as if she were afraid that she would not recognize her husband when she saw him. He walked toward her. He noted, almost as though he were checking her appearance against a description of a missing person, that she looked exactly the way he had remembered her. Her shoulder-length blonde hair fell softly around her face and accentuated the wide-set blue eyes. She had light eyebrows which she refused to darken with make-up, and she always wore the palest possible lipstick. He had never decided whether she was pretty or not, but the quality about her of sweetness, and the clarity of her features, made the question of her beauty almost irrelevant. If her figure was not exactly seductive, it was appealingly trim. She was tall enough so that he had always felt comfortable dancing with her and walking with her. They made an attractive couple. She was the kind of girl whom one imagines in a tennis dress more than in a negligee, but that wholesomeness was exactly what he had always wanted in a wife—or had thought he wanted. It was exciting to think of the awakening that he would be bringing to that innocence and purity, without entirely obliterating any of her sweetness.

The idea of her, abandoned in his arms, seemed even more thrilling to his imagination than anything he had known or anything he could imagine with even the most experienced and adept whore.

At last she saw him and cried out, "Irv!" and they ran to each other. As soon as he had swung his duffel bag down to the ground, they embraced, and after a long moment he pushed her slightly away from him, and, still holding her tightly by the shoulders, stared into her eyes.

"Let's get out of here," he said. He shouldered his duffel bag, then took her by the elbow and guided her out to the exit from the pier.

They found a cab, and got in. He looked at her and asked, "Where to?"

"I've found us a hotel," she answered, and added, as if in apology, "It's very reasonable, nice but very reasonable."

"Okay," he said, and she told the driver the address.

In the cab they were silent, shy with each other. They held hands very tightly, as if each was afraid that the other would disappear into an ectoplasmic mist.

When the cab pulled up in front of the hotel, Irv turned to Cal and asked, "Have you unpacked?"

"Well, no," she said. "My plane just got in."

"Well, the hell with it then," he said. "Driver, wait a minute."

He went inside, got her bags from the puzzled bell captain, and came back to the cab.

"But Irv," Call protested. "It's impossible to get hotel rooms in San Francisco. There isn't a thing available. I was very lucky to get that room!"

"Who said San Francisco was the only place in the country? Let's go to Las Vegas."

She looked at him, dumbfounded.

"But—but it's so expensive."

"Don't worry about it. This is our honeymoon. Remember? We never really had one."

He took her face gently in his hands, kissed her on the nose, and then ordered the driver, "Take us to the airport, please."

On the way to the airport he explained to Cal about his phenomenal luck on the ship and how they would spend some of his poker winnings having themselves a really first-class time. He could see faint disapproval on her face as he told her about the gambling on the ship, but she said nothing. Perhaps she was afraid to say anything to this new, strange husband, who seemed so self-assured, so brisk and confident.

What did she know, anyway, of that odd mood on the ship where money had had no value? They had all felt sufficiently lucky just to be alive, and the pay they had drawn had been like the money in a Monopoly game. In the first-class section of the Western Air Lines plane to Las Vegas, which he could not help but compare to the noisy MATS transport from Korea to Tokyo with those uncomfortable canvas sling chairs, he felt as if a new life was beginning. Here he was with a couple of thousand dollars in his pocket, his wife sitting next to him, and a martini in his hand.

Cal was very animated on the trip, talking vivaciously—even compulsively—and told him about friends, about her family, and all the things she had not been able to write about in the many letters she had sent to him in Korea. He listened in a serene, Olympian way, paying attention to the news of the folks back home in the way a boy might pay attention to the busy peregrinations of a colony of ants. He looked out of the window and admired the mountains, and then the expanse of desert. The pilot called their attention to Boulder Dam and Lake Meade behind it, and then banked and started the plane on its descent to the Las Vegas airfield.

He called The Sands from the airport, and had no trouble getting a room.

"You see?" he said to Cal. "Everybody's in San Francisco."

Her laughter was more than the joke called for, and it betrayed the nervousness that she felt, confronted by this seeming stranger. Kane was aware of this, and was rather enjoying it. He was also touched by it, and he felt the way one feels after having planned a surprise party, during that moment of apparent darkness and silence, just before the lights go on and the party begins. He was practically bursting with glee at the surprise he had in store for her as soon as they reached the privacy of the bedroom.

The cab pulled up to the main building of the great complex of The Sands. Feeling entirely carefree and confident, Kane registered, and, as he did so, he remembered with amusement the self-conscious gaucherie with which he had registered at that motel the first night they had spent together. The room clerk at The Sands was especially cordial to Kane because he was still in uniform, and Kane confided that he was just returning from Korea and that this was his first day back in the States. The room clerk insisted upon sending a bottle of champagne to the room, and wished Mr. and Mrs. Kane a fine time.

Their room was in the Hialeah. All of the buildings in The Sands were named after the major racetracks of the country, and Kane rather enjoyed the breeziness of the gesture. He had never been to a racetrack in his life, but he felt quite at home in the little electric cart that took them from the main building to Hialeah. The bell boy took them inside and ushered them down a corridor. He opened the door and stood back, and they entered what was the wildest room that Kane had ever seen in his life—or even imagined.

The tub in the bathroom was sunken, the bed in the alcove was raised and canopied, and there were great festoons of crimson taffeta hanging from the canopy. The raised alcove with that enormous bed on it looked like a stage, and in fact there was a draw drape of some gauzy stuff separating the alcove from the rest of the room, so that the illusion of the stage was maintained. There was an enormous sectional sofa, and a pair of French provincial armchairs flanking a huge, circular fruitwood coffee table, on which stood a large bowl of fruit and the champagne in the silver ice bucket, which had preceded them to the room.

"Jesus fucking Christ!" Kane exclaimed.

"I beg your pardon?" Cal said.
He looked at her. She was horrified.

With every passing moment Cal realized that the man she had married had changed, and was now a stranger. She had married a boy, a sweet, diffident, rather withdrawn boy, but now she was facing a man, rough, profane, aggressive, and more confident. All the way from Des Moines, where she had boarded the plane, she had avoided thinking about what it would be like to be together with Irv again. She had had the excuse of an examination in remedial reading methods, and had taken a textbook along with her so that she could study it on the flight, but the experience of flying—she had never been in a plane before—had been so absorbing that she had not been able to study. Now that she had landed, had met Irv, had been swept off, and had landed again here in Las Vegas, she was still uncertain of her reaction. She knew she loved him, but who now was the "him" she loved? Not only were the surroundings strange and different—in her daydreams she had always imagined them together on the campus of Iowa State or in her organdy-trimmed room in her family's airy farmhouse outside of Des Moines—but he was different too. So, here they were, in this wild room like some set in a Hollywood movie, in which there was nothing for her to hold on to but the abstract idea that she loved him and was married to him.

She was still gauging her emotional temperature when Irv came up to her, put his arms around her, and kissed her, a long, searching kiss. He held her close to him with one arm and cupped her buttock with his other hand. Instinctively she stiffened, and then relaxed in his embrace. After a long moment he pulled away from her, held her at arm's length, and looked deep into her eyes. Consciously, she manufactured a smile, which seemed to reassure him. He gave a laugh that broke the tension.

"A shower," he said, "the champagne, and then . . ." He broke off and smiled at her—or was it something between a smile and a leer?—patted her on the backside, and went off to the bathroom.

She took off her suit jacket and hung it in the closet. Then, with a kind of nervous orderliness, she began to unpack, putting the clothing from her suitcase and his duffel bag into the closet and the drawers of the massive fruitwood dresser. He had left the bathroom door open, and she could hear him singing in the shower.

After she had finished unpacking, she looked around for something else to do, but there wasn't anything. She sat down in the chair, and stared out of the window at the carefully manicured grass, which only profligate quantities of labor and money could have produced from the arid desert.

Finally the water stopped. A minute later he emerged from the bathroom with a towel wrapped around his waist. He lit a cigarette and offered one to her.

"Irv!" she said. "You know I don't smoke! When did you start?"

"Over there," he said.

He put the cigarette in the ashtray and, picking up the bottle of champagne, pulled off the foil, twisted the wire, and deftly popped the cork. During the course of his exertions with the champagne bottle, the towel he had wrapped around his waist fell to the floor. He did not bother to pick it up. She riveted her eyes upon the champagne bottle, wishing she could think of some way of asking him to put the towel back on, or to put a bathrobe on, or something, but she knew there was nothing she could say. He was her husband, even if she had known him as a husband for only a few short days.

After he had poured champagne into the two glasses, he turned, noticed her face, and said in a teasing way, "Cal, you're blushing!"

She put her hand to her cheek, as if to hide the fact. She could not, however, deny it.

He picked up the towel and retied it around his waist. Then he handed her a glass of champagne. They raised their glasses, looking intently at one another, and drank.

"I unpacked," she said.

"You didn't open any of the boxes, did you?" he asked in mock horror.

"No, should I have?"

"No, no. That was the whole point. Here, hang on a minute."

He put his champagne glass down on the coffee table and went over to his Dopp Kitt, which she had left on top of the dresser. He opened the zipper and produced a comb, with which he combed his hair, and then a small box, which he handed to her.

"Here, this is for you," he said.

He waited expectantly while she undid the wrapping. Inside of the paper there was a small white box. Inside that there was a small plush jeweler's box and, inside that, were the pearl earrings.

"Oh, Irv!" she said. "They're beautiful!"

"Put them on," he said. "They're real, you know."

"Oh, they're so lustrous. Oh, thank you."

She went over to him, kissed him quickly, and then turned to the mirror to put the earrings on and look at herself. She cocked her head, and turned it from side to side to see the pearls against her skin. Then she turned to him.

"What do you think?" she asked, smiling provocatively.

"You're beautiful," he said in a husky voice.

He came up behind her and put his arms around her, cupping her breasts, and kissed her on the neck just below the drop of the earring. He nuzzled his nose under her ear and moved his hands on her breasts. Then he stepped back and undid the buttons on the back of her blouse, slid the blouse off her shoulders, and dropped it on the chair.

"I think I'll have a bath myself," she said.

"Coming up," he said. "I'll run it for you."

He went into the bathroom. She got out of the rest of her clothing and slid into a light nylon robe.

"All ready!" he called.

She went into the bathroom. He untied the sash on the robe, and said, "Hop in. It's all ready for you."

She allowed him to take the robe from her, and got into the tub. She wished she could hide under the surface of the water. In the movies there were always thick bubbles so that you could do that.

But then, to her relief, he left the room. She eased back into the tub. But he returned, carrying his champagne glass, his cigarette, and an ashtray. He sat down on the toilet seat and put the champagne glass and the ashtray on the large marble washstand beside him.

"You're more beautiful than I remembered," he said.

"Did you miss me?" she asked.

"Jesus, yes! Wait till you get out of the tub, and I'll show you."

She winced at his use of the Lord's name and ignored the rest of his comment. He had changed enormously. It wasn't just that she had forgotten the fine details of his personality but that those details had changed, and she could not help but wonder what this all meant for their future together. She wondered whether she would have married the man who was sitting there on the toilet seat so carelessly, smoking, drinking, and swearing, and making his eagerness for her body all too apparent. Still, it was possible that this was all a kind of surface toughness that he had acquired from the men with whom he had been fighting in Korea and that underneath it he was the same sweet Irv she had known, loved, and married.

She stood up and reached for a towel.

"I'll dry you," he said, and he helped her out of the tub.

She stood there quietly while he rubbed the rough, fluffy towel all over her body.

"Come," he said.

"I . . . I . . . I need a moment alone," she said.

"Oh, sure. Okay." He went out alone and closed the door behind him.

In his absence, she had gone to a gynecologist and been fitted for a diaphragm. She felt a little uneasy about the small case she carried around with her, not because it was morally wrong, but because it was somehow so forward, so blatant. Well, she supposed she would get used to it. Aside from the practice with it in the doctor's office, this was the first time she had used it.

When she finished, she closed the case and washed her hands. She glanced at the robe that hung from the hook on the back of the bathroom door, thought of putting it on, but realized how silly that was. Then, squaring her shoulders, she opened the door and went out into the room, where Irv was lying on the bed. He had pulled down the covers and had discarded his own covering—the towel. He looked very Turkish, she thought, considering the picture he made on that preposterous bed with a glass of champagne in one hand and a cigarette in the other—and his penis boldly erect.

As she approached the bed he put down the cigarette, put down the glass, and held out his arms toward her. She glanced down at his erect member, and then fell into his arms, almost as if she were hiding there. His body felt rough and hard against her. He was much more muscular than he had been before he had gone into the Army. But he smelled the same, and when he kissed her his mouth tasted the same. He ran his hands along her body with an assurance that she did not remember. Then, before she expected it, he was on top of her and within her.

It was not painful, but neither was it particularly pleasurable.

It was like fucking a board.

It would have been bad enough under ordinary circumstances, but after his experiences in Japan it was disastrous. Still, he thought, perhaps it was his fault. He had not been sufficiently gradual in his approach, but then he had been so damned eager. On the other hand, he had hoped that she would be eager for him, too, after all that time apart from each other. But apparently she wasn't. Well, maybe he could make up for it now. Deliberately slowing his pace, he tried to consolidated his position by kissing her and stroking her in artful ways. It did not seem to do any good. Finally, determined that it was going to be good, great, better than great, he withdrew gently and lay down beside her.

"Darling," he said, "I've wanted you for so long."

He propped himself up on one elbow, looked down at her face, and stroked her body softly.

"I know, Irv. I've missed you too."

She smiled up at him and, encouraged by her response, he smiled at her. Tentatively, she reached out and touched his cheek, and then, moving her hand slightly, she ran her fingers through his hair. Further encouraged, he leaned over and kissed her passionately, thrusting his tongue deep into her mouth. She met his kiss with her own and moved with her whole body to embrace him. With all his misgivings gone, and confident that she was as eager now for him as he was for her, he entered her again. She stiffened slightly, but in his irresistible need he could no longer hold himself back. Without wanting it to be so fast, and sad that he was no longer able to accommodate himself to her, and that he could not bring her along with him, he felt himself dissolve into a torrent. He collapsed onto her body, exhausted by the force of his climax. She stirred slightly beneath him. He was hardly aware of her stroking his back. After a while, he realized that she was murmuring his name, and he answered by saying, "Cal, Cal, I love you so much."

He withdrew and lay down beside her, exhausted. He was not yet seriously worried about their adjustment to each other. He was still delighting in her body and was confident that the next time would be better, better for her and therefore better for them both. After all, the long separation might have made her nervous and apprehensive, and they had had so little time together before he had gone off to fight.

He sat up in bed, reached for the glass of champagne on the night table beside him, drained it, and then, with deliberate cheerfulness, suggested, "Well, how about something to eat? Let's go take a look around, shall we?"

"Yes, yes. That'd be fine."

He was pleased by the sudden animation in her voice and face, and he leaned over, gave her an affectionate kiss, and jumped out of bed to get dressed. He went to the closet to get his civvies, turned back, and told Cal, "Put on something sexy! We'll have a great time. Okay, baby?"

"Sure," she said. "I have just the thing."

To get from anyplace in The Sands to anyplace else, it was necessary to go through the casino—a matter of design, not chance. So, in order to get to the dining room, they had to make their way through a bank of slot machines, and pass the roulette tables, the 21 tables, and the crap tables. On an impulse, Irv felt in his pocket and pulled out a half-dollar, handed it to Cal, and told her to try her luck at one of the machines. She took the half-dollar, put it in the nearest machine, and pulled the crank. In the three windows there was a blur as the symbols whirled around, then, one after another, they stopped, settled in place, and, much to Cal's astonishment, produced a jackpot. Quantities of half-dollars came pouring out from the tray in the bottom of the machine. An elderly woman at the next slot machine glared at Cal for a second and then turned back to the methodical feeding of coins into her machine.

It struck them both, somehow, as terribly funny, and with a pleasant conspiratorial feeling they scooped up the money into one of the plastic bags that the hotel supplied for the purpose. Still smiling, they went on together into the dining room.

They had a fine dinner, starting with cocktails, which he insisted that she have with him—it had occurred to him that a little liquor might loosen her up and make her relax—and then going on through a thick steak accompanied by a bottle of burgundy, a salad, and a baked Alaska for two. Afterward they ordered coffee royale. They both watched as the waiter put a spoon across the top of the coffee cup, poured brandy into it, lit the brandy, and lowered the spoon, flaming brandy and all, into the coffee. It was delicious.

They had talked little during the meal, content to watch the people around them and enjoy their food and the closeness they felt from their sharing of the novelty of it all. After dinner there was a floor show, and Irv watched Cal's eyes grow wide as the tall, leggy chorus girls wearing G-strings and pasties paraded across the small stage at the end of the room. The girls were, to his taste, too large, too crude, too blatant, but he rather approved of the effect he thought they might have on Cal. After the chorus girls, Dick Haymes came on and sang songs, and then, after a final production number with the chorus girls, there was music for dancing, throbbing, intimate music, to which they danced well together—as they had done so often back in Iowa. Irv was feeling supremely confident of his prospects for a better time with Cal when they left the café to go back to the bedroom.

On the way back, as they passed through the casino, he put a silver dollar down on number twenty—which he picked because that had been the magic number for him in Japan. The croupier spun the wheel. Number twenty won. For his dollar bet he won thirty-six dollars.

"It's incredible," Cal said. "How do they manage to stay in business?"

"Well, not everybody wins all the time," Kane explained. "I'm just lucky tonight, I guess. You make me lucky."

She smiled at him, and, feeling on top of the world again, he escorted her through the lobby and across the cool lawn to the Hialeah and their room.

It could not have been a more auspicious set of circumstances. He was eager and, indeed, determined to share with Cal the delights that he knew could be available from their lovemaking. Surely the love they felt for each other would enhance the physical joys he knew they would feel, and he was most eager to have her feel them along with him.

They went into the room to find that it had been made up and the bed turned down. With great alacrity and joyfulness, they got undressed and fell into bed. He was not going to make the same mistake this time. He would be gradual and would take as much time as she needed. He began simply by holding her in his arms and kissing her lightly. He did this for some few minutes, after which, instead of continuing, he fell asleep.

When he awoke, he found himself curled up around her. They were nestled together like a couple of spoons. It was, he found, delightful and arousing. He began to stroke her, cupping her breast and running his hand along her thigh, until she awoke, too. She stretched out, smiled at him, and kissed him lightly.

"Good morning, Mrs. Kane," he said.

"Good morning, Mr. Kane," she answered, smiling.

He continued to touch her, moving his hand up along her thigh until it was between her legs. He was glad that she had awakened so quickly and in such good spirits. He felt a surge of love for her and he held her close and kissed her confidently. She responded to his embrace, and held him tight to her. They lay together this way for several minutes. This time, Irv was in no hurry. Even if it took all morning, this time he was determined to enjoy her pleasure as well as his own.

She was moving her hands in small circles on his back.

"Touch me," he said.

"I am touching you."

"No, no. Touch me *there*."

"I . . . I don't know how."

He took her hand and guided it gently, and moved it slowly up and down the length of his penis. He removed his hand, and hesitantly she stroked him. After a moment, when she seemed to have accustomed herself to this, he took her hand and moved it lower, so that she could cup his scrotum. She drew her hand away, and then, tentatively, almost reluctantly, as if it were the lesser of the two evils, she returned to her first stroking.

Sensing that she was reluctant and ill at ease, he began to stroke and touch her in a correspondingly intimate fashion. She had let go of him, and now he leaned over and kissed her breast. Then, in a methodical way—he remembered how Satsumi had done it—he began to wander with his lips down to her belly, and then descended ever lower over the soft swell of her abdomen to the thick, blonde puff.

She wriggled uncomfortably under his mouth. "Irv," she said, "please don't."

"But I want to kiss you."

"Please don't. It makes me feel so—so strange."

"All right, then," he said, "you kiss me."

He lay back and put his head on the pillow beside her.

"What do you mean?" she asked. *"There?"*

"Of course," he said.

With his hand, he reached around to the back of her head and began to guide her face downward. Suddenly she stiffened.

"No!" she cried out, "I can't do it. I can't! I can't do it!"

She leapt from the bed and fled into the bathroom, slamming the door. The reverberation of the slam shook the room, and through it he could hear the bolt of the lock shoot closed.

He lay there for a moment, drained of all passion and all feeling. Then, when his mind began to clear again, and he began to allow himself to think, all he could feel and think was his irritation. He was willing to be patient with her, to give her the time she needed to adjust to him and to their life together—but this was ridiculous. This had nothing to do with him, or with natural reticence and diffidence about sex. This had been fear and disgust. Horror. And he was afraid of it, afraid that it was beyond his reach or anybody's. Afraid of it, and saddened by it, and resentful of it, too, because it was so senseless in the way it cheated both of them.

He got up from the bed, lit a cigarette, and got his clothes. From behind the closed bathroom door he could hear the muffled sobbing that was not quite drowned out by the running water she had turned on to mask the sound. He ran his hands through his hair, straightened his collar, and walked across the room to the bathroom door.

"Cal?" he said.

There was no answer.

"Cal, I'm going out for some breakfast!"

He felt his irritation welling up inside him like nausea, and he turned and strode out of the room. He stood in the corridor with the door opened, and waited one more moment. There was no sound from the bathroom. It was only by the exercise of great restraint that he refrained from slamming the door as he left.

He went over to the main building where, in the coffee shop, he went to the men's room, urinated, splashed water on his face, and brushed his teeth with a wet finger. Then he went back to the coffee shop and ordered a breakfast of orange juice, coffee, and bacon and eggs.

After his second cup of coffee, his good humor had begun to return. He left the coffee shop and, walking through the casino, put a silver dollar on black. It was a conservative bet.

There was no one else at the table. The croupier looked around, then spun the wheel and threw the ball. The ball whirled around the outside of the wheel. Then, as the wheel slowed, it began to bounce down into the numbered slots. It came up on sixteen red.

He continued to play, keeping his bets to black and red, occasionally doubling his dollar stake to two, and then, later, going up to five. It was not until nearly an hour had passed that he quit. He had lost two hundred and twenty dollars.

He felt utterly empty. The great zest, ebullience, exuberance and confidence he had felt less than twenty-four hours ago was deserting him. He felt his vitality, his élan, his very manhood, trickling like sand through his fingers. Or trickling like the silver dollars into the croupier's slot.

He wanted a drink, but even though there were hostesses who went around to the gambling tables offering liquor with the compliments of the house, he wanted to get away from the scene of his defeats. He went out through the lobby and into the blinding desert sunshine. He got a cab and asked the driver to take him to a nice, dark, quiet bar in downtown Las Vegas.

"Sure thing, buddy," the cabbie said. "I know just the kind of place you want."

The driver deposited him at the New Yorkers' Bar, which was a nice, ordinary-looking bar. He went inside, and the coolness and blue darkness were refreshing after the heat of the Nevada day outside. He ordered a double bourbon and he sipped it appreciatively. He had not gone through half the bourbon when he was suddenly conscious of the pressure of a thigh against his own. He looked around and saw a striking redhead of about thirty beside him.

"Have you got a match?" she asked.

"Sure," he said, lighting her cigarette. "Can I buy you a drink as well?"

"Why not?" she said, and asked him for a gimlet.

He conveyed the order to the bartender, who produced, almost instantly, a gimlet in front of the redhead, and then retired to the far end of the bar.

Irv looked around for the first time. The bar was virtually deserted. In the corner were the ubiquitous slot machines, but no one was playing them. There were a few customers in the booths. Kane and the redhead were the only ones at the bar. There was a jukebox playing softly in the background. Inside the bar, one could hardly tell whether it was day or night.

"My name is Patty," the redhead said. "What's yours?"

"Irv," he answered, after a moment. He looked her over, trying to make up his mind about her.

"Are you alone in town?" she asked. It was not the question so much as the look she gave him that influenced him. She was available, and a pro. He looked at her for a moment more, and then, deciding to risk a mistake, asked, "Twenty-five?"

She looked at him, nodded, and smiled. They drained their drinks and left together.

It was a great time that he had with her. It was all he had hoped it would be with Cal. It was ironic, he thought. There was no love between them. There was only money. And yet, there had been a kind of zest and inventiveness to their lovemaking. He had been delighted by her flaming red pubic hair, which had looked so startling against the very pale skin of her body. And she had been amused at his delight.

He left her, feeling good and strong and, back at The Sands, he tried his luck once more. He won back his two hundred and twenty dollar loss in less than half an hour, topped that with another hundred and ten dollars, gave the ten to the croupier, and went back to the room to find Cal.

They went back two days later to Iowa State University, where they found an apartment. Irv stuck it out for two months, at the end of which time he knew that he could no longer stand the round of classroom sessions, homework, papers, and all the dumb rah-rah stuff of the kids who were his fellow students. Each evening alone with Cal in the apartment was more oppressive than the last. They were like a couple of roommates—except that she was pregnant. Every now and then, less and less frequently, he would make an attempt to woo her and to make love. After each failure, he would read yet another marriage manual, but even though he gave them all to Cal to read, too, none of them helped. The two of them grew no closer. The pregnancy made her more awkward and more irritable. And more secretive about her body.

It was partly to get away from I.S.U., and partly, he had to admit to himself, to get away from her, that he decided to go to New York. He had no particular idea of what it was that he wanted to do there, or of what it was that he wanted to do with his life. It wasn't just to make money. He wanted to do something important, something useful. He wanted to amount to something.

Surely there would be a place, a way, an opportunity to do that in New York.

If he had to find something, if he had to make up some way of being useful, then, in New York, he might find some way to help other young people avoid the disaster that he had so narrowly averted himself and that had apparently overtaken Cal entirely— this damned repression, this accursed inhibition, this hypocritical and unnatural fear of the body, and the denial of the joy of sexuality.

He told Cal that as soon as he had found a job and an apartment he would let her know, and that as soon as she had finished her final term, she could join him. Perhaps, away from the stultifying atmosphere of the Midwest of her childhood and girlhood, she too might join him in understanding what life had to offer.

It was, anyway, a hope. The only hope they had.

5

The telephone on the small walnut night table began to ring. It made a muted noise, but even that soft tone was enough to wake Richard Patterson from his sleep. One hand reached out and picked up the phone, and, in a voice still gravelly from sleep, Patterson said, "Thank you, Jean, I'm awake."

He put the phone back on its cradle. He lay in bed, awake but not yet up, considering the day ahead of him. He had twenty minutes in which to bathe and shave, and then his breakfast would arrive. Often he used five of those minutes to collect himself and to plan the strategy of the day's campaign. The sun streamed in through the window. He knew it was going to be another hot day, but the soft purr of the air-conditioning machine protected him from the heat and the glare of the outside world. It was curious, he thought, and he considered air-conditioners—this one in the apartment-hotel, another one in the limousine, and yet another in his office in the Department of Justice. He sometimes chafed at the isolation he felt. He was a part of the government that was supposed to be of the people, by the people, and for the people, but even the vary air he breathed was purified and filtered. It was so hard to know what was really going on out there, where the people were walking around in the muggy air, but then, for that matter, it was just as hard, or even harder for them to know what was going on inside, where the action was. And it was, anyway, a damned sight more comfortable on the inside. And more fun, too.

Thinking of action, he decided that he had better begin. He threw the light cover off and got up. In front of the full-length mirror, he stood for a moment, studying himself, and then began the regimen of five minutes of exercise with which he started each day. He wasn't in bad shape at all for a man of fifty-one, he thought as he surveyed his image in the mirror. There was just the faintest hint of what would have been a paunch—if he hadn't been keeping those muscles taut. He was scarcely breathing hard after he had gone through the ritual, touching his toes, doing deep knee bends, and going through the stretches and gyrations for the torso muscles. His legs were still young, and did not have that corded look that men's legs get if there isn't any effort to keep in shape.

He went into the bathroom, stepped into the shower, and turned it on, first very hot, and then very cold. He gasped at the sudden alteration of the temperature as the cold water hit. Then he stepped out and began shaving. As he was patting Houbigant's *Pour Hommes* on his face, he heard the outer door of the suite open, and the slight rattle of the dishes on the cart as Kermit brought in his breakfast. He wrapped a towel about his middle and strode out into the large, still-darkened living room. Kermit was just about to draw the draperies and admit the morning light.

"Good morning, sir," Kermit said. "It looks like another scorcher."

Kermit turned from the window back to the cart and began setting up the breakfast. He held out the orange juice, which Patterson took and carried back to the bedroom. It was his habit to drink it while dressing. He took the glass and answered, "Yes, but that's what we get for having the capital in Washington. Way back, when they decided on Washington, they never thought that anyone would hang around here in the summertime."

"I guess that's right, sir," Kermit said, smiling.

Patterson went back to the bedroom to dress. He came out shortly, in his trousers, shirt, and stocking feet, to sit down and eat. He had the same breakfast every morning: two poached eggs, two slices of protein toast, coffee, black, and one English banger, the pork sausage for which he had acquired a taste during World War II, when he had been a fighter pilot stationed in Britain.

He sat down and unfolded his *Washington Post*, which he read every morning at breakfast. *The New York Times* he saved for the ride to his office. In a way, it was a carry-over, a habit merely, for most of the news in the papers was already familiar to him, having passed over his desk a day, or even weeks, before. And even the kind of treatment the different papers and columnists gave to various stories and issues were predictable enough. Still, it was not a bad habit, he thought. He had worse.

The front page of the *Post* was mostly devoted to the aftermath of a recent Latin American coup. That was a knotty problem, but it was State's problem. He glanced at the lead paragraphs, found nothing new or surprising, and then looked at the pictures of people crowded on beaches and the usual feature stories about the sizzling weekend. The Albany race riots had quieted down. It had been rainy up there, and the rain had helped to maintain the truce that the Justice Department had been instrumental in arranging the week before. The mayor was meeting with all the interested parties, and, with luck, Albany would simmer down. What they needed up there, he thought, was a snowstorm. All over the north, what they really needed was a return of the glacier.

There was editorial comment about the riots, but the paper only repeated the genial platitudes it had been expounding for years, urging caution, moderation, optimism, and good will. Patterson knew how much he trusted any of those things—damned little. There was little good will left, little reason for optimism, and with caution and moderation there would be nothing but more riots, and no hope whatever for any change. The trick was to talk caution and moderation in public while in private action and negotiation he was being as honest and as tough as he could be. And as drastic as it was necessary to be. But when the papers parroted the public pronouncements, it was annoying and depressing. The editors weren't in office. They could afford to speak openly, without using the cipher of politics. Why in hell didn't they? It'd make things easier, maybe, for the people who actually had to do something.

For diversion he turned to the paper's entertainment section, where he was not particularly surprised to see a small, close-cropped picture of Jill in a large display ad for her new picture—*Do Not Fold, Spindle, or Mutilate*. He suddenly realized why he had woken up feeling so elated. She was coming to Washington tonight, and they would see each other. It wouldn't be for long, and she could only steal one night from the schedule her publicists had arranged for her. He hoped that there would be no sudden crises to keep him tied up during those few precious hours. What he wanted was a nice, dull, ordinary day of Washington summer routine, where he could leave the office promptly at five.

He took his second cup of coffee back to the bedroom with him and finished his dressing. The trouble with the civil rights movement was that there was no leverage in it any more. The mood of it was wrong. The grand old days when Burke Marshall could walk down the streets of a southern town in his shirtsleeves, turn back a mob of whites, and appear in the paper the next day as a hero were all gone. It wasn't that simple any more. The liberals were still saying the same things about wanting to give the Negro equality and opportunity. But the Blacks didn't even like to be called Negroes—Whitey's word. And the riots had turned off a great many of the uncommitted, good-hearted, liberal-leaning whites. The other side was more appealing and far richer to any politician now, and he wasn't going to have any part in that appeal to fear and that hue and cry about safety in the streets and law and order. It was just too cheap and cynical.

There was nothing to do but share Ralph Ellison's view that it was getting better, that the riots of the twenties had been much worse, and that the riots had been progressively less violent and destructive during the thirties and forties. But meanwhile, he had to go through the motions and deal, not with the reality, but with the political implications, which were a reality of another kind. None of it engaged his passion—nothing but one, small, private facet of the business, the one thing that had remained unchanged. The Bureau still stood around at every disorder, at every riot, taking careful notes, making sure their hats were on straight. The hats identified them in the newsreels and in the television films as what they were—Tyler's men. And it was Tyler's object never to offend the men upon whose cooperation and good will his work sometimes depended, the local sheriffs, the local police chiefs, the local authorities. The Bureau's fabulous record of arrests, prosecutions, and convictions depended on the cooperation of these local authorities, and even the most antediluvian red-necked bull of a sheriff was still the man with whom the Bureau had to deal in cases of bank robberies and car thefts. Tyler was unwilling to alienate these men. An integrated university or an integrated neighborhood was not something that you could tally up in a statistical survey, nor was it useful to present to a congressional appropriations committee.

Patterson, since he had become Attorney General, had often criticized Tyler for his reluctance to get involved with the really big crime syndicate boys, and for his indifference to civil rights; but still, through countless administrations and right through to the present moment, Tyler sat there, aging only imperceptibly, growing a little more jowly and moon-faced each year, the first appointee of any incoming President, ruling the Bureau, and making the Attorney General's job all the harder. Tyler had not done anything that was actually, provably obstructive, so that there was nothing Patterson could actually say. Tyler was too foxy for that. He had outlasted countless Attorneys General, and Patterson knew that his own chances of toppling Tyler were remote indeed. There had as yet been no open break. The two men were polite and formal with each other. Patterson had avoided the open enmity that had grown up between Tyler and other Attorneys General, but neither man made any pretense of real friendliness or even respect.

He supposed that the main thing Tyler disliked about him was his road to the top. Tyler had been an obscure bureaucrat who had risen to take over the bureau by getting out and gunning down famous bandits and killers. Patterson had come along on the Ivy line, and the aura of privilege and ease clung to him. The high road, Patterson knew, was low enough, but Tyler's view of America was distorted, limited to the lower middle class, of which the patrician Patterson was obviously not a part.

It was all there, all obvious as hell. Tyler's mania about hats, about haircuts, about dark socks, all gave him away. Patterson's own background had never seemed remarkable to him, because of course all his friends had the same background, shared the same assumptions, cultivated the same tastes. He was a product of the northern New Jersey suburbs, where his father had been a successful corporation attorney. Princeton had followed Lawrenceville, and Harvard Law had followed Princeton. Then, after World War II, Patterson had returned to the States, eager to take up the clerkship that had been offered to him but had been suspended because of the war. He was also more than a little eager to try out those qualities of leadership he had discovered in himself in the Air Force. He had come to Washington, where, against all probabilities, and quite contrary to his own expectations, he had remained ever since.

The telephone rang again, interrupting his thoughts. It was the one ring signal that announced to him that his limousine was waiting downstairs. He slipped into the jacket of his gray glen-plaid suit, picked up his black kangaroo attaché case—a birthday present from Jill—and, grabbing the *Times*, descended in the elevator to the waiting car. He was conscious of the eyes of strangers recognizing him. He rather enjoyed it, he supposed. He returned their stares with the greeting of a warm smile, a trick he had picked up from a short-sighted Southern senator, who always smiled greetings out of defensive necessity, and then stepped into the long black Cadillac with the US-7 license plate.

The driver closed the door with a satisfactory *thunk*, and went around to get into the car. With a quiet purr the limousine pulled away from the curb and sailed into the traffic of early-morning Washington. Patterson returned Osborne's "Good morning," and then turned his attention to the *Times*. He had about twenty minutes before the car would pull up at the Justice Department.

M. R. Tyler, the Director of the Federal Bureau of Investigation, sat behind his large oak desk, going over the time sheets of the Oklahoma City office. That was the post to which difficult agents were sent for discipline and reformation. If Oklahoma City didn't work for them, there was always Nome, but Tyler was reluctant to send men there unless they were particularly promising. It was easier simply to fire them.

The first half hour of his day he always passed this way, inspecting the time sheets and checking the overtime that he took as evidence of enthusiasm and dedication. The activity put him in the requisite frame of mind for the day's business. It was a fine way of warming up, nicely satisfying and reassuringly routine, and it also kept him in touch with the activities in the field offices and with each of the individual agents with whose careers he liked to keep in close touch. Even if he had only met them for that one time, when they had been brought into his office for the ceremonial handshake at the end of the training period, he still felt a personal interest and kept a personal eye on every one of his agents in all of the fifty states.

His office was unusually warm this morning. He did not have air-conditioning. He thought there was something artificial about it and that it kept people from working their best. He was also convinced that air-conditioning caused colds and a general weakness of the physique. In the thirties and forties, when he had done some of his best work, it had been during the steamy Washington summers. His office was airy, however, with cross ventilation. It was furnished in Spartan simplicity. Across the deep blue carpet, on which his desk floated like a solitary island in a tropical sea, he could look at the opposite wall, where there was a huge enlargement of Norman Rockwell's "The Four Freedoms" framed in oak to match the desk. In back of him, on the walls around the windows, were portraits signed, "To M. R. Tyler with great respect and affection," or a similar sentiment, of all of the six Presidents under whom he had served.

Directly to the right of his desk was a heavy pair of bronze flag-holders, with the flag of the United States in the place of honor and, to its left, the flag of the Bureau. There was a straight-backed chair to the side of his desk. Tyler wanted people who came in to talk to him to be sitting up straight, to be alert. He was not interested in comfort or ease, either for himself or for his visitors. Besides, the bad posture that he thought was one of the worst symptoms of an effete age had a disastrous effect on the internal organs, compressing them and putting unnatural strains upon them. Like those old creole matrons in New Orleans who made their daughters sit on stools for hours, he felt that anyone ought to be able to sit up straight on a backless bench indefinitely without any display whatever of discomfort or fatigue.

There was a knock at the door, and then, even before Tyler could say, "Come in," the door opened and Henry Dillard, the Associate Director of the Bureau, entered. Only he and Miss Pennybacker entered without the express invitation of the Director. Dillard was in his middle forties. He wore his salt-and-pepper hair medium short, neither so short as to offend the Director, who considered crew-cuts to be a sign of immaturity, nor so long as to approach the kind of bohemianism Tyler also found repugnant. Dillard had a weathered face, which, with its network of wrinkles and its pale blue eyes, was quite impassive and all but impossible to read. He was in his shirt sleeves. Tyler thought that men who worked in their shirt sleeves were busy men; he seldom put his jacket on, himself, except for conferences with the Attorney General or with the President. He liked to think of himself, for all the grandeur of his position, as just another working cop. Dillard knew his superior well enough to follow Tyler's lead when it mattered, so he affected shirt sleeves too.

"Sit down," Tyler said. "I'll be with you in just a minute."

Dillard seated himself in the chair beside the massive desk, carefully keeping his spine from touching the back of the chair, and waited, holding the sheaf of papers and manila envelopes in his hand.

A few moments later, Tyler looked up and said, "Miller."

"Miller? Jack Miller? Oklahoma City, isn't he?"

"That's right," Tyler said, evidently pleased that Dillard was keeping up as closely as he. "I've been looking at his time sheets. An hour here, and an hour and a half there. He doesn't seem to be putting his heart into the job."

"I think he's had some family problems," Dillard said. "His wife's been sick." He was neither giving excuses for the agent, nor throwing him as a sacrifice to the Director, but merely stating a fact.

"Well, we'll keep an eye on him. Let's see if he shapes up in a couple of months."

He put the overtime sheets on one side of his desk and turned his attention to Dillard, whose job it was to bring in every morning a summary of what had gone on during the past twenty-four hours. Tyler reached his hand out for the manila envelope Dillard gave him. Across the face of the envelope, in large red letters, was the "Top Secret" stamp. Tyler held it in his hand for a moment, as if he were trying to guess its weight, and then, putting it down, asked, "Anything interesting?"

"Kansas City has come through with our bank robbers," Dillard reported. "Two young punks who'd moved up from gas stations."

The Director was pleased. He allowed Dillard one of his rare, wintry smiles. "Anything else?" he asked.

"Nothing special," Dillard replied. "It's all in there. The usual car thefts. I think our statistics this month will be on the high side."

"Not surprising," the Director said, scowling again.

"There is one thing," Dillard suggested after a moment's pause. His diffidence alerted the Director. This was, clearly, what Dillard had come in to talk about.

"Oh?" Tyler asked, the heavy brows knitting over brown eyes that were still piercing in spite of the pouches of slack flesh beneath them.

"I had a phone call from Pat."

"Billingsley? What's bothering him?"

"He says we are."

"That's ridiculous!" Tyler snorted. "But go on."

"Some kid came to see him last week. From the Justice Department. Said he just wanted to ask him a few questions. Pat said he didn't stay for long, and he didn't ask much, but he wanted to know what the hell was up."

A slow flush had begun to tinge Tyler's cheeks as he listened to Dillard's report. No special agent in a field office would initiate a thing like this on his own responsibility. Tyler knew, then, that it couldn't be anyone from the Bureau. It had to be one of Patterson's own people, one of those fancy Harvard lawyers he'd collected around himself. But why Pat? Pat Billingsley had been with the FBI for fifteen years, and in that time he had compiled, Tyler thought, an amazing record, having climbed from trainee to Special Agent in charge of the Los Angeles office, and finally to Deputy Director for the Middle Atlantic States—that part of the country which Tyler believed to be more thickly infested with lefties, comsymps, and commies than any other. Pat had found favor with some wealthy Texas oilmen who had backed him when he had decided to go into business for himself, five years before. With their backing, and with his staff—all of them former FBI men—he had risen in those five years to a position in the private security field where he was a rival of Burns, Pinkerton, and Wackenhut.

As far as Tyler was concerned, Billingsley was all right, and more than all right. He was furious at Dillard's news, for an attack on Billingsley was tantamount to an attack on Tyler himself.

"It wasn't just the young lawyer," Dillard went on, "and it isn't even the Justice Department all by itself. D. J. McIntyre is up for audit."

McIntyre, Tyler knew, was one of Billingsley's most enthusiastic backers, a multimillionaire from the Southwest who was a great fighter for freedom and a great enemy of Communist conspirators. He even sponsored, out of his own pocket, a daily radio program that tried to bring Americans back to their basic responsibilities. Tyler had, several times, been a guest on those programs, and had found them to be an encouraging restraint on, and one of the few outlets for criticism of, the rampant left.

"Are you sure it was a Justice man?" Tyler asked. "What did Pat say the name was?" He reached for the thick directory that lay on one side of his desk.

"Ed Froelich," Dillard said.

Tyler riffled through the pages of the Justice Department roster. "Friendly, Friml, Froelich. Yes."

He closed the book with a loud report and reached for one of the three telephones on his desk. One connected him immediately to any of his field offices, the second was an outside line, and the third was a Department of Justice line. It was the third phone that he picked up, and after dialing two digits he said, "Miss Ryder? I'd like to see Mr. Patterson this morning, if that's convenient for him. This is Mr. Tyler."

He grunted, nodded, said, "Thank you," and hung up. Then he turned back to Dillard, and with a satisfied smile announced,

"I'm going to see him in an hour, and we'll get this cleared up. You get back to Pat and tell him that I'll call him after lunch."

"Nine-twenty? I'll see you then," he said.

"I can hardly wait," she said, and her famous throaty whisper carried three thousand miles across the country. She paused a second, and he could hear her breathing in his ear.

"Neither can I," he said, and he hung up the phone, rather more slowly than with the usual crisply efficient gesture that was just short of a slam.

Jill Jefferson had been speaking to him on his private wire. Almost immediately, his intercom light flashed.

He pushed the button. "Yes, Miss Ryder?"

"Mr. Tyler just called you, Mr. Patterson," she said. "He'd like to see you this morning. I penciled him in for eleven. Is that all right, sir? Your calendar is open for that hour."

"Yes, that's fine," Patterson said. "Did he say what he wanted to see me about?"

"No, sir."

"Well, all right. Eleven will be fine."

He released the button, leaned back in his leather-upholstered chair, and ran his fingers through his still thick, slightly wavy hair. This was it. He had blocked it out that morning, hoping that he had still a few days before Tyler discovered anything about the Billingsley investigation. But it had hit the fan, and Tyler would be out for bear.

He felt a curious kind of detachment, wondering what tack Tyler would take, what he would do. There were so many different weapons the old fox could choose from. It was not for nothing that Tyler had been one of the most powerful men in Washington for nearly thirty years.

Patterson thought back to the day, five weeks before, when Jack Randall, the junior senator from Nevada and ranking minority member of the Senate Judiciary Committee, had come to see him, even more furious than usual, and, as it turned out, justifiably so. The two men had been in the same eating club at Princeton, although in different classes. Their relations had always been cordial, though not intimate.

"What kind of shit have you been putting in the chili bowl, Dickie boy?" Randall had demanded.

Patterson had winced. This was Randall's Senate style, his campaigning style, the jes'-folks public figure he had learned to cut. Back at Princeton, at Colonial, he had been a rather more elegant and reserved young man.

"I beg your pardon?" Patterson had asked, knowing that it sounded stuffy, but also knowing that he just could not compete, could not scale the scatalogical heights of Randall's rhetoric.

"Remember Dexter Miles? He was in my year. Ivy, I think."

"Oh? What's troubling him?"

"He thinks you are."

"What are you talking about?"

"Miles is a lawyer now, with a practice in Carson City. Doing right well, too. Anyway, last week he had a young engineer in his office, putting in air-conditioning, and the young fellow told him his office was being bugged. Showed him the wires and everything. He's since found out that his phones are being tapped, too. Office and home. Now, that ain't right?"

"What makes you think it's us?" Patterson asked.

"Well, who the hell else would it be?"

"The syndicate, maybe?"

"Miles? Miles doesn't think so. And I don't think so. They need him."

"Well, look," Patterson had explained, "you know as well as

I do that there isn't a bug or a wiretap that Tyler's people put on anybody without a written authorization from me. And there hasn't been any such authorization."

"Mule shit. You don't think they improvise? You know goddam good and well they do," he had said, shaking his finger at Patterson.

"But they have no reason to. We have no investigations going in Neveda that would remotely require such a thing."

"I'd hoped that was so," Randall had said, rather more calmly, "but then the problem is still serious. Maybe more serious."

"What do you mean?"

"Here's a lawyer, just like you or me, not only with the ordinary rights of privacy that every citizen ought to have, but with a special privilege to privacy with his clients. And here some pissant bastard goes bugging him. Now if it isn't one of your boys or one of Tyler's boys, then it must be the Billingsley beef."

"Billingsley? All he does is guard racetracks and sneak up on hotel rooms."

"No, no, you haven't been keeping up. They've got big backing now, and a contract with the state of Nevada, and they're all of them graduates of Tyler's academy. Billingsley's even got most of his men sworn in as deputy sheriffs in all the counties out there, and let me tell you, Dick, I don't like it. I don't like it one bit. It's a big billy-goat turd in my ripe olive bowl of life."

Patterson winced. "What can I do? Billingsley's in Nevada."

"The hell you say! He's big. He's incorporated in Delaware, operates in six states, and is fair game for you. And there's that little old Section 65 of the Communications Act of 1934, at which you might have a look, during one of your contemplative moments."

Patterson made a note of the citation on his memo pad.

"I'd be much obliged to you, Dickie," Randall had said. "For one thing, it'd save me the whole unpleasant business of having to hold an investigation, and all that messy kind of thing."

"Are you threatening me?" Patterson had asked, smiling, as if it were a joke, but still gazing with a steady intensity at his visitor.

"Why, no. Nothing of the kind. I'm simply coming by to tell an old school chum that there's great political capital to be made out of this, and I'm allowing you the first place in line at the old traveling pussy wagon."

"I'll be glad to look into it," Patterson had answered, with bland calm.

"I was hoping you would, and, if I may, I'll drop by again, in a month, to see you and find out how you're coming along. I do like to report to my constituents, you know."

Randall had picked up the large white Stetson he affected, swooped it aloft in an exaggerated courtly gesture, plopped it onto his head, adjusting it by pushing the back of the hat with the palm of his hand so that the brim of the front drooped down over his forehead, winked, and then turned on his heel and left, calling, "Bye, now," over his shoulder.

Patterson shook his head, now, remembering that vaudevillian exit. Vaudeville was dead—but the Senate lived on.

There was only one job in America that a lawyer could want more than that of Attorney General. There were three old men on the Court. None had as yet indicated that he was about to retire, but the actuarial tables were all on Patterson's side. And so, he was sure, was the President. His close association with the President, and his record as a lawyer over the past twenty years, he thought, were enough to give him at least an inside track. Now, three and a half weeks after Randall's visit, he realized that the make-or-break moment might well be upon him. That was why he had so carefully avoided this supremely important question that morning, when he had been ordering his plans for the day. He was between Randall's devil and Tyler's deep blue sea. Nobody in Washington who crossed Tyler got away without paying for it some way or other. Patterson tried to imagine what the worst could be, what the bottom line was, and, while it was not utterly disastrous, a quiet retirement, or a continuing practice with a firm in New York, was not at all what he had in mind for his future.

He buzzed Miss Ryder and called for the Billingsley folder. He would look it over very carefully before Tyler appeared. When she came in, carrying the large manila folder, he gave her careful instructions about the procedure for the meeting with Tyler at eleven. "At two minutes to eleven," he said, knowing that Tyler was punctual to the minute, "I want you to bring in coffee. Use the 'foreign judge' china. And a plate of butter cookies. Don't announce him. Get up, come to the door, and show him in."

"Yes, Mr. Patterson," she said, and left the room.

He would talk with Tyler over there, he thought, looking toward the informal grouping at one end of his office—the love seat and two easy chairs arranged around a teak coffee table. It would be one way of avoiding the man-desk-man position, which seemed to be combative, and which would set up a barrier between them even before they began to talk. Also, it might put Tyler somewhat at his ease. He did not like to talk with people except in his own office, and seldom was required to do so. Patterson was, of course, Tyler's titular boss, but Tyler had carved out his own empire and had his own appropriations from Congress, and his own network of congressional and senatorial friends and supporters. Until now, Patterson and Tyler had maintained distant but perfectly polite relations. While each man was aware of the suspicion with which the other viewed him, this had not affected their working arrangements. Justice used the FBI when it had to; the FBI came to Justice when it was necessary for it to do so.

Patterson was entirely aware that such elementary devices as the coffee and the seating arrangement would not make things very much easier, but if they helped even a little bit, they would be worth while. Certainly, he decided, they could do no harm.

At 10:58 Anne Ryder brought in the heavy silver tray, put it on the coffee table, asked if she should pour the coffee, and, after he shook his head no, went back out to her desk in the outer office.

The last echo of the final chime of the antique banjo clock on the wall had not yet died when there was a knock at the door. Patterson rose and crossed the room as Anne opened the door. To sidestep the delicate problem—Tyler? Mr. Tyler? Certainly not Marvin!—he held out his hand and said vigorously, "Good to see you! What can I do for you?" and guided Tyler over to the love seat in the corner of the room.

"You'll have some coffee, won't you?" Patterson invited, and, without waiting for an answer, began to pour.

"Thank you," Tyler said curtly. "Good of you to see me on such short notice."

"Except for a call from the Chief, I'm always at your service, you know," he returned. Patterson winced inwardly at his own use of the phrase, "the Chief," which was not at all the way in which he thought of the President. But these were Tyler's words for the President, the words he had used to refer to all six Presidents under whom he had served—perhaps, Patterson thought, whimsically, in the corner of his mind, because he could not remember their right names.

"Cookies?" he offered. He felt like a little old lady, holding out the plate of butter cookies to this jowled bastard and delaying the moment when they would get down to the hard-nosed business.

"No, thank you," Tyler said, "at my age I can't afford such things. I never touch sweets."

There was something smug and self-satisfied in the way he'd said it, and Patterson could imagine him patting his belly, proud that the muscles were still firm. Or perhaps he had a bulletproof vest, which made his belly firm from the outside, working as a kind of corset. My God, Patterson thought, I'm becoming as silly as a schoolboy.

He checked his face to make sure that the lines were suitably grave and concerned, passed Tyler the cream and the sugar, both of which Tyler declined, and waited for the Director to speak, as if he had no idea in the world what could be on his mind.

"I understand that you've begun an investigation of Pat Billingsley," Tyler began. It was not a question but a statement.

"Yes?" Patterson responded cautiously.

"Has Pat been up to anything that I ought to know about?" Tyler asked. "After all, he was one of my boys."

It was a hard question to answer, and a hard question to duck. Patterson imagined that, at one time, Tyler must have been at least minimally diplomatic, supposed that he would have had to be until he'd made it to the top of the bureau; but, if it was true that power corrupts, it was also true, apparently, that power dulls, too.

"To tell you the truth," Patterson said at last, "I'm not sure."

"Then why are you bothering him?" Tyler demanded.

"He's had a bug and a tap on a lawyer out in Nevada."

"Who?" Tyler wanted to know.

Patterson was instinctively cautious.

"A good lawyer," he said, "a friend of a friend of mine."

"But what's his name?" Tyler asked, bulling ahead.

"Is that really relevant?" Patterson countered. "The point is that bugging and wiretapping of that kind are against the law, and Billingsley ought to know that."

Tyler changed his tack slightly. "Why are you so sure it's Pat?"

Patterson answered patiently, "It isn't you. It isn't me. Who else could it be?"

Tyler was silent for a moment. "I don't know," he began. "I don't know that Pat is doing it. Mind you, I'm not suggesting that he is. But if it were true that he has been doing such a thing, then I'm sure he must have had some good reason. I can vouch for him. I've known him for years, and he's never done a thing that wasn't one hundred per cent above board."

"Oh, come on, now," Patterson began, but Tyler cut him off.

"Why do you think those people backed him that way when he left the Bureau? He's a good man, a good investigator, and a good American."

The two men glared at each other.

"It seems to me," Tyler went on, "that you have enough to do without bothering a little investigator out West."

"He's no little investigator, and you know it. He's got offices in six states, and big backing, and he's big business. He's got a staff of seven hundred men, and I'm not entirely sure that I very much like these large private police forces. Free enterprise is one thing, but there are certain activities of the government that ought properly to be left to the government. Ours is one of them."

Tyler waved his hand impatiently, as if to brush away these irrelevant objections.

"Look," he said, "I vouch for Pat Billingsley. Now, what more could you want?"

There was a silence in the office. Deliberately, Patterson raised his coffee cup to his lips, savored the coffee, swallowed it, put the cup back down on the coffee table, and then answered, "I'm afraid that this time I need more than that, Tyler."

The red flush that covered Tyler's face when he was angry now started to shoot up from his neck, suffusing the jowly face. A vein stood out in his forehead, throbbing. But when he spoke, his voice was controlled, even icily calm. He began again, looking straight at Patterson. "I was here twenty-six years before you got to town, and I shall probably be here for ten years after you leave. I know what I'm talking about. There's no reason for you to doubt my word."

"I'm not doubting your word," Patterson said, in a conciliatory tone. "If I were the only one who was interested, your word might be sufficient. But there are other people involved as well, other people who are interested."

"Who else is interested?"

Paterson was on the point of telling Tyler that it had been Jack Randall who had come to see him and had brought the matter of Dexter Miles and Patrick Billingsley's security business to his attention. It was a tempting prospect to turn Tyler's anger away from himself and divert it to Jack Randall's desk and person. But the very attractiveness of that diversion of Tyler's vindictiveness and power angered him. The idea that he should have to worry about a subordinate in his own department, this bureaucratic prick, who had, he'd been told, a Norman Rockwell painting in his office, and a locked file of dossiers on every important official, every senator or congressman with whom he dealt, with the President himself, for all he knew—it was insupportable. It was giving in to a moment of sheer orneriness and contrariness to buck him, to fight him. Nevertheless, he found himself doing just that.

With a reasonableness that barely disguised the malice underneath it, he said, "If Billingsley is clean, that's what we'll find out. Isn't that what you've been telling people now for years? That if they're innocent they have nothing to fear from an investigation?"

"Well," Tyler countered, "if this is that kind of disinterested and high-minded investigation, why didn't you turn it over to the Bureau? We could have handled it."

"I thought of that," Patterson said, "but it occurred to me that Billingsley is a friend of yours, and I thought it would be considerate of me to save you the embarrassment of having to run an investigation on a friend of yours. I know it's something I'd never like to have to do."

"I wish I could believe you, Mr. Patterson," Tyler said, "but I don't. If this were simply a matter of some two-bit congressman or six-bit senator giving you a hard time, then the most natural thing in the world would have been to come to me. I've been dealing with congressmen and senators—yes, sir, and with cabinet officers—for nearly thirty years. I was dealing with these people when you were playing soccer at prep school . . ."

Patterson wondered how the hell Tyler had ever found out that he'd played soccer. Patterson had played jayvee soccer for Lawrenceville, and, so far as he could remember, had not mentioned it to anyone for twenty years. Obviously, Tyler was letting him know that there was a dossier on him, too. Well, screw that, he thought.

Tyler continued. He was standing, now, and talking not so much to Patterson as to a spot on the wall just above his head. "Mr. Patterson, I'll say it once more. There's nothing that you have to investigate in Pat Billingsley. That's my final word on the subject. All you have to write in your file is that Pat Billingsley is a friend of M. R. Tyler. And then look at that, and study on that, and study on that well."

Tyler squared his shoulders, said good morning, and left the office.

Patterson looked down at the coffee table. He noticed that Tyler had not touched his cup of coffee. He got up, stretched, and walked to the window behind his desk. He looked out.

What had the threat been? Surely, it had been a threat, but of a vague kind. There were a couple of bills that were going down to the Senate that Patterson thought vital. It was conceivable that Tyler could rally his senatorial friends to see to it that they never got out of committee. It would not be a public fight—or would that be what Tyler would want? If he knew about soccer at Lawrenceville, he knew more than that. He knew, for one thing, about Jill.

Nobody in Washington cared whom you slept with, so long as you kept it quiet. Tyler had so many ways to make an awful lot of noise.

Jill Jefferson glanced across the aisle once again. It was stupid, she kept telling herself, stupid as hell. After all, what was the guy anyway? Nothing! That was the whole point, wasn't it, of being a pretender? You weren't the real thing. And this guy who was the Pretender to the Spanish Throne was a nothing. But still, he was the guy who would have been the king, if the Spaniards still had kings, and when she thought of that, and the whole crazy idea of kings and thrones and crowns, she felt her head pull around as if her nose were steel and the guy were a huge magnet. And then it started all over again, and she felt stupid, because this was exactly what kept happening to her all the time, and was, in fact, the reason for her having taken this flight. The attention of the reporters and the photographers and the rubberneckers would all be on him, the non-king, instead of on her.

Because she was, in her way, a queen. Queen of the silver screen, as those old Hollywood pulps used to say, and she'd read them in the Cohoes Ethical Drugstore and, like any other kid, she had dreamed of having all that happen to her. And now that it had happened, she was still gawking, still turning her head to look at the Pretender, as if she were still that skinny kid with the big boobs and the frizzed hair in that ratsy drugstore.

The crazy thing was that she was as much a pretender as he was. For one thing, she wasn't Jill Jefferson. There wasn't any such person. She was Jill Kerzjenski. Or had been. But as they'd said out at the studio, you can't put a sneeze up on a marquee, and so they'd given her "Jefferson" as a new last name, because it had the same initial as Jill, and the double initials had worked well for Brigitte Bardot and Marilyn Monroe and might work again.

But she wasn't Jefferson or Kerzjenski either, on the plane, but Jones, traveling incognito, and booked onto this flight so that, when Don Carlos or whatever his name was strutted down the stairs, she could sneak by and into the airport and the waiting car, and maybe not be noticed. She spent so much of her damned life trying not to be noticed, trying to keep out of the way of photographer and gawkers, that it seemed as if she were right back where she started but with everything reversed—a big movie star dreaming about the wonderful life of some kid in a Cohoes drugstore about whom nobody cared and who was at least left alone and in peace.

"Is there anything wrong?" the stewardess asked.

Jill looked up, then looked down at the virtually untouched tray before her.

"No, no. Nothing's wrong. I'm just not very hungry, I'm afraid."

"Shall I take this away, then?"

"Please."

She was never very hungry. Anorexia, Dr. Parker said it was. What good that did, giving it a name like that, she hadn't the vaguest idea. Of course it fed the fat Dr. Parker, and the fat Mrs. Parker, and all the fat little Parkers. A little touch of anorexia wouldn't do any of them any harm. But she had it. And it was, or so he claimed, because she had a dislike of taking things into her body. It wouldn't be just a dislike of food or anything obvious like that. From that kind of obviousness, fat Dr. Parker couldn't feed himself. So it had to be sexual, of course. Fat, dirty-minded Dr. Parker made everything sexual. Well, okay, but if that was the problem, why was she able to make love? What sense did it make for her not to like to eat?

But there was no point in getting angry at him. He liked it. He said that she was manifesting hostility and that it was transference, and he seemed so damned pleased. It was frustrating, actually.

But still, it was true that she hadn't been able to eat the African lobster tails. She supposed it could just as easily be anorexia as anything else. And it certainly was true that that spindly little girl in Cohoes had not been fantastically happy. A life like that could screw you up good and proper. The way it worked was kind of funny, though. You get what you want, and then you find out that you can't enjoy it, because it isn't what you thought it would be or because you're so damned tired and knocked out that you just don't care any more or aren't able to.

Except this time. This time, maybe, it was different. She didn't trust it all the way yet. She was still nervous about putting too much weight on it. But the thing that she and Richard had going looked like it could be different. She hoped it was. But there were all those other times, from Mr. Kendrick on, when she had felt the bump of the letdown. The way she had learned to avoid that, was not to hope, not to allow herself to think for a minute that there was anything more to it than the two people using each other, an arrangement in which she got a boost or a free ride or a contract or a part, and he got a free piece of what was now the most famous, the most desired, the most expensive ass in the country. In the world.

And that had been okay with her. Simple and honest and clear cut. All the sappy ideas that most people have about love had not impressed her much. In fact, what she had figured out back there in Cohoes was the difference between the stars and the public, between the lucky few and the unlucky many. The few, the ones who made it, got rid of those jerk ideas about true love and happily-ever-after, and they traveled lighter and got farther. Love was a luxury, she had decided, and something she could do without. For a while, anyway. Until she had climbed up there and made it big. And she had climbed.

She had begun by winning a beauty contest and going to Albany, and parlaying that into a trip with Leo Shuman out to Los Angeles. And it had been a gas, that trip. She'd had to keep Leo company, but he had been less demanding than the boys at Cohoes High usually were, and he was giving her more than a movie and a fudge sundae for what he got. So it had seemed to her to be a pretty good deal. And out on the coast, she'd connected with Alvin Rosemont (né Rosenberg) who had got her her first contract with a studio. . . .

It was a trite story, a carbon copy of hundreds of others, and Jill knew that. The difference was that she had been lucky and had made it. Which did not affect her thinking much. The point was that you had to be in a position to take advantage of that lightning flash of luck, have to maneuver into the open fields where lightning sometimes strikes. She'd scrabbled and scrambled, and got herself into such a position. It was, she rather thought, a weird combination of unflinching honesty about oneself, and a little dreaming thrown in. Because it could go the other way, too. She'd seen that. Girls came out and did a little hustling to get themselves contacts or contracts or parts, and then they just kept on hustling, because they'd been doing that anyway, more or less, and what the hell was the difference?

Well, there was a difference. For one thing, money was cheap. Even the hundred or two hundred bucks was cheap as opposed to the long-shot chance at the big money. And you hedged your bet anyway, by telling yourself that it was just sociable. And you had to do that, and think that, and keep on thinking that, because every now and then, as these things turned out, you could actually wind up being friends with the guy. Or even more than friends.

As now. As with Richard Patterson.

What a simple, clear-cut thing that had looked to be at the beginning. They had met at a charity, at one of those dinners for Hire the Handicapped—which the studio had put her onto because everybody's got to have a charity, and as long as you're taking the deduction and doing the bit for your accountant, the publicity department and your own career might get their little boosts from it, too. So you specialized, concentrating on one particular charity. Hire the Handicapped, they'd found for her. And that was okay. Funny, even, because everybody out there in rube-land assumed that somehow, somewhere, at some stage of her life, she'd been handicapped, and no matter how often she denied the conclusion to which so many reporters and feature writers leapt, the legend persisted. They were sure that she had broken her back or her legs or her neck, or maybe all of them, and, through a long period of painful retraining and rehabilitation, had learned to dance again.

To hell with that. But she'd gone to their crummy dinners, and had met Patterson at one of them. He'd been there on the campaign trail, trying to raise money for the man who, when he got elected, would turn around and give him the Attorney General's office. They'd met, and talked, and fallen into bed—not so much because of any overwhelming attraction, but mostly because they were both safe. Neither one was some obscure celebrity-fucker, out to score. Both were important and established, and . . . Well, it had happened before, in something like the same way, and for much the same reasons. That week in Baja California with Ralph Day, or that cruise to Bimini with Ted Mannheim . . . but this, with Richard, had been even better, better than she could ever have imagined. Better, in fact, than she would have allowed herself to believe.

And so, now, she was sneaking into Washington on the way to New York and the publicity appearances there to see Richard again, as she had been doing off and on for six months now. And gawking at Don Carlos, in whose shadow she would sneak.

The plane landed, and Don Carlos turned out to be unnecessary after all. She waited until most of the passengers were out of the plane, and then, instead of leaving by the forward exit for the first-class passengers, she went back to the tourist exit. She hurried through the crowd at National and out onto the curb where Richard's driver had parked the car—the cream-colored Pontiac, not the official limousine. Bonita, Jill's maid, would be getting the luggage and taking a cab to the hotel. And in New York Clifford Bradley, her press agent, would be checking into the suite at the St. Regis. It was all so very complicated!

She relaxed in the back seat and let the air-conditioning do its work, cooling her down from that momentary blast of heat she had felt between plane and car. And she thought about Richard and about the fact that she had been thinking about him a great deal lately. Rather too much, in fact. Or, to be honest about it, she had to admit that she was just plain scared. If she had learned anything, it was not to want any particular thing, any special role, any special person, too much. It was better to keep these things in reasonable proportion. Fun and games, and good-bye, Charlie. But it was tough, sometimes. In a way, she felt like a Pretender, too, sometimes. It was as if underneath everything she were still that same gawky girl, or, even worse, one of the other gawky girls who believed the whole song and dance about love and rapture and the little house with the picket fence and the roses . . .

She had slipped before, had convinced herself that she was in love—with the capital L—with Bobby Washburne, the quarterback of the Los Angeles Rams, and that had turned into a disaster of epic proportions, in glorious Technicolor and breathtaking Cinemascope. Better to play it cool, take it easy, get what fun there was out of a thing, and then let it alone. But another marriage?

And yet, that's what she was thinking about, wasn't she? There she was, all alone in the car except for the driver, thinking her own thoughts, and arguing like mad against them. Which side were her real feelings on, then? It was one of those trick questions of fat Dr. Parker. Or it was one of those tricks of her own mind, which Dr. Parker had helped her to guard against.

Somewhere, down at the bottom of all the tricks and confusion and deception, there was that nagging feeling she'd had more and more frequently since Richard had come along that she was sick of it all, sick of the whole craziness of making movies. She had enough money, and her face was famous in every corner of the world. Men might not know who their president was, or their premier, or their king—whadya think of that, Don Carlos?—but they knew who she was. And they wanted her. All of them. She had nowhere to go, she reflected. There was nowhere to turn except to Richard. Because she could not go back to the senior class of Cohoes High and start over again. It was a bit late for that.

A crazy business. That it was. She knew she was not an actress. She was bright enough and honest enough to have noticed that she was a well-trained animal who could move around a set, who could project love, hate, and desire—mainly desire—or caricatures of a director's notions of these emotions. At whatever angle she was photographed she always came out looking beautiful, a trick of the bone structure of her face. She had no desire to go on the stage, she had no desire to make any more money. There was nothing she really wanted any more. She remembered those days of being hungry, of being skinny, of wanting, always wanting something, but now she didn't want anything any more—except Richard. The question was, she thought, did Richard want her? Not simply as a playmate—the most glamorous playmate in the world—but as his wife. His first wife had died several years before. He had two almost-grown children off in boarding school, and he lived alone. What had amazed her from the beginning, what had struck her with almost overwhelming force, was that he was the first man she had ever known who didn't want anything from her, who only wanted her for herself. But did he want her as a wife, or did he want her simply in his bed?

For once the shoe was on the other foot. Richard Patterson represented the only thing left that she did want. She wasn't even sure what it was. Class? Solidity? Respectability? Or all of them? He was intelligent, assured, eminently successful, gay, warm, and, with her anyway, uncalculating. For God's sake, he was the Attorney General of the United States! What did he need from her? But from him she hoped for a great deal.

With Dr. Parker's help, she had worked out one of her main recurring problems. Tough as she tried to be, she was continually mistaking a feeling of gratitude for a feeling of love. She didn't think it was that same thing this time. She was too aware now, too self-conscious of her own feelings.

As if to reassure herself, she opened her alligator purse and took out a small gold compact. She opened it and looked at her face. The light in the car was dim, but she could still see herself by the intermittent flashes of brightness as they passed the streetlights on the parkway leading from the airport into the city. She looked rather flushed and a little tired, and she decided to shower before she called Richard. It was at times like this that she wondered what people kept seeing in her face. Without makeup, and directly, not through the artful eye of the motion picture camera, she was not at all a classic beauty. She looked rather too thin. There was a sharpness about the chin that the makeup man in her last picture had commented on—that she would have to watch in the years ahead. She closed the compact with a deliberate snap and thrust it into her bag, as if she were thrusting her own appearance into its recesses. She looked out of the window at the greenery of the park through which the car was passing, but her mind was still on herself.

She could not inspect her body in any easy compact mirror, but she thought about that, too, trying to see it through Richard's eyes. Her body, too, photographed very well, promising, seducing, inviting in every curve, but she had never recovered from an adolescence when she had been the first girl in her class to mature —and she still felt all hips and bosom. Men had often told her that no man would want to sleep with one of those flat-chested models from the pages of *Vogue,* but each time she saw one of those tall, willowy, ethereal creatures she felt again that old disgust at her own grossness. The success she had had in motion pictures—which should have reassured her—she was inclined to dismiss as merely the result of the machinations—and attentions of Manny Youdelman, the studio head, who had had two enormous fat wives and seemed to go for flesh.

They pulled up in front of the Federalist House. Bill got out, ran around the car, and opened the door, and Jill got out and gave him her jewelry case. She went inside, signed the register, and was shown up to her suite.

There were three enormous vases of summer flowers, and, in the bedroom on the night table, there was a crystal bud vase with the largest, most perfect yellow rose that she had ever seen. She smiled and felt reassured. Things would be just fine.

From the shower she could hear Bonita come in and start the unpacking. She turned off the water, got out, and padded naked to the bedroom. She picked up the phone and asked for Richard's suite. He answered the phone almost immediately.

"Darling!" she said, adding unnecessarily, "I'm here." Stupid, she thought, but then talking to him she always felt thick-tongued and foolish. The eagerness of his answer, however, made her feel better. It didn't matter at all what she said; he was only waiting for her call.

"May I come up?" he asked. "I'm starving."

"You mean you haven't eaten yet?"

"No, I've been waiting for you."

"That was silly," she said, "but sweet. I've just gotten out of the shower," she added. "Give me five minutes."

"I'll call down for dinner," he said, "and then I'll come up. What would you like?" He became very brisk and businesslike. "The same old steak and salad? You didn't eat on the plane, did you?" he asked.

"God, no," she said.

His voice dropped. "When I finish eating," he said, "I'll still be starving."

She laughed, deep in her throat, and hung up.

Bonita came in and combed Jill's long honey-blonde hair. She started to do it up, but Jill shook her head. "No, just brush it loose." Then she slipped on a bright Pucci jumpsuit and a pair of green ballet slippers that picked up the sharp acid green of the print. She wore no bra because, despite her fears about the grossness of her body, her breasts were firm and high.

"Bonita, has the bellboy shown you your room?"

"*Sí, señora.*"

"All right, then, I won't need you any more tonight. I'll call you in the morning when I want you."

"Very good, *señora. Buenas noches,*" the maid said, with a slight flutter to her voice and a giggle at the end.

Jill enjoyed having a maid who spoke so little English. She knew enough to do the simple things Jill wanted her to do, but she didn't bother her with conversation. The most irritating she ever got was when she gave that faint, high-pitched giggle whenever she was excited. And she became excited rather easily. The high life she fancied her fabulously beautiful mistress enjoyed, she, too, enjoyed, although vicariously.

The door closed behind her and Jill paced nervously in the living room, waiting for Richard to join her. She lit a cigarette, posed herself carefully on the couch, changed her mind, got up, fluffed up the pillows, sat down in an easy chair, changed her mind again, got up, crossed the room, stubbed out the cigarette, and was about to try the couch again when she heard a soft knock at the door. She crossed to it quickly and opened it. They stood for a moment, looking at each other.

"Miss Jefferson?" he asked. "May I come in?"

She laughed, stood back while he entered the room, and, after the door was firmly closed behind him, flung herself into his arms. They stood there, each savoring the closeness of the other for a long moment. Richard slid his hands down her back. When they broke apart she felt very shaky.

"Oh, God, it's good to see you," she said.

"It's good to see you," he said. "And feel you and taste you too."

There was a knock at the door. As she crossed to an easy chair and sat down, he opened the door. It was room service with a large silver bucket.

"I thought we might want that while we're waiting for our dinner," Richard said as the boy carried in the tray with the two glasses and the champagne. He put it down, looked at Richard, and asked, "Shall I open it, sir?"

"No thank you, I'll do it," Richard said, as he felt in his pockets for some silver and signed the check.

He expertly twisted the loop, pulled the wire cage off the top of the bottle, removed the foil, and then, with slow, continually increasing pressure of the thumb, popped the cork. Jill had watched countless leading men mess up this particular gesture in any number of high society films. Usually they splashed the far wall with champagne. Once, David Dodge had splashed a Panavision lens with champagne on the sixteenth take of the same scene. She had supposed that after the day's shooting all the technicans had gotten drunk on all that champagne. This was one of the things she liked best about Richard. He did everything with a minimum of effort, deftly, and without any fuss. His was the reality they were mimicking out there on the coast. He poured the wine into the glasses and they held them up for a moment, silently toasting each other.

"I'd say, 'To us,'" Patterson said, "but then we couldn't drink, could we?"

"Can we think it?"

"Freedom of thought is the most basic freedom of all, I should suppose. We can think anything we please."

He held out his glass to touch hers, and the mock seriousness collapsed into grins before they drank.

It was, nevertheless, an awkward moment. They had not seen each other for six weeks. They could not leap off instantly into bed where they could re-establish in the simplest and most direct way the intimacy they had enjoyed—if for no other reason than that the room-service waiter would be appearing at any moment with the dinner Richard had ordered. But there was another reason, harder to define but no less important for that. They had passed beyond the merely sexual, or so Jill had begun to think. To allow herself to think. And now she wanted to look around and explore this new territory, to see if it was really like what she had imagined. Indeed, she wanted to see if she—and they—were really there.

They had met at that stupid banquet, and had exchanged a few bits of commonplace small talk, and he had invited her out for something to eat. As a joke, mostly, because she had eaten so little of the dinner they had been served. She had accepted on a whim, for no good reason except that he had interested her by his good looks, and his cultivated manner, and by the difference that she could see between him and the ordinary Hollywood specimens of success and power. They had gone for a drive together and he had taken her home without so much as the shadow of a pass—which also had been, at the very least, amusingly different. And pleasant. And they had seen each other again and again, and only after some months, and at her invitation, had he come up one evening to her hotel room in New York for a nightcap—and had stayed until the next morning.

Dr. Parker's opinion was that she had been trying to prove to herself that he was "just like all the others" in order to prevent herself from becoming any more seriously involved with him. But he had failed miserably to be like all the others, being a man who took love affairs very seriously and . . . and he liked her. And was not trying to use her. Not for anything. There was nothing in the world that she could do for him. That nasty business with Bobby Washburne had affected her in more ways than she'd known, even at the time. And it had hit her pretty hard, even then.

He had not been the simple, gruff, masculine athlete she had taken him to be. Not at all. He had married her for reassurance, because it was a great proof of his virility—to the world and to himself—to marry a girl like Jill Jefferson, wasn't it! And besides, he had had only two or three or maybe four seasons left in which he could expect to perform well and keep on playing for the Rams. And then what? Coaching? Selling insurance? Settling down into the ordinary world of ordinary people? No, he had wanted to become a photographer. He had taken sports photographs as a hobby and was good at it, and he had figured that through Jill he could set himself up as one of those high-priced fashion photographers, maybe. And he had taken pictures of her—and sold them to that magazine!

The divorce had followed not long thereafter. And the anorexia had set in, a symptom, Dr. Parker had explained, of her disgust with men, and with herself, with her body, with her own sexuality. With all sexuality. And what she loved about Richard was the surprising gentleness he had shown—surprising only because she had not expected any gentleness from any man—when she had told him about it.

It had been another test, her telling him. And again, he had betrayed her gloomy expectations, but with such charm and grace. He had even joked with her about it, suggesting one evening after a dinner they had had together at Chauveron, when she had eaten with rare gusto, that he was very pleased with her, and even flattered, because a meal was a lot tougher to fake than an orgasm.

And he had smiled at her, looking rather impish and mischievous! And he had called her his little waif!

But still, it was hard to pick up from where they had left off. Their lives were so separate, not only geographically but every other way as well. The things they did were so public, so thoroughly covered in the press, that the large questions were irrelevant. And they were both so wholly occupied by their careers, that there was precious little left over to bring out for private sharing. It was at such moments that that old nagging fear came back to Jill—that this was not different or special, but just a more elaborate version of the same old game of musical beds. Or, no, maybe it had nothing to do with the moment, or anything at all except herself and all those problems with which Dr. Parker was trying to deal.

They drained their glasses. With relaxed poise, Richard asked how her flight had been.

"Fine," she said, "just fine."

There was a pause, and the silence seemed to have a sourness to it that she could taste. Her own or his—what difference did it make? But then she thought of the Spanish Pretender, and how she had, despite all her efforts, kept staring at him. She told Richard about the reason for her flight on that plane, so that she could dodge the reporters. And then it hadn't been necessary at all, because she'd just got out of the tourist exit, which nobody ever watched.

"It's a scene out of *Back Street*," he said, wryly, and they both laughed.

The ice was broken. He was himself again, and not the figment that she kept trying to substitute for him.

"A lousy movie," she said.

"Yes, I guess so," he answered. "But, by God, you do remember it, don't you? I do. I remember a lot of those so-called terrible movies . . ."

The room-service waiter arrived with their dinners—roast beef, braised potatoes, glazed Belgian carrots, and a salad for Richard, and a Newport steak and endive salad for Jill. He pulled the plates out of the warming compartment beneath the table and set them on the snowy cloth with something of a flourish as he removed the metal covers. Then, with a slight bow, he said that he hoped they would enjoy their meal and left.

"I hope so, too," Richard said. "I still don't know how hard to push you."

"Dr. Parker said . . ."

"Yes? What did the good doctor say?"

"You resent him?"

"Oh, I don't know. A little maybe," he admitted.

"Good."

"Why is that good?"

"Because it means that you're jealous of him," she said, adding, "or, at least a little, maybe . . ."

"Maybe I am. Do you want me to be?"

"Maybe a little," she said.

"I'll drink to that," he replied, and he refilled their champagne glasses.

"But what is it that Dr. Parker said?"

"That the pushing wasn't important. It was the fact that you are concerned. And . . . and that I am concerned, and am trying to please you. So I eat. I make all-gone, like a good little girl."

"You are a good little girl. Or, maybe not so little," Richard said, indicating by a glance his appreciation of her figure.

It was, at least, partly Richard's concern. It was also partly the fact that she and Dr. Parker had worked through to the probable beginnings of her difficulty, having dredged up her memory of her mother's death—from peritonitis following a botched kitchen-table abortion of a child she had been too old to bear.

"What kind of abortion?" Dr. Parker had asked.

"What I said. A botched kitchen-table abortion."

"Surely you didn't witness the abortion?"

"No."

"Then what makes you think it was performed on a kitchen table?"

"I don't know. I just assumed. Something I'd read maybe."

"Perhaps. But the association, you see, of kitchen tables and kitchens and food with the abortion is possibly of some significance . . ."

She had not told Richard about all that, not yet. But the important thing was that she was getting better, that she was able, now, to eat nearly a whole Newport steak, and most of the endive salad, without feeling even the slightest wave of nausea. Even the waiter seemed pleased, as he came in to clear. Or, no, that was just his manner, she supposed.

He left the coffee pot and the plate of petits fours, and wheeled the table out. Richard, after lighting a small brown Havana cigar —shipped to him in the diplomatic pouch from London—poured them each a cup of coffee and moved to the sofa. She brought her cup over and joined him. They sat there, saying little, sipping the coffee and enjoying each other's presence. As he drank his coffee, his fingertips idly stroked her forearm.

"New?" he asked, "isn't it?" He touched the cloth of her jumpsuit.

"Yes, do you like it?"

"It's hard to say. I'd have to see it on a hanger."

"You what?" she asked, and then laughed.

And then, abruptly, she got up, pulled the zipper down the front, and, in a deft liquid motion, stepped out of the jumpsuit. She was naked.

Patterson put down his coffee cup. "I was only joking," he said, "but, my God, I'd forgotten how beautiful you are."

He got up and ran his fingers down her torso, from the shoulder, over the breasts, to the slight swell of her belly, and down her smooth thighs.

"It's funny," he said. "You ought to feel silly standing around like that. But I'm the one who feels silly, standing here with all these clothes on. Let's take these in there, shall we?"

He picked up the champagne glasses and led the way into the bedroom.

"By all means," she said. "It doesn't do to have the Attorney General feeling silly, does it?"

She lay down on the bed and watched him while he undressed. She held the champagne glass out to him, and, after he had finished getting out of his clothes, he took the glass, took a sip, and then put the glass down on the night table. Deliberately, he lay down beside her, and, gently, he took her in his arms. He kissed her, lightly at first, and then more deeply. He began his lovemaking with great restraint in order to draw out each moment for as long as possible, and also out of a kind of respect—and even reverence—for her, who had been so frequently abused by the world and its men, whose lovemaking was usually as gross as their persons.

From the first night they had spent together she had been surprised by the intensity of her response to him. They seemed closest to moments of pure love when their bodies became the medium for the expression of that love. Having shed the public garb of movie actress and of statesman, they were simply themselves, less than themselves and more. For the first time in her life, she had understood what people meant when they said that the physical relationship could be a vehicle for the expression of a spiritual one.

He stroked her, gently at first, and she could feel her nipples tighten under his caresses. He continued to caress her until she was eager for him to enter her. And he did, with ease and assurance.

This was the moment she had thought about all day, all the way from Los Angeles to Washington, the moment when she would feel the weight of Richard on her and the warmth of him in her, and the security that that feeling gave her was like no other feeling she had ever known in her life.

His warmth covered her body. She ran her fingers up and down his back, down to his buttocks and then slowly up again to his shoulders, savoring the feel of his firm flesh. He lay upon her and within her without moving, and the two of them exchanged kisses and murmured endearments. It was as though they were floating four feet off the bed. She had been surprised by his singular technique the first time they had gone to bed together, and he had acknowledged to her, afterwards, that although he was no longer an eighteen-year-old boy there were certain compensations that came with age and experience. The control and the refinement in the taste for pleasure. its very elegance and gentleness were not only compensations, she thought, but ideals in themselves.

She was familiar with the coarse grab, the quick thrust, the grunt and the quick withdrawal, and then, later, the loud snore. Richard took his time, bringing her up gently, and then slowly allowing them both to rest before the intensity of passion carried them over the crest. He moved vigorously within her, and her breath came in short gasps. She felt she could stand it no longer. He sensed this, stopped abruptly, and held her gently to him. Then he rolled over on his back, bringing her with him, so that she was sitting astride him. To higher and higher plateaus they climbed, and at each one they stopped for a new vista. At one moment she could stand it no longer, and the words she had wanted to say for so long came bubbling up.

"Richard, I love you," she said, no longer caring whether it was clever or politic to say so. She only knew that she had to tell him how she felt.

His head was then buried between her breasts, and he looked up and said, "Oh, my darling. I love you, too."

Finally, when her pleasure was so keen it was nearly inseparable from pain, he continued and accelerated his pace, almost mercifully allowing her and himself the relief of release. He collapsed on top of her and she stroked his hair, pushing the famous forelock back, and kissing the tip of his slightly upturned nose. He raised himself on his elbow and looked down into her celebrated blue eyes. Gently he withdrew from her body, kissing her as he did so, and lay down beside her on the bed. Then he reached over to the night table, lit two cigarettes, and gave her one.

They were silent for a few moments, and then she turned to him, propped herself up on one arm, and said, "Richard, I meant what I said before. I *do* love you. You don't have to love me, but I want you to know that I love you, and I've never felt this way about anyone before. Loving you is what's important for me." Then she laughed self-consciously, adding, "That's all," and took a deep puff of her cigarette.

He thought for a long moment before he replied. Then he reached over to the night table for one of the tulip glasses that was still half full of champagne, and extended it to her. She took a sip and handed it back to him, and then he drained the rest of the wine. He looked down at her and said quietly, "I love you, Jill, and I wish there were some way I could show everyone how very much I do love you." He traced the contours of her face with small, delicate kisses.

"You don't have to say anything," she began.

"No, no, I want to. You see," he said, "I hope within a year or so to be beyond all this political stuff, to be in a position where none of it matters any more. And then I'll be able to say to the whole world, 'I love Jill Jefferson,' and be able to show them and you precisely what I mean by that love."

"You're not thinking of leaving politics, are you?" she asked.

"I won't be leaving politics," he said, and then added cryptically, "It will be beyond politics."

"Oh?" she asked, but he did not say anything more.

He simply smiled and said, "I know it's superstitious. I don't want to talk about it any more. Just trust me. And trust that we will have a future together. Can you do that?"

"Of course I can, darling," she said. She lay there quietly, smoking her cigarette, savoring the joy that his words had brought her. She knew that the only job in America that Richard could look forward to that was beyond politics was one on the Supreme Court, where the appointments were for life. It was with some difficulty that she restrained herself from asking him to confirm the guess she had made, but she respected his reluctance to discuss something that had not yet happened but that he very much wanted to happen. It was not at all foreign to the kinds of superstitions that actors and actresses scrupulously observed on the Coast, and the superstitions of her childhood in Cohoes. For years, Jill had kept an Indian head penny in her left shoe . . .

Whether it was to avoid any further discussion of this sensitive topic, or whether it was thoughtfulness, she could not tell. At any rate, Richard got out of bed, went into the living room and brought back two fresh cups of coffee. Now all their restraint was gone, and they sat in the bed, naked, drinking their coffee, telling each other funny stories of things that had happened in the past six weeks, and feeling the warmth and intimacy that they had known at each of their previous meetings. Richard told her that he would spend the night, and finally they fell asleep, curled up close together in the center of the bed. She left a call for five-thirty.

When the phone rang she answered it, thanked the switchboard girl, nudged Richard, and fell back to sleep, almost at once. When she half awoke some time later and turned in her sleep, reaching out for him, he was gone. When she really woke up she found a note tucked under the ashtray on her night table. It said, "I meant what I said. I love you. R." And then, "P.S. I'll call you about 10." She smiled when she read it.

When the phone rang at six-thirty in Richard Patterson's suite he was already awake—he had been awake since Jill had nudged him at five-thirty and sent him back to his own apartment in the hotel. He had taken a long hot bath and then stretched out on his bed to think about the confusing day before and the wonderful night he had spent with her. He muttered his automatic, "Thank you, Jean," to the switchboard girl, and began his usual morning ritual, the shave, the breakfast, clothes, the *Washington Post*, downstairs to the waiting car, and the *Times* into work.

The two letters were clipped together, and attached to them was a note scrawled in Jack Nelson's unmistakably bold handwriting—he used a green Pen-tel—saying, "Look what Mother Tyler has kicked off now." Patterson glanced at the first letter:

THE MOTHERS' LEAGUE FOR A DECENT AMERICA

2825 St. Georges Avenue   Rahway, New Jersey

July 12, 196—

The Honorable Richard Patterson
Attorney General of the United States
Department of Justice
Washington, D.C.

Dear Mr. Patterson:

It is with a growing concern not only for our young people, but for our entire nation, that I write to you today to protest against the ever-increasing flood of filth and smut which is washing away the traditional moral values that have made our country a strong, Christian country.

The recent tragedy in Boston, Massachusetts, in which a young man, his mind fevered by the images and words of filthy magazines cynically published to prey upon weaknesses and inexperience in our youth, wantonly and savagely raped and murdered Marcia Church, a defenseless young woman, serves to give added force to the recent remarks of our nation's greatest authority on crime and its causes, Mr. M. R. Tyler, your associate and the Director of the Federal Bureau of Investigation of your department.

Speaking in Wheeling, West Virginia, he said, "The Communists will use everything and anything in their power, no matter how low or how devious or how filthy, to gain every advantage and control over the minds and hearts of Americans. Here we have an unwitting alliance of our foreign enemies and our domestic criminals, one working to overthrow us, the other to enrich itself by weakening us."

Our organization is dedicated to the proposition that the mothers of America know what is best for the American people. They are, I have no doubt, rejoicing in the Kremlin at this further evidence of our national moral decay and flabbiness.

Our freedoms must be preserved, and in the interest of preserving freedom I ask you, Mr. Patterson, vigorously to stamp out these parasites who are sapping and corrupting our life's blood.

Waiting the favor of an early reply, I am, sir,

    Very sincerely,

    Mary Regina Sullivan (*Mrs. Michael O'B. Sullivan*)
    Executive Secretary

Patterson shook his head. What he felt was a combination of amusement and disgust. The letter was, obviously, just another one of those pieces of crank mail that came into the office. Jack Nelson had sent it up for him to see as a kind of mock protest at the kind of nonsense they had to put up with downstairs. Or was it just a joke—was there a point to it? Had Nelson been calling his attention to Tyler's speech in Wheeling? He remembered vaguely reading about the murder, a sordid business up in Boston about two weeks before. It had been an unattractive business, but he had dismissed it from his mind almost immediately upon turning the page. It had been only a brief account in *The New York Times* and there had been no mention of it at all in the Washington paper. It had not been that extraordinary or surprising a case; he knew—and he knew that Tyler knew, too—that crimes against persons increased drastically in the summer and fell in the winter. Crimes against property correspondingly rose in the winter and fell in the summer. The rape-murder, while regrettable, was not at all unusual.

He was about to put the letter in the Out basket when he realized that there was a second sheet, a second letter. This one, while on the same stationery, was from a Father Francis X. Gavigan, who was listed on the letterhead as chaplain for the organization. He skimmed the letter quickly, slowing down to read the fourth paragraph, which made a not uninteresting suggestion:

> I do not appeal to you, sir, solely on theological or even religious grounds, but venture to point out that there are obvious political advantages that would accrue to you from such a work. This does not seem to me to be incompatible with my reasons for writing to you, for in the mysterious and complicated workings of Divine Providence, many disparate and diverse influences can be brought to bear for the same noble end. . . ."

The letter was gibberish, Patterson thought. He remembered Jimmy Walker's famous comment, "No girl was ever ruined by a book." He remembered, too, his own adolescence, when he hardly needed any stimulation for the ideas—banal and universal as they were—that were the standard fare in the magazines to which this Mothers' League was objecting. That the Boston rapist had been reading girlie magazines, or even hard-core pornography, had nothing to do with the rape itself. For the right kind of person—or the wrong kind—the women's underwear section of the Sears catalogue could be sufficient incitement.

He threw the two letters into his Out box to be returned to Jack Nelson without comment. Nelson could deal with them, could answer them any way he chose. But something about those letters stayed with him. There was some peculiar conjunction; some odd combination of things in those letters that kept dancing around in the back of his head. It was more annoying than anything else because, clearly, the whole business was foolish and repellent. Still, there was a nagging insistence about them. He picked up a manila folder, opened it, but did not even look down at the yellow legal pad with its notes that lay on top of the papers inside. Instead, he looked off at the Barnett Newman painting on the wall opposite his desk. In a way, the Newman painting was an indication of the fluctuations of his intelligence, for, when he was feeling sharp and bright, the painting was a series of areas held together by the two vertical strokes, and was all of the things Newman said it was. On the other hand, when he was dull and stupid, it looked like nothing more than two navy blue stripes on a royal blue canvas.

It looked like stripes now. Or, no, the two areas of blue seemed to be squeezing the darker blue vertical between them. He was that vertical. Or, no, Tyler was that vertical. It was the mention of Tyler that had stayed with him. Mrs. Sullivan had mentioned

Tyler's speech. Father Gavigan had talked about political advantages. And here he was, involved in what he was sure would be a head-on collision with that old bull over the Billingsley business, indeed over the whole issue of wiretapping and bugging.

Suddenly it all fell into place, as clearly as a prepared slide under a properly focused microscope. He would disarm the old bastard, beat him to the punch, steal his thunder, fight him on his own ground. He would attack with Billingsley, but he would protect his flank by doing something about "the rising flood of filth and smut." How could Tyler attack the man who was using the power of the Justice Department, the power of the Federal Government, to wage a crusade in which he so ardently believed? He couldn't, by God. It was, he supposed, a trifle shady, but then politics is the art of the possible. Anyway, the constitutional safeguards, and the attitude of the Court, were such that the freedom of the press was pretty safe. He didn't have to worry about that so much as the freedom from wiretapping. To bring an action and have it thrown out of court didn't bother him at all. And if there had to be priorities in civil liberties, the privilege of an attorney talking with his clients on the telephone took precedence, he supposed. Supposed? Knew! The question of the rights of publishers was vaguer, depended on "community standards," and would clarify itself some day, he hoped. He could, he told himself, only do so much.

He pressed a button and asked his secretary to get him the newspaper clippings on the rape-murder in Boston. "All of them," he said. "Everything you can get. Tabloids, news magazines, the works." He continued, "Look in the files for any previous correspondence from the Mothers' League for a Decent America."

"Yes, sir," she said.

He pressed the buzzer down again. "Oh, by the way, this is all *very* confidential." He closed the manila folder that lay on his blotter. He was too much involved in this new scheme to have the requisite calm and patience for the kind of careful analysis that the material in the folder demanded. On the other hand, there would be a wait before the material for which he had just asked would appear. He looked at the banjo clock on the wall and realized that Jill would probably be awake by now. He picked up his private phone and called the Federalist House, asking for Jill's suite by its extension number.

"Hello?" Jill answered the phone herself.

"Jill? Dick. I called up to say good morning."

"Oh, darling," she said, "it's such a wonderful morning." She laughed lazily and they both were silent for a moment, remembering the night before.

"Did you find my note?" he asked.

"Yes," she said. "Bonita put it on my breakfast tray. I'm having my second cup of coffee now. I'm still in bed. Can you get away for lunch?"

"No, I don't think so," he said. "Not if I want to come up to New York this evening to be with you for the weekend."

"Of course," she said. "Are you madly busy now, or can we chat?"

"No," he said, "I'm not busy. As a matter of fact, I'm just sitting here waiting for some papers, and thinking about you."

"I wish you could be right here," she said.

"For ten minutes?" he joked.

"Well," she said, "we could have a cup of coffee together."

"I just had a cup of coffee," he said.

"One can always have another cup of coffee," she said.

But he was not listening. His mind was wandering back to his interview with Tyler, to the two letters, and to the campaign that was beginning to form in his mind. "Tell me," he asked, "have you ever seen a magazine called *Tomcat?*"

"Everybody has. It's even in the dentists' offices."

"But I've never seen it. I sleep in the barber's chair, and my dentist takes me as soon as I walk in the office."

"Well, it's kind of glossy, and it's got a lot of stories and stuff, and in the middle there's a great big picture of a girl without any clothes on. It's supposed to be very risqué or something, but it isn't. It's kind of dull, I think."

"Do you know who puts it out?" Richard asked. "One of the big companies? But I don't suppose you'd have any reason to know."

"As a matter of fact," Jill said, "it's published by a man named Irvin Kane." She paused for a moment, then she added, almost involuntarily, "He's a real creep."

"Oh?" asked Patterson, picking up her comment and her tone of voice. "Do you know him?"

Reluctantly, she said, "Yes, we've met."

"Tell me about him."

"He's just a creep, that's all," she said, obviously unwilling to talk about him.

"But tell me, tell me. What makes you say that?"

"What is this?" she asked. "Are you thinking of taking out a subscription?"

"No," he said, "this is serious, Jill."

"Well, I'm serious too," she said. "He's a lousy human being. And he makes a lot of money by being lousy."

Patiently, with a combination of the incisive courtroom manner of the cross-examiner and the charming, genial, and affectionate persuasion of the lover, he bullied and coaxed the story from her.

"It wasn't the pictures," she said. "I've told you about that. That was all Washburne's doing. But . . ."

"Yes?" he asked, trying to hide the impatience he felt. "What is it, Jill?"

"Well, I knew a girl . . . We were friends for a while . . . I mean, good friends . . ."

"Yes?"

"And she actually lived at Kane's place. For a couple of months or so. She'd been in the magazine, too, with the same kind of pictures, and then she'd gone to the place he has out on an island in Boston Harbor. To do publicity, it was supposed to be. He has the girls go out to openings of supermarkets or automobile showrooms, and that kind of thing . . ."

"Well? What happened to your friend?"

"Well, I mean she was . . . She'd been around and all. And she sort of expected that he'd, you know, maybe make a play for her. But from what she told me, it would have been better if he had. Because the way it was . . . well, it was worse. He kept her there for two months or so, never making a pass at her himself, but pushing her at any man who happened to be in the house. And—and the way he got his kicks was watching them go off to the bedroom together. It was creepy. She had the feeling all the time that what he really wanted to do was to go on into the bedroom and watch the whole thing. It was just crawly!"

"What happened to your friend?"

"Oh, she just left after a while. She went back to the Coast. That's where I got to know her. And she told me."

"I see."

Patterson had always been tolerant of other people's sex lives and other people's kicks, but beyond his tolerance, and indeed beyond his acceptance of the varieties of sexual enjoyment, there was still a kind of primitive revulsion that he felt at peculiarly dramatic departures from the normal. The sight of attractive women was certainly a reasonable thing to enjoy, either as a prelude to lovemaking, or even in and of itself. But this? It was, as Jill had just said, "crawly."

Had she told him that at one time in the remote past she had slept with Irvin Kane, he could not have been so repelled. This story of what had happened to a friend—or was it a friend? Was she telling him the truth about that? Had Jill been telling him about herself? He put the question itself out of his mind.

"I'm sorry to have had to tell you all this over the phone this way," Jill said, "but you made it sound so important."

"It is," he said. "There's something I have to decide, and this has been very helpful, believe me." He paused, and added, "I'm sorry I had to make you remember all this nastiness."

There was a pause, during which he wondered whether he had gone too far, whether she now suspected that he suspected.

"Do you remember our discussion last night?" he asked.

"Yes," Jill said.

"Well, I meant it. I do love you . . . and I'll see you in New York about ten."

"Good," she said. "Oh, darling, it's so wonderful to love you. I'll see you later." And she hung the phone up slowly.

Miss Ryder entered his office carrying a stack of clippings and copies of the latest two issues of *Tomcat* magazine. She looked at him quizzically as she put them down on his desk, but she was far too good a secretary to say anything. She stood there for a moment and then left.

He immediately turned to the material, opened the pages of the magazine, flipped through it, and then went through the clippings. The fourth or fifth clipping that he came to arrested his attention. It was the sob sister's column on Frank Scully's room, describing the piles of *Tomcat* magazines, the pictures of the gatefold girls all over the walls with the unprintable comments scrawled all over their bodies. Patterson could well imagine what those comments were. It was all pretty distasteful, he thought. Still, it would do. It would be the perfect way of disarming M. R. Tyler and his loyal followers. A man who went after smut, they believed, could do no wrong. It was a simplistic view that Patterson found every bit as distasteful as the magazines and clippings on his desk, but that was the world of politics in which he had to function. And if this was the price of a successful attack on bugging and wiretapping, he was, he thought, prepared to pay it. The civil liberties of Irvin Kane seemed less important than the privacy of Dexter Miles.

No, that was not right. That was hardly an appropriate attitude for a lawyer to take. For an Attorney General. But, still, he was a man before he was a lawyer, and he could not help but weigh Jill's distaste for the man. And his own? If what he had suspected about Jill being that "friend" were true, then, by God, yes. His own. And, besides, he was only the lawyer. In an adversary system of justice. He wasn't the judge. The judges would decide. That's what they were for.

And for his own part? It wasn't, he told himself, any act of vengeance. The object was not to go after Irvin Kane. That was only the means. And what did it matter if he was not reluctant now to go ahead? Wouldn't that be helpful and desirable? Of course it would.

And he was not reluctant, he decided. Not at all.

6

The steam swirled around Irv Kane in thick clouds. He could hardly see his knees. The temperature was set at 200, and Kane could feel the sweat form and then drip down his naked body. It was relaxing in the steam bath, and a wonderful restorative. All of the dirt, all of the nasty poisons buried down in his pores were cooked out and he felt cleansed and purified. Not only that, the intensity of the heat was such that he was unable for the while to think about the menace that had suddenly loomed up to threaten his entire empire. Here, in the miniscule steam room in a corner of his private bathroom, in his private Boeing 737, six miles above Kansas, he was able to feel safe and remote from the turbulence of the weather—which, according to the pilot, was two miles below them—or from the human weather below that. He reached for the sponge that lay in the ice water just outside the door and squeezed it over his head so that the cold water poured down in refreshing rivulets over his forehead, neck, and shoulders. But, even after the sponge had been squeezed dry, he continued to clench it with increasing tightness and anger—as if it were not just a sponge, but Richard Patterson's heart.

Finally he had had enough. He reached outside the steam room and flicked the lever to "off." As the steam valve abruptly turned off he stood up, turned on the cold faucet and stood gasping under the needle spray of icy water. Then, turning off the cold water, he emerged from the small steam closet. On the heated towel rack was a large fluffy towel embroidered with the head of a tomcat. He wrapped it around himself and walked over to the mirror, where he surveyed his face. No, he didn't need a shave. He looked at his eyes and at his skin. He always felt so rejuvenated by a steam bath that it was a surprise to him that it didn't change his appearance as drastically as it changed the way he felt.

He pressed a coral button and almost instantly Cato appeared with a large bottle of scented rubbing alcohol. Kane stretched out on the rubbing table and closed his eyes, giving himself over to the ministrations of Cato's nimble fingers. It was important for Kane to be in top condition when he reached Los Angeles and saw Jill Jefferson.

It was, he knew, an unpleasant thing that he had to do—even an ugly thing. Hell, he knew that it was blackmail—no more and no less. But his back was against the wall. And it was a miserable, low, sneaky, dreadful thing that Patterson was doing to him. To revive, for no reason at all except political opportunism and personal ambition, the Comstock Act of 1873 applying criminal penalties to an American publisher who was presumably protected by the Constitution of the United States of America. . . .

"Oooh." He grunted as Cato began a manipulation of the

muscles on either side of his spinal column with his strong, flat thumbs.

For a few minutes, the only discomfort with which Kane had to put up was the pleasurable pain of Cato's vigorous massage. The mental torture was, at least for a while, submerged. But, at last, Cato stood back, ready to see if Kane wanted any more. It was reluctance to continue this kind of childish hiding from his real, urgent, and important problems that made him say, "No, thank you, Cato, that's fine. I'd like an oyster pizza in about ten minutes in the lounge."

"Yes, Mr. Kane," Cato said, and went forward to the galley where, along with the infrared oven there was the special oven with the extra-high controls that Cato used to prepare Kane's pizzas on the Tomcat plane that Kane called TC-1.

Kane got off the table and went into the small dressing room adjoining the bath, where he picked out a light blue shirt and a dark gray Italian silk lounge suit. He surveyed his tie rack and then picked a navy blue heavy silk Dior tie with a pale blue fleur-de-lis pattern that matched the shirt. He looked at the rack of shoes, tentatively selected a pair of black calf desert boots, but then decided that he would wait until the last minute before putting them on. He much preferred to go around barefoot.

He padded out, over the tangerine nylon carpeting, through his bedroom and into the lounge where Carmen and Debbie, the two Kitties along for publicity work, were watching a quiz program on television. In the corner, at a small desk, Freddie and Charlie, his two assistants, were going over his itinerary and typing out a short speech that he was going to make at a dinner the following night. Sitting on the overstuffed tangerine sofa was Jack Garsythe, *Tomcat's* advertising director. He was sprawled out, intently reading *Motor Trend*. Across the room from Garsythe, sitting cross-legged on the floor, practicing the game of pick-up-sticks that Kane had bought for her at the airport, was Darlene, his current girl.

Kane sat down next to Darlene, and she picked up all the sticks and held them clenched in her fist, then opened it suddenly and let them fall in their random patterns on the floor. She carefully picked up the black stick to use as a lever to separate the others, and then, in rapid succession, a red, a blue, and a green. She had picked up eight sticks when she moved one. Kane said, "My turn," and took the plastic sticks from her. He opened his hand with such force that they scattered in a large circle in front of him and he was able to pick up fifteen of them before he jiggled a red one, trying to flick it off a pile of tangled sticks. She had another turn, but by this time he had lost interest in the game. It was not taking his mind off his problems, as he had hoped it would; it was only preventing him from thinking about them with the clarity and the decisiveness they required. He got up, and without saying so much as a word to her, walked over to one of the easy chairs near a window, sat down and, swiveling back and forth, stared at the blank blue sky above and the solid bank of clouds below the plane.

Cato appeared with the steaming oyster pizza on a platter. Kane took a piece and then nodded to Cato to distribute the rest around the room. He took two bites and then, getting bored with that, too, called to Cato and dropped the uneaten half of the wedge back onto the now half-empty tray. He asked Cato to bring him a Scotch and water. Cato's impassive face showed no surprise at this unusual request from Kane, who rarely drank, but, with even more than his usual promptness and expeditiousness, he disappeared and reappeared with the drink on a small plastic tray. Kane took it, hardly noticing that he was doing so. Sloshing the liquor around in the glass and staring out of the window at the blankness of the cloud bank, he continued to roil and boil in frustration and rage against Patterson and the miserable thing that the man was trying to do to him. To have held a press conference that way, and to have referred to Irvin Kane by name, and to have called him a pornographer—it was libelous. He wondered whether he ought to sue. Patterson? The Department of Justice? The United States Government?

And, even worse, to be mentioned in the same breath with purveyors of pervert magazines—magazines whose pages were filled with pictures of women wearing high boots and tight belts and carrying whips—and to be associated with the makers of Lesbian movies—it was just *too* outrageous and unfair.

He had thought that Richard Patterson, like the President who had appointed him, was a liberal, decent man. But now, with this vicious and unwarranted attack upon *Tomcat* and all that it stood for, Kane realized that the fight he had been leading against the forces of prudery and sexual reaction in America was only begun. He wondered about Patterson's sudden, puritanical fervor. He had met Patterson, and had found him a typical, urbane, upper-middle-class Easterner. He was neither a Fundamentalist nor an anti-smut crusading Catholic, but a white Anglo-Saxon Protestant. Patterson was doing it—he had to be doing it—for purely political reasons. He wasn't a prig. Everybody knew about his thing with Jill Jefferson. Or, no, not everybody, but everybody who was anybody. But then, if he was doing it for political reasons rather than because of principle, he would surely be open to persuasion—other political pressures—that would be just as strong, or even stronger.

He was sitting there, brooding, about Patterson's threat to prosecute him under the old Comstock Act when Darlene came over to him and, either bored with her pick-up-sticks or eager to change his mood and be of help and service, started stroking the outside edge of his right ear. He shook his head. "No, not now, I'm thinking. Can't you see I'm thinking?"

"I'm sorry," she said, and pouted as prettily as she could before she retreated to the sofa, where she sat down beside Garsythe and, picking up an emery board, began to file her already perfect silver-frosted nails.

Kane got up suddenly and went aft to his office, a small, simple, but elegantly outfitted room with a bronze and walnut Platner table that served as a desk. He sat down in the chair behind the desk, picked up the light blue phone and waited until the pilot, Terry Armstrong, answered.

"Yes, Mr. Kane?"

"How are we doing?"

"We should be over Denver in about eight minutes. And our ETA is still two-thirty, Los Angeles time."

"Wonderful," Kane said. "Will you put me through to the mobile phone operator? I want to call Bud Sloat in the *Tomcat* building."

"I'll put the call through for you and call you back when I've got him, Mr. Kane."

"Thank you, I'd appreciate that," Irv said, and hung up.

He felt a small moment of satisfaction and power. He was the master of a four and a half million dollar jet aircraft with two superbly trained pilots and a navigator, all of them dedicated to the job of getting Irv Kane wherever he wanted to go. Sitting there, in this luxurious office, in this incredibly expensive plane, he felt invulnerable—or nearly so. But the shadow of Patterson's power dogged the plane, just as, looking down at the checkered fields of the Midwest, Kane could see the shadow of the Boeing 737 trailing along after the plane.

"Son of a bitch," he said aloud.

A few minutes later, the phone buzzed discreetly. Kane picked it up immediately.

"Bud?"

"Irv! How are you? Where are you?"
"I'm fine. In a little while we'll be passing over Denver."
"Great!"
"Bud, I've decided. I'm going to use everything we've got."
"Oh?"
"Yes."
"I thought you'd decided before you left."
"Well, I did. But I've been thinking about it, and I've decided that my decision was right."
"I hate to point this out, but if you were all that sure, you wouldn't have gone over it all over again. You wouldn't be calling me now, would you?"
"Why not?"
"Just to tell me I was wrong and you were right?" Bud asked. "Come on, now. You're still not sure! And you want to argue with me a little and then react to what I tell you so that you can work yourself up to being sure. Isn't that true?"
"Okay, maybe. Maybe it is. But . . ."
"But what?"
"But tell me again."
"Tell you what again?"
"Your reasons. Your reasons for me not to do it."
"Will you listen to me?"
"Of course I'll listen. That's why I called you. To listen."
"All right," Bud said, and for an instant he paused, gathering his thoughts and ordering his arguments.
"First of all," he began, "there's nothing we've got to worry about. The Roth case is clear, and we're as safe as we can be. There's nothing to these threats of Patterson's. And I think he knows that. And even if he doesn't, the courts will. So I think it's unlikely he'll ever push this thing into the courts in the first place, and it's almost a certainty that, if he does, the courts will throw

it right out. And that isn't just my opinion, but the lawyers', too, and yours, if I remember correctly."

"Okay, Bud, but there's still a risk. A small one, a very small one, but a risk, and if I can avoid even that small risk, then why shouldn't I? Especially if I'm right."

"If you believe you're right, then you shouldn't. Why risk your moral edge? I think there's another risk you run this way. What if it doesn't work? What if something goes wrong, and it backfires? Then, instead of just a political advantage, you've got Patterson out for your skin—for revenge. For honor. For real . . ."

"I don't see how it can go wrong."

"As an old professor of mine used to say, it's a contingent universe."

"What the hell does that mean?"

"That nothing is certain."

"Except you."

"Well . . . you are too, aren't you?" Bud asked.

"I have to be. It's my magazine. I built it. I run it. I take the responsibility for it . . ."

"Are you questioning my loyalty to the magazine? Or to you?"

"No, not at all. I'm just pointing out the difference in our positions. Assume the worst, and what happens? Whose magazine goes under? Who pays the fine? Who goes to jail? You can be calm about all this, but I can't."

"A calm opinion may have something to recommend it."

"But there is something to be said, too, for passion. For a feeling of necessity. The world is not such a reasonable place as you suppose. Or such an attractive place, either. I know it's a pretty unattractive thing I'm thinking of doing. But it's irresistible. And I've got the stuff. I've got the ammunition. And I've got to use it."

"You don't *have* to do anything."

"Don't you?" Irv asked. "Well, maybe *you* don't, but I do. I feel it."

"I don't know what you want of me, then. I can't argue with feelings, and—and I don't know. The divine right of publishers."

"Maybe that's it," Irv said. "Maybe that's it."

"Well, good luck then."

"Thanks," Irv said. "And thanks for telling me what you think. It's been helpful."

"Any time."

"Right."

Irv Kane hung up. He hadn't accomplished much by the call. But then he felt a little better, a little surer. And that was all he'd hoped for. It wasn't the divine right of publishers, after all. But the divine right of principles. And principals. Bud was all right, but he was an employee. And what did an employee know? What could an employee ever know? You had to live with it, own it, have it own you . . .

He looked out of the window at the white ocean of cloud below them now. He took a deep breath. He thought for a moment of Patterson, and what he could be after. And he smiled, thinking of how deftly and efficiently Patterson could be stopped.

Patterson, at that moment, was sitting in his office in Washington, thumbing through a copy of *Tomcat*, one of a whole pile of back issues he had requested. He had no particular purpose in doing this, or, at least, there was nothing specific for which he was hunting. He scarcely even read the magazine with very much attention. Rather, he turned the pages, slowly, rhythmically, getting the feel of the magazine and trying to find some response from within himself.

It was not doubt. It was nothing so simple as doubt. It was a deeper question, or series of questions, that had come up as a result of that trip to Newark he had recently made. Of all places. Newark was such a dreary town, such a non-place, neither suburb of New York nor city in its own right. It was just there, across the river, as Hades was across the river from the Elysian Fields. And he had gone there to get some sense, not of the issues themselves—which could be better studied in the calm of a library—but of the resonance of the issues. Their political ramifications. Was it Oliver Wendell Holmes who had said an idea is nothing until it meets some challenge out in the real world of action and events? Something like that. And it sounded like Holmes.

Anyway, with that kind of desire—or curiosity, really—to let the idea encounter some objective challenge out in the world, with a wish to cut through the foam of intellection and get to the hard core of fact, he had worked the Mother's League for a Decent America, had worked them deliberately, so that they were emboldened to invite him to come up to address them on the subject of decency and morality in books and magazines—which was, of course, just what he wanted. The point had been to get out of Washington, and get away to somewhere else, somewhere that was nowhere at all—like Newark—to meet the women in their absurd hats and their tacky dresses and their sensible shoes, and to see and hear and smell what was going on out there in the country.

It had been a sensible, a reasonable, and even a laudable idea. What public official could think of doing otherwise? But then, as he had discovered, he was no public official, except by accident. He had never run for anything, never gone through the ordeal of banquets and barbecues, and dinners and picnics and meetings and speeches, had not shaken hands or kissed babies, or posed with the president of the Jaycees . . . He had never known the stink of it, the sour smell of subways and crowded buses, the dust of bus terminals, the dryness of airports. And the shock of this trip had been something for which he had been quite unprepared. The others, the representatives and senators and governors, and the President and Vice President, they had all gone through it, endured it, been toughened by it, had even learned from it.

Or, perhaps, even now, even from this one amateurish venture, he was learning what they learned. At least he was beginning to learn. But what a difficult lesson. How subtle and complicated. He had not made it easy for himself. For all of his deliberate planning, his picking a spot with shrewdness (close, easy to get to, densely populated, but yet not one of the centers of sophistication and culture), he had forgotten who he was and who they were, and how many millions of miles stretched between his world and theirs.

He had given his speech in Newark, telling the ladies what they wanted to hear, playing on their simplicity and on their belief, even though he knew better. They took books seriously, those women. As subliterates always do. They believed that good books cause good actions and bad books cause bad actions, because why else would one bother with them? The labor of reading had to have some effect, had to be for something, didn't it? And who was going to tell them that after the Bible, and Plato, and Dante, and Shakespeare we didn't seem to be a whole hell of a lot better off?

So he had got up there to tell them that the moral fiber of the country was rotting, and that they were the only safeguards left between where we were and total ruin. And of course they believed it. And he found, after a little while that he was not just playing them, appealing to their prejudices and biases, but that he himself was being played, was spouting for them what they wanted to hear, as if they were playing him, as if he were the dummy and they were the collective ventriloquists. And he had asked himself, up there on the platform at the little lectern, whether this might not be demagoguery, and whether demagoguery might not be the ultimate form of democracy. Because the demos speaks through the demagogue!

As he was doing. The puritanism that he had come up to use took hold of him, and, for the ten or fifteen minutes of his talk, it was real anger, real concern, real outrage that he was spouting up there, at these men who confuse and mislead our young people, at the erosion of liberty into license, at the exploitation of nudity for profit that was the oldest profession . . .

And after the speech they had had their tea. And the women had confided in him, telling him stories of the seduction of nieces, of the forced marriages of nephews, or nephews of neighbors—all of which was directly caused, of course, by the filthy magazines and vile books that they bought at their candy stores and drugstores. As if you had to be able to read to get a girl in trouble. He had listened and nodded, allowing them to take the nods for agreement. And then Father Gavigan had invited him to inspect a display of literature.

On the long folding table at the back of the room, Father Gavigan had set out about thirty magazines and books—an incredible array of the worst junk that Patterson had ever seen. There were pictures of women in waist-cinchers, getting spanked by other women or by men, or being tortured with the most elaborate machines. The books were sleazy-looking paperbacks with names like *Swamp Tramp* and *Space Cuties*. That last one had caught his attention because of the weird picture on the cover, which showed an interior of a rocket ship full of half-naked women and a pair of Buck Rogers-type male spacemen. It was the stupidity rather than the prurience of the material that Patterson found depressing. But the women took it seriously. And so did Father Gavigan.

And he? What did he think? What did he really think?

He hardly knew; now that he had come back from Newark, where he had gone to make this little test sounding, he was less sure of what he thought he thought than he had been before.

He looked at the magazine without seeing what he was looking at, and then closed it. He had been, once, a part of that world. Or his forebears had been. And he might become a part of it one day, when he got old. But, in the meanwhile, he had his career to think of, and his original purpose—the maneuvering of M. R. Tyler for the soundest and surest purpose. And he had Jill.

It was funny, in a way, that he should find himself allied with these New Jersey women against displays of sexuality when he was one of the most fortunate of men in that sphere. Jill Jefferson was the embodiment of the American Dream, and it was he whose bed she graced and shared. And in an affair that was illicit and, in the eyes of those women—if they had known of it—sinful. Get that in a cartoon, Irvin Kane, he thought, and you will have a profoundly philosophical publication.

Well, maybe that was what Kane was trying for. One could never tell. He wondered again what he ought to do, how he ought to proceed. And it seemed after a while only to be a strategic problem. The thing was to begin, to seem like a crusader, to make some noise—until Tyler was beaten on the wiretapping thing. And then? If the timing worked out properly, he could always just let the whole thing drop. Let it die away, slowly and without much notice. The pretense to action was not an unusual thing in Washington, was, in itself, a traditional kind of political action.

Father Gavigan and the ladies from Newark and Rahway and Elizabeth would be disappointed. But, then, that was their nature and their destiny. They would always be disappointed. They had even worked out a way of life and a way of responding to life so that they enjoyed their disappointment. It was familiar, and therefore comforting. He would not deprive them of that.

Irv Kane paced back and forth across the huge living room of the bungalow he had taken at the Beverly Hills Hotel. He was not exactly nervous. What was there to be nervous about? But he was certainly not relaxed. It was something like irritability. Annoyance. After all, he was sure that she would come. She had said she would. And he knew that she knew that she had to come. There had been no allusion to anything, no threat, no muscle at all, but he knew, and she knew, and the knowledge had accompanied their conversation, as much as the slight hum of the telephone wires.

He had called her at the studio. Freddy had placed the call, had waited out the switchboard and the private secretary, and then had handed the phone to Irv with Jill Jefferson on the line.

"Jill, how are you? Irv Kane," he'd said, as if neither his people nor her people had existed. The fiction one maintained was that one had simply picked up the phone and called, and that the other person had simply picked up the phone and answered. All very casual and friendly.

"Irv! How nice to hear from you! What brings you to town?"

"Actually, I came to see you, dear. I have to talk to you."

"Yes?"

"Can you come by after work? I'm at the Beverly Hills."

"It's—a little awkward, Irv," she had begun.

"It's important," he had cut in. "If it weren't, I shouldn't have come all the way out here."

"Let me think a moment," she had said. And he had let her think. And he had been thinking, too. About the simple logistical problems involved in her visiting him at the hotel.

"Perhaps at around seven?" he had suggested. "I'm out in Bungalow Eleven."

"Well, if it's that important, I suppose I can move some other things around."

"I'd appreciate it."

"All right," she had said. "I'll see you around sevenish."

"I'll be waiting."

They had not said goodbye. The tug of war had already begun. He had yielded a little, naming a time after dark, and telling her that he was in one of the bungalows to which she could come without being seen, arriving and departing quite easily and privately. But he had not yielded much. And she had agreed to come. Which meant, which had to mean, that she was aware of the necessity. She had not forgotten. Of course not. But, then, she was not a stupid girl.

He flopped into a chair, put a cigarette into the little ivory holder, and lit it. He took a few puffs, then stubbed it out. He got up, checked the machines that were lined up along one wall, and went back to the chair. Then he got up once again, went to the table in the dining alcove, and took a pear from the basket of fruit the manager had sent over. He looked at his watch. It was ten past seven. Almost savagely, he bit into the pear.

Before he had finished the pear, the bell rang. Cato appeared from the kitchen, went to the door, and opened it. He helped Jill out of her black raincoat and accepted the silk kerchief she had worn on her head. She took off the large sunglasses she had worn and put them in her purse.

It had been, Kane reflected, the absolutely standard movie-star-incognito getup. But perhaps out here that was the safest one, the question being *which* movie star.

"It's good to see you," Irv said. "It's been a long time. What is it? Five years? Six?"

"About that," she said.

"Here, sit down. Would you like a drink?"

"I could do with a sherry," she said, after a moment's hesitation.

"Good. I'll have one, too," he said to Cato, who nodded and went out to the kitchen to get the drinks.

"You're looking good," Irv said. "Better than ever."

"Thank you." There was little or no self-consciousness to it. Her looks, after all, were her stock in trade, and a compliment to them was a compliment to the experts who had put her together, who kept her looking the way she did.

"I saw your latest picture," Irv said. "Liked it. I liked it a lot. You've done damned well."

"I've been lucky," she said.

It was not the words of the conversation Irv Kane was attending to. What they were actually saying was banal and commonplace. And both of them knew it. The important thing was the chemistry, the degree of tension or relaxation she displayed, and which would be as much in evidence in these exchanges of small talk as in anything else. And, of course, they were waiting for Cato.

He appeared with the sherry glasses on a small round tray. And disappeared.

"Success!" Irv said, raising his glass.

She responded by raising her glass wordlessly and sipping the pale sherry.

"Six years!" he said. "A long time. I imagine you must be wondering why I called you, and why I asked you to come over here."

Jill hesitated, then said, "It's always great to see an old friend. But I *was* puzzled. I mean, from everything I read, it seems you're a very busy man."

"I'm not all that busy. Besides, it's very important for me to see you now."

"Oh?"

"Surely you've seen the papers," Kane said. "Your friend," he went on, emphasizing and underlining with his voice the word "friend," "Mr. Patterson, has started some kind of a campaign, and he seems to be after me."

Jill waited a moment and then said, "Yes, Richard Patterson is a friend of mine, but I know nothing about what he's doing. He doesn't consult me, you know. He rarely even mentions what he's doing." Clearly she had decided to respond to the word "friend" in its most general sense, and not rise to the innuendo in Kane's voice.

"But Patterson would surely listen to you if you were to suggest things to him. He would be open to persuasion from you, wouldn't he?"

"I don't know, and I don't want to find out," she said. "What are you talking about?" she asked.

"I want him to cut it out," Kane said bluntly. "He is going after my hide, and I won't have it. I want you to call him off."

"I don't think I can. I don't think I could if I tried. I don't think he'd listen to me," she said. "But even if he would, why should I?"

"Why shouldn't you?" Kane countered. "After all, you and I have worked together, you've appeared in the magazine, you've been a guest of mine at the Mansion . . ."

"Yes, Irv," she said, "but does that give you any claim to ask something like this of me?"

"But what the hell is he doing? He can't condemn me and my magazine, he can't condemn the kind of business I'm running without condemning you as well. And, after all, from what I hear you and he have a very good thing going, too, don't you? Serious, even."

"That's very unfair of you," she said, "What Richard does in private has nothing to do with the stand he takes on public issues. I mean," she said, as if she were explaining a lesson to a backward child, "he's the Attorney General of the United States of America! And I'm certainly not going to suggest to him what he should or should not do. He knows that a lot better than I do."

"Nonsense," Kane said. "You know the kind of operation I run. And he may be the Attorney General of the United States of America, but for God's sakes, I'm a citizen of the United States of America. More than that, I'm a publisher in the United States of America, and I've got the goddam freedom of the goddam press. He can't interfere with me this way. This is outrageous, and I won't have it!" he said, with rising fury.

"Well, then," she said reasonably, "why don't you write him a letter? If you've done nothing wrong, Irv, there's nothing for you to worry about."

"I've always found," he said "that in my business dealings it's often well to have an intermediary, some kind of spokesman, an agent, if you will. You have an agent, don't you? Somebody who negotiates for you? And takes care of your interests?"

"Yes," she said, "but that has nothing to do with this."

"Well, I don't know but that it does," Kane suggested.

"Look, Irv, she said, getting to her feet, "I wish you well. I wish your magazine well. But my relationship with Richard Patterson is strictly private. And what he does in his public position is his business, and I don't and won't have anything to do with that." She paused for a minute and then added, "Is there anything else you wanted to see me about?"

"It's not that easy. Sit down."

Jill listened, not to his words but to the menace behind them, and obeyed him, sitting back down in the armchair, listening now to what he had to say.

"I've got something here I want to show you," Kane began.

"All I want you to do is to take a look at this and then we may have something to talk about."

He got up, crossed the room, and flicked the switch in a large leatherette-covered box that lay on the floor next to the television set. Then he turned the knob of the set on.

"What is this?" Jill asked in a puzzled voice. "This is your life, Jill Jefferson?" She managed a small laugh.

Kane joined in the laughter. "Not far wrong," he said. "Not far wrong at all."

"What is it?" she asked, not joking now, and even a little nervous.

"You'll see."

He pushed a button on the Ampex machine, and then recrossed the room, sitting down in the chair opposite Jill's to watch her watch the tape that was projected on a blank channel of the television screen. "You'll see," he said again.

She stared at the screen, puzzled and wary. The screen flickered for a moment, and then she saw a scene that she did not at first recognize. A group of people were sitting on sofas and chairs, and there was a large, marble coffee table in the middle of the grouping. One of the men reached into his wallet and withdrew a couple of bills, which he threw down on the table.

"You recognize it?" Irv asked.

"No, I don't think so."

"Here, I'll turn on the sound."

He got up, turned a knob, and the man's speech came through the audio of the television set.

"Make it a sporting proposition, I say," he was saying. "Like a horse race or a prizefight."

As the second man, closer to the camera, leaned forward to put his money into the pot, she saw the profile of the first, which had been obscured before. She recognized him. She remembered the scene, the awful evening. . . . And then Irv Kane watched her reaction as she moved from recognition of the moment itself to the further realization that he had recorded it all on tape, that he had it still, that he was showing it to her.

It had been the last night of her stay at Tomcat House, and the reason for her leaving. The four men—she couldn't even remember all their names now—had been visitors. And one of those men had been Martin Wyner, the producer. The son of a bitch. Or, no, not any more of a son of a bitch than most producers were. It was, she supposed, the power that corrupted them all and in pretty much the same way. But they had all been there, and Wyner had set up this competition, the prize being a part in his next picture. The contestants had been Inge Peterson and Jill Jefferson, both of them girls with a few pictures behind them and a big question mark in front of them. And the competition had been the four men. Who could work her way through the four and finish first. It was like that awful description of the bullpen in *Mamie Stover*. In fact, it had been the description of that bullpen in the Huie book that had given Wyner the idea.

Mamie Stover's claim to fame had been her ability to service four marines in four minutes, or something like that. And she had had some elaborate four-compartment booth through which she moved, turning sex into an assembly line job. And Wyner had always wanted to try it. In anybody else, it would have been just a fantasy, something to think about on lonely nights. But for a producer who could dangle contracts as bait, anything was possible. Or damned near anything. And she had been possible, then. Her wrecked marriage, her six-week-long drunk, her acceptance of the offer to come to Tomcat House, had all set her up. And Wyner had come along to pluck her—but good.

The money on the table—it had been four hundred dollars— had been for the loser. The contract was for the winner. And she and Inge had agreed. What was the difference between getting laid once and getting laid four times? And they had drunk enough so that the idea of the contract seemed plausible. The damned thing was that they seldom came through on those casting-couch deals. This one hadn't. Oh, Wyner had given her a thousand bucks to square things. But there hadn't been any contract, or any picture. And yet she had come out to Hollywood expecting that there would be one, and had stayed in town, and had fallen into another picture. So, in a weird way, it had all worked out.

Except for this. She watched as the men threw their money onto the marble table. And then the scene shifted to the other room, the room into which she had gone with one of the other men.

She watched herself getting laid. She remembered how it had been, and how the first two had been fairly easy. The tough part had been the second two, who had already had Inge. Wyner had been the most difficult. She had had to work on him like a trainer in a cockfight trying to revive a damned near dead bird. She had had to suck him and play with him and get him hard, and then she had had to work him like crazy to get him to come. . . .

She shuddered, not so much at the memory of the thing itself, but at the idea that Kane had filmed it all, or taped it. Had watched it all, as it had been happening, and then again later, over and over, for all she knew.

"Turn it off," she said.

"But the best part is still to come."

"I know what the rest of it is. Turn it off."

"All right."

Kane went over to the leatherette-covered machine and snapped the knob. The television screen went dark, and the image diminished to a round circle of light that shrank to a last lingering pinpoint.

"You are a filthy bastard," she said to Kane in a dead voice.

"That may be," he said.

"It's blackmail."

"That's right," he agreed. "Call the police." He indicated the phone with a wave of his hand. "Call the sheriff. Call the Attorney General. Call anyone you like."

She remained in her chair.

"Your friend Patterson is threatening everything I've worked for and everything I've got and I'll fight him with everything I've got. I have to."

"What if I talk to him," she began, after a long pause, "and he won't listen to me? What if I ask him to stop his investigation and he won't?"

"A man will do a great many things for a woman he loves," Kane said. "You've just got to make him believe it's worth while."

"I don't know," she said.

"Look," Kane said, "he's doing this for political reasons, and if he's got a good political reason to stop, he'll stop."

"I don't know," she repeated numbly.

"Well," Kane retorted, "it's worth a try, isn't it?"

"And if I fail?" she asked at last.

"Well, then, Mr. Patterson—and others—will have a new film for their collections. And we'll both go down together."

"I see."

"I hoped you would."

Irv Kane got up, crossed the room, went to the kitchen, and asked Cato to get Jill's coat and scarf. And he offered to have Cato drive her home.

"No, no thank you. I can manage."

"Are you sure? It's no trouble. I'd be happy to—"

"Don't put yourself out."

She opened the door and walked out of the bungalow without looking behind her.

Kane watched her walk along the winding path that led between banana trees and orange trees and all sorts of tropical bushes and shrubs. She disappeared for a moment into semidarkness, then appeared again as she passed through a distant pool of light, and then disappeared for good as the path curved out of his field of vision.

He closed the door. He had played his card. Now he would have to wait and see what happened. It felt good, he thought. She had behaved about the way he had expected. Maybe a little better, even. He looked around. He saw the half-eaten pear that he had put down on the plate next to the fruit basket. The air had turned its flesh brownish. It was disgusting.

"Cato," he said, "get rid of that. And then get those things packed up. We're leaving."

The phone buzzed in Richard Patterson's office and he picked it up. "Jill!" he said. "What a nice surprise. Where are you?"

"I'm at the Federalist. They don't need me for shooting for a few days," she said, "and I missed you so much I decided to come and see you. I'd like to talk to you, too," she added casually, almost as if it were an afterthought.

"Darling, I'm so happy you're here, I'll talk to you about anything—if talking is all you want to do." His delight was spontaneous and strong. "I'll be back at the hotel in half an hour. I'll shower and come right on up."

"Fine," she said.

He blew her a kiss and hung up.

In her hotel suite she remembered her last visit to Washington, when her anticipation had been almost unendurable. She remembered how she had paced, in the same way, but for such different reasons. Now she doubted everything. Did Richard love her enough to give up that part of his campaign which was directed at Kane? Never mind that, did he love her enough to forgive her? How much would she have to tell him? Could she persuade him to leave Kane alone without having to tell him about the existence of that television tape? Could she tell him about its existence without telling him everything about it? And if she had to tell him everything, would he understand that the Jill Jefferson of five years ago was a different girl from the woman she was now—from the woman he loved? She had read somewhere that all of the cells in one's body changed every seven years, so that actually she was even physically a different person. And emotionally she was now in large measure his creation because she had found with him a new kind of life and new reasons for living.

There was a discreet knock on the door, and she ran to open it. "Richard!"

He stepped into the room quickly, closed the door behind him, and took her in his arms. "I couldn't think of a more wonderful surprise if I tried," he said, and kissed her. It was a long, intense, but at the same time domestic and familiar kiss in the good sense, as if she were a wife of long standing, assured and relaxed in the love of her husband. With his arm around her, he led her over to the sofa and they sat down together, holding hands and basking in each other's presence.

"How long can you stay?" he asked.

"I have to be back on Monday," she answered.

"We'll have a wonderful weekend," he said. "Perhaps you'd like to go out to the country. There's a splendid inn about twenty miles of here, outside of Alexandria. But," he said, changing his tone, "you should have let me know you were coming. It's just a matter of wild luck that I'm free. There was a conference I was supposed to go to in New York tomorrow, but it's been cancelled." He added more gently, "But I've always liked surprises." At length he stopped talking. He looked at her and for the first time noticed that she was nervous and pale. Her eyes looked huge, even larger than they did in the exaggerated pictures of her in the magazines and on the screen. He noticed that she had not answered him, had not responded to any of his banter, or his comments. She had just been sitting there, clinging tightly to his hand and letting him talk.

"What is it, darling? Is anything the matter? You look upset."

She rose and crossed the room quickly to stare out the window. He followed her, put his hands on her shoulders, and turned her around to face him. He said gently, "Whatever it is, it can't be that bad."

She burst into tears and buried her head in his shoulder. They stood there together for a long time as he gently patted her back and waited for her crying to exhaust itself. Then he led her back to the sofa and they sat down. He waited, unwilling to push her, and knowing that she would come to it in her own good time.

"Richard," she finally said, "do you love me?"

"More than anything," he said fervently. "You know I do."

"If I asked you to do something for me, and I didn't tell you why, would you do it?"

"I can't think of anything I wouldn't do for you, Jill," he replied. "You mean more to me than I could ever tell you."

"You wouldn't ask me why?" she pressed. "You'd just do it?"

"Darling, what's wrong? What is it?"

She hesitated. She had not been able to get that initial agreement, the promise that he would do anything, without asking any questions. But then that was a child's dream, a fantasy. Even if he had promised—which he hadn't—he would have had to break the promise. And his very refusal to grant her the impossible terms for which she had asked was, in a curious way, reassuring.

"Would you call off your campaign against Irv Kane?"

"Would I what?"

"Would you leave him out of it? Leave him alone?"

He got up abruptly from the sofa where they had been sitting together and walked back and forth.

"Call off the whole thing? Or just the thing with Kane?"

"With Kane," she said.

He looked at her for a long time, and then started to pace again. "Is that why you came to Washington?" he asked. "To ask me that?"

"Yes," she said.

"I see."

"Do you?"

"Well, yes, I think so. I mean, I may not see it all, but I see that it's important."

"Nothing has ever been so important to me."

"Nothing?" he asked, raising his eyebrows a little.

"Important to us."

"Oh?"

"Believe me."

"Oh, I believe you. But why? What's happened?"

"Because—because he isn't a pornographer. He doesn't belong with those other men you're investigating."

"You didn't come all the way from the coast to tell me that. What has Kane to do with you?"

"Nothing. Not a thing, now."

"But once he did, is that right?"

"What are you doing," she asked, "cross-examining me?"

"Just asking," he said.

"Do you have to? Couldn't you just—trust me? Believe me? It'd be so much better if you could . . ."

"If I could, I would," he said, "but I'm not just Richard Patterson in this, and you know that. As Richard Patterson, the man who loves you, I would do anything I could for you. Just because you asked me to do it. But I'm also the Attorney General of the United States, and that Richard Patterson can't just stop a thing like this for no reason at all. I don't even say 'wouldn't' but 'can't.' I'm not my own man. I'm a member of the President's cabinet. I'm the head of an executive department. I just can't turn these things off and on like water in a spigot. I wish it were that simple."

"I wish it were, too."

"Come on, now. Nothing can be that bad!"

"It's bad."

"I can take it," he said, forcing a smile. "Come on, try me. Have a little faith and belief and confidence in me, why don't you? You're trying to carry too much of the burden alone."

"Can you help me?" she asked, half pleading and half challenging.

"I don't know. I can try."

"Can you call off the thing with Kane? Divert it?"

"I don't know. I can try. But tell me why, Jill. You've got to tell me why you're asking. You've got to trust me . . ."

"Yes, I guess I do," she began. "It's—oh, it's so awful."

"Knowing that you're unhappy is awful. And not knowing why is as awful as anything I can think of."

"It's something that—that Kane knows about me. That he's threatened to use . . ."

"Blackmail, you mean?"

"Something like that."

"Oh, God," he said. He shook his head. "I wish we had the setup they have in England. There you can bring a man up on a blackmail charge and no one would ever have to know either that you brought the charge or what it was that he was blackmailing you with. We should have that, but we don't."

Then, having provided the general remark for a change of

mood and a momentary respite, he returned to the more specific question. "Well, what is it?"

"That's the tough one, isn't it?" she said, as if she were not really there, but commenting on the scene. Or, it was as if neither of them were really there, but were up in some gallery together, watching this melodrama. No, that was only what she wished, what she wanted.

"Well? You've got to tell me. You might as well get it over with, huh?"

She hesitated. He turned her face gently by holding her chin between his thumb and forefinger.

"Nothing is that bad," he repeated. "You know I love you, and you know I want to marry you. And I'll do anything I can to help you."

"Yes," she said, "I know."

"Then it's easy, isn't it? Tell me."

And she did. She told him. She had thought that it would be enough just to tell him about the tape Kane had made, and that it wouldn't be so bad that way. After all, the idea that she had got laid wasn't so unspeakable as the fact that it had been before a camera, and the blame for the camera was all Kane's—who had installed the hidden machines, and operated them, and now was using the tape to blackmail her. But it wasn't enough. Patterson was, after all, a lawyer, and with the relentlessness of a seasoned trial attorney he kept at her, wanting to know exactly what had been shown on the tapes, and who her partner had been.

"What difference does that make?" she wanted to know.

"I don't know. You tell me."

"It doesn't."

"Then tell me. Who was it? Was it one man or more than one?"

"More."

"How many?"

"What's the point? Two? Two thousand? What difference could it possibly make?"

"It could make a difference to me."

"But if you say that, then he's won. Don't you see? Irv Kane has won, and I've lost. We've lost."

"Two? Three?"

"Four."

"One at a time, or all at once?"

"One at a time. Jesus, what do you take me for?"

"Look, I've got to know. If I decide to go ahead and fight this thing, nail him, then I've got to know what he's going to throw at me. At us."

"But I don't want you to fight him. I want you to let him alone. Drop it. Don't you understand? All that you can get out of this is shame and disgust."

"We've been skating close to that already, haven't we?"

"Have we?" she asked. "Look, it was a long time ago."

"I know that."

"It's a crummy business. It's a tough life."

"I know that too."

"You don't go to movie-star school the way you go to Harvard Law School. They don't have exams, and a whole lot of offers from the studios for top graduates. You claw your way up. Or crawl."

"Or whatever."

"Yes! Or whatever."

"All right," he said. "Now what else was on the tape?"

"I've told you what was on the tape."

"Everything?"

"Yes," she said. And then, having gone this far, she decided that it could make no difference, that she might as well go the rest of the way, and tell it all, leaving it to him to take it or not take it as best he could. If it was another test that she was rigging for him, as Dr. Parker would of course say, well then, so be it. Let it be a test. And good luck. "No," she said.

"What else was there?"

And she told him about the bet, and about Inge Peterson, and the contest, and how all that was on the tape, too.

She finished, and waited for his reaction. What would the courtroom wonder do now, she asked herself. He had worked her the way he would have worked a witness in the box. And had got her to collapse and spill it all. Very nice, dramatic little operation it had been, too. And now? What did the scenario call for? Was she to collapse into tears and let him comfort her, and make better? It was odd that she felt herself resenting the way he had treated her. After all, she had been the one who had brought him the huge pile of shit to eat. And . . .

But she noticed, suddenly, that he was sitting there, just sitting there, without saying anything, without moving, just sitting there, holding his head in his hands.

He had broken. After all that bullying, he had been the one who had broken. And the realization of that was worse than if he had stood up and slapped her. If he had beaten the hell out of her, it would have been better than this. But he was just sitting there.

She waited. She waited a very long time. And then he picked his head up, looked at her, and said, very softly, "Whore!"

"Thanks," she said.

"You whore!"

"Thanks a lot," she said.

She got up, went over to the bar, and poured herself a drink. Just straight whiskey. Then she poured one for him, and brought it over to him. He took it, without saying anything, dazed, the way a patient in a hospital takes his medicine from a nurse.

"What does he want?"

"He wants you to leave him alone."

"No," he said. "No, not for anything!"

"If you don't, he'll start sending out copies of those tapes."

"He— But how could you do a thing like that? How—how could the studio let you do a thing like that?"

"I told you, I didn't know he had that damned machine going. I didn't know he had the machine at all. And the studio didn't give a damn about me six years ago. I didn't give a damn about me. Not until I met you. I didn't care what happened to me. And I'm a different person now. You've made me a different person. Don't you understand that? That was all a long time ago!"

She wanted to touch him, but she was afraid to. She was afraid. And that was probably the worst thing that had happened.

"Richard," she said, "don't you understand? I am what you've made me."

He looked up at her. "What a hell of a position you've put me into."

"I know. I'm sorry."

"So am I," he said. "I mean, I love you, and I wanted to marry you . . ."

He went on. There was an entire diatribe, a long lecture that she didn't hear. It was like watching somebody talk in one of those old, silent, absurd movies. She had been with him, listening to him, understanding him, and then, suddenly, that one word, or not really the word so much as the tense of the word, had changed everything. "Wanted" was what he had said. And the rest of it was all talk, and for what she heard of it, it could have been in some foreign language that she'd never even heard of—Patagonian or Sardinopalian or High Swabian. The jaw moved, and the lips, and the tongue flapped up and down, and sounds came out. And then sounds stopped coming out. Apparently he had finished.

She walked back to the sofa, sat down, and buried her face in her hands. "Richard, what can I say? I'm sorry. If I had known then that I would meet you, that we would love each other, that all this was possible—of course, I'd never have done it. But then I was just drifting and I didn't care about anything."

"You were drifting without brains," he said, almost snarling as he turned toward her. "How the hell could you be so stupid?" And again, out of a rage that was not only directed at her but at himself, too, seeing his plans and his dreams dissolving, he came over and shook her. "How could you be so dumb?"

She went limp as he stood there, holding her upper arms in his steel grip, and he finally flung her back on the sofa.

"I'll call you tomorrow and see what we can salvage from this mess—but don't expect me to be very helpful. And I'm not letting up on Kane. If anything, he's a filthier pig than I thought, and he deserves anything we can dish out to him. What I'd really like to do is string him up by the balls." He paused. "I haven't decided yet what I'd like to do to you." He walked out and slammed the door behind him.

She longed for the release of tears, but they were all gone. All she could do was sit there, numbly, realizing that her life had crashed around her. All her hopes, all her dreams, all her love for Richard was as nothing now. The only thing in her life that had any meaning, and reality, was destroyed. She was nothing, but she was not the nothing she had been years before. Now she *knew* Richard's assessment of her as nothing better than a two-bit whore. What was there for her to do? Who was there? She could call the studio, she could get a press agent who would pat her hand and give her drinks, but what friends had she? She could pour all of it out into the uncomprehending ears of Bonita—but that was all. During the past year she had focused all her emotions, all her capacities for both love and friendship on Richard. And he was gone.

There was someone, she remembered. She went into the bedroom and dialed a number—the number of her psychiatrist in Beverly Hills. The phone was picked up and she heard a metallic voice say, "Dr. Parker is in Hawaii. He will be back on the twenty-fourth. If you need help immediately, please call Dr. Meyer Leichter at Crestview 2-1414." Click.

So there was no one. Not even Dr. Parker, who had pulled her across chasms of despair before. She curled up on the bed, holding her knees and rocking herself, suddenly chilled and empty. Finally she realized what she could do to spare Richard humiliation, to spare him the embarrassment of having his love for her smeared and sullied by Kane and his tape. Not only that, it would be a way of insuring that Kane would suffer, too. She could save the man she loved and destroy the man who had destroyed her. It was all so simple, so easy, so direct, now that she had thought of it. Lots of people had died for lots stupider reasons than this.

She got up from the bed and went to the small traveling case on the dresser. She took out two Miltowns, gulped them down without any water, and lay down on the bed, waiting for them to take effect.

After a while she felt relaxed, neither high nor low, but slightly floaty. She got up, went back to the case, and took out the small, curved razor that she used for shaving her legs. She turned the handle, opened it, and extracted the Wilkinson Sword razor blade. She went into the bathroom and filled the tub with hot water. Then she took off her clothes and surveyed herself in the full-length mirror for a few minutes. It was, she decided, a good body. She wished that she had done better with it. She felt sorry for it. All the organs there, working away, not knowing what was going to happen to them in a matter of moments.

She walked back into the bedroom for a moment, looked at the phone, and wished that she could call Richard—just to talk with him a little. But, no, that was impossible, wasn't it? Which was sad. Very, very sad. She sighed, and went into the bathroom. It didn't make any difference anyway. There was nothing she had to say to him that her last gesture would not say with more force and clarity. He would know now, finally, how very much she had loved him. And he would know what he had to do.

She got into the tub, picked up the gray sliver of steel, and quickly, with only a short gasp at each of the two strokes, slit the veins in her wrists. The pain was over quickly, and she lay back, watching the bath water turn pink before her vision blurred and she slipped under the water.

Richard Patterson left the bar where he had been sitting for several hours drinking. He walked unsteadily from the table where he had been drinking George Dickel in double shots all evening. He had been an ass, he told himself. At his age, in his fifties, what the hell was he interested in. Fame? Glory? Immortality? Jill loved him, and she needed him, and he had let her down. Now he didn't care whether she had posed for every stag movie ever made, she was his girl and he loved her. And her love was something he believed in. She was right. What she had been six years before was not what she was now. If he never made the Supreme Court, if he never made anything, if he had Jill with him, life would be joyful for the twenty or twenty-five years they had left. And after that, what the hell difference did it make? He had got his name in the World Almanac forever, in the list of Attorneys General, so what difference did it make whether he was on that page, or the one that listed the Supreme Court Justices? He would be dead anyway. Immortality didn't keep you very warm.

He paid his tab and left the bar, waving away the cabbie in front. He decided he needed fresh air to clear his head. He would go back to the hotel and tell her how sorry he was. He would do anything she wanted—even let that slimy bastard go. He didn't care. If that would make her happy, okay. And if she could stand it, they would ride out the tape. He'd go after Kane and then resign. They could keep their heads high no matter what he did with the tape, and no matter to whom he showed it.

He walked along the quiet streets back to the hotel, thinking of Jill and feeling for the first time in months very good. Really good. Younger, freer, more himself.

When he got back to the hotel he noticed two squad cars parked discreetly across the street. But they did not interest him. He assumed they were an escort for some foreign dignitary staying at the hotel. He walked through the revolving doors and was immediately conscious of some sort of muted excitement in the lobby that communicated itself to him in an almost psychic way. There was a tension in the atmosphere, almost an electric charge as if on a dry day the carpet was giving off sparks of static electricity. Emotionally, psychically, it was that kind of dry day. He decided to go back to his apartment, wash his face and then go to her suite and tell her what he had decided, and to apologize to her and beg her to accept his love.

In the elevator, going to his floor, he said, without really caring, "Something seems to be up, Max. What's going on?"

"Oh, Mr. Patterson," the operator answered. "It's really wild. That movie star, you know, Jill Jefferson, the gorgeous one, they just found her dead in the bathtub. She killed herself, I heard. Blood all over everything. I'm not supposed to say anything," he added, "but seeing as it's you . . ."

Patterson felt as if he had been kicked in the stomach.

The elevator stopped at his floor, and he stood there for a moment.

"Something the matter, sir? Don't you feel well?" the operator asked.

"No, that's all right." And he left the elevator, walking like a zombie.

He staggered into his apartment, unaware of the tears that were streaming down his cheeks, and flung himself on the floor.

The racket of the rotors subsided, and Irv Kane emerged from the helicopter that had brought him from Logan to the island. Nina waved, and he waved back.

"Hey, what a hell of a nice thing to do!" Irv exclaimed as soon as he was close enough to Nina to talk. "Damned fine of you!"

"My pleasure," she answered. "Welcome back. How was the trip?"

"Just fine. That new advertising sales office in San Francisco is all set up. Better than I'd hoped. Really fine looking. And I stopped off in Evanston to see the printing plant and check the plans for the telex system. In a couple of months we'll be able to supervise the whole printing operation from right here! It's all fine!"

"Good," Nina said. "Glad to hear it."

"Everything okay back here?"

"Just fine. Bud has the flu, but he'll be all right."

"Oh?"

"He thinks it's one of those twenty-four-hour things. He's a little better today. Still wobbly, but better."

"Good."

They walked toward the main entrance to Tomcat House. Nina was puzzled by any number of things, none of which was important enough or even definite enough to be worrisome, but still had her straining as if to hear or to see something just beyond the threshold of perception. Why had Bud asked her to come out to meet Irv, and why had he told her to lie for him and to say that he was sick? And what was the point of her telling Irv about Jill Jefferson's suicide? Bud had been very mysterious indeed, carefully instructing her to mention that unfortunate but irrelevant news item. It was irrelevant, wasn't it? It had to be. What could that have to do with anything? Irv had gone to San Francisco and to Evanston. And, in Washington, the movie star had killed herself. Still, the tone of Bud's request had been serious, and oddly sympathetic. The way he had said, "Irv will want to have somebody around. And not me. So it had better be you. And . . . Well, you'll see." And he had refused to say anything further about it.

They went on into the house, and immediately Irv kicked off his shoes and took off his socks. He wiggled his toes and announced that it was good to be home.

"Any problems with anything?" he asked. "The photographs came in on 'The New Zeal in New Zealand'?"

"They're in. And they're fine," she answered. "No, there aren't any problems. Except . . ."

"Yes?"

"Well, Bud wanted me to ask you if you'd seen the papers."

"No, I haven't. Why?"

"The story about Jill Jefferson."

"What about her?"

"She's dead. Killed herself."

"Oh, my God!"

"Did you know her?"

"Yes," Irv said. "I knew her. Oh, Jesus! Get me a drink, would you?"

"Scotch? Bourbon?" she asked. "What?"

"Anything. I don't care. But strong. And soon!"

She poured a large Scotch into a rocks glass and brought it to him.

"What is it? What's the matter, Irv?"

He did not answer. He took a large swallow of the whiskey and exhaled audibly.

"What does her death have to do with you?"

"Everything!"

"What are you talking about?"

He sat there silently, and she was reluctant to press him. She could wait. He seemed to be formulating something, to be hunting for some way of putting it. His brow was deeply furrowed, and every now and then his head would shake slightly from side to side, in negation—but of what thought or what formulation she had no idea. At last he looked up at her and asked her a question that surprised her.

"Do you think *Tomcat* is a good thing?"

"Yes, of course."

"I mean, that it is useful and helpful? That it helps people to get over some of their hang-ups and problems about sex and about themselves?"

"Yes, I do."

"Because that's the point, isn't it? I mean, sure, we may make money. But so do doctors, don't they? And lawyers, and psychiatrists! There's nothing wrong with making money."

"No," she said.

"But we're helping people. My God, they're so fucked up out there, they don't know whether they're coming or going. It's awful. Do you know what I cut out of the paper last month? I cut out a story about a kid in Oregon who was so strung out with guilt feelings about his sexual urges that he castrated himself! Can you imagine? I mean, our crazy society is in trouble. And if *Tomcat* can help people, even if only a little bit, reassure them, teach them how to enjoy themselves, or to be comfortable with themselves, then it's a good thing, isn't it?"

"Yes, Irv, of course it is," Nina answered. "But what brings all this on?"

"I just can't figure it. It's a lousy world. You play it straight, and you lose. You play it crooked, and you still lose. And the whole point of the game is to do something that's worth doing, that's worth while, that's needed!"

"Yes, it is needed, but—but what is it? What's the trouble?"

"What isn't the trouble? I stopped in Evanston to see the printing plant, you know, and I called Indianapolis. To talk to my ex-wife."

"Oh?"

"I wanted to arrange for Karyn's visit. I mean, I haven't seen my own daughter in two years, except for six hours once. And I've got the right to see her. And Cal, my ex-wife, was going on about what a terrible thing the magazine was, and what a terrible influence I was being, and how she hated to have Karyn come to this den of iniquity here . . ."

"And that's upset you?"

"That . . . And something worse, much worse. It all seems to be falling in on me, all at once."

"What does?"

He sat there for a while, thinking again, not saying anything. And then, instead of answering her question, he reached out, took her hand, pulled her down beside him, and held her in his arms. Or, no, it wasn't quite that, either. The motions were the same, and the result was the same, but from the moment she put her arms around him, responding to his gesture, it was somehow perfectly clear that it was he who was seeking comfort and even shelter in her arms, for he did not seem to be making any sexual overtures at all. He laid his head upon her shoulder and clutched her, and she could feel the rhythm of his breathing and the weight of his head, and she patted the back of his head and stroked his hair, feeling at the same time entirely mystified and yet happy to be of some use and of some comfort to him. Whatever it was, it was bad.

Then he sat up and said, "I don't know what's the matter with me. Tired, I guess. Yes, that must be it. I must be tired."

It was an obvious retreating back into himself, a face-saving manner of disengagement. Or was it an excuse for not pursuing the moment, taking it from what it had been to something more, upstairs, perhaps, in his private quarters? Or maybe it was both.

As gracefully as she could, she stood up, went to the bar, and poured herself a dollop of Scotch. She had done nothing wrong, had not even had the opportunity to mess anything up. But still she felt a certain edginess, an embarrassment, and a sadness that that moment was all there was going to be. He had not been able to confide in her, to tell her what the matter was, nor had he been able—or willing—to take other kinds of wordless comfort from her. She downed the Scotch.

"Why don't you take a nap for a few hours, then?" she suggested, taking her cue from him.

"Yes, I think I will. That's a good idea."

"You'll be all right?"

"Sure. A little rest and I'll be fine."

"I'm sorry to hear about—your argument with your ex-wife."

"Well, those things happen, I guess."

"I guess they do," she said.

He did not answer.

"Well, I'll get on back to the office, then."

"Okay," he said. "And . . . thanks for coming over."

"Any time."

"With better news, I hope."

"I hope so, too," she said, not at all sure what he was talking about.

Feeling thoroughly uncomfortable, she left him.

Irv Kane went upstairs to shower. He was not going to think about it. Not yet. The whole idea of Jill Jefferson's suicide was too monstrous, too awful . . . grotesque! People only did that in fiction. They didn't really kill themselves. Certainly not this way, for spite. And that's what it had been. Had to have been! It was the only way she could have managed to turn the tables on him so efficiently and so finally. But not now. He wouldn't think about it now. Because it was unpleasant, and useless—especially useless. It would only be later, when he was calmer, and rested, that it would even be worth bringing up for attention and for thought. But not now. The news was still too fresh, and he was too stunned. And tired. Or, no, he wasn't tired. He had only said that to Nina, to get rid of her. But it was funny, because, having said it, he had started to feel it. Very peculiar.

Anyway, it had worked. He had got Nina out of the way. Because she didn't know, and he didn't want to tell her. And that was interesting. It was as if he had been afraid that she would just accept the information that he had caused Jill Jefferson's suicide—had practically killed her—as if it were nothing. And he didn't want that. On the other hand, he didn't want her to disapprove, either. It was very strange, but somehow important. And that wasn't good. Was he getting involved with her emotionally? No, he didn't think so. He wouldn't allow it.

He thought of that moment, downstairs, when he had reached out to her for comfort and she had been willing to offer it. And it hadn't been right, hadn't felt right. Not to him, anyway. And not to her, either, he supposed. But, still, he wondered about her. He wondered whether she had a lover. He supposed so. What sort of guy would it be? But he put that out of his mind. What difference did it make to him, anyway? Or did it make a difference? He was annoyed to find himself thinking about her in this way. It was unfair, both to her and to himself. If he didn't want her that way, and he didn't—or didn't think he did—then whatever she did on her own time was her own business. He even wondered whether he could get her if he wanted her. Yes? Probably. But the hell with it! No, that was ridiculous.

It was better, though, than thinking about Jill Jefferson. And that was ridiculous, too, but horrible. Like the fellow in the museum of the New York City Morgue who had urinated on the third rail of a subway, and had been electrocuted by the current running up the stream. They had the charred penis in a bottle, there, on display. Funny and horrible. And ridiculous. And all the more awful and horrible for that.

He stepped out of the shower, grabbed the hooded terry-cloth bathrobe from the heated towel rack, and slipped it on. He had to do something. Had to keep occupied and busy. That was the trick. If he could manage to stay busy enough, he wouldn't be able to think at all.

He crossed the room and sat down at the large marble table that served as a desk. He flipped open a metal file of color transparencies, shoving the tray into the feeder for the viewer. Rapidly, he started pressing the button that operated the feeder so that candidates for Kalendar Kitty appeared in the lens, one after another. He looked at each of them briefly but critically, observing that this one was too low slung in the bosom, this one too broad in the hips, this one too short in the legs, this one fine in the body but sluttish looking in the face, and this one—there was nothing the matter with the one in the lens now. She was not bad at all.

He made a note of the number in the upper right hand corner of the slide and continued with his viewing.

He spent perhaps twenty minutes going through the hundred shots of the hundred different girls in the slide file, and then, with a list of five possibles, he got up, stretched, took off the terry robe, and lay down on the linen-covered Barcalounger. He reached for the button, turned the switch, and gave himself over to the steady vibrations of the chair.

It was difficult, nevertheless, for Kane to clear his mind entirely so he could take the greatest possible advantage from the physical pleasure and stimulation of the vibrating chair. It was just so damned unfair. He hadn't wanted it to happen this way. He hadn't wanted her to kill herself! It was so stupid doing a thing like that. It hadn't been his fault that she'd gone down for the four guys in Tomcat House six years ago. She'd done that on her own hook. And he hadn't intended to use the tapes at the time he'd made them. They'd been made in fun, and for his own enjoyment. It was only circumstances that had put him into a position where he'd been able to use them, where it had been irresistible. . . . Still, he felt more terrible than he had ever felt in his life. No, he felt worse when Buchanan was killed. But this was the next worst. And Patterson would be down on him now, in spades. But he would deal with that later.

Right now, he was—what? Hungry? No, he wasn't hungry, nor thirsty, nor eager to talk to anyone. But, really, neither did he want to be alone. He switched the vibrator off, got up, and padded naked across the room to the console, where he began adjusting knobs and throwing switches. One after another, rooms in the house flashed onto the screen of the monitor. Cameras, the television cameras hidden behind one-way mirrors, louvered ceilings, or in air-conditioning vents, probed the bedrooms, the common rooms, the bathrooms, so that he could look into any of them at any time of the day or night. But the public rooms were empty, and though the private apartments were occupied, nothing was going on. The reporter from *The Manhattanite* was taking a nap. The novelist who had come to Tomcat House to discuss a possible biography of Kane was sitting in his undershorts, typing. The nightclub entertainer who was visiting as Kane's guest was sitting in a chair, watching television and working over a racing form.

There were also half a dozen girls in residence. Four of them were playing bridge. He turned on the audio. They were talking about the forthcoming marriage of one of their friends. It was disappointing, but, then, it was not a very good time of the day.

Still, even if this particular moment had not yielded anything particularly interesting or amusing, the activity itself was vastly reassuring to Kane. The feeling of power he got from being able to spy on anyone in Tomcat House, to watch what they were doing, to listen to them talking, and without their knowing about it, raised him from the depression in which he had been floundering helplessly. He turned another switch and the machine went dark. Then he got up, went across the room to the wall safe, and twirled the dial on the Mosler lock. The door came open, and he pulled out a sixteen-inch reel of television tape. He brought it back to the console, put it on the machine, and threw the switches. He sat back to watch as his own room flashed onto the screen of the monitor. He saw himself lying on the lounger behind him, and he saw Bambi lie down beside him. With a kind of abstracted attention, he watched the image of himself lying there while Bambi stroked him, kissed him, and then rubbed her body against his. He watched his own growing tumescence, and noted, with particular satisfaction, the expression he had not caught at the time but which he now saw, on the tape, on Bambi's face. It was something that combined pride and relief at having been successful in arousing him.

She had known the score all right, and she had played the game pretty well, and for a long time. She had also been a sweet kid. He wondered where she was now.

He watched, more attentive now, as the Kane on the screen responded to Bambi's attentions. He saw himself roll over, mount the girl, and then, lying there on her and in her, reach down to turn the vibrator switch on.

In a curious way, from this point on, the tape was boring. There was nothing more to watch, really, except his hand going down from time to time to turn the knob that increased the strength and frequency of the vibrations of the chair. Out of sheer restlessness he turned the machine off, rewound the tape, and started it again, but this time he ran the tape at triple speed, watching with amusement as the semispasmodic gestures unfolded at an incredible rate. This time, Bambi ran into the room, ripped her clothes off in a frenzy, kissed him with a demoniac fury, stroked him as if her life depended upon it, and, in response, his penis shot up like a jack-in-the-box. He jumped on her like a Keystone Kop in a comedy chase. It was funny, but, in an odd way, it was arousing, too. That was the way it ought to be done sometimes, he thought. Brisk and efficient.

He picked up the phone and dialed 2. He waited for a moment as the phone rang in Suzanne's room.

"Yes?" she asked.

"Irv," he said.

"Hi!"

"Come on up, why don't you?"

"Sure," she said. "Be right there."

He hung the phone up and pushed the button that activated the elevator. Then he rewound the tape, took the reel off the machine, and returned it to the safe. He found another reel, Jill Jefferson's reel, and put it on.

With a kind of glum detachment, he watched her go through her tricks, the thought occurring to him as a surrealistic accompaniment that this was at the center of her life. She hadn't known it at the time, but this evening, these four men, these few hours of sexual athleticism were at the heart of her whole experience, and would someday sum up the whole force and substance of her life. It was something that not even Patterson could understand, nor she, any more—because she was dead, now, wasn't she? It was only he, Irvin Kane, who knew, who understood, who could look down and see it all, the way God could . . .

He snorted, and took the tape off. But the Olympian feeling continued as he put on another reel and watched, with a curious blend of amusement and physical excitement, the antics of a visiting bishop as he ran into his bedroom, ripped his clerical clothing off, ripped the costume off his Kitty Kompanion, and, with a speed and aggressiveness that would have been impressive in the most incredible sex maniac, proceed to bang the girl.

There was a wonderful cartoon quality to it all. It was as if Kane was watching Mickey Mouse making love to Minnie Mouse, and that cartoon aspect, which brought to mind in some oblique way the old Flash Gordon comic books he had seen in the Army, struck him as being the last word in the purity of sexuality. There was something marvelously dehumanized about it. It was reduced to its ultimate idea, without any of the awkwardness, the fumbling, the complications of personality, the *longueurs* of "relationships." It was brisk, and, in a surrealistic but still convincing way, all so clean!

The elevator door opened, and Susie came in. She was wearing a pair of electric blue stretch pants and a matching cashmere sweater. She came over to Irv, put her arms around him, and pressed her face against the back of his neck.

"Hi, honey! If I'd known it was going to be a party, I could have taken my clothes off in the elevator," she said.

"You don't have to bother," he answered, without taking his eyes from the screen.

"I don't?" she asked, puzzled.

"No," he said. "Just get down there and get started."

There was a pause, during which she was reacting, trying to decide if it was a joke or if he meant it seriously. Or, if it was serious, trying to decide whether she was going to take offense. But he was not paying attention to her at all. His attention was still fixed on the speeded-up monitor, where, now, a New York publisher was putting his glasses on the night table, ripping off his tweeds, and leaping onto his Kitty like a Pony Express rider behind schedule.

"That's not very friendly," she pouted.

He took his eyes from the monitor, looked at her, flashed a quick smile, and said, "Indulge me, baby, huh?"

He looked back at the screen and, in a moment, felt the girl's lips close upon him.

But it was out of synch. He could not expect her to perform at the rate of the performers on the monitor. That would not have been humanly possible. Instead, and with some reluctance, he turned the knob and slowed down the publisher's cavortings to a normal rhythm. He watched the plump white buttocks plunge.

He felt himself approach his own climax.

He turned the audio knob, and he heard the publisher exclaim, "Oh, that'th terrific! That'th nithe!"

He smiled, but his smile faded instantly. He was close now, and he looked down at the girl's face between his legs and, realizing the absurd poignance of her situation, allowed himself to feel some connection with her.

"Oh, that's terrific," he said, mimicking the publisher. "That's nice," he said. He stroked her hair, and then, suddenly, with both hands, he clutched her head hard.

After she had left, he took the tape off the machine, and replaced it with the new tape they had just made.

He threw the switch and watched on the screen as Susie came in from the elevator. He leaned back and watched the whole scene again, first at the regular and then at the fast speed, smiled to himself, and went back to the marble desk.

It took only a couple of minutes for him to pick the Kalendar Kitty from the five possibles. He also made a note to himself to get Susie a present.

And Jill Jefferson? She, he decided, had been a nut.

7

Anne Ryder looked up as Richard Patterson strode past her desk and into his office. She did not mind that he had not said "Good morning," or even that he had not said "Good morning" to her for the preceding three weeks. She was thinking only of the suffering of the man, and trying to find some way of helping him. He needed help. She could see that. If only he had been one of those boisterous types who are able to let off steam when they have to, or get drunk or get into a fight. But he was not like that at all. He bottled it all up. There were dark circles under his eyes, and deep lines that marked his brow. There were dark circles under Anne Ryder's eyes, too, for that matter, because she had been doing the only thing she could think of doing for him, the only thing he had asked of her—and the impossibly long hours of drudgery he put in, trying to lose himself in the sheer volume and intensity of work, had taken its toll of both of them. She was tired, bone tired. But she would rest up on the weekend. He would take his briefcase home with him, work, read, write, read some more, drive himself until he dropped into the oblivion of exhaustion. The lips showed it. That white face, and the thin, compressed line of the mouth gave it all away. But there was no reasonable way for her to extend sympathy, for her to show any interest in his suffering, for her to make any gesture—except to stay with him, typing and taking dictation on through the evening and into the middle of the night. One session had gone until two-thirty in the morning.

Patterson had broken out the George Dickel, and had sipped his way through the last few hours of that marathon session, but with no visible effect whatever. He had offered her a drink, which of course, she had declined. She would have collapsed at that late hour, and with that kind of fatigue waiting to combine with the alcohol. But that was just what he wanted for himself. To collapse. To break down. To stop thinking and feeling and hurting.

She sighed, picked up the mail she had sorted for him, and brought it in to him.

"Thank you, Anne," he said, and managed a wan smile.

She nodded, but he was already flipping through the letters, and she didn't want to intrude upon him, even with a simple "You're welcome." She turned to leave, but he surprised her by asking her for some coffee.

"Certainly, Mr. Patterson," she said. "I'll get it right away."

He had not had coffee in the office since that awful day. And she was hopeful about his asking for it now. Perhaps he was getting over it. Perhaps he had been right, and the only thing for him was what he had done—to work himself to exhaustion until the hurt began to fade.

She looked back at him before she left the room. It was just a glance, just a quick look, but it was enough. He didn't look the way an emotional convalescent ought to look. He was worse, rather than better. There was an intensity about his carriage, even in the chair, that wasn't quite right, that didn't jibe with the request for coffee.

But she had no time to contemplate. He had asked for coffee and coffee he would have. She went off to brew some in the electric percolator.

The coffee was still brewing when the buzzer sounded on her phone.

"Would you get me Tyler, please?" he asked.

"Yes, Mr. Patterson."

She dialed Tyler's secretary, announced that Mr. Patterson was calling, and, when Tyler was on the line, buzzed back for him to pick up the phone. She was about to hang up, but she paused. And then, because she had paused, brought the phone back to her ear. It was the first time in twenty years of government service that she had done such a thing. But she had a feeling, an entirely unfounded but persistent hunch, that this call had something to do with this noticeable variation in his mood. And it was not a bad kind of spying. Her only motive was her concern for him, her eagerness to be helpful somehow. She knew, of course, that she could not have explained this to anyone, could hardly explain it reasonably to herself, but there it was, an impulse, a need to do it, this once. And she left the button unpressed, and the phone she glued to her ear.

The call, however, was not informative. It was a curiously laconic exchange.

"Tyler, this is Patterson."

"Yes, sir. What can I do for you?"

"I'd like to stop by and see you this morning, if I may. It's important that I speak with you."

"Certainly," Tyler said. "My time is always at your disposal. Whenever you want to come over, I'll be waiting to see you."

"Thank you," Patterson said. "Thank you very much. I'll be there in perhaps twenty minutes."

And he hung up.

Miss Ryder was disappointed. The adrenalin was still coursing through her bloodstream from the act of eavesdropping. She knew that the call had been as important as she had guessed. Perhaps even more important. It was not exactly Mr. Patterson's habit to go over to see Tyler, to leave his own office and go to Tyler's. It was very strange. But she was outside it all, unable to penetrate into the center of this new business any more than she had been able to penetrate into the mind or heart of her agonized superior. She had the feeling, suddenly, of terrible uselessness. Irrelevance and uselessness.

Rather wearily, she got up, went back to the coffee maker, poured a cup for Mr. Patterson, and brought it in.

"Thank you," he said. He did not even look up.

The gold point traced the lines over and over again. The long yellow legal pad was covered with the designs that were not even designs but merely doodles, random outpourings of a small unoccupied corner of a largely preoccupied mind. The patterns varied, some of them being mostly sinuous, others being angular, and still others squarish, as if they had been done not with a fountain pen on a pad but with one of those Etch-a-Sketch toys. What they all had in common, however, was a kind of inward turning. The progress of Patterson's pen point was that of a frantic insect, scurrying back over the same ground over and over again, as if in search of some morsel of food, some scent, some trace of familiar life. Or of an ant whose hill has been flattened by the heel of a passing child, and which covers the known ground over and over again, looking for one of the holes that leads down to safety and to home.

There was no end to the searching. Perhaps the end was that which Patterson himself imposed from above, looking down at the increasingly displeasing tangle of lines and abruptly blotting them out by an even heavier scratching of the pen so that, after the passage of some minutes, the entire pad was a series of ominous black blots, connected with each other by crosshatched lines. He pulled off the sheet of paper, crumpled it into a ball, and threw it in the direction of the wastebasket. It bounced off the rim, and fell between the basket and the wall. Patterson was not surprised or even disappointed. Nothing seemed to be going well for him.

He took up the pen and started a new doodle on a clean sheet of paper, but the pen started to skip. It was running dry. He considered filling it in order that he might continue, but, made aware of what he was doing by this failure of the pen, and faced with the embarrassing necessity consciously to refill the pen in order to continue this childish, mindless activity, he simply screwed the cap back onto the pen and put it down on the blotter. If there was an answer, it was not to be found in these patterns on the yellow pad. He would have to work it out for himself.

He had been scrambling around in all kinds of futile directions, had ridden one train of thought after another, and had found all of them to be inward-turning and useless. It was distasteful and depressing. Still, there was no way to get around it. It was as if the whole position he had taken, the entire code by which he had lived, had suddenly been stripped away from him. He had thought himself to be all of a piece, and was therefore all the more distressed to discover that the attractive civilized surface in him—as perhaps in all of us—was only a thin veneer.

Here he was, the Attorney General of the United States, presumably a man who should be devoting himself to the carrying out of, and even to the improvement of, our legal system, and whose actions ought to be characterized by judicial restraint. Nevertheless, in the light of this sudden personal bereavement, he found himself thrown back to a more ancient and more savage kind of law. He disapproved heartily of what he had been thinking of doing, what in fact he knew he would inevitably do, but his disapproval was not important. There was nothing else he could do that would make him feel like a lawyer, make him feel like a man. The only law that could satisfy him was the primitive law of revenge—a tooth for a tooth, an eye for an eye, and a life for a life. Or, in this case, a bug for a bug.

After all, that was what had killed her. It hadn't been that orgy so much as the fact that Irvin Kane had been eavesdropping on the orgy with that electronic equipment, and it was as if the electronic rig in Tomcat House had been a pistol Kane had held to Jill Jefferson's temple. There was nothing for Richard Patterson to do but to take up the same weapon, to fight gunfire with gunfire, and to do Kane to death.

The answer had not been so intricate or so remote and difficult to find, after all. He had, each time, been drawing it for himself on the pad. It had not been the series of tortuous lines that had been important, but the scratching out of the designs, the great heavy blots with which he had obliterated them. It would be that simple. No, there did not have to be anything involuted or subtle, but it could be as blunt as those black blots, those ideograms of revenge, or, at the very least, Rorschach blots, which, to Patterson's tired eyes, meant revenge—so that it amounted to the same thing.

The irony of it was that now, seeking the kind of revenge that

Jill deserved and that he demanded, all of the niceties of legal ethics were instantly expendable. And the ambitions he had entertained were now, after her death, unimportant and irrelevant. All he wanted was some kind of satisfaction from the world and from Irvin Kane.

His own involvement, his own inability to respond soon enough to her need, when she had expressed it to him—this was something he could not bear to think about. He tried to keep it hidden away. It was, nevertheless, the source of that final push, that extra shot of moral adrenalin that enabled him at this moment, finally, to make his move.

He had worked it all out. He had not even had to think about it consciously, but it had simply presented itself to him in a flash, as to an experienced chess player to whom suddenly a line of action will appear through the pieces on the board. There, opening up before him, the one simple, elegant combination of moves pops up to the mind's eye and leads to the inexorable mate. Patterson, having had that moment of clear vision, got up from his desk. He looked down and noticed the cup of coffee Miss Ryder had brought in. He picked it up and sipped it. It was only lukewarm, but he drained it anyway, in three large, hurried gulps. Then he went into his private lavatory, took off his coat, hung it on the hook on the inside of the door, and, pushing his cuffs up, proceded to wash his hands and face. It was a way of attaining a kind of instant calm and freshness. But it was not just that, any more than it had been just that for Pilate.

He looked at his face in the mirror. He supposed he looked tired, not that he cared all that much. He even ventured a small smile at the pretentiousness of the comparison that had suggested itself to him. He was not Pilate at all. He was one of those fellows at the gate, one of those with hollow eyes and clenched fists, shouting out, "Crucify him!"

And, by God, he would.

"Shall I call for the car?" Miss Ryder asked as he passed her desk.

"No, thanks. I feel like walking," he told her. "I should be back in an hour or so."

"Yes, sir."

He wanted the visit to be as inconspicuous as possible. He left the building, walked to the corner, and found a cruising cab. He darted into the anonymous leatherette interior and sat back.

"The FBI Building," he told the driver.

"FBI it is," the cabbie replied.

"Always a pleasure, sir," Tyler said, rising from his desk chair and coming out into the middle of the room to meet Patterson.

Always? Patterson wondered for a moment just what the hell Tyler was talking about. He had never been in this office before, though God knows it had been described to him often. He looked at Tyler's death's-head grin, which was genuine enough. And then, of course, it struck him that his very appearance here was, to Tyler, a clear indication of victory, and the welcoming comment made sense. It was winning—particularly winning in a battle with a superior—that was "always a pleasure."

With a certain degree of graciousness, which of course he could afford, Tyler escorted Patterson to the chair beside his desk. A plain straight-backed chair.

"Would you like a cup of coffee?" Tyler offered.

"No thanks, I just had some," Patterson said, and, for some reason, he was glad that it was true.

"All right, then. What can I do for you, sir?"

He was enjoying it thoroughly, Patterson realized, and he decided that that was just as well. Let him get all the fun out of it there was, and put that in the balance, too, along with the offer. Patterson was beyond caring how he tipped the scales in this encounter, just so long as he tipped them.

"I'll get right to the point," he said. "Both of us are too busy to play games."

He paused for a moment, not just for the dramatic effect, which would have been his effect, but for Tyler's sake, too. To let him have the full savor of his triumph. "I think we can do business."

"Oh?" was all that Tyler allowed himself. It was barely a question.

"Your buddy. Billingsley. I'm willing to forget him."

"I'm glad to hear that, sir," Tyler said. "I told you he was a good man. A good detective. A good citizen . . ."

"Oh, cut the crap. You know what I think of Billingsley. But I'll forget him . . ."

Patterson waited for Tyler to ask.

"And?"

"And you help me with a favor in return."

"Welcome to Washington," Tyler said, with surprising wit, for him. "What's the favor?"

"Actually, it's something that ought to appeal to you anyway. You're on the board of the Mother's League for Decent Literature. You ought to find this very congenial."

"Irvin Kane?"

Patterson had to admire the man. "Yes," he said, "Irvin Kane. I want to nail him. I want him in a jail cell sewing mailbags. I want to break up his God-damned empire. I want to destroy him."

"Not unreasonable," Tyler said.

Patterson thought for a moment, trying to decide whether Tyler meant that the objective of destroying Kane was not unreasonable, or whether he meant that he understood Patterson's motive.

"How can we help you? How would you like us to do it?"

"I don't have to tell you how I've always felt about wiretapping and bugging. It's a lousy way to get somebody. And I'd always thought I'd rather let a hundred guilty men go than become guilty myself in the way I went after them. I don't feel that way any more. I'd do anything to get that bastard. Even bugging."

"You can't use it as evidence."

"I know that. But it can give us leads. I can use it to get to his editors, to his assistants. There may be a way of getting around the 'redeeming social value' if I can get some of these people to admit that the intent was to titillate, and to arouse prurient interest. We might get a conviction that way. And that would make it tougher for all your smut peddlers."

"It could. It could at that."

"I want to know what goes on in that damned mansion of his. I want to hear every word that gets said in that house. I want to hear the toilets flush!"

The intensity with which Patterson spoke had its effect on Tyler. He enjoyed it, but he was impressed by it, too.

"If that's what you want . . . ." Tyler said.

"That's what I want. And it's what you want, too, isn't it?"

"I've expressed my views about filth merchants many times. I'm not one to defend Irvin Kane."

"And Billingsley is off the hook," Patterson repeated.

"I appreciate that," Tyler replied.

"I do think you might ask him to be a little more circumspect," Patterson suggested. "I'm not taking any moral tone about it. I can't afford to do that. Not any more. But I think it makes sense, politically."

"I agree with you entirely," Tyler said. He spoke slowly, partly for effect and partly because he was enjoying himself. "There are certain things we do—certain things we have to do—that are best done with circumspection."

"Yes," Patterson said, conceding the point, the set, the match. "Yes, I see that now."

He stood up. There was nothing left to say now. Tyler stood up, too, and walked across the room to see him out. It was done.

"I was very sorry to hear about . . . the death of . . . your friend," Tyler said.

Patterson looked at him through narrowed eyes. Was there mockery in Tyler's condolence? Just for an instant a kind of rage flickered through Patterson, but he did not show it. And he decided, in the moment of near-exhaustion that followed that burst of emotional energy, that Tyler had probably meant it straight. Why not? If Jill's death had got Tyler what he wanted, he could afford now to extend some sympathy. It could very well be sincere, Patterson decided. And, if anything, that made it even less welcome.

But what the hell! He didn't have to like Tyler. He could still think of Tyler as a sanctimonious, hypocritical, maneuvering son of a bitch! The point was to use him, to use all that twisted, repellent, egomaniacal competence for his own purposes. When you set out to shoot a man, why be particular about the gun you use?

He left Tyler's office. It was only downstairs and outside that he realized they hadn't shaken hands. He wondered whether he should have remembered to do that, but at the same time he was glad he hadn't.

A low haze, once rich and thick but now threadbare, hung over the water. Occasionally, through one of the worn places, a glint of early morning sun shone through to touch the gray surface of the harbor. There was little wind, and the water, calm and indolent, nudged the lapstrake sides of the small fishing boat with an abstract regularity. Overhead, gulls wheeled and turned, scanning the water for fish or bits of edible garbage. From time to time one of the birds would swoop down, hit the surface, and make a stab at the water's larder.

In the boat Charles Olson watched the birds, following their graceful turns with his eyes but not really thinking about them. In a curious way he and those birds had a great deal in common. The kind of scanning attention they paid the water was very like what his own job required. Sitting there in the bow, he smoked his pipe and, every now and then, twitched one of the hand lines that trailed over the sides of the boat. He shivered in the morning chill, even though he had two thick sweaters under his weather suit and a warm fisherman's cap with the earflaps down. Beside him, on the small seat, there was a pail containing a few fish jumping in futile attempts to escape, or just lying there, in terror or resignation or whatever it is that fish feel. At the end of the day, he would throw most of them back. He would, perhaps, take back a couple of them for dinner. That would make it all the more rewarding.

He was only pretending to fish, to be a fisherman. On the bottom of the boat, near his feet, under the sun-bleached tarpaulin, was the most expensive, most efficient tape recorder that Sony made, further improved by Olson's own considerable ingenuity. Under that tarp of innocence the spools turned and the tape ran and the machine recorded every sound that came out of or into the telephones of Tomcat House. With his left hand, Olson checked the hand lines for a bite. In his right hand was what looked to be an ordinary fiberglass rod, but was, in fact, an antenna. Down on the bottom of the bay, spliced into Irvin Kane's private cable, there was a small, efficient bug that transmitted up to the antenna. And in the house, transmitting to another channel on the tape, there was another bug.

Olson was cold, and hungry, too. He lifted the tarp to look at the machine, not only to check its performance but to see how much tape was left on the big spool. At the end of the reel, he would have a cup of hot coffee from the Thermos bottle. He had promised himself that reward, and the prospect of the coffee made his scanning almost avaricious. Like those gulls overhead, he was hungry, and the hunger kept him alert. It was the hunger and the pleasure he took in the intricacy of his machines, the delight he found in the sophistication of his techniques. The gulls, too, probably enjoyed their soaring and swooping, bathed in their own grace, and delighted in their flight. It would have been only some uninitiated observer from shore who could have supposed that there was anything boring about Olson's vigil, or tiresome about the gulls' search for food. The time passed easily enough, and each moment was quietly satisfying.

There were, at that early hour, few other boats out in the harbor. Half an hour earlier a tug had pulled a garbage scow out of the harbor, and now, off in the distance, he could see one other fishing boat heading out to sea. On the other side he could see the shoreline, and the erratic sparkle of sunlight on glass as the random chances of the mist played with the geometry of light. Olson was used to being alone. He spent most of his time this way, with a recorder, his reels of tape, his dials, and his microphones, monitoring the talk of one person for the benefit of another. He had learned a kind of patience from this line of work, and had developed exactly that sort of free-floating attention that could absorb in just the right way the life and the motion of the harbor.

It had long ceased to surprise him that people were willing to pay his fees—two hundred dollars a day plus such extraordinary expenses as, for instance, the rental of this boat. He had been working long enough so that he didn't question it any more. It was that kind of world. It was not his responsibility anyway. He was just a technician, and could not afford to take any interest in what the motives of his clients might be, just as he couldn't afford to pay attention to the information that his machines were gleaning. He was like one of those fishermen who never eat fish. Every night he went home to Dorchester and, after dinner at six o'clock, went down to his workshop in the cellar to tinker with his equipment, refining it, improving it, playing with it. It was his not entirely boastful joke that, if he wanted to do so, he could bug the private john of the President in the White House. Through the sewer. But of course he didn't tell people that. He had wondered, once, whether to write to the White House, but had decided against it. There was no point in calling attention to himself that way.

Not that the government didn't know about him. On this job, he had a pretty strong suspicion that Mr. Brown—the man who had called on him—was a government man. CIA, or DIA, or FBI. Not that Olson cared, one way or another. He just did what he was asked to do, collected his fee, and forgot about it. And that was a part of his value to his customers. Brown had asked him to put a tap on Irvin Kane's mansion out on the island, and he had been delighted because the technical problems were interesting. The mansion was out there in the harbor, and he had had to modify a lot of the equipment to adapt it to underwater work. Once that was done, it was the standard routine. He sat out in the boat, fishing, and living from one cup of coffee to the next, getting wet in the rain, shivering in the cold, and collecting one man's words for another man's ears. At night, his partner came out and covered for him. On the next job, his partner would take the day turn, and he'd work at night.

He looked under the tarp again. The reel was nearly finished. He took out a fresh reel from the box, got it ready, and, when the moment came, made the switch. He used the headphone for the change, just in case anything should come over during the twenty seconds or so between tapes. But there was nothing at all. There hardly ever was. Still, it was a good habit. He checked the recording levels, and then, satisfied that the machine was working perfectly, he reached down for the Thermos.

Carefully, intently—he had been waiting for this for the past forty-five minutes—he unscrewed the top of the vacuum bottle and poured the coffee into the red plastic cup. He closed the Thermos, tucked it down under the seat, and pulled out the bag of doughnuts his wife had given him as he'd left the house in the small hours of the morning. He took a bite of a doughnut and licked the powdered sugar from his lips. Then he took his first sip of the strong coffee.

It was only then that he looked up. He'd heard a sound. It was a motor. He looked around him, and saw the small Boston Whaler that was approaching. There were two men in the Whaler, probably going out to a larger boat somewhere. They didn't look like seamen. A couple of sports, Olson decided, on their way out for a good time, fishing or just sailing around and drinking. One of them waved to him. He held up the doughnut, answering their greeting.

The Whaler came on fast. What were they, crazy? Or were they out to have a look at him? Well, there was nothing he could do about it. He took another bite of his doughnut and waited.

The boat passed. It was going too fast for him to worry about any curiosity on their part about his presence out there in the harbor. But it was too close for that speed. If he'd been fishing he'd have been sore as hell. And, as it was, he was displeased. The boat continued on, receding now, but the wake it had kicked up hit Olson's boat, bobbing it, and causing him to spill some of the coffee out of the plastic cup. It hit his knee, dribbling down the rubber boot, and formed a small brown puddle next to his foot. Thanks to the boot, he hadn't been burned by the hot coffee. He was glad of that. But then he looked at the cup, now at least a third emptied. He wondered whether to refill it or not. If he did, he'd have to take less coffee each time he changed a reel for the rest of the day. No, he'd take his loss now, he decided. All he would allow himself to do was to drink the coffee that was left in the cup more slowly than usual, drawing it out for as long he could.

There was no sense brooding about it. He'd have another full cup to look forward to. In forty-two minutes or so. And after four more reels, he'd have earned himself a sandwich.

Patterson leaned back in the wooden chair and flipped the ash off the end of his cigar into a tin ashtray bearing an ad for the Tastee Tower of Pizza, We Deliver. Across the desk sat a man Patterson knew only as Mr. Brown, in the regulation dark suit with the chrome cuff links showing, and the absurd hat that made him look more like a gangster in one of the B movies of the forties than an FBI agent of the sixties.

Across the room, at a workbench, in the bright light of a hanging fixture that looked like one of the lamps over a pool table in any pool hall, Olson stood and soldered two wires together, entirely oblivious of the other two men in the room, or to the voices coming over from the speaker of the tape recorder on the desk between Patterson and Brown.

Patterson adjusted the tone control, increasing the treble. "Who was that?" he asked.

"The woman was Nina Kirby," Brown said. "The man who spoke just before her was Bud Sloat, Kane's managing editor."

"Yes, I know who he is. Where's Kane?"

"He comes on in a minute or two. You'll be able to hear him just fine. He was right next to the picture. He comes in real clear."

"The picture?"

Brown explained how the bug had been attached to the frame of the Degas—Kane's Degas, on its way back from the Boston Museum of Fine Arts, where it had appeared for a while on loan.

"I see."

"A neat job," Brown said.

"Fine," Patterson said. Actually, it was awful, but then everything about this whole operation was awful. The cheap room, the ridiculous hat on Brown's head, the whole plan of it. And yet, in a perverse way, he took a considerable satisfaction from the very sordidness of what he was doing and what he had got himself into. At the very least, it all confirmed for him the feeling that he so desperately needed—the feeling that he was, at last, doing something.

He glanced across the room at Olson, the ultimate automaton, the *1984* hero, who was all technique and no thought, soldering away. He leaned forward and strained to hear the voices. The voices mingled in a blur that was hard to follow. But then there was a silence. Kane's voice, clear and recognizable, greeted his assembled hirelings, each of whom returned the greeting. Then Kane addressed the group.

"I've asked you all here this morning for a special reason," he began. "*Tomcat* is about to strike out in a new direction, with a new project. And I'll need your help. All of us will have to pull together on this one. This could be the biggest, the most significant, the most important thing any of us have ever done in our lives. I'll be frank with you. We've done well. We've done very well. We've run an original investment of a few thousand dollars into tens of millions, and we've done it by being sophisticated, entertaining, and by being bold. We've taken a few chances, but we've been right in our guesses, and have been pretty accurate in the way we've sized up the taste and mood of our audience. Now, it'd be easy to sit back and relax. We could keep on growing, along with the population. We could just consolidate what we've already done. But we've got to the point now where we can actually make a contribution, where we can do some good. And I'd like to go in that direction.

"You all know me well enough to understand that I'm no missionary. I'm no crusader. I'm a businessman. But as a businessman, it strikes me that there is an amazing opportunity just now, a huge market to be tapped out there in America, and the right time to tap it. And we have all the resources and facilities with which to undertake the task. What I propose is simply that we undertake a new program—a program of publishing pornographic books!"

There was a pause on the tape. It was not difficult for Patterson to imagine the mood of that silence. The audacity of the idea was impressive even to him. But what was it? Some kind of joke? A put-on? Or did Kane mean it? And, if he did, what could he be thinking about? Was he a lunatic? Had he simply flipped out? Patterson could not help but smile. Kane was playing right into his hands. It was too good to be true.

In order to savor the moment, he tried to conjure up in his mind's eye the expression in the room with Kane. Shock? Excitement? Skepticism? Or blank incredulousness?

Obviously Kane was waiting for the effect of his last remark to sink in, for it seemed to Patterson an interminable time before Kane continued: "I'm perfectly serious. I think the time is right for this. The decisions of the Supreme Court have taken virtually all the teeth out of the old repressive laws by holding that any book is acceptable if it has redeeming social significance. Now most book publishers have been getting their writers to put in some kind of upbeat ending, or to include some large issue somewhere so that they can print and sell their stuff and claim that it has redeeming social significance. We can take the old classics of pornography—which are, by the way, mostly in the public domain—and get important critics and professors and psychiatrists to write introductions to them, and get the same social significance that way—"

"But, Irv, *why?*" That was the female voice. Nina Kirby, the feature editor of *Tomcat*.

"For one thing, there's the money. But for another, I think it's a good idea. I've been thinking a lot lately about pornography, and I've decided it's a good thing. It helps a lot of people out. The very old, whose lives, sexually, are mostly limited to fantasy, and the very young, who can get the same pleasurable fantasy experiences, but also need the reassurance that they aren't depraved and monstrous—those are the main readers of pornography. And with improved medical care, the population is growing enormously at both ends of the spectrum. There are more very old people and more teen-agers now than ever before, not only absolutely, but relative to the gross population."

"What about the supposed harm, or the risk of harm, that these laws were trying to prevent?" asked someone with a deliberate baritone voice. Patterson wasn't sure whether it was Bud Sloat, or perhaps Walter Randolph, the associate publisher who ran the business end of the publishing.

"I don't believe it. I just don't buy it," Kane answered. There was a pause, and then Kane continued, "In the only scientific study of this of any weight or worth, the Kinsey Institute study of sex offenders, the finding is that sex criminals tend to read pornography and erotic literature rather less than a random sampling of the population does. And in Denmark, where they have had absolute freedom of the press and where pornography is sold openly and legally, there hasn't been any significant change in the crime rate. Nor has there been any change in France, where they used to have greater freedom and latitude than they do now. I think people who read this kind of thing in a habitual way and with any regularity tend to be rather passive about their sexual lives, generally. They're not going to run out and rape anybody. They're not that kind."

"What about the Moors murders?" That was the female voice, Nina again.

"Those two English murderers?"

"Yes, what about them? Brady, I think his name was, had fifty volumes of pornography hidden away, and he and that girl friend of his were sex criminals."

"I'm not saying that sex criminals never read pornography. But Brady was cutting up cats and torturing them, burning them alive, when he was six. And he certainly hadn't been reading pornography at that age. I think he was just crazy. And he would have been crazy without the books."

"But, Irv."

"Yes, Bud?" So that baritone voice had been Randolph, Patterson thought.

"Even allowing that you're right, and granting everything that you've been saying as valid and true and legitimate—which it probably is—I still wonder if this is the right moment, the right moment for *us*. You know that the Justice Department is looking for some kind of club to beat your head in with. And if you go ahead with this, you'll be giving it to them on a silver tray, all wrapped up in a nice satin ribbon!"

"That's exactly the point! I'll be giving them a balsa-wood club."

"I don't understand."

"Balsa wood is very light."

"I know what Balsa wood is. But I don't see anything fake about this club. It looks pretty substantial to me."

"I disagree on two counts," Kane said. "First of all, a book has more weight, more prestige, is more of a holy object somehow, than a magazine. And if we can get Patterson to go after us on the books, our chances in court will be better. Second, there is more latitude for the printed word than there is for pictures. The only troubles we've ever had with vigilante mayors and local censorship boards have been because of our Kalendar Kitties, not because of any of the text matter of the magazine. You can describe in words any damned thing you want, but show a picture and you're in trouble. It may be that MacLuhan is right, after all, and that this is the post-Gutenberg age. I don't think so, but the public feeling about these things is pretty clear. So, with books, with printed words in them, we've got all the traditional protections, and all the respectability we could want. Plus we'll have these prestige names doing our introductions for us. And the whole enterprise will be very lofty in tone."

"Aren't you worried about being so lofty that he'll leave you alone?"

"No, because the ads will be gut stuff, and as direct as we can make them. The ads will be pure turn-on! But you can't go to jail for your ads, can you?"

"No, I guess not," Bud said.

"I like it," Nina said. "And what I like most about it is that if Patterson goes after the books you're safe, and if he doesn't go after the books he looks silly. I mean, to go after the magazine when your book line is more adventurous, and the ads for the books still more bold . . ."

"Exactly," Kane interrupted. "I've figured a way to hide behind my own skirts." He laughed, and asked, "Ingenious?"

"Too ingenious," Bud answered. "I think you're fooling yourself. I think you're making it easier for Patterson, rather than harder. And I think he'll go after you across the board, hit you everywhere, and score wherever he can."

"I can't stop him from doing that," Kane answered. "I can't

stop him from doing anything. But I can be damned sure that I've got the strongest ground to stand on. And to fight from."

"And you think pornography is that strongest ground?"

"Yes. It isn't so much the pornography itself, but the issue of freedom. And the whole business of repression and inhibition that made me start the magazine in the first place. In the voting booths of the market place, the American public has shown that it supports me. And even if it didn't, this is what I believe in. And if the pressure is on, and I'm going to get shot at, then I want to be doing exactly what I please, exactly what I believe in. This is no time to play it safe."

"Are you sure this isn't just recklessness?" Bud asked.

"I don't know. Maybe. Maybe it is. But I don't mind getting shot off the field, if that's going to happen. The only thing I refuse to be is scared off the field. You see my point?"

"I see it, but I'm not sure whether you're not rationalizing."

"That's just a word for thinking we don't agree with, isn't it?"

"You mean that *I'm* rationalizing?"

"Bud." That was Nina Kirby again. "Why are you really so negative about this? Are you actually concerned for the success of this venture? Or are you hedging? Is it that in a book you—Bud Sloat—can't hide behind the quality fiction, the sociological articles, the psychiatric articles, that give the magazine the prestige to publish the nudes?"

"Nina, for God's sake, I'm not going to psychoanalyze myself at this meeting. How do *you* feel about the porno business?"

"Frankly, I don't care—I don't really care about the issues. And I do believe Irv has a point—his *raison d'être*."

"Look." Bud said then. "I yield to no one in my admiration for what you've done with *Tomcat*, Irv, but I still think that this time you may be going too far. If this is such a sure thing, why aren't any other publishers doing it? What is there that frightens all of them off? Their accountants? They can't stand the idea of making all that money?"

"Timidity," Kane said, "just plain timidity. There are a few small-time operators with paperbacks out on the coast. They are mostly undercapitalized, and they don't have the outlets. But for the rest, they're just scared."

"Well, what are you going to do about outlets?" Bud asked.

"We've got a deal, after all, with Raleigh and Novak. They distribute for us. They'll keep right on distributing."

"But that's only for bar manuals and joke books . . ."

"And our fiction anthology. And our fashion guide."

"I still think old Raleigh will object."

"We'll handle him," Kane said. "I'm sure we can handle anyone."

Patterson heard the sound of a door opening, and then heard Kane say, "I'll take it in the next room, Jane." Then he said, "That'll be all. Nina, Bud, wait for me here, would you?" The tape rolled on. Patterson heard the noises of chairs moving and men's voices talking, eight or nine, he supposed, who were no doubt leaving Tomcat House to return to the Kane Building.

Then Nina said, "You didn't seem too happy about Irv's idea."

"No, I'm afraid I wasn't happy about it at all."

"Why not?"

"I think he's going too far. All these years, he's thought of himself as a pioneer and an adventurer in the frontiers of publishing and—well, he hasn't been. He's been living in some comfortable outpost town, where the occasional report of Indians on the warpath makes for conversation at the bridge tables. But with this he's really going out there. And he's going to blow it. Everything. He's going to lose it all."

"Maybe that's what he wants to do."

"All right. Fine. But then what happens to all this? What happens to us?"

"Are you afraid?"

"No, I'm not afraid. I just don't like to take chances when it isn't worth it. If it were something really important, really worth while, then it'd be a different thing. But *this?*"

"It's a living," she said, echoing what he had said so many times.

"But that's all it is. He's beginning to take himself seriously."

"He always has taken himself seriously," she reminded him.

"But he's risking our necks now."

"He's been feeding our faces long enough, hasn't he?"

"I guess. But, Jesus! Have you read any pornography? I mean, the real hard-core stuff? It's so damned dull and dreary."

"I've read some. I thought it was funny."

"Oh, wonderful! But you see what I mean."

"I see. Look, we'll talk about it later. He's likely to come back any time. Say something nice. Something more affirmative. And tonight we'll talk about it."

"That sounds like a swell evening!"

"We'll talk about it, and then maybe we'll turn on."

"Funny," Bud said. "We turn on with grass—" Patterson could not help smiling to himself as he heard Sloat continue—"which is supposed to be immoral and illegal and—well, everything but fattening. And he sits here in this absurd house and turns on with his damned plans. And that's what's really dangerous."

"That's funny?"

"Sure it is. Some day, the government is going to wise up and discover that pot is a lot less dangerous and subversive than sobriety. It makes for a docile, manageable citizenry."

"An ingenious idea," she said.

"Isn't it?"

"What is?" Ah, that was Kane's voice again. "What's an ingenious idea?"

"Why, yours," Bud said. "Your idea about publishing."

"Oh? I thought you were less than delighted with it."

"No, no. I think there's a certain element of risk, but you know that. I was just playing devil's advocate, there, to try to help you clarify what you think about it. I mean, I hadn't had time even to begin to decide what I thought about the—fine details of it."

"Oh? Well, then. I'm glad to hear that. I was really puzzled and disappointed by your lack of enthusiasm."

"No, I think it's fine. There's that risk, but then, it's your magazine, and you're a big boy."

"It's my magazine," Kane said.

"And if you want to go out shooting for bear, we're with you."

"Good," he said. "And—thanks."

"No thanks necessary," Bud said. "You run a good show here. I'm glad to be part of it."

"Still, thanks. I—I just had a very distressing call. Trouble at home."

"Oh?" Nina said.

"Yes," Irv said, "and I'm afraid I'll have to go out there. I'll try to be back tomorrow. If I'm held up, I'll call."

"If there's anything we can do," Nina said, "anything I can do . . ."

"Thanks," Irv said. "I think it'll be okay."

"I hope so," Nina said.

"That's about it," Brown said.

It was jarring, Patterson thought, the sound of the agent's voice, live, not on tape, reminding him where he was and exactly what he was doing in this dingy room in Boston. He told himself there was no point in being greedy. He'd got an awful lot right there. "Thank you, Mr. Brown. That's just about enough."

The powerlessness, the inadequacy, the feeling of helpless struggling, all those things that the luxury and extravagant comfort and cost of the Boeing 737 had been supposed to ward off, keep out, fly over like bad weather—they were all returning. Even here, high up in the air, they reached him. He nursed his drink, staring into the glass and watching the ice cubes vibrate with the vibrations of the jet engines, or looking out of the window at the weird, mountainous arrangements of the clouds below, and still he felt like nothing. Like shit.

Well, that was Cal's gift, wasn't it, her bitch ability to make anybody feel like shit. But it wasn't just Cal and her poisonous emanations. If it had been just been Cal, he could have dealt with her, could have dealt with his feelings. It was more than Cal, or Karyn, or the news about Karyn, and the knowledge that there was going to be a perfectly dreadful scene. It was this returning to Indianapolis, like a criminal to the scene of his crime, like a dog to his vomit. Indianapolis! Fabled in song and story! The city of love and of light and of laughter! The city of shit! Even Newark had its troubadours, however mangy—Leslie Fiedler and Philip Roth! But Indianapolis? The capital of nowhere! The city to which Irv Kane's father had fled, trying to find a hole into which he could crawl and pull in after himself. And he'd found it. Indianapolis, and a job teaching shop in a junior high school, and odd jobs in the summer, and lucky to get them during a depression. Indianapolis, a city from which all good men, all hopeful, bright, promising, uncrushed souls fled as Lot from the city of Sodom, not looking back!

That was it! That was what was wrong. He was not only looking back but going back, returning to that vile ville. And that rinky-dink house with the rambler roses and the chintz curtains and the pickled pine hutch in the kitchen that Cal liked for its ugliness, humdrum prissiness, its ghastly charm. With all that, what difference did it make that there were real reasons to be depressed and glum? The para-real reasons, the fortuitous peripheral reasons were powerful enough.

Irv Kane drained the drink and held out the empty glass. Cato took it, and returned it full. Kane promised himself that this would be the last one. He didn't want to show up half drunk. Didn't need to. It would be bad enough as it was, without any help from the Scotch. In fact that was just exactly what it would be like —a bad drunk. Something to live through and then sweat out and throw up, and take Alka-Seltzer over. On the other hand, he didn't want to face it all stone sober. He wasn't that much of a masochist. A topical anaesthetic was what he wanted. A little something to numb the sharpness of the pain. He took a swallow of the fresh drink and closed his eyes, trying to think about nothing at all.

But all through the descent, and through the long ride in the limousine from the airport to the house, the possibilities of the argument kept appearing before his unwilling mind, the way chess combinations must appear to a tournament player even after the big match he has just lost. Or cards. It was more like a deck of cards, tattered and limp, with some garish picture of a horse or a ship or a pot of flowers, that some personal daemon kept shuffling and shuffling before his eyes, in an endless succession of losing hands.

All right, so she was knocked up. No problem there. There were abortionists to be had. Even legally. There were psychiatrists who were, for a price, understanding about these things. Or there were all those doctors in Japan, a thousand bucks away, ready to scoop out the little bastard like a speck from a glass of milk. It was the only sane thing to do. It would be just pointless and stupid and cruel for a fifteen-year-old girl to have to go through a whole pregnancy and give up the child at the end of it. And it would be even worse, even more pointless and more cruel to allow her to marry the guy, whoever he was. But Cal, he was sure, would favor . . . favor what? He was not sure of the terms, but only of the cruelty, and the stupidity, and the repressive, benighted, sour rage that she would have for him. How she would translate that quagmire of emotional fetor into a practical suggestion Kane could not begin to guess. But he could not allow himself to hope that it would produce anything reasonable or useful. Or humane.

The car pulled up to the curb in front of the house. The driver got out, came around, and opened the door, and, only because the driver was standing there, Kane got out. He would have preferred to sit there in the back seat, thinking for a little while longer. Or not thinking, but just catching his breath, getting ready. It was like the first plunge into a cold pool in early summer. It really didn't do any good to stand there on the diving board and wait. Probably it made the dive more difficult, and the shock of the cold water even worse. Still, one had to wait, to argue with the reluctance of one's own body. And as often as not it was the expectant look of some friend, or even a stranger—even a child—that would help the courage to perk and boil up. And then the plunge . . .

Well, he had nothing to gain by waiting. And he supposed that the sooner he went in, the sooner he would be out, and back in the plane, and on the way back to Boston.

"I don't expect to be too long," he said.

"Very good, sir," the driver said, touching his cap.

He manufactured a smile and then went up the brick walk to the front door with the—Lord, yes—brass eagle door knocker and the doorbell that sounded the first measure of the Westminster chimes. In the instant between the ringing of the chimes and the opening of the door, it struck him that even if the sex thing had gone better, they still wouldn't have made it together. Their tastes were too different. Their views of the world, their . . .

But the door was open, and she was standing there, looking at him.

"Well, come in," she said.

"Thank you."

"She didn't tell me she was going to call you. And if she'd told me, I don't think I'd have let her. But maybe it's a good thing that you're here."

"Thank you. I only want to help."

"Good," Cal said.

She led the way into the living room where Karyn was sitting. Irv went over to Karyn, kissed her, and then sat down on the couch beside her.

"All right," Cal said, "now what I'd like you to do is explain to her that all those things you keep printing in that filthy magazine aren't true, and are just a way of making money. I'd like you to tell her that her idea of all the things you stand for is wrong and stupid, and that you and that magazine of yours is exactly what got her into trouble this way."

"What?"

"You heard me!"

"You're crazy! You're out of your mind!"

"Go ahead and tell her, or get out!"

Irv stole a glance at Karyn. She looked scared to death.

"Look, Cal," he said, "she called me, and I've come to see her. Now if you're going to take this insane attitude, I'll just take Karyn with me, and we'll talk things over out in the car."

"You step out of this house with her, you just put one foot out the front door with her, and I'll be on the phone so fast to the newspapers that you won't get to the corner before the extras hit the stands with the story of the daughter of *Tomcat*'s publisher getting herself into trouble."

"You had her here with you. She was in your custody! I'll come up smelling like a rose."

"You think?"

"I know!"

"Then go ahead."

"Only if you make it necessary! I want to talk with Karyn, and I think it would be a good idea if you were here with us while we talk."

"Why is that such a good idea?"

"Because she has to deal with both of us. Because she's got to listen to me and know that you've heard what I'm saying—so that you won't undermine it all the minute I leave."

"No, I won't have to do that. I'll sit here and watch you do it all by yourself."

"Very funny!"

"I think so!"

He waited for a moment, took a deep breath, rubbed his hand over his cheek and around his chin, and then looked at the young girl beside him, his daughter, his very frightened daughter, the girl whose flesh was a part of his flesh, and yet whom he scarcely knew. He had not seen her for six months, because of the press of business, and he hardly knew what to say to her or how to begin. And yet, in a way, that made it easier. He was not so much pitching the argument to her, directing the discussion at her, but merely making it in a general and ideal way, expressing his best judgment in the best way he could. That was what he had to do. He would do what fathers ought to do, cleanly and honestly.

"How do you feel about this, Karyn?" he began, in a gentle and reasonable tone. It was warm, but not too familiar, nor too presuming.

"I'm— Oh, daddy, I'm so sorry!"

"I'm sorry too," he said. "Sorry for you. But what do you want to do now?"

"What can I do?"

"Do you want an abortion?"

"Mom says . . ."

"Never mind what Mom says. What do *you* want?"

"Aren't they dangerous?"

"No, not if they're done right, and early enough. You could go to Japan. They're legal there. And it would be done in a hospital . . ."

"Over my dead body!" Cal erupted.

"Yes, if necessary," Irv said, smiling at her.

"But isn't that murder? Mom says . . ."

"Is that what she said? That it's murder? That's nonsense."

"I knew you'd say that," Cal interrupted. "It's what a smut-peddler like you would have to say, isn't it?"

"Will you shut up?"

"Why should I?"

"Because," he said, getting up, "if you don't I'm going to shut you up."

He advanced toward her, and, even without his realizing it, he had clenched his fists. His lips were a tight, white line, pressed together as they were in anger. "I'm going to warn you one more time," he said, "to let Karyn and me talk this out, and to sit there with your mouth closed and your filthy little mind out of sight."

"*My* filthy mind . . ."

"Yes, yours! Because you're the one that thinks sex is dirty and filthy and horrible. Because you're the one who never told Karyn the things a girl ought to know about so that she let herself get pregnant when it wasn't necessary. Because you're the one responsible for this, more than I am, or the magazine is, or even that boy—whoever he was."

"Jim Montgomery," Karyn volunteered.

"I don't even want to know. It doesn't make any difference."

"It doesn't?" Cal asked. "We could put him in jail for statutory rape!"

"Wouldn't you just like to do that, now? Wouldn't that be just fine! Ruin the boy's life for him, and make you feel good. Right?"

"It's what he deserves."

"It's what you deserve," Irv said.

"It's what you deserve," Cal countered. "You have the temerity to accuse me of being responsible for this, when I've tried to protect her, to shield her—"

"And you see what a sensible plan that is."

"It would have worked if the whole country weren't going down the toilet bowl, with degenerates like you flushing it for all it's worth . . ."

"Are you quite through?"

"Are you?"

"No," he said. "We haven't solved anything."

"There's nothing to solve. There's not even anything for you to do except make your ridiculous speeches and get Karyn upset and get me disgusted, and then you get back in your big car and drive away."

"And what about the pregnancy?"

"It will do what pregnancies usually do. She'll have the baby, and then put it up for adoption. And perhaps she'll learn a lesson from it. Perhaps she'll learn something about responsibility and the consequences of one's actions."

"Or learn how to hate sex so that if she does get married some day, she'll be so twisted up inside that she'll wind up the way you did . . ."

"Which would be better than staying married to someone like you, all sex crazy and surrounded by those fancy whores you show in your magazine . . ."

"They're not whores, they're just pretty girls."

"They're whores."

"They're—Look, isn't this a little silly?" He shook his head, and then turned to Karyn. "I'm not going to argue with your mother. I won't be able to convince her of anything. And when you get a little older, you'll be able to understand what I mean. Maybe you understand already. But the question now is what we can do for you, what you want to do. Do you want to go to Japan?"

"Yes, but I'm afraid."

"It'll be all right. I'll go with you."

"You won't take her out of the country. You can't. I'll get a court order!" Cal exclaimed.

"Look, it's for her sake that I'm doing this. Why must you be so pigheaded?"

"I'm pigheaded, as you insist on putting it, because I'm right. I don't approve of rape. Even statutory rape. And I don't approve of murder. I guess I'm just old fashioned. I don't even like those whores of yours. Which makes me practically un-American, doesn't it? But I'm still the girl's mother, and I'm going to do what's right and what's best."

"You won't let me take her to Japan?"

"No."

"Not even if that's what she wants to do?"

"I don't care what she wants to do."

"Well, that's clear enough, isn't it?" he asked. The question was for Karyn's benefit. He looked at her, and she returned the look, eyes wide with—affection? Trust? Understanding? Appeal? Or all of those things?

Well, he had not done so badly. He had threatened Japan, and that was what Cal would be guarding against. And he could set up an appointment with a doctor right here in Indianapolis and sneak Karyn off to have it all done without Cal's knowing about it. It would be a little tricky, maybe, but it would work. All it really needed was Karyn's cooperation. And he was sure he had that.

"All right," he said, getting up again, "I'll discuss it with my lawyers and see where we stand."

"What are you talking about?"

"I want to find out whether I don't have grounds to demand custody for myself. Or whether I can't have my visiting rights worked so that I can take her wherever I want. Or I may bring an action against you—for blackmail. Or I may see about having you committed to an institution for observation. You never know what these lawyers are going to suggest, do you?"

"You don't scare me," Cal said. "Not the least little bit."

But the very denial was reassuring to Irv Kane. He had no way of being sure how much he had got her worried, but she was at least a little bit worried. And there was some satisfaction in that.

"Good-bye, then," he said.

He walked toward the door. Cal remained in the Windsor chair where she had been sitting. And Karyn came to the door to say good-bye, as he had expected she would, as he had been counting on, in fact. For it was only then that he could whisper to her while he touched her loose chestnut hair, "Call me the day after tomorrow. Call me in Boston, collect. I'll have something worked out by then. I promise you. Trust me."

"I do," she said.

"Good."

He kissed her on the cheek, and then left.

On the whole, he felt pretty good about it. Cal's attack, her entire attitude, had been so outrageous as to be actually reassuring, not only about Karyn and the abortion, but also about his whole career, his publishing of *Tomcat,* and his plans for the new book series. Repression, ignorance, fear, and a perverse distaste were not going to get anybody anywhere. And those things would be the objects of his campaign, to make inroads against them wherever and however he could.

In a more practical and immediate enterprise, the finding of an abortionist for Karyn, he had even less difficulty than he had expected. The Chicago advertising office came through in less than twenty-four hours with the names of five men in Chicago, two in Cincinnati, one in Indianapolis, one in Scranton, and two in Washington, D.C. And all of them were well recommended. The range of cities he had given was not only a way of disguising his own purpose in asking for the information, but also to extend the number of possibilities for Karyn. After all, with the plane at their disposal, they could fly to Chicago or Washington and back in less time than anybody else in Indianapolis could drive to Fort Wayne.

He considered the list before him, and then set up two appointments, one in Chicago and one in Cleveland. Then he sat back to wait for Karyn's call.

It came in late at night. She had waited until her mother had gone to bed, and had sneaked downstairs to use the phone. Cal had forbidden her to call Irv at all, and she apologized for the lateness of the hour.

"That's okay. Really. I wasn't sleeping. And I understand about your mother's attitude. I expected it."

"But it just doesn't make any sense."

"No, it doesn't, does it?"

"No. Especially now. When—when there's no problem any more."

"What do you mean."

"Well, I don't know, exactly. But I got my period this morning. I guess it's either a miscarriage, or the doctor made a mistake. But there's nothing to worry about any more."

"That's wonderful news."

"And I wanted to call you right away. But mother wouldn't let me. In a way, I think that was worse than anything she said to you when you were here."

"Don't worry about it. I'm not."

"But you've been worrying all day, and there was no need for it. Don't you see?"

"Sure, I see. But what I see that's more important is your concern, and your thoughtfulness. And that makes me much happier than your mother makes me unhappy. And, anyway, it's such good news!"

"Isn't it!"

"But next time, you'll be more careful, won't you?"

"But there isn't going to be any next time. I won't ever do a thing like that again. I promise."

"Nonsense. First of all, you ought not make promises that you can't keep. And that's a silly promise anyway. The only promise I want from you is that you'll be a little more careful and sensible. Sex is for making love or for making babies. You can decide that perfectly well. That's what science is for. You understand me?"

"Yes, I understand."

"Good. I'll write to you soon. And I'll see if I can't arrange things so that you can come and visit at Christmas."

"I'd like that."

"Me, too."

"And . . . thanks, Dad."

"Any time," he said, with a chuckle. And it felt good to hear her chuckle back before they said good-bye.

He felt good. Better than good, he felt absolutely graced. Blessed. It was partly the fact that she was still alive, that her spirit was not yet so badly warped or crushed that it might not recover and grow, that his daughter was growing up and might yet grow up right. That made him feel good, of course. But beyond that, there was the mad, absurd, unpredictable luck of the miscarriage, or the faulty diagnosis, or whatever it had been, the pure delivery from trouble and threat to safety and calm. And for that to happen this way . . .

Well, it didn't do to push it too far. And being a more or less sensible, practical person, Irv Kane did not try to push it, or want to let himself rely on it. But in some way, deliberately left in the shadows of his mind—where, in fact, the glow that it gave off was more noticeable, like one of those glow-in-the-dark light pulls—there was the notion that he was riding a wave of luck or that the wheel of fortune was with him. It was a sign, a mark of grace, an indication of—well, nothing in particular, but a general kind of assurance. From fate, or the gods, or God.

He tried to counterbalance the feeling by labeling it as foolishness, as superstition, as primitive hocus-pocus. But the mere act of labeling it was not enough to make it go away. It was still there, still glowing, still alive. And if he was careful and sensible, he told himself, and did not rely on it or let it dictate his plans or affect his plans in any way, its presence, its simple existence there in that dark corner of his thoughts, could do no harm. On the contrary, there was a kind of confidence that could only be helpful. When one expects to win, one often does win. And he expected great things.

The whole sourness of the business with Jill Jefferson was wiped away, erased, as if the translation from the Slough of Despond to the Delectable Mountain had not happened to Karyn except incidentally, as a part of the process by which it was to happen to him.

That it had happened, that somehow things had changed, had improved, had gone back to the way they had been before that awful mistake, that he had been saved somehow, was certain. He was sure of it, and he felt good; he felt so good that he was sure of it.

8

"You like little girls?"
"No."
"You dislike little girls! Eh?"
There was no answer.
"You like older women?"
"How old?"
"I don't know. You tell me how old. Forty? Fifty?"
"What do you mean, 'Do I like older women?'"
"Sexually! Do you like older women sexually?"
"No."
"The women you like. You like fat women or thin women?"
"I don't know."
"Well, *I* don't know. You got to tell me. What kind of women you imagine when you masturbate?"

"I don't know. Girls. Twenty, twenty-five years old. Good-looking."

"Voluptuous? Big breasts? Big behinds?"

"Yeah."

"How many times a day you masturbate?"

There was no answer.

"Two? Three? Four times?"

"Sometimes four."

"Sometimes more than that?"

"Sometimes."

"Five? Six times?"

"I don't know. I don't keep count, for Christ's sake!"

"Sometimes six times?"

"Yeah, I guess so. Some days, six times."

"That's too much."

Dr. Zathmiry leaned back in his chair and lit a new cigarette from the butt of the old one.

"You want a cigarette?" he said to Scully.

"Yeah, thanks."

Dr. Zathmiry extended the pack to Scully, watching as he took one, put it in his mouth, and then, out of habit, patted his pockets, looking for a book of matches. Dr. Zathmiry waited for a moment while Scully's mind performed exactly according to expectations. There was the habitual response, the frustration of the habitual response, and only then the conscious thinking that necessity brought forth. It only took a few seconds before Scully realized that he was no longer at Walpole State Prison but at Bridgewater State Hospital now. None of the inmates at Bridgewater were allowed to have matches. So, the offer of the cigarette served two purposes, establishing a bond of friendliness, however slight, between Zathmiry and the patient, and also putting the patient in his place and emphasizing the dependence that was a part of the patient's situation.

"How about homosexual experiences? You had homosexual experiences?"

"You mean with queers?"

"Yes, sexual experiences with other men."

"No," Scully said, with vehemence.

He was, Zathmiry concluded, overreacting. Probably some kind of latent. Continuing along this line of thought, he wondered whether Scully might not have been channeling aggressions he felt toward himself, transferring them to another object and expressing his rage and anger through the rape-murder of the girl. He would be punishing the girl for not being male, and, at the same time, proving his manhood by having intercourse with a girl.

"Tell me," Zathmiry asked, "when you masturbate, what kind of thoughts you have?"

"I don't know. I guess I think about screwing."

"You think about screwing? Who do you think about screwing? That girl? The girl you killed?"

Scully shifted uneasily in his chair, took a puff of his cigarette, flicked the ash into the ashtray on Zathmiry's desk, and, after some further hesitation, admitted, "Yeah, sometimes."

"Why do you think about her and not other girls? You ever . . . you ever have intercourse with other girls?"

There was no answer. Scully looked down at his feet.

"Come on! Come on, tell me!" Zathmiry ordered. "You don't tell me things, I can't help you. I'm here to help you. I'm a doctor!"

There was another pause, but this one Zathmiry decided to wait out. He tilted his head back so that the glare from the overhead light bounced off his glasses and shone into Scully's face. It was a trick he had learned long ago in Prague.

"No," Scully admitted, finally, in a barely audible tone.

"That was the only girl you ever had intercourse with?"
"Yeah. The only one."
"Why not other girls? You didn't like other girls, too?"
"Yeah, I liked other girls. But they didn't like me that much."
"And you were angry at the other girls because they didn't like you? Is that it?"
"No, they were pigs, anyway."
"You ever commit other crimes?"
"No."
"Just this one thing? Just this one crime?"
Scully nodded.
"Speak up, please."
"That's right," Scully said.
"You never stole a car? You never stole money?"
"Oh, when I was—I don't know, maybe fourteen—me and some guys went shoplifting once. I guess for the excitement. But I never did it again."
"But no other sexual crimes you committed?"
"No."
"You felt bad after you killed the girl?"
"Yeah, I felt bad. Sure I felt bad."
"Is that why you tried to kill yourself at Walpole?"
"I don't know. I guess partly that. But mostly I guess it was because they were going to kill me anyway. I didn't want to wait for that. It was horrible. It—well, it didn't make any difference. To die then or in two months. It seemed stupid the way they were trying to keep me alive so they could kill me."
"So it was more fear than guilt."
"Yeah, maybe."
"So you didn't feel very guilty about killing the girl."
"Yeah, I felt guilty. I felt bad. But . . . But, I didn't mean to kill her. It was an accident."

"You raped her. That was an accident too?"

"I don't know. I don't know how it happened. I didn't plan to do anything like that. I didn't mean for anything like that to happen. But . . ."

"But? What happened?"

"I don't know. Something came over me, I guess."

"You have fits of dizziness sometimes? You have fainting spells ever? You have sometimes your memory doesn't work too good?"

"No, no."

"Only this time? Is that right?"

"Well, I kind of remember *what* happened, but I don't remember why it happened. Or how it happened."

"So, tell me, why you masturbate so much?"

"I don't know. There's not too much else to do around here. I mean, you kept me in that cell without any clothes on for two weeks."

"We did that for your own protection. You tried to kill yourself. You got clothes on, you could try to hurt yourself with them. But you could watch television now. You could play ping-pong."

"I'm not very good at ping-pong. And I don't like television much. It's boring. And this place is full of loonies. They talk to themselves."

"This place is full of loonies! You think you're all right? This is a hospital. We have sick people here. We try to help them."

"Nobody's doing anything for me."

"I'm talking to you. Am I not talking to you right now?"

"I'm not sick."

"Do you think just ordinary healthy people go around raping and killing people and then trying to kill themselves?"

"I don't know. Sometimes, maybe. You had me here for a month before the trial and you let me go. You said I was perfectly okay."

"No, no. We said you were able to stand trial. That means that you could understand what was going on. We didn't say that you were perfectly okay. That's a different thing. Now we're here trying to figure out how we can help you. How we can make you better. How we can make you so you wouldn't do this kind of thing any more."

"What difference does it make? They're going to kill me."

"Now, now, don't be like that. They haven't killed anybody in Massachusetts in twenty years. And as long as you're here nobody can hurt you. They can't take you out of here to execute you. This is a hospital."

"I'd rather be dead than spend the rest of my life here. These loonies give me the creeps. And these questions bother me. At least back at Walpole everybody left me alone. I sit there in that cell all by myself and then I come out here and you ask me questions about how many times a day I masturbate. That's not right."

"Look here, Scully, I'm going to help you."

"The only way to help me is to send me back to Walpole and let them kill me. They wouldn't let me kill myself, let them kill me."

"That is not a healthy remark, Scully," Zathmiry said. "Nobody really wants to die." Dr. Zathmiry pushed the button that was concealed on the inside of one of the legs of his desk. The door opened and the guard appeared to take Scully back to his cell. He waited as Scully stubbed out the cigarette butt, and then the two of them marched out.

Zathmiry reached for his Stenorette, held the mike in one hand, and, with the other, massaged his temples. Then, with his thumb resting lightly on the button of the mike, he looked through the metal grille and the dirty glass and out into the bleak, soiled February sky. It was so tiresome, so hopeless and tiresome, trying to treat these people. They were mostly retarded, they were crazy, they were sick, they were disgusting. Here he was, a psychiatrist, trained in Vienna, and simply because he had made a wrong political choice he was condemned to be here, too, to be in this slop sink, this hellhole of humanity, underpaid, overworked, harried, harassed, and tormented. And working with human garbage of the most objectionable sort. He had not seen such a bunch since they had cleaned out the prisons in Prague to find recruits for the German Army in 1944. It had been his task to separate, not the wheat from the chaff, but the usable chaff from the unusable chaff. He remembered how they had taken all the sexual criminals and had, by a very simple operation, rendered them entirely harmless and safe, and perfectly adequate to serve as cannon fodder for the Fatherland without any danger of their raping the wives of the officers or the wives of the civilians in the towns through which they were retreating.

Suddenly a faint smile lit Dr. Zathmiry's lined, tired face. Perhaps he could take credit now for a discovery of his, for the technique he had perfected then. It was a small, simple operation, and it worked. No more would Scully be masturbating five, six times a day. No more, even if by some preposterous mischance he were to be taken out of here or taken out of prison and put back into society, would he be a danger to the girls on the streets and in the apartments of the United States. It would be simply a small matter of sectioning the perineal autonomic nerves. Two small cuts and that was all there was to it.

He had discovered this in Prague, while discussing with a colleague one of the unfortunate side-effects of the operation for prostatic carcinoma, or, rather, an occasional regrettable result of that operation. When the autonomic nervous system was interfered with, the blood vessels of the penis could no longer retain the blood. It was the blood entering the penis in greater volume than the blood leaving that resulted in the tumescence, but when all this was interfered with the circulation of the penis was entirely normal and regular, like, say, that of an arm. On the other hand, like an arm, it wouldn't get stiff.

Dr. Zathmiry pushed the button of the Stenorette and proceeded to dictate: "Scully, Frank . . ."

He glanced down at the file on his desk. "4320514. Convicted first degree murder following rape. Referred for observation and treatment following attempted suicide at Walpole State Prison. Diagnosis: latent homosexual, paranoid undifferentiated schizophrenic. Poorly integrated personality structure. Chronic masturbator. Recommendation for treatment: Sectioning perineal autonomic nerves for psychiatric prophylaxis. Signed, Tibor Zathmiry." He released the button and then smiled. Then he pressed the button again. "Request permission to perform operation as indicated. T.Z."

He doubted that O'Neill would know what the hell he was talking about, and he was sure that he would not have the presence of mind to inquire what it was. He would not want to betray his ignorance. So very American of him, Zathmiry thought.

It took a week for the tape to get transcribed, sent up to O'Neill's office, work its way up to the top of O'Neill's In basket, and get itself read, initialed, and returned to Dr. Zathmiry. It was not the time that had elapsed, therefore, that bothered Zathmiry. He was accustomed to that sort of inefficiency. But the notation scrawled on the bottom of the first page, "Call me, please!" seemed foolish. In the first place, if O'Neill wanted to speak about it on the phone, why hadn't he called in the first place? But more annoying was the likelihood that he would require of Zathmiry an explanation of what the procedure actually was. A great nuisance!

He picked up the phone, called O'Neill, and, after the routine exchange of cordial greetings, got down to business.

"About Scully. You had some question?"

"No, not a question, so much as a comment."

"Yes?" Zathmiry asked.

"I think in Scully's case it would be unwise to perform such an operation."

"You disapprove of the operation itself, or of the application to Scully?"

"I didn't say I disapproved."

"But you said . . . What *did* you say?"

"I said I thought it would be unwise. Politically, if you will."

"If *I* will? What do you mean?"

"For one thing, Scully is unusual in that he is represented by a team of lawyers. Very expensive. Very meticulous. They might make an issue of this, don't you see?"

"Good. Let them make an issue. I think it is a sensible procedure for this kind of problem. Gets right to the root of the difficulty, don't you see?" He allowed himself a restrained chuckle.

"But it could bring more attention to us than either of us want. Administrative chores for me. Hearings. Review boards. Paperwork. And for you . . . well, publicity."

"I see."

"I thought you would."

"But it is an interesting idea. It's a shame, really."

"We have other rapists, other child-molesters. Other patients whom your suggestion might . . . benefit."

"And in another case that was less . . . sensitive, you'd have no objection?"

"I don't know. There is something of a legal question. I might consider it. But then, when I am on vacation next month, it wouldn't have to have my official notice, would it? Or my written approval."

"I understand."

"Good."

"And thank you."

"Quite all right."

Zathmiry hung up. He sat, brooding about O'Neill and his reasonableness. Not such a bad type, after all. He had to protect his own skin, but then that was the nature of the game. And he had given as much leeway as he could to Zathmiry. Another man might not have done so much.

He got up, went to the files in the outer office, pulled out three or four large reddish-brown manila envelopes. Levin. Fremont. Smith. Maloff. He flipped through them, looked up at the ceiling, and then decided.

He leaned forward, flipped the pages on his desk calendar, and made an appointment for Levin, #4320996.

RALEIGH & NOVAK, INC.
BOOK PUBLISHERS
719 Fifth Avenue
New York, N.Y. 10022

September 11, 196—

Mr. Irvin S. Kane
Tomcat Magazine
Kane Building
235 Arlington Street
Boston, Mass.

Dear Irv:

I have been studying the material you sent me, and I have been discussing it with my associates here, and with our attorney as well. I am inclined to agree with you about the need for such an undertaking, and about the beneficial results that such a line of books might have. And of course I agree with you about the freedom of the press and about our theoretical right to proceed with the series.

What bothers me, though, is the likelihood that there will be legal proceedings, and that the cost of such proceedings will almost certainly destroy any profit that your firm or ours might be likely to realize—at least during the first couple of years. I am also disturbed to learn that the burden of legal action is likely to fall more upon Raleigh and Novak than upon Tomcat, Inc. As the distributors of the series, we would be vulnerable to these prosecutions in a more direct way than you would be.

Ours has been a most pleasant and profitable association. And I should be delighted if a way could be worked out so that we might continue to distribute Topper Books—all of them except this new series. Perhaps if we were to wait for a more favorable moment, or to move in a more gradual way toward this admittedly desirable goal?

I am, truly, sorry to have to write to you in this way, and to have to convey such disappointing news. But this is what I am told, and I have no choice but to turn around and tell you what my people tell me.

Let me know when you plan to be in New York. We'll have dinner together. Murial sends her best regards, as I do mine,

       Cordially,

       Alan D. Novak
       Editor-in-chief

  The prig! The prig! The pusillanimous pompous ass. The prize ass of Fifth Avenue! The hypocritical, cowardly jerk of a publisher!

  Irv Kane crumpled up the letter into a tight ball, and as hard as he could he threw it against the wall. It bounced off and fell to the floor. The goddam stupid son of a bitch! The living shit. King of the shits. Emperor of the shits! Tsar of all the shits!

He crossed the room, picked up the letter, and brought it back to his desk. He smoothed it out, looked at it, and picked up his dictaphone. "Alan D. Novak, Raleigh and Novak, 719 Fifth Avenue, New York, 10022. Dear Alan. You are lower than whale shit and there isn't anything in the world lower than that. I'd kick you right in the balls if they were big enough to kick. If I could find them. If you had any. But you don't. You are an asshole in gold-rimmed spectacles. I am very grateful to you for your letter, and the occasion it provides for me to tell you at last what I think of you. Fuck you. Sincerely, Irv."

He played the letter back so that he could hear it. Then he erased it. He felt a little better, but not much. It was just infuriating. Fat-ass Novak, with all his protestations of pioneering and crusading, and all his famous liberal posturing, and all his prestige and power, and all the money he had made from Kane's books, with all of that, had turned around and stabbed him in the back. Or, worse than that, Novak had stabbed Kane's project, his brainchild. Well, he wasn't going to hold still for it. He would go ahead anyway, distribute his books himself, and make even more money. He'd show Novak. He hit him in the only place where it mattered, right where he lived—in the pocketbook. He'd make the series so successful, and so profitable, and such a financial triumph that Novak would kick himself every morning, noon, and night.

But the problems of setting up a distribution operation with salespeople and accounting and bookkeeping people, and warehouses—it was going to be a big job. A damned nuisance. He wondered whether, before he tackled a thing like that, before he sank a lot of money into such an ambitious project, whether he might not approach some other publishers. And then, as his anger subsided into the coolness of calculation and planning, he wondered whether he ought not try Novak one more time. He was a jerk, but he had a good sales staff. And he had all the damned equipment—the computers and the whole works. And the fact that he was a jerk could be used, could be used against him. There was a principle of jujitsu in which one used an opponent's weight against him, letting him throw himself. With all the weight of stupidity of that fat head of his, Novak could kill himself if the right grip and the right throw could be found for him. But what? How to work it?

He picked up the phone and asked for Bud Sloat. In a matter of seconds, he was put through to Bud's office in the Kane Building.

"Bud? Irv."

"Good morning. What's up?"

"Just got a letter from Novak. He's chickening out."

"Are you surprised?"

"Yes and no. I didn't think he was all that much in the guts department. But I did give him credit for a little more greed than he seems to have."

"Maybe he had it once. Twenty years ago."

"But that doesn't do us any good now," Kane said.

"No, it sure doesn't. What do you think we ought to do?"

"I don't know. That's what I called about. It seems to me that we can go any one of three ways. We can set up our own distribution system. Or we can hook in with another publisher—or try to. Or we can give Novak another chance."

"I don't understand. What would make him change his mind?"

"Mind? What mind? He's got a little ganglion up there. But if we can stimulate that little ganglion, and make the frog jump, we might make it jump our way. You follow me?"

"In a general way. But how do you think we can make him jump?"

"Well, you know Alan. He's a pompous ass in public, but in private he's a would-be swinger. The real reason he's been distributing our books all this time isn't the money he's been making from doing it. Although that doesn't hurt, I suppose. But the real reason is that he likes to come to our parties and flash a gold Tomcat lighter, and all that shit."

"You think?"

"Yes. And he's not exactly averse to having a chick thrust at him every now and then, either. Remember the party we had for the launching of the international edition?"

"I remember."

"Well, I think maybe it might be a good idea to have a party for Novak. Have him up here. Let him make like a big Tomcat. And then talk business with him."

"Well, I guess it could be worth a try. We can't lose anything by it, can we?"

"No. That's why it's worth a try," Kane said. Then, after a pause, he continued, "And we ought to do it up good and proper. What do you think of getting Josie Thompson for him? You think he'd like her?"

"Unless he's turned queer, he'll like her."

"Good. You'll find her and set it up?"

"Whatever you say," Bud answered. "She's in Dallas, I think."

"Get her. Set up some publicity appearances for her. Supermarket openings. Rotary raffles. Anything. And put through a voucher for five hundred for her. That ought to do it."

"When do you want to have your party?"

"We'll shoot for a week from Saturday. But I'll have to invite Novak first. If he accepts, we'll set it all up. I'll talk to you this afternoon."

It was a relatively simple matter to get Alan Novak to accept the invitation to the party. And the party itself was no problem at all. The machinery for such exercises was there, waiting to be set into action at Irv Kane's word. And with the word given the orders went out, and the invitations, and, as reliably as at a small eighteenth-century court, the food and the liquor and the entertainers and the courtiers assembled to make an evening of it. And it went well enough. A novelist got drunk and vomited all over one of the carpets. And the president of a Midwestern company that manufactured tie clips, cuff links, money clips, and key rings, and advertised these things in the pages of *Tomcat*, took a fancy to Nina and became rather annoying in the fervor with which he tried to force his attentions upon her. But mostly it went well, in a civilized manner. Every so often a couple would disappear. And, after a while, would return. And everyone avoided letting on that the absence had been noticed. And after a while, as it got later, and people got drunker, nobody did notice any more. Nobody except Irv and Bud and Mike Costello, who stood behind the bar making excellent drinks but was in fact the unofficial bouncer and keeper of the peace. It was quite late indeed before Alan Novak and Josie made their move past the bar and into the hall that led down a half flight of stairs to a series of ten bedrooms.

Costello came up to Kane with a drink on a tray. "Your Moscow Mule, sir," he said.

Kane accepted the drink, nodded, and, at that signal, excused himself. He crossed the room, stepping into the elevator, and ascended to his own quarters. There, at the console, sipping the Moscow Mule, he watched Novak perform with the titian-haired beauty who had been the Kalendar Kitty of the previous April. Novak was scarcely the model of healthy virility, requiring a good deal of encouragement and active help before he was ready to play, and, even then, was very brief. Josie, honest craftsman that she was, managed to coax a creditable performance out of him, but it was hardly an "A" feature production.

Kane got bored watching. He drained his drink, then turned off the television set and returned to the party. He was ready to talk business now. And so, obviously, was Novak.

Kane stationed himself at the bar, near the door to the bedroom corridor, and was not at all surprised, although he acted as if he were, to see Novak emerge from the doorway.

"Alan! Been looking for you! Having a good time?"

"Fine. Just fine."

"Good," Kane said. "Good. I like my old friends to have a good time. A fine time."

"Well, you sure do know how to give a party, Irv."

"You enjoy it and I enjoy your enjoying it. That's what parties are all about, right?"

"Right," Novak said.

He was no longer embarrassed but a little patronizing, just a touch, having decided, Kane was sure, that he, Kane, was more than a little drunk. Which was fine. Novak would be off his guard that way.

"Look, Alan, about that series . . ."

"I was terribly sorry about that. Truly, I was . . ."

"So was I, Alan. So was I. After all, we've known each other for years. You and I, and Muriel. Right? And I admire you. I mean, you're a good publisher, and a good sport, and a fellow who knows how to have a good time. Right?"

With studied nonchalance, he poked Novak in the ribs, winked broadly, and nodded.

"Irv, I . . . I mean, you . . ."

Kane let Novak sputter along for a second and then cut in, interrupting, and letting him off the hook. And also ending the Joe E. Brown act of the genial party drunk.

"Forget it. Look, strictly business. This series will do fantastically well. Nobody gave *Tomcat* a chance when I started, and you see what it's done. And the books will do even better. I just don't like to see you throwing away money. Your money. And that's what you're doing. You're throwing away potential profits of several hundred thousand a year. No risk! That's a shame. I like you. I like to see you have a good time. To enjoy life, and all the good things . . ." He nodded in the direction of the bedrooms, but this time without hamming it up. "And I like to see you do well in business. For both our sakes. So, give me a sensible answer."

"Irv, if it were just me, I'd go for it. I swear I would. Because I believe in you and I believe in anything you do. But we're on the point now of negotiating a merger with one of the big duplicator companies. And this would kill us. This would make the merger impossible. That's the reason. The only reason."

"Well, why in hell didn't you say so two weeks ago?"

"Because this thing is so damned delicate that the slightest rumor would kill it. . . ."

"And you didn't trust me?"

"I trusted you. But I didn't trust your secretary. Or, for that matter, mine. I didn't trust your phone or mine. I didn't trust anything but your own live ear."

"You're getting a little paranoid, Alan."

"You think so? I tell you, down in the city even the God-damned urinals are tapped! It's a damned crime."

"Guess you're right about that, Alan."

"Irv, if there's anything I can do, put in a good word with—a competitor, I'll be glad to help out. Anything, old friend." It was an uncomfortable moment for Novak, and it gave Kane more than mild pleasure to see the hypocrite squirm.

"Okay, Alan. Sure, if I need any help from you I'll be sure to call." He turned his back on the publisher and added, over his shoulder, "Enjoy yourself, Alan. This might turn out to be a most memorable evening."

Bud picked up a new manuscript from the pile, glanced at the reader's report, weighed the manuscript with his hand, and sighed. He put it down for a moment, looked at it, and then picked up the brandy bottle. He poured another splash into his snifter, raised it to his nose, and inhaled. Then he settled back in his chair with the short story manuscript. He was still reading the first page when the doorbell rang. He was puzzled. The doorman had not called up to announce anyone. The doorman announced everyone except Nina, and she had her own key. He wasn't expecting her, anyway. Or anyone else. Was it a neighbor who wanted to borrow some sugar, or a screwdriver? He tightened the belt on his Viyella bathrobe, put the typescript down on the table beside the chair, and went to the door. He opened it.

There were two men standing there in the hall.

"Mr. Sloat?"

"Yes?"

"My name is Harris," one of them said.

In a smooth, practiced gesture he displayed an open wallet, which held his identification. Bud glanced at it. Harris was an FBI man.

"Yes, what can I do for you gentlemen?" he asked.

"We'd like to come in if we may."

"What's this about?"

The other man reached into his jacket pocket and pulled out a paper.

"We have a warrant," the other man said.

"A warrant?"

"A search warrant. We'd like to take a look around."

He handed Bud the paper. Bud looked at it. It was, indeed, a search warrant.

"I don't know what you're expecting to find," Bud said. "I haven't done anything."

"If you haven't done anything," Harris reasoned, "you haven't got anything to worry about. May we come in?"

Bud stood aside.

"Sure, come on in. What choice have I got?"

They did not bother to answer, but stepped immediately into the foyer and on into the living room. Bud stood at the arch of the living room and watched them circle. Their eyes scanned the bookshelves, the furniture, the statues, and came to rest on the coffee table. The one who had identified himself as Harris went to the table, and, almost casually, opened the silver cigarette box. He picked up a pinch of the dried leaves, crumbled them between his fingers, sniffed them, and put the pinch back in the cigarette box. He picked the box up, put it in a manila envelope, sealed it, and looked up.

"I'm afraid you'll have to come with us, Mr. Sloat," he said.

The speed with which they had come in, homed in on the cigarette box, and found the marijuana, made Bud realize that this had been no fishing expedition. They had known what to look for and where to look for it. There was something very peculiar about it, and Bud was baffled and alarmed.

"May I call my lawyer?" he asked.

"You can do that downtown," Harris told him.

"Can I get dressed? Can I get out of my bathrobe and put on a jacket?"

"Of course."

Harris nodded to the other man, who followed Bud into the bedroom and stood there while Bud took off his robe, put on a tie and a jacket, and turned out the light. Then he went to the front hall closet and took his raincoat.

"Okay," he said. "I guess I'm ready."

The two men nodded, and escorted him out of his apartment, waited while he locked his door, and then went with him to the elevator. They rode down in silence, and in silence walked out through the lobby to the black sedan waiting outside the entrance to the apartment house.

It was not until the car had driven away and they were several blocks from the apartment that Bud realized he should have probably taken his toothbrush.

The three of them rode in silence. Harris sat in the back seat next to Bud, while the other one drove. The flashes from the street lights winked into the car and washed the impassive faces of the FBI men, bathing them in an unnatural pallor. It was not until they had been driving for five minutes or so that Bud recovered himself sufficiently to tear his mind away from those foolishly distracting surface things, and to try to think about what had happened, what was still happening, in a coherent way.

It was such an obvious setup. They hadn't even gone through the charade of a search. He wasn't being paranoid, he thought. It was simply inescapable that somebody was out to get him. Why? What for?

It was so unlikely for him to have been hit on the marijuana thing. He didn't buy the dangerous little nickel and dime bags from kids or pot heads but purchased his Acapulco Gold in hundred-dollar lots—a year's supply—from a Coast Guard commander he had known in college. So it had to be something else. It had to be a handle, or a club, that they were wielding over him. But what could it be for? And who were *they?*

There was no immediate answer that came to mind. He knew that it was important to stay calm, to think clearly and reasonably—

he remembered what the penalty was for possession of marijuana. Unfortunately, he had enough of it so that, under the law, he could be considered a wholesaler, even though it wasn't true. And the penalty for possession of that quantity ran up to ten years. But it was ridiculous. This whole thing was ridiculous. And yet it was frightening, all the more frightening because it was ridiculous. These guys weren't FBI agents. They were fugitives from some Kafka novel that had not yet been written. It was all pure fiction. But, no, he was real—and they were real.

The car turned into Government Square—it had once been Scollay Square—and Bud looked around, puzzled. Where were they taking him? Why here? This wasn't a police station. Was this where the FBI office in Boston was? But at this hour of the night, why would they be taking him to the office? Wouldn't they be taking him to a jail somewhere? Wouldn't they be booking him?

He wanted very much to ask them where they were taking him, and what was happening. But, at the same time, he was unwilling to give them the satisfaction of knowing how afraid and uncertain he was.

The car stopped. Harris got out and waited for Bud to follow. Then the other one got out, and the three of them walked up the four steps and into the deserted lobby of the large office building.

An elevator man sat there, at the end of a bank of elevators. He was wearing a gray coverall and reading *The Record-American,* the stub of an unlit cigar between his teeth. He looked up, saw the three men approaching, and, with obvious reluctance, tucked the paper between the stool and the wall. He got up as they approached, stepped into the elevator, and waited for them to follow him.

Nobody said anything. The elevator man didn't ask what floor, nor did the agents offer a number. It was a sequence out of an old silent movie, except for the faint hum of the motor down below and the rustle of the cables in the elevator shaft.

The elevator door opened and Bud followed Harris out into the corridor. They walked together down the corridor, their heels making an impressive tattoo on the crushed stone floor. At the end of the hall Bud could see the translucent glass door with light showing through it. It was the only lit door along the entire hallway. There was no marking on the door, no indication of what sort of office it was. There wasn't even a number on it.

Harris opened the door and stepped aside to let Bud pass through.

It was rather a bleak-looking reception room, painted government green and with asphalt tiles in black and white on the floor. There were two green steel desks, a green steel bookcase, entirely empty, and two green steel and leatherette chairs. Behind one of the desks an older version of the two agents who had come to pick up Bud sat in his shirt sleeves, eating a ham sandwich and drinking coffee out of a cardboard container. There was a crossword puzzle, half done and stained with a circle from the bottom of the coffee container, in front of him on the desk. He looked up, said, "Thank you, boys," and Harris and the other one, the still anonymous one, went out again, closing the door behind them.

"Good evening, Mr. Sloat. Have a chair."

Bud sat down obediently. It was even more confusing, more uncertain and, in an odd way, even more frightening than it had been before. This kind of thing didn't happen in real life! Or did it? Well, he was finding out.

The man in the shirt sleeves picked up the telephone, pushed the intercom buzzer, and announced, "He's here." He listened for a moment and then said, "Yes, sir." He hung the phone up, looked at Bud, and said, "In there."

"What's in there?"

"Go in the door and you'll find out." The man had returned to the crossword puzzle. He did not look up.

Bud shot a glance toward the door that led out to the corridor. Through the translucent glass he could see the two figures, Harris and the other one, standing there in the hall. Although his palms began to sweat, he felt chilled. He went to the door the man had indicated, put his hand on the knob, paused for one last second, and then turned the knob and went inside.

Leaning against the desk, his feet crossed, his right palm supporting part of his weight on the glass top of the desk, his collar open and his tie loosened, was Richard Patterson.

Bud recognized him instantly. For a split second Sloat was afraid he was going to laugh.

"Good evening, Mr. Sloat," Patterson said. "Won't you sit down?"

Bud looked at the chair. He was about to sit down, when, having recovered himself somewhat, he asked, "What the hell is this?"

"Sit down," Patterson said patiently, "and I'll tell you."

Bud sat down in the chair that Patterson had indicated, reached in his pocket, and pulled out his cigarettes. He was still looking for his lighter when Patterson flipped him a pack of matches. Bud made a stab at them, but missed and had to turn around and grope under the chair to find them. He lit his cigarette and watched Patterson walk around the desk and sit down at the chair behind it.

"Interesting career you've had, Mr. Sloat," Patterson began.

"I beg your pardon?" Bud said, not quite believing that he'd heard what he thought he had.

"Very interesting," Paterson went on. "First a teacher, then a reporter, and then a novelist. And now, managing editor of *Tomcat*. An odd progression. Are you happy?"

"Am I what? I'm not sure I understand."

Patterson turned away from Bud and looked up at the wall,

where there was nothing, nothing but the dusty picture molding and the dreary, bureaucratic green. But it didn't make any difference because the point was the pose, even without any excuse at all. And Bud had to admire the absolute assurance of the man who sat behind the desk.

"It'd be nice if you could go back to fiction," Patterson suggested.

To be kidnaped in the middle of the night—legally kidnaped, but still, kidnaped—and to be brought by two FBI men to an office building where the Attorney General of the United States sat and contemplated your artistic career . . . It made no sense. No sense at all. It was down the rabbit hole with Alice. And Bud was sure that at any moment Patterson would turn into the Queen of Hearts and start to bellow, "Off with his head!"

"Do you like to travel, Mr. Sloat?"

"Travel? I suppose it depends on where it's to."

"Anywhere. Europe. The Far East. South America. Anywhere at all."

"Yes, I like to travel."

"Good. I rather thought so."

"Mr. Patterson, do you mind if I ask a question."

"Not at all."

"Just so I can be sure that I'm not losing my mind, would you please tell me what all this is about?"

"What I want to propose to you," Patterson said, "is perfectly simple. I think it would be a fine idea for you to go off for a year or two and write. And I think it would not be difficult to arrange a grant from the National Foundation for the Arts so that you could do this."

"I don't know what to say," Bud began. "I suppose that such an offer—even at this hour of the night, and under these circumstances—is an honor. And . . . But I have a job, and I'm happy there, and well paid."

"Are you happy there? Wouldn't you really rather be writing again?"

"I am quite capable of deciding when I want to write. And of arranging my life so that I could write if I decided to do that."

"Oh, well. Of course. I understand your feeling about this. But let us assume that you were going to write a novel. Wouldn't you rather write a novel with a setting in Rome—where you've gone to visit several times—than a book with, say, a prison setting?"

"Mr. Patterson, what are you talking about?"

This time, the Attorney General turned his head in the direction of the door, beyond which the FBI men were still waiting.

"I'm talking about two to ten years, Mr. Sloat. Two to ten years, and a record."

It was coming clearer. Bud didn't know what it was that Patterson wanted, but, whatever it was, he wanted it very much indeed. That elaborate a carrot, and that elaborate a stick . . . Strangely enough, he felt somehow reassured. At the very least, he had returned to the world of the plausible and the possible.

"What do you want?" he asked.

"Your cooperation."

"I see. My cooperation. To help you get Irv Kane?"

"To help save the taxpayers some money. You see, we're going to get him anyway. We're going to get him whether you cooperate or not. And if you can save us a few thousand or a few hundred thousand dollars, it seems only fair to me that you should benefit by it a little."

"What do you want me to do?"

"You've decided then?"

"I've asked you what you want me to do."

"No, I'm afraid you have to decide first. Then I'll tell you what we want."

Bud sat there for a moment, thinking. On the one hand, there was the prison term. Clear and sure. And on the other? Irv and the magazine and the goddam book series. If only Irv had listened to him when he'd warned that the time wasn't right, that the risk was too great, that it was jeopardizing everything. Was he to suffer because Kane had ignored what he'd told him? All right, suffer a little, suffer reasonably. But that much? Ten years? And he'd be off in Rome . . .

"All right. Anything you want. What?"

"Good. I rather thought you might be reasonable about this. I hoped you would. And it may turn out that there isn't anything for you to do. I hope there won't be. What we have in mind for you is a kind of supportive role . . ."

Bud listened while Patterson explained the plan. There was to be the prosecution under the Comstock Act, which was the way Patterson wanted to get Kane. But in the event that the courts were unwilling to convict for that, there was a second arrow in his quiver—procuring, living on the proceeds of prostitution, keeping a disorderly house, and violation of the Mann Act. Patterson knew about the arrangements for Alan Novak, knew everything, every last detail.

"Then what do you need me for?"

"As a witness. The kind of evidence we have is not admissible in a court."

"Wiretaps?"

"What difference does it make?"

"None, I guess," Bud admitted. "But— That's how you found my marijuana!"

"We came in with a warrant, searched, and found it, Mr. Sloat," Patterson said, smiling. "That was all strictly legal."

"Yes, you would have seen to that, wouldn't you?"

"We saw to that."

"I see," he said. And then, after a pause, he asked, "And that's all you want? For me to testify, if it comes to that?"

"Well, that, and—you might keep us informed about Mr. Kane's progress with his new book-publishing venture."

"I see."

"Why not? You were against it from the start, weren't you? Why should you have to suffer for a decision that you didn't ever make? That you opposed?"

"All right," Bud said.

"Yes, of course. And, you understand that our arrangement is confidential. Because it would be better that way. No matter what else happens, this little business about the marijuana can stick. Any time. There's no way out of that, I'm afraid. There was no entrapment, nothing. The only way out is the way you've elected to take. Wisely, I think."

"I understand."

"Good. Mr. Harris will be glad to give you a lift home, I think."

Bud got up. He did not offer to shake hands with the Attorney General. Nor did the Attorney General extend a hand to him. He stood there for an instant, looked at Patterson, and then turned and left.

Richard Patterson waited until the outer door had closed. Then he sighed, rubbed his eyes with his fists, and yawned. He felt awfully tired. Still, he was not quite done. Not quite. He picked up the phone, dialed a number, and waited for an answer.

"Hello?"

"This is Patterson," he said. "You can fold it up now. It's all done. We're in."

"Yes, sir."

He hung up the phone. He supposed that he ought to feel good. He ought, he thought, at least to feel something. But he felt only tired, and grimy. After all, what difference did it make? None of this was going to bring her back. And without her, what difference did anything make?

"Shit!" he said, aloud.

"Sir?" the FBI man asked, coming in to answer what he had taken to be a call.

"Let's go," Patterson said. "The airport."

Arthur Marx sat behind the huge Regency desk in his oak-paneled office and asked his secretary, "Would you play hostess, dear?"

He looked toward Kane, who was stretched out on the green leather sofa and asked him, "You'll have a Bloody Mary, won't you?"

"Sure. Thanks," Kane said.

"Two Bloody Marys, please," Marx ordered, and the girl went to the cabinet that was concealed in the oak paneling, pushed a button, and, after the panel slid open, proceeded to mix the drinks. It was an imposing room, deliberately created to increase and enhance Marx's stature and presence. The first few times that Kane had been in the office he had been puzzled by the discrepancy between the standing Marx and the seated Marx. When he stood, the attorney was only five feet, four inches tall, but when he sat behind his desk, he could look the tallest client in the eye. Once, under the pretext of restlessness and involved thought, Kane had paced about the room, and, in the course of his pacing, had walked behind the desk, where he had discovered the carpet-covered platform under Marx's chair. Not that Marx had, himself, tried particularly to conceal it. But he didn't exactly make a point of demonstrating it, either.

Kane had been amused by his discovery, and by other discoveries as well. Once, when they had been conferring late in the afternoon about a complicated series of contracts, he had watched the sun set behind Marx, and had noticed that the window behind the lawyer was made of stained glass. That in itself would perhaps have been remarkable enough, but the glow of the setting sun on Marx's head and shoulders continued past all reasonable time, and, at a quarter of nine it was still there, bathing him in an impressive halation of back lighting. Marx worked that trick, Kane had discovered, by a spotlight mounted outside the building and aimed back through the window at an angle.

It was amusing, but in a way it was also reassuring. The kind of ego this device betrayed, the sensitivity about his height that the platform suggested, the touchiness and aggressiveness of the man that Kane knew from their years of business together, were all highly desirable in an advocate. Clearly, as clearly as anything, Kane could see that Marx had been the runty kid who had got beat up a lot and who had learned to fight with his tongue. It was that scrappiness, as well as the brilliance and boldness of Marx's mind, that Kane was hiring and for which Kane paid a retainer of thirty thousand dollars a year.

Kane accepted the Bloody Mary from the secretary, took a sip, and enjoyed the tartness of the drink. He felt good. He felt good because he had Marx in his corner, now, when he needed him most. It didn't matter that litigation cost extra, he would be getting his money's worth—in legal representation, in publicity, and in sheer amusement value. It would be fun to watch Art Marx work.

The secretary had put the Bloody Mary down on an aluminum coaster on Marx's desk and was on her way out.

"No calls, please," Marx instructed her.

"Yes, sir," she said, in a clipped English accent, and closed the door behind her.

"I must say," Marx began, "that I admire your insouciance."

"Oh?" Kane said.

"Sure," Marx said. "My God, that was an arraignment this morning, and you behaved as if it were your goddam wedding. I had the car out there in back so that we could have gone out the side door. We could have avoided all those reporters and photographers. But you went out there, smiling and waving and posing for pictures, and you're holding a press conference this afternoon? That's real *chutzpah*."

"Well," Kane said, "I'm relying on you. You told me I had nothing to worry about, so I'm not worrying."

"You don't," Marx said. "But usually it's the lawyer who's calm. The client tends to get nervous. But here you are, on bail from a criminal proceeding and you're behaving as if you've been elected governor."

Kane laughed, swung himself to a sitting position, and took another sip of his drink. "What are you trying to tell me, Art?" he asked. "Are you worried?"

Marx put his fingertips together. It looked almost as though he were praying, the way he had his elbows spread on the blotter, fingertips touching and his chin resting at the apex of his index fingers. "All I can tell you is what I've told you before," he began. "This should be a civil action, and, as a matter of fact, there shouldn't be any action at all. The governing case here is the Roth decision, and the redeeming social value of material in the magazine is demonstrable and obvious and evident. The thing that bothers me—or, no, I won't say 'bothers,' let me say 'puzzles'—yes, the thing that puzzles me is why Patterson is doing this. It's such a goddam obvious witch hunt. I've met him, and he's a reasonable fellow. As a matter of fact, he's a very intelligent man—

not, I thought, a prig or a prude. If he were stupid, I could understand it. I never thought that he was that politically ambitious. Where the hell can he go? Does he want to be President? And even if he did have political ambitions, it just doesn't make sense for him to put so much on the line in this kind of a campaign and lose. If he just wanted to make a big noise about smut he could go after whips and spurs. Or those homo magazines. But to bring an action like this against you based on the theory of the Ginsberg conviction and to do it with a kind of obvious creaking of machinery . . . What puzzles me is what he thinks he can get out of it. If I knew that I'd feel a lot more confident because legally we're in a great position. It's the strategy of it that I just do not understand. He doesn't have a leg to stand on. This intent business —except in something like a homicide there is no such thing. How can you prove intent? And this advertising thing? That's ridiculous. You could lock up General Motors because they say that Cadillacs are sexy. You could lock up Colgate because they say their toothpaste is appealing and makes you look layable. There isn't a mouthwash company that wouldn't have every goddam executive in jail if advertising were a standard. It's laughable."

Kane waited for the wave of oratory to subside. The force of the question had long since been clear to him, and he was sure that Marx had known it was perfectly clear but had gone on anyway from the sheer love of rodomontade.

"You really want to know?" he asked Marx. "You have to know?"

"I don't like the sound of that," Marx said, sitting up straight and fixing Kane with his famous, piercing cross-examiner's eye. "You've got something to tell me?"

"Yes," Kane said.

"Then tell me! If I'm to represent you, I've got to know what the hell I'm representing, don't I? I have to explain that to every two-bit holdup man that comes into this office. I should think it wouldn't be necessary to explain it to you. If you don't tell me the truth I can't represent you. I mean, just as a practical matter, I don't like surprises. When I get up in a courtroom and ask a question, I've got to be damn sure that I know what the answer's going to be. It's only Perry Mason who finds out things on fishing expeditions. If any real lawyer behaved the way he does, he'd lose every week."

"All right, all right," Kane said. "I tried to get Patterson off my back about eight months ago. Only it backfired."

"Yes?"

"You remember the stories about Patterson and Jill Jefferson?"

"Sure I remember. What has that to do with anything?"

Kane lit a cigarette, took a puff, inhaled, and then blew the smoke out through his mouth and nose. It was a long bit of business, a kind of deliberate stall so that he could gather his wits and gather his words and find a way of telling Marx what had happened. He valued the man's opinion of him. He began, reciting in a very matter-of-fact way the story of his attempt to get Jill Jefferson to intercede for him with Patterson. It was not a pleasant story, and he did not enjoy telling it. He was not worried about Marx's personal reaction; Marx had a pretty strong stomach. He was certainly not worried about Marx's professional reaction either. But it was the necessity of having to face it himself, having himself to say it aloud for the first time that subdued him. God knows he had suffered private moments of anguish. His recitation, at first impersonal and detached, began to fray just the slightest bit as he reached the conclusion of the story and got to the part about the interview he had had with Jill at the Beverly Hills Hotel, and about her suicide three days later. "And so you see," he said, "what I tried to do was to blackmail her. I never expected that it would turn out the way it did. But it did," he said flatly.

The word "blackmail" hung in the air. It was the closest thing to a confession that Kane had ever made—or had ever had to make.

Marx had listened in utter silence, and, now that Kane was finished, he remained silent for several moments more. He sighed once, rubbed his chin, and then said, with an air of finality, "So. That explains the puzzle."

"It's not a pretty story," Kane admitted.

"No, it isn't," Marx agreed, "but neither is it a pretty story when an Attorney General of the United States uses his position and the powers of government this way for a personal vendetta. Now that I know why he's doing this, I don't think we have anything to worry about."

Kane wished for a moment that Marx had not been such a professional after all, wished that Marx had allowed himself some kind of personal reaction. It was unimportant what kind of reaction Marx could have shown, but something, anything. It was bad enough to have to cough it all up and confess it that way, but it was even worse to perform the act of confession without some kind of response—absolution or condemnation or sympathy or antipathy—anything would have been preferable to this purely strategic professional mask. It was, then, with a combination of resentment and admiration that he commented, "You know, Art, you've got a pretty strong stomach."

"Yes," Marx agreed, "that's my business. That is the name of the game."

There was a silence during which the two men looked at each other. It could not have lasted more than a few seconds. Still, it was the closest thing to an intimate moment that Kane could remember with Marx—with any man since Buchanan had been run over that day in the streets of Tokyo.

"Freshen your drink?" Marx offered.

He had half risen out of his chair. He intended obviously to fix the drink himself, which was not his style at all. Kane noted this, appreciated it, but declined. "No, thanks," he said, "I'll need my wits about me."

"Don't worry," Marx said. "Just tell them that you have every confidence in me and in the Constitution, and duck any direct questions."

"I'm not worried," Kane said, "the reporters love to eat and drink at the Mansion. They're all my friends."

Kane stubbed his cigarette out in the blue-green ceramic ashtray and asked Marx, "So—where do we stand? What happens next?"

"You've pleaded not guilty and you're out on bail. Trial is set for three weeks from today, but we'll extend that, and very probably they'll extend it, too, so that nothing much will happen for two, two and a half months. We'll waive a jury, I think. In New York we might go with one, but up here, in Boston, I think the risks are too high. The questions here are mostly precedent questions that have to do with the law, and I think there's a good chance that the judge may simply throw the case out. If it does go to trial, we have an excellent chance of winning, and even if we don't, we're sure to win on appeal. There's nothing for you to do except relax. All I need from you is a list of clergymen on the advisory council, psychologists, literary critics—especially those who owe you favors. We'll see if we can get some enlightened high school principal or prep school headmaster, which is more likely, to testify for you."

"Great," Kane said. "We're in good shape, then."

"I think so."

Kane fished under the sofa for his loafers and slid them on. Marx took advantage of the moment to descend from his platform and come across the room so he could escort Kane out.

"Oh, there's one other thing I wanted to ask you about," Marx began.

"Yes?"

"This Scully business. How far do you want to go with this? I'm sure we're going to lose the appeal in the Massachusetts Supreme Court. That damned judge in the Criminal Court conducted that trial like a ballet. There isn't a real error in the record. They'll either keep him in Bridgewater forever or ship him back to Walpole, and eventually the governor will commute the sentence to life. Shall we drop it now or shall we go on with it?"

"But where is there to go on to?" Kane asked.

"I'm not sure that there is anything, really, but one of the young fellows in the office, one of the stars of tomorrow of Marx, Bronstein and Engels, has written a very interesting memo about the confession angle and the circumstances of Scully's arrest. He's been watching the trends of decisions in the Supreme Court, and he thinks it might be worth a shot at a writ of certiorari. If they're willing to hear it, are you willing to go on paying?"

"Sure," Kane said. "Take it as far as it'll go. If you think there's even an outside chance, go with it."

"It's really a kind of interesting point . . ."

"I'm sure it is, counselor, but I wouldn't understand it anyway."

"Okay, okay," Marx said, "but lay off that counselor stuff. That's what gangsters call their lawyers."

"Well, after all," Kane said, "I'm out on bail—just like a gangster. Who has a right better than me?"

They both laughed. Marx reached up to pat Kane on the back and escorted him out of the office, through the elegantly decorated reception room and out into the hall, where he waited with him until the elevator came.

It was not the act of love itself that, however pleasant it had been, however tender and even however loving, was still something familiar to Nina, something she and Bud had shared many times before. Nor was it the way in which he continued to embrace her, pushing her hair gently out of her eyes and stroking her cheek and the side of her neck, as he looked down at her, smiling. She appreciated that and enjoyed it. But it was the statement, the declared words, which he uttered almost casually, almost as if they, too, were a part of their shared embraces. He had just rolled over, and, as he lay back from the kiss that invariably accompanied their separation, said it.

"I love you, Nina."

She was startled out of her post-coital languor. She opened her eyes and propped herself up on an elbow. She looked down at him intently, trying to decide how he meant it—and trying to decide, too, what her response ought to be.

"When did you decide that?" she asked, with a little smile. She was playing for time, trying to find out what had prompted his declaration, and trying to gauge, herself, not only what she ought to say but what she wanted to say. Did she love him? It was not a question that she had had to ask herself before. She was not even sure any more what love was. Oh, when she had been nineteen and twenty she had had the same romantic ideas that all girls of that age are burdened with. But now, having outgrown those childish notions and having been plunged into a world of sophistication and urbanity, a world where she could "love" a man for two years without ever getting close to him, and where she could make love with another man for the same two years without ever having analyzed her feelings for him—now she was entirely at a loss.

"I don't know when I decided, really," he said. "It's occurred to me more and more in the last few months that you make me very happy. And no other woman has ever made me so happy for such a long time. You know," he went on, "after two marriages I'm not sure I know what love is all about. But I do know that I want to be with you and I want to take care of you." Echoing her thoughts he continued, "You know, I think I knew more about love at fifteen than I do now at forty-five."

"I'm afraid of the word 'love,'" Nina said, "but all the things you said, I feel, too."

"I don't know," he said. "I guess I'm going about this in the wrong way." He leaned over and grabbed two cigarettes from the alabaster cigarette urn on the night table, lit them both and passed her one.

She was not going to rush him, not going to prompt him. Even though she knew that he had something important to say she wondered whether he might not be using the pause as a dramatic or rhetorical device. But whatever it was, she knew that it was something that would affect the course of their future friendship. She sat up, propped the pillows higher so that she could sit up straight, and pulled the sheet up to her waist.

She was ready, now, for a serious discussion.

She was not ready, however, for his next question. He turned to her, took a deep drag on his cigarette, exhaled noisily, and asked abruptly, "Will you marry me?"

"I don't mean to sound ungracious," she began after a moment, "or ungrateful. But I don't understand why you want to get married. What do you want with a third wife? We've been so happy together this way for the last two and a half years." Her voice trailed off, and then she went on. "The only thing that would be different if we were married is that we could have a child," she said softly.

"Wouldn't you like to have one?" Bud asked. "I support two children, but I don't feel like a father at all."

"Yes," she said, "I'd like to have a child. I'd like that very much. I think we'd be just as happy married as we have been this way," she went on.

"Then you will?" he said with some eagerness. "Then you will marry me?"

"I don't know," she said. "Let me think about it. I've always been honest with you, and it's more important now that I be honest with you than it ever has been before. And honest with myself, too. I won't marry you just for a child, even though I want one. It would have to be because it was the best thing for *us*. If I said no," she continued thoughtfully, "would it be the end?"

"Not the end of my feeling for you," he answered, "but it would work out the same way. It would be the end of this."

"Oh?" she asked. "What do you mean?"

"I'm going to be leaving *Tomcat*," he said.

"Where are you going?" she asked.

"As a matter of fact," he said, "I'm leaving the country. I'm going to Rome. And I want to take you with me."

Now it was her turn to stall. Now she needed to think. The idea of their just continuing the way they were, working for *Tomcat*—working for Irv—and yet getting married . . . it didn't make any sense. But to start a new life together, to change their scene, the very thought seemed plausible, possible, and even attractive.

"Could you get me a drink?" she asked. "A question like this . . . well, it needs, at the very least, a brandy and soda."

"Sure," he said. "Be glad to."

He got out of bed, kissed her on the forehead, and padded off to the bar in the living room.

She was tempted. No other man had been so easy to get along with, so pleasant to be with, so interesting to talk to, so gay and so much fun—and so good in bed. This business with Irv—or, hell, it wasn't even that—these fantasies about Irv, were getting her nowhere. She remembered a moment, seven months before, when he had reached out for sympathy and affection, but had drawn back into himself and had been unable to accept the compassion and the warmth she had always been ready to give. That should have settled that beyond any doubt. And it had, she told herself, it had settled it.

She could, on the other hand, perfectly well imagine a life with Bud. Civilized, warm, amusing, with enough intimacy to satisfy her, and yet with a respect for each other's privacy and individuality. And she yearned for a child. She was, after all, thirty-two now. She had, she supposed, about five years left, and in ten years, if she had let these five go by, she knew she would bitterly regret it.

Bud came back, bearing the two highball glasses of brandy and soda.

"*Ciao*," she said.

"Is that yes?" he asked.

She smiled and nodded. He put the brandy glasses down on the night table and embraced her.

"Oh, that's wonderful!" he exclaimed. "I'm so happy. We'll have a good life," he promised.

He kissed her tenderly.

"Yes," she said. "We will."

He reached for the glasses and handed her one, and then, looking deeply into each other's eyes, they clinked glasses and drank a toast to their future.

It was after she had had two sips of the drink that she turned to him and asked him, "What will we be doing in Rome?"

"Guess," he said.

"I can't."

"Oh, come on, try to guess."

"You're going to be a correspondent?"

"No."

"You're going into PR?"

"No, no. Guess again. It's better than that."

"You've just inherited a million dollars . . . oh, come on, Bud," she said, laughing, "tell me."

"I'm up for a grant. The National Foundation for the Arts. To work in Rome. What do you think?"

"Marvelous, darling," she said, excitedly. "What a wonderful thing. How long have you known about this? Why didn't you tell me before?"

"It wasn't so important," he said, "as knowing whether you would come with me."

"Oh," she said, "that's very sweet. Really," she said, "I mean it. When do we go?"

"Any time," he said.

"Not before Irv is finished with this business. We have to stay around until the trial is over. They'll let you wait for that, won't they? It's no real problem," she went on. "They'll acquit him, of course. But still, if both of us are going to be leaving the magazine we've got to give him some time to find our replacements and help him break them in."

He was silent.

"If it goes up to the appellate courts it will go on for a year," Bud began.

"We wouldn't have to wait for that," Nina said. He wouldn't need us for that, anyway. I just don't want him to think that we're running out on him."

"But we are," Bud said. "I have."

"Bud," she said, sitting up. "What do you mean?"

"Why do you think I was offered the grant to Rome?"

She looked at him, uncomprehending, blank.

"You have to know this," he said. "I had no choice. They caught me. They found four ounces of pot, and they offered me the choice—jail or Rome."

"And what did you have to do?" she asked, very subdued and feeling quite physically sick. She had not liked what she had heard so far, she did not want to hear more, but she had to. She had to hear it all. There was too much riding on it. It was too important. "What did you have to do?" she asked again.

"They wanted my cooperation on the case against Irv."

"And you gave it to them?"

"What would you have done?" he asked.

She did not answer.

"Of course I gave it to them. I gave them everything they wanted. Damn it, I had no choice. It was the only sane thing to do. I did it to save my skin, I did it for our sake, I did it—"

"You didn't do it for *my* sake," she said, standing up beside the bed.

"What good would it have done anybody for me to have gone to jail for ten years on a charge like that? What would you have done? I mean, you've been here with me, you've smoked pot, too. They could have caught us both together and put the screws on both of us. I tell you, I had no choice."

"Crap!" she answered. She had started to get into her clothes, with nervous, clumsy fingers.

"Don't be such a fucking girl scout!" he said angrily. "You tell me what you would have done."

"I wouldn't have sold Irv down the river that way. I don't know what I'd have done. Maybe I'd have gone to Irv to tell him.

Maybe I'd have gone to the papers. Maybe I'd have gone to Irv's lawyer about it. But I wouldn't have betrayed him."

"Look," Bud said, "it isn't me you're angry at, it's the world. It's the crummy world."

"I'm not angry at the world, Bud. I'm not even angry at you. I'm just sick and disgusted."

"So you still care for him?"

"My God," she said, "you don't understand anything!"

"Yes, I do. You've been hung up on him ever since you came to *Tomcat*, and you're still hung up about him. That crazy, egotistical son of a bitch!"

"Him? *He's* a son of a bitch? And you don't think you've done anything wrong?"

"I don't know," he said. "I don't make that kind of decision. I do what I have to do."

"That's very noble."

"No, it isn't noble. I'm not trying to be noble. For God's sake, what does nobility have to do with anything? You think Irv Kane is noble? Do you know what Patterson wanted from me?"

"I don't want to know."

"You ought to know. It'd be good for your moral education."

"My moral education? With you as the professor?"

"Yes. He wanted my testimony against Irv for pimping. For procuring."

"For what?"

"You heard me! It's what he's got tucked up his sleeve for Irv if the pornography business doesn't work."

"Pimping?"

"Of course. For advertisers. For big writers. For Alan Novak."

"Oh, dear."

"Yes. 'Oh, dear!' Noble, isn't it?"

"But why? What has Patterson been trying to do? Why has he been after Irv that way?"

"Don't you know?"

"No," she said, defiantly, "I don't."

"It's revenge, sweetheart. Revenge for Jill Jefferson's suicide."

"What are you talking about? What could Irv have to do with that?"

"You remember Irv's trip out to the coast to see Jill Jefferson? And you remember that she killed herself a couple of days later? You broke the news to Irv, remember?"

"I remember."

"Well, he went out there to pressure her into pressuring Patterson to lay off, to call off the dogs, to leave *Tomcat* alone. My God, can't you see it? It was blackmail! It had to be. He had something on her, and he was using it. And she took the only way out he'd left her!"

"Blackmail?" Nina asked, stunned. "I . . . I don't believe you."

"Irv is too noble for that, huh?"

"Blackmail with what? What was he using?"

"I haven't the vaguest idea."

"I didn't think so. It's all guessing, isn't it? It's exactly what your kind of mind would come up with!"

"Try to explain it some other way, then."

"Maybe it just doesn't make any sense at all. Maybe there is no explanation."

"Just imagination, huh? But the pimping part of it is true enough. And he knew that I'd had my hand in that. That I made some of the calls. So, you see, he could have got me to testify anyway. He could have done it all with nothing but the threat of a perjury rap. And I'd have had to do exactly the same thing."

"You still could have gone to Irv's lawyers, or to Irv."

"The point, as I say, was to save my own skin. We're too important to let a thing like this, a crazy gesture, a delusion of nobility, ruin us. And our life together."

"What life together?" she asked. "Do you think I could marry you now?"

"I don't know. That's for you to decide."

She did not answer. She stepped into her shoes and walked out of the bedroom through the living room and into the foyer. She stopped at the door, picked up her pocketbook, opened it, rummaged through it for a moment until she found the key to his apartment. She dropped it in the tropical fish bowl on the hall table before she opened the door and went out. She was tempted to slam it behind her, but she refused to give him that satisfaction.

In the taxi home she began to cry, but whether it was for herself, for Irv, for Bud, or for all of them, she could hardly have said.

9

He had, at the first, been entirely absorbed in the proceedings, fascinated by every detail. It was as if he had been in a theater, rather than in a courtroom, and had been gripped entirely by the artfulness of the playwright, the skill of the actors, the brilliance of the set decorator. Odd things captured his attention entirely, as for instance the way in which the clerk of the court kept pushing his tortoise-shell spectacles back up on his nose. They didn't fit quite properly, and, from time to time, he would reach up with the index finger of his right hand and push them back where they belonged. The timing of those gestures was deliciously random. The mood of the room fascinated Irv Kane, too: the paneling, the portraits of former judges, mostly dead and all of them obscure, unknown figures, the quality of the light that came through the high, arched windows, so filtered and so anemic, even in midsummer, as to require the help of the elaborate chandelier, which was itself so ornate, so old, and so high, as to require, in turn, the help of the more recent sconces around the walls. All these things, during the *longueurs,* leaped out at Kane, and his nimble mind toyed with them.

But then, when the case got under way, when the prosecution began to call its witnesses, its experts, its educators, its psychiatrists, its social workers, its critics, Kane's attention matured, and, instead of feeling like a little boy in a room full of mysterious grownups, he felt like an old man. There was no intervening moment of mere equality, of simple parity. He leaped suddenly to age, to wisdom, to crankiness, even. It was all nonsense. All foolish palaver. The psychiatrists were full of shit. The social workers had no idea what they were talking about and, if they had ever actually done any social work, Kane was certain it had to be in the Land of Oz, where nothing real penetrated through their green glasses.

There were references to the Moors murder trial in England, and to the Scully case in Boston. It was irrelevant. Kane knew that even before Marx wrote him a note, with his old-fashioned gold fountain pen, about the absurdity of the entire line of argument: "Question is whether, 'To the *average* person, applying contemporary community standards,' material appeals to prurient interest."

Kane read the note, nodded, and folded it in halves, quarters, eighths, sixteenths ... he could not fold it any more. But the anger he felt, an old man's rage, burned in him, and it was with a savage frustration that he gave up the attempt to fold the paper once more. With a great act of will, he put the small piece of paper into his pocket.

After a while even the rage faded. It had got to be boring. The dreary obviousness with which the United States Attorney presented witness after witness, trying to build his stupid case became insufferably dull. Kane found that his mind was wandering, away from the witnesses, away from the courtroom, and back to the problems of the business, the trivial, persistent problems, foolish things like the renewal of the royalty contract for the Tomcat pajamas. It was a dumb thing to be thinking about, he told himself, in the middle of his trial. Hell, even if the trial weren't going on, it would be a dumb thing to be thinking about. On the other hand, anything else was better than this.

He tried to pay attention again. He tried to listen, to think, to scheme along with Marx. Most of the issues were procedural, and he was ignorant about the procedures of the courtroom. And no matter how hard he tried to force himself to listen and to follow, he was dogged by the conviction that it didn't really make any difference anyway. Marx had told him there was a good chance they would win right here. And that it was an absolute certainty they would win on appeal. So there wasn't even any suspense to it, any feeling that there was much at stake, that he was really involved.

It was only during the recesses, when the court adjourned for lunch, or at the end of the day, when he sat with Marx across a table at a restaurant, or went up to Marx's office for a drink, that it became even faintly interesting. It was at those times that Marx explained to him what the strategy of the United States Attorney seemed to be, and what the plans were that he had for their defense.

"What they're doing is what any prosecutor tries to do. They're attacking across the board, firing a shotgun and scattering arguments in every direction, figuring that something has got to hit somewhere if the pellets are dense enough. But I don't see that there is too much to worry about. The advertising is gamy, sure, but the ads don't have anything to do with the point at issue. And the possibility that young people might read the books is a little disturbing, but the whole notion of censorship by age groups is unconstitutional and dangerous. And I imagine they'll try to bring in books or pieces of books to try to get what they can from the shock value—but that's where the Roth decision applies, and that's where the appellate courts will have to follow the rule about the work as a whole from the Woolsey decision in *Ulysses*, and the average adult from the Roth case. The prosecution will rest in a while, and I'll move to dismiss. And we just might make it, right there. If I were on the bench, I'd think very seriously of throwing the whole case out. I really would."

"I'm glad to hear it," Kane said. He was sure that Marx was not just whistling in the dark. If Marx was hopeful, then there was good reason to hope. Lawyers were like doctors, after all. They always made out that the problems were dark and grave so that they could take all the more credit for coming in to save the day, the patient, the client, the case . . . and so they could charge all the more, too.

On the other hand, Marx had been his guidepost in the decision finally to go ahead with the books. The expenditure of better than $150,000 in direct mail advertising and ads in the journals, and all the money that was tied up in the books themselves had all been spent, more or less, on Marx's say-so. It would be, to say the least, awkward for him to have second thoughts about the decision now.

"Dessert?" Marx asked.

"No, I don't think so. Just coffee for me."

"Two coffees," Marx told the waiter. And to Kane he said, "Relax! You've been sitting there with your forehead all wrinkled for the last three minutes. It's lousy for your digestion."

"Okay," Kane said. "If you say so, I'll relax."

And he did. He went sauntering back into the courtroom, ready for all the annoying irrelevance now, because Marx had assured him that it would be ultimately harmless. In fact, ultimately, it would be helpful. All this publicity, and all the coverage! You couldn't begin to buy this kind of time and space.

Still, it was tiresome. The prosecution was coming on in its holier-than-thou tone. And the judge was a joke. Marx's only fear about the initial trial was owing to Judge Berigan's age, and his famous remark about sex being man's greatest weakness. Berigan was in his sixties, and Kane was sure that he had long ago forgotten what it was like to be alive.

The prosecution droned on. They called still more psychiatrists and sociologists. And they all yammered along about the great harm that these books could do, especially if they fell into the hands of young people. One, Dr. Mull, took a slightly different line, criticizing not the sexuality but the object-ness of the sexuality, the way in which the sex was divorced from emotion and sentiment. The prosecuting attorney asked him to be more specific, and Dr. Mull reached into his briefcase and pulled out a copy of *The Amusement Park*.

"The passage that begins on page 37, for example, is most definitely a passage which dissociates the sexual from the emotional and is dangerous rather than helpful to the growth of the young person."

"Would you read the passage, Dr. Mull?"

"Objection," said Marx. "The book is submitted in evidence. There is no particular advantage to be gained by reading aloud from it. The book was not intended to be read aloud!"

"On the contrary, the publication of the book allows for any ordinary use. One could read aloud from it. And the advantage," the prosecutor explained, "is that we have the eminent and able

Dr. Mull here with us, so that we can discuss the passage and deal with it directly."

"You may read the passage," Judge Berigan said. "Objection denied."

> *We walked further down the midway, laughing, enjoying the lights and the crowd, and ourselves, and we came to the arcade of chance. There were, inside, gambling machines, not unlike the conventional slot machines all over the world. But here, instead of the one-armed bandits, there were big-pricked bandits. Lines of women played the machines, the operation of which was quite simple. Each "machine" concealed a man. They stood behind a screen and placed their members through a small aperture. The women, standing in lines in front, paid a half dollar for the privilege of sucking—*

"Objection!" Marx shouted at the top of his voice. In a more moderate tone he requested a conference with the judge in his chambers. Judge Berigan granted the request for a conference, and Berigan, Marx, and Joseph Fineberg retired to the chambers for five minutes. When they returned, Marx had made his objection once more, pointing out that material could not fairly be excerpted from a book and that either the whole book would have to be read or none of it could be read. He rattled off a series of citations. The judge granted the motion.

"Very well," Fineberg continued. "Would you tell the court, then, Dr. Mull, what comment you have to make upon the book as a whole."

"My comment," the witness said, "is this. Not only is the passage prurient and calculated to arouse lustful thoughts and emotions, but it is destructive to the precious idea that there is a connection between sex and love, between sex and reproduction, between sex and anything else at all. Sex can be a beautiful expression of the affection between two people, or of hope in the future as we propagate the race of man. But this passage and, indeed, the tendency of the entire book, I believe, is destructive to any meaning, any possibility of connection between gross sexuality and anything else."

"And do you think, Dr. Mull, that there is any danger in the publication and circulation of such a book as this?"

"Well, it seems to me that if there is any force or effect to books at all, then this book is dangerous. And if we believe that good books can cause good, then I think we must conclude that bad books can cause bad."

"Your witness."

Marx got up and cross-examined.

"Dr. Mull, you read this book?"

"Yes."

"The whole book?"

"Yes, of course."

"And have you been corrupted by it?"

"I'm not sure I know what you mean."

"You've just said that the tendency of such a book as this is to corrupt, to destroy meaning and beauty of sexuality, and to mislead. Well, then, as one who has read the book, have you been corrupted, or misled, or has sexuality changed in your view to something less beautiful or meaningful?"

"Well, I'm a scholar . . ."

"We know your credentials and your position. What I'm asking is whether you, personally, have been corrupted or misled. Yes or no."

"Why, no, but . . ."

"Thank you, Dr. Mull. No further questions."

The prosecution rested. Marx moved that the complaint be dismissed because the prosecution had not proved a case. The judge denied the motion.

Marx called the first of Kane's experts, who testified, one after another, about the celebration of eroticism, the harmfulness of repression, the social and scholarly significance of the books that Kane had published, and the probable effect of their publication on the welfare of the community. Kane listened, or tried to, but a peculiar ennui overtook him. It was, he supposed, helpful enough. And relevant enough. But the real witnesses, the appropriate witnesses would have been Satsumi, and Cal, and . . .

But that was impossible. And the trial was only a ceremony, an approximation of the real world, not that real world itself. So the experts paraded, his against theirs, like intellectual chess pieces.

At last he was called, and he walked up to the stand and was sworn in.

"Your name?"

"Irvin Kane."

"Your address?"

"Tomcat House, Eagle Island, Boston."

Marx began with the preliminary questions, as they had gone over them before, in Marx's office. It was immediately established that Irvin Kane was the publisher and controlling stockholder in *Tomcat* magazine, and the principal owner of Topper Books, Inc. The circulation of *Tomcat* was established at 4,700,000, and then Marx began the serious questioning by reviewing the censorship fights that Kane had already had on the magazine, eliciting from Kane the opinion that the wide acceptance of the magazine itself, of which the 4,700,000 copies a month provided ample proof, was a demonstration that he was merely marching in step with community standards.

The questions continued through Kane's belief in the social significance of everything he was doing, in his views about the importance of liberating the American public from the myths of their Puritan heritage, and finally to his particular concern with disaffiliated youth and with the absolute importance and, indeed, urgency of dealing with young people with honesty and candor.

The direct examination was relatively brief. It was now up to the United States Attorney, Joseph Fineberg, to complete his testimony with the cross-examination. Now his beliefs—and his composure—would be put to the ultimate test.

Fineberg was a husky, "scrappy"-looking fellow, the kind of person who in television and movies was played by Martin Balsam. He also had Balsam's receding hairline and that odd face, which combined a kind of ferretlike look with impressive sincerity.

The questions began in a predictable enough way. Fineberg asked questions about the figures that had been projected for the profits of the book program for the next three years. He didn't ask the questions blindly, but obviously used information that had been fed to him. His questions required only yes or no answers.

"Is it not a fact, Mr. Kane, that your projected profits for three years were in excess of two million dollars?"

"Yes, they are."

"And yet you still maintain that your motive for this is purely altruistic and idealistic and not self-seeking?"

"Yes, sir, I do. This is a part of the free enterprise system as I understand it. To do things that are good for the public and yet to make a profit through the doing of them. I don't think there's been a law passed against that yet."

"Just answer the questions, please, Mr. Kane."

"That's what I'm trying to do."

Fineberg turned and stood there for a moment, holding his chin in his hand and looking very thoughtful. Then he went to the table on which he had piles of papers and law books, and picked up an illustrated brochure. He held it in his hand, tapped his chin with it, and then crossed back to the witness stand. He extended it to Kane.

"Do you recognize this paper?"

"Yes, it's one of our direct mail advertisements."

"Would you read it, please?"

"Oh, I've already read it."

"I mean would you read it aloud, to the court, please?"

"Objection!" Marx called out. "There is no reason why Mr. Fineberg can't read the pamphlet to the court. This is an enormously irregular procedure!"

"Would you be distressed or embarrassed by reading the ad, Mr. Kane?" Fineberg asked.

"No, I don't think so," Kane said.

"You can read it, Mr. Fineberg," Judge Berigan said.

"Very well, your honor," Fineberg said, and he cleared his throat and read the pamphlet. "It is illustrated by a drawing of two men and three women, all of whom are shown to be strolling across a rolling landscape, which is in fact the body of a woman. There is a clearly discernible nipple at the top of the hill to the left of the picture, and there is a navel in the middle of the valley toward the right. The caption of the illustration reads, 'There is a pleasant glade, down yonder . . .' And beneath the illustration there is a headline that reads, 'Daring? Bold? Adventurous? Shocking? And under that, in smaller type, 'We don't think so, but there are many who do. And that's why Irvin S. Kane, the Publisher and Editor-in-Chief of *Tomcat* magazine, undertook to publish Topper Books. To kick a few more bricks from the ugly wreck of Victorian prudishness! To reaffirm the older, healthier idea that sex can be fun, can be funny, can be exuberant, can be lively! To entertain the psychologically mature reader who has an appreciation of the ribaldry and earthiness of Chaucer, of Boccaccio, of Apollinaire! And to provide, perhaps, that little shock to the timid, the frightened, the fearful, the prudish reader who might be liberated from the hidebound constructions of literature of a generation ago, and who would be better off—both in literature and life—for having been so liberated!

" 'This attractively printed, handsomely bound series of books will be available by subscription at a specially attractive price of only $2.00 per volume (plus 35 cents for postage and handling). These same books will be sold at bookstores for $3.50! Among the first volumes in the series:

" '*Taylor East and Mrs. Beasley* by Jack Towne. The story of a nymphomaniacal wife of a prep school housemaster, and the twelve boys in her charge!

" '*The Amusement Park* by John Folger. A surrealist trip to a sexual playland, like nothing you've ever read—or imagined—before!

" '*The Sex Life of Jesus* by Eugene Spoonfeld. An irreverent fantasy about Jesus and Mary Magdalene, and how they spent forty days in the desert—*together.*

" '*Jane Amor, Space Nurse* by Robert V. Kessler. The first woman on the moon—along with six astronauts!

" '*Every Night, Joseph!* by Andrew Peters. Another Biblical fantasy, this one about Joseph and Potiphar's wife, and the impossible demands the tormented and misunderstood woman put upon her young admirer!

" '*Galley of the Girls* by Neil Farber. A cruising ship of prostitutes in the War of 1812! This little-known incident in American history will surprise many, amuse all!

" '*Aphrodite Examined* by John J. Slutton. The mad scientist develops a substitute for women—and falls in love with it himself!

" 'Order now! With a charter subscription to the Topper Books series, you will get a year's subscription (original or renewal) to *Tomcat*, absolutely free! All books sent in plain, lilac wrappers.' "

There was a ripple of laughter through the courtroom.

"Why lilac?" Mr. Fineberg asked, good-natured and charming.

"Well, it's a plain wrapper. But brown is such a dreary color," Kane replied.

"Is it not true that this copy is designed to pander? That this entire advertisement is calculated to appeal to the basest instincts?" Fineberg snapped.

"I don't know that any instincts are base," Kane replied calmly.

"Well, then, put it another way," Fineberg said, smiling. "Would you let your own daughter read the books in your Topper Books series?"

"Yes, I certainly would."

"And would that be with your former wife's approval?" Fineberg shot back.

Kane felt the anger welling up within him.

"I can't answer for her," he said.

"Is it not a fact that she objected strenuously to your daughter's visit to your home and to the unhealthy influences to which she would be subjected there?"

Marx leapt to his feet. "Objection, your Honor. The question is irrelevant, incompetent, and immaterial."

"On the contrary," interjected Fineberg, "we're trying to establish the character and competence of the witness as an adviser and counselor to young people."

"The witness will answer the question," Berigan said.

"Yes," Kane snarled, "it's perfectly true. In fact, this is why I undertook to publish this entire series. The kind of maladjusted prudishness that was being inflicted on my own daughter enraged and sickened me and I felt that something had to be done about it—not just for her, but for every son and daughter in the country."

"Why do you consider yourself an authority on what's good for adolescents?"

"I don't consider myself an authority on what's good for adolescents. Good, healthy, open sexuality is good for every one."

"For fourteen- and fifteen-year-old children?" Fineberg demanded.

"For everyone. Sure, fourteen, sure thirteen, even twelve!"

"No further questions," Fineberg said with a faint smile, and he turned and strolled back to his table.

The court adjourned. In the moment of noise and bustle as the press and the spectators crowded to the door, Kane turned to Marx. "Did I blow it?" he asked.

"You tried hard enough," Marx said wryly.

The following morning there were the summing-up speeches from both of the lawyers, and then the case went to the judge.

Ten days later Kane was found guilty and was sentenced to five years in the Federal penitentiary. Marx filed an immediate appeal. Kane's bail was set at fifteen thousand dollars, which he posted, and he returned to Tomcat House.

For Patterson, the moment was unexpected, entirely surprising, and somehow disappointing. Perhaps, he thought, it was disappointing because he had not been able to work himself up to it. It had taken him so very much unawares during the reception at the White House.

He had been discussing the Trade Metals Act with Michael Ford, the Secretary of Commerce, and drinking champagne—the domestic champagne the President had insisted upon for all his receptions—when Senator Randall came up, replendent in his dinner jacket with the beaded Balenciaga vest and the garnet studs in his ruffled dress shirt. Both Ford and Patterson greeted him.

They chatted for a while inconsequentially, and then, after Ford excused himself to freshen his drink, and the two men were left alone, Jack Randall turned to Patterson and said, "Got to hand it to you, buddy. I sure do appreciate the way you handled that little business for me."

"That little business?" Patterson asked, uneasily.

"You sure did wipe Billingsley's ass for him good."

"Oh, well," Patterson said. "Always glad to help an old buddy."

"And I'm always glad to return a favor," Randall said. "And I'll be able to do that, I hear, right soon." He winked and drifted off into the East Room.

The Marine Band had begun to play "Hello Dolly," and Patterson was busy trying to figure out what Randall could possibly have been talking about. The Billingsley business was perhaps explicable. Somehow or other, Tyler had evidently managed to drop a hint—or even more than a hint—to Billingsley. Had he done so it would not have been out of principle but because he disapproved of any kind of bungling that brought public attention to anyone in that line of work. He remembered Tyler's having said that he would advise Billingsley. Apparently it had been fairly explicit advice. Patterson doubted whether the bug had been removed. If anything had changed, probably it had just been the kind of equipment that Billingsley was using. It would be something now that would not be detectable by the antibug engineers Randall's friend employed.

But it was the other part of Randall's comment that really puzzled him. What kind of favor was he contemplating in return? Randall was on the Judiciary Committee. Patterson tried to think what business he had with them, what was pending, what was coming up. Nothing seemed to fit the terms of Randall's expression and that odd wink. He had already dismissed it as Western bombast when, not half an hour later, the President himself ambled up, grabbed Patterson's elbow in that characteristic "jes' politicians" gesture, and whispered into his ear.

"Dick"—nobody except the President of the United States ever called him Dick—"there's going to be a vacancy in three months. Old Cahoon is stepping down and the place is yours."

"A vacancy?"

"On the Court."

"Why me?" Patterson asked in amazement.

"You're a nice fella," the President said, "and a damn fine lawyer. Besides, the Jews and the Negroes and the Irish all have their seats up there. I was thinking of giving this one to a paisan, but the last good lawyer they turned out was Cicero. So I decided to go way out, and hit that last minority group."

"Minority group?" Patterson asked.

"Us Wasps," the President said.

He guffawed and walked away, leaving Patterson wincing in a peculiar mixture of horror and delight.

He only wished he could have told Jill of the absurd way in which his final triumph had come.

At the head of the long green-baize table, Chief Justice Lester Summerson looked up. His hooded eyes, deeply shadowed, gave him the look of a startled lizard, but that was a mere accident of the configurations of his lined, mottled face and his prominent cheekbones and receding jaw. It was not an expression, for his face was impassive, showed nothing at all of what was going on behind those eyes, and would have been desirable in a poker player. Walter Chubb, the third ranking of the nine Justices, the one upon whom the Holmes mantle had fallen—he was called by the newspapers "The Great Dissenter," just as Holmes had been—looked from Summerson to Krook, the Junior Justice. In a characteristic gesture, he ran his hand through his shock of white hair, rubbed his reddish face, and looked back at Summerson.

It was a struggle between the two of them, between Summerson and Chubb. The terms of the struggle had been made perfectly clear, weeks before. Summerson, usually a reasonable, rational, judicious fellow, had commented in the robing room that he was unhappy about the tendency of the Court's decisions on pornography, censorship, and the line he thought had been blurred lately, the line between liberty and license.

"What?" Chubb had asked. "What are you trying to tell me?"

"Just what I'm saying. My God, have you looked at the books that they're publishing these days? And advertising? In *The New York Times* Book Section, even! Some of those things are terrible! You used to have to smuggle those books in from France. Now they're illegal in France and legal here!"

"Is that such a bad thing?"

"It damn well is! You know, if somebody sent one of those books to one of my daughters, I'd punch him right in the nose," Summerson had declared.

"Is that a dare?" Chubb had asked, wryly.

Chubb was, for all his sixty-two years, a vigorous man, a big-game hunter, a still formidable tennis player—although he limited himself to doubles, now—and, more to the point, a former captain of the Yale boxing team.

"No, not a dare," Summerson had answered, but without the snort of indignant amusement that Chubb had expected. He really took the damned business seriously.

How seriously, Chubb had found out only later. The Kane case was on the docket. That had been what Summerson had been talking about, really. But Chubb had not expected this . . . manipulation. This maneuvering. Summerson, exercising his prerogative as Chief Justice, had moved the case up on the docket. And had managed to bring it in at the tail end of the spring term. That meant that old Cahoon would be sitting on it, and would be voting on it. And that meant a vote for affirmation of the conviction. Two votes, really. It would be both Cahoon and Summerson. The old conservative and the liberal with the old hang-up—for the Chief Justice was rather priggish and prim. Which made it tough for poor Kane. He'd need five votes. Not just five votes out of the nine, but five out of the remaining seven. And James Tulkingborn would probably vote to uphold the conviction, too. He was neither a "liberal" nor a "conservative" but an independent, quirky man whose devotion to the law was such that neither faction could rely upon him. He was that "swing" vote that neither side could count on.

And that left Chubb himself. And Skimpole. And probably Dedlock. Vholes? He tended just the slightest bit toward a conservative position. And Krook? Well, they would soon see.

The old tradition—one of those laws that the Court itself could not have overturned, even had it wanted to do so—required that the Justices discuss cases in order of their seniority, beginning with the Chief Justice and working downward, but that they vote in reverse order of seniority. The point was to prevent the junior Associate Justices from being influenced by the votes of their seniors. But no tradition could prevent those men who were likely to be influenced from actually being influenced. The discussion made it clear, usually, which way the votes were going to go.

Summerson began. He objected to Kane's entire enterprise, to the spirit of it, and to the effects he had seen in the publishing business of the earlier decisions of the Court. He had dissented in the Roth case, and felt, still, that he had been right to do so.

Chubb listened, and grudgingly he even admired the old fox. He was actually coming on as the underdog! Nervy old coot!

Cahoon agreed with what Summerson had said. Of course. No surprise there.

Then it was Chubb's turn.

"I'm afraid I don't see it that way at all," he began. "Sure, Kane has gone pretty far, but if he did, it was with the Roth case behind him, and with the assurance we had given him that any social significance could redeem. I don't see how there can be any question but that social significance is there, in his magazine and in his book program. Some of us may not like his books, but the very fact of their publication is socially significant. I never liked that qualification myself. I thought it was damned vague. And I still think so. My own position is that talk about sex is perfectly natural and that no legislation or judicial decision is the appropriate way to control it. But given the position that the Court has taken, we'd have to say that his whole program of publication was utterly trivial and entirely without significance if we were to affirm. I don't think so, and I'd favor reversing the lower court."

He could have said more, but he didn't think it would have helped. Nobody gets converted after the first couple of minutes, anyway. Was it Twain who had said that? he wondered. Anyway, it was true. And all there was left was to sit and wait, to listen, and to count.

Skimpole wanted to reverse. And Dedlock. So it was three to two. Tulkingborn wanted to affirm. And Baythorne. None of these votes was surprising, although Chubb had tried to keep alive a small, faint hope for Tulkingborn. Anyway, it was four to three for affirming.

Chubb had already given up when he heard Vholes take a surprising turn. Vholes was not at all sure that the suspension of the Post Office Department's review board and the subsequent decision to prosecute Kane in a criminal rather than in a civil proceeding was not a violation of Kane's rights, and, in effect, an *ex post facto* law. And he disagreed about the legitimacy of any of the discussion of the advertising that had taken up so much of the original trial. The publication itself, he said, should be the only consideration.

So. It was four to four. Even Stephen. And which way would the Krook bend?

Krook cleared his throat and began. Chubb listened, impatiently, to the introductory remarks. Krook still sounded as though he were teaching a class at Columbia Law School, and he tended to lecture. The lectures were good as lectures go, Chubb had to admit, but they were a little out of place. It was, no doubt, an effort that Krook was making to overcome the feeling of awe at just being there, being one of the nine men who protect the Constitution of the United States and exercise power and judgment as no other nine men in the world could do. Well, Chubb could indulge that. If it helped him to feel that he belonged and enabled him to think for himself, let him lecture.

". . . and so I'd say that the age of the audience is not the controlling factor," he was saying. "The principle of freedom of the press is not to be limited by the audience to which the publication is aimed, except at great peril. The idea of dividing up the public into groups and of saying that this group can have so much freedom and this group can have a little less is repellent to an egalitarian society. A person is entitled to the freedom to read, no matter what his age."

Chubb wiped his face with his hand. This time it was deliberate, an aping of his tic, and done to hide the smile of satisfaction and relief that he felt might erupt on his features. He was glad he did so, for in a moment, with Krook's name not yet dry on the mental reverse list, Krook reversed himself.

"The relevant question is the intention to pander, to arouse prurience of thought and attitude, no matter what the audience may be. And I think that the advertising campaign submitted in evidence in the trial in the District Court points very clearly to that concluson—that Kane's intention was to pander. And that intention falls outside of the legitimate area of publishing guaranteed freedom by the Constitution."

Chubb realized that he had been staring. For a second? Ten? Thirty? He had lost all idea of time, shocked as he had been by the eccentricity of what he had heard. He had taken it in, and then, after a kind of mental double take in which he had confirmed what he thought he'd heard, he had experienced a physical sensation—the adrenalin, no doubt—as his body had reacted to Krook's comments. It was an appalling idea! To judge a book on its advertising was . . . absurd! Why, you could publish the Bible, advertise it as a hot book, and then, because of the advertisement, it would *be* a hot book.

It would have been laughable, except that Krook had tipped the scale. It was five to four, now, affirming. And the decision would be written, and would be a precedent for other decisions. More harm had been done by that grotesque and—there was no other word for it—stupid line of reasoning than most men get to do in a lifetime of selfishness, indifference, greed, and anger. And even worse, he had lost all confidence in Krook, in the man's common sense, in his reasonableness. And without common sense and reasonableness, the law was nothing better than a huge toy in the hands of irresponsible children!

He deflected his outrage to a smaller target, to a more manageable issue, about which he could think and to which he could respond with more balance. It was Summerson who had done it. Five to four it was, but if Summerson hadn't moved the case up, Cahoon would have gone off.

Chubb wondered whether Summerson would assign the decision

to Cahoon, and let him have a last fling, or give it to Krook, to show that it wasn't a power play, and that the Junior Justice had his own head and his own voice. Probably the latter.

The voting went just as Chubb had figured it would. And Summerson asigned the decision to Krook. Which left Chubb to write, if he wanted to, another great dissent. He volunteered for it. And they went on to the next case.

It was three weeks later, on a Monday morning, that Krook read the majority opinion he had written. Chubb rocked uneasily in his chair, looking out at the courtroom. His gaze fell on the frieze at the back of the room, above the columns. One of the figures—Justice, she looked to be—was bare-breasted. Chubb wondered what Kane had done that was any more explicit, any more prurient, any more objectionable than that. He ran his fingers through his hair, wiped his face with his hand, and resumed his rocking.

"Nina!"

"I heard the news this afternoon," she said. "I had to come to you."

The news. It had not been necessary for her to say what news. Kane's final appeal to the United States District Court in Boston for a compassionate reduction of his sentence had been denied. His jail term was to begin in three days, the following Monday. At eight o'clock in the morning, he was to report to the U.S. Marshal's office in Boston and board the bus for Portsmouth Federal Penitentiary.

"I'm glad you came," he said. "I've been sitting here, trying to finish some last-minute paper work. But it's awfully quiet. Nobody is here except the servants. Would you like a drink? Or something to eat? How about a pizza? The condemned man ate a hearty pizza."

"No, thank you," she said. "I'm not really very hungry."

"Neither am I," he admitted. "Sit down."

She sat down on one of the Barcaloungers. There was a moment of embarrassed silence. It was as if she were visiting someone in a hospital, someone with terminal cancer. There was nothing to say, or there was everything to say and therefore nothing to say. The reality that lay between them was like an inert lump, proof against all inroads of conventional conversation.

"I just don't know what to say," Nina began finally. "It's so terrible. It's just such an awful, stupid thing."

"Thanks," he said. "I've been reading about it."

"You've been what?"

"Reading about it. I've been reading the *Handbook for Conscientious Objectors* that the Central Committee for Conscientious Objectors puts out."

"I don't understand."

"It's the only book I know about that has what I'm looking for. It's a guidebook for people who are going to prison. A how-to-do-it book. It's kind of interesting. Did you know that there are 1,051,200 minutes in a two-year stretch? Marx says that on a five-year sentence I'll be in probably for twenty to twenty-four months. So at the most there are 1,051,200 minutes . . ."

"Irv, don't," she said.

"No, no. It's really fascinating. It says here that 'Time becomes the endless preoccupation of the man in prison. It is reckoned not only in months, days, and minutes—' That's where they have the figure about how many minutes there are in two years—'but in Sunday dinners to be eaten, counts to be endured, or the number of miles of prison spaghetti yet to be consumed.' Can you imagine that? Miles of spaghetti!"

She attempted a smile.

"But it does say that you've got to do your own time, and take each day as it comes, without looking back. Or forward. It's full of all kinds of little bits of information, too. All I get is twelve dollars a month to spend at the commissary for 'Candy, tobacco, oranges, magazines, and other items.'"

He laughed at the absurdity of the twelve dollars a month. For him! But Nina had buried her face in her hands and had begun to sob quietly. "Oh, Irv," she sobbed, "stop it!"

He stopped his recitation of interesting details from the handbook, and, more embarrassed by her display of emotion than by the silence that recitation had been intended to break, he crossed the room and stood next to her. Awkwardly, and with a kind of nervous hesitation, he took her shoulders in his hands, and with small, tight, nervous motions, patted her ineffectually.

Her sobbing continued unabated. He had to do something else, something more direct, more comforting, and, because his nervousness and constraint had gone unnoticed—her face was still buried in her hands—he was able to try again, this time by sitting down beside her. He perched uncomfortably on the edge of the lounger.

He put his arms around her shoulder. He was surprised, but not at all displeased, when she took her face from her hands, looked directly at him with large, tear-filled eyes, and exclaimed, "Oh, Irv!" She buried her head in the crook of his shoulder.

He held her lightly, and then with increased firmness, as, losing his self-consciousness, he realized what a depth of compassion and affection she was expressing for him. He held her with more authority and protectiveness, but still the crying continued. Finally he put his hand under her chin and lifted her face. He had thought to wipe away the tears with his handkerchief. But, with her face lifted close to his, and as he looked down at it, poignant, tear-strained, it happened.

It had to happen. All along, it had been waiting for them.

Whether she had moved toward him first or he toward her, neither of them could ever remember. But there they were. They kissed.

He supposed, when he thought of it later, that there had been only the most minute differences between that kiss and any other. The physical activity, after all, was not so highly differentiated. But, still, it was the difference between a raw, young jug wine and a rich, lyrical mature claret. It was, moreover, the maturity of it, the fact that she was not one of those polyurethane girls but a real woman, who felt like, and tasted like, a real woman as they clung to each other. At first they were taking comfort from each other's physical presence, but then, imperceptibly, the embrace became a sharing and taking and giving of delight.

They separated just for a moment and looked into each other's eyes, sharing their amazement and their wonder, and suddenly hungering for each other, with a hunger that had been building for three years.

"Oh, Irv," she said, tremulously, but this time the meaning was altogether different. "I've loved you for such a long time!"

"Nina!" he said tenderly, and pulled her back against him.

Together, as though in a slow-motion film, they sank down on the lounger. They kissed again, and this time Irv ran his hand up Nina's leg, under her dress, and up her thigh. There was a particular excitement for him, one he had not felt for years and was scarcely able to remember—the apprehension, however slight, that she might reject him, stop his hand, break away from him. She was no bought-and-paid-for Kitty whose affections were guaranteed, but a real woman, and all the more desirable for that.

But there was no resistance. She moved over to accommodate him next to her, and then, to his inexpressible delight, ground her hips against his. He reached around and, with his other hand, began to undo the zipper of her shift.

"Wait," she breathed. Extricating herself from his embrace,

she sat up, swung her legs down, finished the unzipping, and slid the dress off, letting it fall into a heap at her feet. She reached around, unhooked her bra, hunched her shoulders slightly, and let it fall. He hooked his thumbs into the elastic of her half slip and, in one motion, he peeled it down, bringing the pants with it.

Nina lay back on the lounger, naked and basking in his gaze.

For his part, her beauty was as sharp as a physical blow. "You're —you're lovely," he said. The very pronunciation of the words was difficult because his mouth felt dry and his tongue thick.

Still staring at her, he stood up and began to undress. He drew his cashmere sweater off hurriedly because he did not want to take his eyes from her even for an instant. He could hardly believe that for all these years, for all of these countless months of discriminating among the candidates for Kalendar Kitty, he had missed by so much the whole force of female beauty. There was none of the airbrush ideogram about Nina; on the contrary, she was a real woman, rich in the individuality of her flesh, and the fact that she had lived in her body for a while only made it all the more desirable.

In his eagerness and euphoria, the thought occurred to him— only for an instant, but with preternatural clarity—that such a treasured object as Nina's body demanded a possessor worthy of it and able to appreciate it. He was glad, really glad, that they had waited this long, because only now was he really ready for her and able to take her and to appreciate her as she deserved. None of the countless, nameless, undifferentiated Kitties who had trooped through the Mansion had ever made him feel like this, had ever made him feel like a man!

He stepped out of his trousers and, for a moment, stood over her, looking down at her, warmed by the dazzling glow of open love she was offering him. She reached her arms up to beckon to him. Feeling, for the first time in his life, more than a man and even like a god, he descended upon her.

She received him with a cry of joy.

In the beginning the light and the darkness, the heavens and the earth, the sea and the dry land were separated, one from another, but for them they all came together again, merged and mixed, and together they fell back into the original chaos, the original void at the center of which, in a blinding flash of light, they made the world new together.

Now, now that he had after all these years of searching finally found it, finally found her, the supreme irony was that in a matter of days, even hours, he would be sent off to jail. He would be imprisoned, now that he had finally found the freedom for which he had been searching all his life. Overwhelmed by the thought of it, his own eyes now began to fill with tears, and this time she comforted him, drawing his head down to her bosom and stroking his hair.

"I've been looking for you all my life," he said, "and at last I've found you. And here you were, all this time! Right here. Oh, I love you!"

He lay there for a moment, and then continued. "It'd be funny, so damned funny, if it weren't so awful. I mean my having to go . . ."

She closed his lips with her fingertips. She did not want to permit him even to pronounce the word "prison." But there it was, looming over both of them.

"There's time yet," she said. "We still have a little time."

"Yes," he said, and then, raising his head, he looked at her. "In a way, with what's hanging over us, it makes it all the sharper, doesn't it? I mean, every single moment."

"Some people have sixty years and never feel the way we do now."

"I know. I've never felt this way before."

"It won't be so bad," she said. "It won't be forever. And I'll visit you. And we can always think about what it will be like when you get out again. And you've got something that can comfort you, can carry you through it, and keep you going . . ."

"Yes," he said, "I've got you."

"You *do* have me. Of course you do. But you've also got truth, the knowledge that you haven't done anything, that you don't deserve to be there. And your innocence will sustain you."

There was a long pause. His head was still nestled on her breast. It wasn't quite the way it had been before, though, because there was a tenseness now, as the agonizing guilt overwhelmed him, and then he realized that the guilt separated him from her, isolating him. Resolved not to allow this to wall them off from each other, he decided to share it with her.

But could he? Did he dare? Could he risk it all, risk their moment together, their new-found love, by confiding in her his terrible secret? Yet he had no choice. It would be so cruel, so very wrong to go away and let her wait for him, as he knew she would do, and then come out and have to tell her. Or, even worse, to go away and come back and never tell her, and always to have this other prison of the mind incarcerating him.

"I'm not innocent," he said at last.

"But you are!" she insisted.

"No, no," he said. His tone was such that she could not stop him now. "I'm not guilty of what they're sending me to jail for. But, in a rough way, it works out, I guess. Did you ever wonder why Patterson was after me?"

He did not wait for her to reply, but continued, as if he were afraid that any loss of momentum might ruin his resolve and that he might not be able to overcome the inertia, the awful temptation to remain silent.

"He was after me because I tried to blackmail Jill Jefferson with one of my tapes. And she killed herself. In a way, I guess, I was responsible. Yes, I was responsible. I killed her, really."

There was nothing she could say to refute his own self-indictment. She believed the facts of it. He had no reason to lie to her, certainly not now. She knew that whatever she said now would mark their entire relationship, would shape it, either stunting it or, perhaps, if she were lucky, allowing it to grow straight and strong and to ripen. Yet, by the same token, she had to tell him what she really thought. To be untrue to herself now would mean being untrue to both of them. It struck her, in a brief instant, that this was very much like the confessional moment she had gone through, months before, in Bud's bedroom. She had been honest in her reaction then, and it had worked out right. She would have to be honest now. Whatever the consequences.

If Irv did love her, it would have to be for her honesty as much as for anything else.

"How awful, Irv. How awful for her. And how awful for you to have to live with."

For his part, Irv was surprised to find that his main feeling was one of release. Arthur Marx had never been able to come out and say it, but her simple, honest "How awful!" was true, and yet limited. She had not got up, as he had feared she might. She had not picked up her clothes, nor had she fled from the room. She was still there, still holding him, still lying beside him. Perhaps he was not a moral monster after all, but only a flawed mortal.

"Do you want to tell me about it?" she asked softly.

And he told her. He told her about the tapes, about the way he had filed them away in his safe, and about the way he had flown out to Los Angeles to confront her with this old tape of her performance, and had used it as a club to try to get her to influence Patterson, whose investigation had just begun. Jill had either told Patterson, had tried to influence him and been rebuffed, or had not dared to tell him at all. Whichever way—and it made no difference—she had taken her own life, and he had put her in the position where she felt she had to.

While he had been talking, she reflected on the enormous difference in her response to Bud's confession. Bud had confessed to a simple betrayal, but Irv, now, was confessing to a kind of murder. The betrayal had repelled her; for Irv's complicity in Jill Jefferson's death, she had only compassion. The difference, she supposed, was that she loved him.

There it was, the only thing that made any sense, the only thing that there was for her to tell him.

"What can I say?" she asked. "It's a terrible thing. But I love you. I love you, anyway. I don't think there's anything you could tell me that would keep me from loving you. What you did was bad. But I can't believe that you are a bad person, a bad man."

Irv Kane was not at all sure he deserved to hear what Nina was telling him, but whether he deserved it or not he could do nothing less than accept her understanding and be grateful for her love.

He reached up, embraced her, kissed her, and he contemplated the hours they had left.

"In a way, I'm glad that there's nobody here. We have this whole house to play with. For the first time since I built it, I think it will really be fun to be here. There couldn't be a better place for us to enjoy ourselves in."

"No," she said, "there couldn't."

"I've finally come to the point where I can really use this place, where we can really enjoy it—together."

"Yes," she said. And then she thought for a moment. "Shall we go for a swim?" she asked.

"Wonderful idea."

They got up and, still naked, walked across the room to the elevator. Even on the way to the elevator and, inside, on the ride down, they held hands. It was just inconceivable for them not to be touching.

They swam in the pool, they ate different kinds of pizza, they took steambaths, they played badminton in the gym, they made love, they romped like Adam and Eve in the garden before the fall. It was not until the small hours of Monday morning that Irv told her, in a serious moment, "You know, I'd have asked you to marry me if I weren't going into prison for a couple of years."

"Yes, I know," she said, simply. "There'll be time for that."

"We'll have all the time in the world," he said. "But I didn't want to be unfair to you."

"You couldn't be."

"I know what you mean. I have the same feeling about you."

He looked at her, and then, in the same tone but with a slightly different timbre, he asked, "Would you do me a favor?"

"Anything."

"There are some papers Arthur Marx is preparing. Would you go over to his office some time today, after I've gone, and sign them?"

She promised that she would.

It was not until that afternoon that she went to Marx's office. She had not seen Irv actually get on the bus. He had not wanted her to come. Marx had driven him to the Marshal's office. And Irv had signed the papers just before he had gone into the office to begin serving his sentence. Marx had brought the papers back to his office, where they waited for Nina's signature.

The papers gave to Nina, for the duration of Kane's imprisonment, a power of attorney over the entire *Tomcat* empire. He had signed control of a good seventy million dollars over to her.

A week later Nina went back to the island. She had had to hire a boat to take her out there—the hydrofoil was in dry dock—and she had walked up the path from the wharf to the front door.

There was no doorbell. She had never noticed that before, but, then, the door had always opened at her approach. Now that the television cameras were turned off, and now that the household staff was gone, all except Cato, she stood around wondering how to make her presence known. The smooth seams of the door might well have been on a mausoleum.

Not knowing what else to do, she knocked, banging as hard as she could upon the heavy door. She waited, knocked again, and waited some more. Then she took off her shoe and with her heel pounded on the door until she was exhausted. She had all but given up, had all but decided to go back to the mainland and call Cato, making an appointment with him to open the door, when he appeared.

A broad smile creased his wrinkled face.

"Ah, Miss Kirby," he said. "Come in. Good to see you. I was not expecting you, was not expecting anyone. The grocery man comes only on Wednesday. It's very lonely out here. Nothing to do, no one to talk to. No parties, no Kitties, no nothing. Very bad."

She walked inside and looked around. The place was immaculate. Cato was keeping it up, doing his work conscientiously. But the look of the place, the living room with the great dust sheets over the furniture and the linen bag over the chandelier, screamed out the emptiness of the house.

Nina explained that she had to go up to Irv's private quarters to do some work.

"Let me make a pot of tea?" he offered.

"I'd like that. Thank you."

"Shall I bring it up, Miss Kirby?"

"No, no, I'll come down when I'm finished and we'll drink it together in the kitchen."

"Oh, very good, very good," he said and scurried off to the kitchen.

Nina wandered through the house, opening doors, peering into the great empty billiard room, the pool room with the huge drained pool in the middle aching like a cavity, the gym in which the click of her heels seemed to be off the sound track of a gothic movie. And, finally, she went to the elevator and rode up to Irv's rooms.

She had never seen them so neat before, the papers stacked in tidy piles on the desk. There were no empty glasses, no ashtrays, no crumpled-up pieces of paper surrounding the wastepaper basket, no books with ragged pieces of paper to mark a place, no marked-up magazines, and no pictures, none of the hundreds of pictures of the magazine layouts or Kitties. They were all gone. This had been the room of her greatest happiness, but somehow it seemed to have fled, too, along with Irv.

She opened her purse, rummaged around until she found her green Gucci wallet, and, opening the little golden-hand clasp, she extracted a small slip of paper that Arthur Marx had given her the day before. It was the combination to the safe.

"Irv wants you to open the safe," Marx had said. "He said that you would know what to do with whatever it is that's in there."

"You don't know?" she had asked.

"I haven't the vaguest idea," he had said. He had looked at her curiously, but she had said nothing, had betrayed nothing by her expression or her manner, remaining entirely impassive and noncommittal.

Now, alone in the room with the combination in her hand and the safe before her, she was nervous indeed. She twirled the Mosler dial—there were five numbers—and as she reached the final number she was disappointed, having expected some kind of click, some kind of feel, but there was nothing. She tried the handle tentatively. Quite easily and quite silently, it gave way and the thick door swung open.

Inside there were a score, perhaps two dozen, maybe thirty large reels of tape. She pulled them out and carried them into the bathroom. One at a time, she opened the large, shiny metal cans and unreeled the tapes, letting them drop like spaghetti into the bathtub. It took her five or six minutes to do each reel, and after ten reels the pile in the bathtub had grown to an impressive size. She had no idea how tape burned, and she was afraid that if it flared up even the spray from the shower would not be enough to extinguish the blaze. She went back into Irv's room, got some newspaper, and, wadding it up, brought it back and mixed it up with the tapes. Then, taking her lighter, she lit the newspaper and watched the paper flare up and the tapes melt. There was no dramatic flash of flame. The tapes didn't burn so much as they just reduced to snakes of black ash, shriveling and writhing like live things.

Now that she had found out how they burned, she thought of taking the rest of them and burning them in a fireplace. But there was no fireplace in Irv's rooms. And she did not want to go downstairs where Cato might see her. So she started with the next batch of the tapes, unwinding them into the tub. The air-conditioning was still on, but she was sweating from the exertion and there was an odd, pungent odor from the melted plastic.

She had destroyed more than two-thirds of the collection, and was filling the tub for the last time, when she hesitated, stopped, and thought about what it was that Irv might have intended for her to do.

Had he wanted her to see any of them? He had not indicated

anything through Marx. If he had, Marx had not conveyed the message, or even the tone of it. She supposed that the very blankness of the message was a kind of message itself—she could do whatever she wanted. So, then, what did she want to do? It was her last chance to see any of them, if indeed she wanted to do so. She thought about it for a moment and then decided that she would put one on the machine and at least see what it was all about. She would not have to watch the whole thing if she didn't want to, she could turn it off at any time. She was not committing herself, really. Or was she?

She opened another can, and this reel she carried back to the console. After puzzling at the controls for a moment, she put the reel on a spindle, threaded the tape along the marked arrows in the plastic facing of the machine and into a blank reel that she retrieved from the bathroom floor. She went back to the controls, found the "on" switch, turned it, and watched a while before she was able to adjust the machine properly, and some time before she figured out that it was not the console but the television set itself that needed adjusting. But, suddenly, there it was.

It was Irv, sitting at the same console, stark naked, and watching the same television screen that she was watching now. Why was he naked and what was he watching? She squinted, trying to make out what the figures were on the tiny screen within the screen, and she was still trying to read the images when she saw a Kitty—was it Suzanne?—come in, come up to Irv, and talk with him for a moment.

Then, abruptly, Suzanne knelt down and put her head between Irv's legs. For a moment Nina stared in frozen fascination, and only then, by an act of will, did she manage to move her hand, which seemed to be made of lead, to the knob and turn the infernal machine off. She pulled the reels off the spindles and ran back to the bathroom, where she flung them into the tub, pulling them off the reels in an almost hysterical frenzy. It was as if the tapes themselves were unclean, were contaminated, were the carriers of some dreadful plague. With trembling hands she wadded up another piece of newspaper, flung it into the tub, and lit it, and only after she watched the last of the tape writhe and melt was she able to get hold of herself. She walked back into the bedroom and fell upon the lounger on which they had first made love.

It was awful. It was worse than awful. She could understand now what Jill Jefferson had gone through. But, too, she could understand what Irv had gone through—the odd torment of his whole life had been there on the screen for her to see. In that brief second she had seen not just an obscene act but the inner suffering of Irv's mind—and body.

More than anything else, she felt sad. She felt sorry for him, sorry for what he had gone through, what his life had been, and angry too at whatever it had been that had twisted and stamped him into that terrible mold.

Then, in a wave of longing, she wished he were there, in this room, on this very lounger, in her arms.

But he had been. And he would be again. After all those years, and all those tapes, he had finally made it, had broken through the barriers of inhibition and fear and the necessity to overcompensate, to prove himself over and over again and to record his proof on those endless reels of tape. It had never been enough for him simply to do the thing, but he had had to prove to himself over and over that he had done it, and from that proof take hope that he could do it again. Now he knew that he had made it. And she knew that he knew. It was with a feeling of exhilaration and joy that she finally got up, went back to the bathroom, and, taking the two reels that were left, calmly opened them and threw them into the tub and destroyed them too. As the last of the tapes melted and dissolved, she felt that she had released him from the bonds in which those coils had held him.

She turned the faucets on, washed the last traces of black ash out of the tub, picked up her bag, and went downstairs to have tea with Cato.

The courtroom was crowded but silent with the hush of expectance. Associate Justice Walter Chubb had moved his chair. Now he was sitting to the right of Chief Justice Summerson in the fourth seat from the left, as the judges appeared to one viewing them from the courtroom. Cahoon was gone now, and Chubb and the rest had all changed their positions. Now, in the chair on the extreme right, Richard Patterson was sitting, beginning his trip, his ride on the most important game of musical chairs in the world.

Patterson was reading the decision. It had been unanimous, and the Chief Justice had assigned it to Patterson as a courtesy, an initiation. The decision was being read aloud in its entirety because of its enormous importance. The whole procedure of criminal law would be affected. It was not so important that Frank Scully would go free. He had committed the murder—a nasty murder—but the one murder, or the small, individual guilt that derived from it, was less important in the long run than the procedural principle that this appeal had given the Court an opportunity to formulate—or to reformulate. No longer would any suspect be made to confess—or even be allowed to confess unless he was warned that his confession could be used against him, unless he was aware of what the legal implications of what he was doing were. The Gideon case had plugged one loophole in the chain of armor protecting the rights of citizens. Every man was entitled now to legal representation in felony cases. The Scully case would cover that interval between the arrest and the appearance at the police station of competent counsel. It was perfectly reasonable for Patterson to have written the decision. Having been, after all, an attorney general, this fell more or less into the area of experience from which he had just come. The administration of the law and of the court had been a part of his duties. And he had been well known as a champion of scrupulous observance of due process —of which Chubb approved entirely. The decision he had written that was being handed down today, the Scully case, would do a great deal to prevent the abuses that had plagued the administration of justice in the past.

It was, nevertheless, ironic and amusing for Chubb to remember that at the time of Scully's arrest there had been much in the papers about his collection of *Tomcat* pictures. After all of Patterson's crusading against smut—and against Irvin Kane—it seemed very quirky indeed that Patterson should now be reading a decision, the effect of which would be to free Scully, the man who had been called "the Tomcat Murderer," while Kane languished somewhere in a Federal prison.

Chubb ran his hand through his hair and remembered what he had learned years ago in law school, that the business of the lawyer and of the judge, too, was not justice, after all, but the law. When the two could be made to conform it would be an ideal world. Which this wasn't. Not yet.

". . . it was not the unanimity of the decision but perhaps the fact the Richard Patterson was the author of the opinion that some Supreme Court watchers in the Capitol today find especially interesting. It had been feared in some quarters that Richard Patterson, known to be a fearless crusader against pornography, would maintain the conservative balance that had prevailed for some years. The fact that Patterson not only concurred with but even wrote today's landmark decision suggests that the role he may play in the Court may in fact be pivotal. Some analysts have even speculated that he may turn the balance so that the liberal wing of the Court may prevail. It should be a very interesting term."

The film clip of the commentator gave way to a commercial that gave way in its turn to a weather report.

"The cold front moving down from Canada," the forecaster explained, "will bring drier, cooler air to Indianapolis for the next few days with chances of frost in low-lying areas . . ."

Cal Kane drew the covers over her and snuggled deeper into the warmth of the bed. The small Sony on the dresser a few feet away droned on with the day's sports results. She was not interested in them. The *Tonight* show would be coming on in a matter of minutes. She threw back the covers, got up, went to her closet, and, reaching up to the shelf, pulled down a plain brown hatbox. She brought the hatbox back to the bed and slid it underneath the dust ruffle. Then she got back into bed and watched while Ed MacMahon went through his nightly patter and finally said, "And here's Johnny!" Carson came on, there was applause and music, and when the applause died down he went into his monologue.

Cal reached down under the bed, pulled the hatbox out, and, from the drawer in the night table, took out a jar of vaseline with which to lubricate the silicone rubber in her vibrator. She reached down and plugged the electric cord into the outlet, and then, pulling the vibrator down under the covers, she inserted it into her vagina. She lay there for a moment, feeling the length of the thing inside her and listening to Johnny Carson go through his monologue; he was looking at her and she looked back at him. When she could stand it no longer, when the suspense was too much for her, she depressed the trigger of the hand grip and the small motor began to move the probe in and out at a rapid rate.

It had become a kind of game. The point was to finish with him. She worked it by using the in and out motion until just a few moments before the monologue was over, and then, for the last two or three jokes, she switched to the up and down movement.

She had done it frequently enough so that three nights out of five her moan of pleasure coincided with the crescendo of applause for him.

For her. For them.

Tonight was one of the successful nights.

She withdrew the vibrator, put it back into the hatbox and tucked it under the bed. Then, far over, she reached out and turned the Sony off.

She nestled down into the bedclothes and drifted off into sleep, a deep, contented, dreamless sleep.

About the Author

The outrageously celebrated Henry Sutton is the alter ego of David Slavitt—poet, novelist, playwright, and critic. Born in White Plains, New York, on March 23, 1935, he was educated at Phillips Academy, Andover; at Yale, where he was house scholar; and at Columbia, where he received his master's degree. Before he split his literary personality, he split for Cape Cod, leaving behind a glamorous position as motion picture critic for *Newsweek* Magazine but realizing his ambition to retire at thirty. He now lives in Harwich, Massachusetts, with his (and Mr. Slavitt's) wife and three children, and when not writing with both sides of his pen he can be found somewhere asail at sea.